CHAPTER ONE

"C'MON, JACK! You used to be game for any lark!"

Jack Carrington, captain in the 1st Foot Guards, peered over a stack of half-unpacked linen at the young dandy accosting him from his doorway. "I'm happy to see you, too, Aubrey, and while I appreciate the flattering enthusiasm for my company which led you to hunt me down before breakfast, I'm not interested in going anywhere. I didn't reach London until late last night, and as you can see, I've yet to settle into my rooms. Can this excursion not wait?"

Receiving the rebuff with no noticeable dimming of his enthusiasm, Aubrey Ludlowe crossed the room and, pushing aside Jack's portmanteau, poured himself some ale from the flagon on the desk. "Can't wait. Besides, why unpack? Leave it for your man."

"I sent my batman to rejoin his family as soon as we landed and haven't yet had time to find a replacement."

Aubrey waved his hand. "Let your new man attend to it after you hire him. The lesson begins shortly, and if we do not arrive soon, all the best seats will be taken."

Surprised, Jack swallowed his ale in a gulp. "You want to drag me away at barely past dawn to watch a *lesson?*

Since when did you develop such enthusiasm for education? Not while we were at Oxford, to be sure!"

Aubrey set his mug down with a thump, his expression affronted. "'Tisn't a matter of some rubbishy book-learning! Nay, 'tis more important than that. Indeed, 'tis the most important thing going on now in London, what with the Season not yet begun. Every gentleman of note will be present. Stands to reason there must be a decision soon, and good friend that I am, I don't wish you to miss having a chance."

Jack stared at Aubrey. "A *lesson* is the most important event now taking place in London?" he asked, trying to sift the most intelligible bits from his friend's speech. A sudden thought occurred and he leaned forward to sniff the air. "Are you sheets-to-the-wind, Aubrey?"

His friend chuckled, seemingly much less offended to be accused of being drunk at seven in the morning than at the suggestion he'd taken up scholarship. "Nay, though I don't mind a little nip first thing, to revive the spirits. A sirloin wouldn't come amiss either, but we haven't time." Aubrey snatched the folded shirt from Jack's hands and tossed it on the bed. "Wear regimentals, since you're half dressed in them already, but we leave now. The fencing master closes the doors promptly at seven-thirty."

"You're haranguing me to go to a *fencing* lesson?" A sudden vision filled Jack's head—smoke, screams, the rattle of musketry and clang of blades, himself with saber slashing. Shaking it off, he said grimly, "No, thank you, Aubrey. My fencing skills are quite proficient enough. Pray God, I shall never need to hone them again."

Julia Justiss
will whisk you back to
Regency England—
where you can escape into
a world of passion and privilege...
deceit and desire!

**Coming soon in new
easier-to-read large print....**

THE COURTESAN

Julia Justiss

MILLS & BOON

First published in Great Britain 2005
by Mills & Boon, an imprint of Harlequin (UK) Limited,
Large Print edition 2011
Eton House, 18-24 Paradise Road, Richmond, Surrey TW9 1SR

© Janet Justiss 2005

ISBN: 978 0 263 22162 6

AudioGO 2 2 AUG 2011

Harlequin (UK) policy is to use papers that are natural, renewable
and recyclable products and made from wood grown in sustainable
forests. The logging and manufacturing process conform to the legal
environmental regulations of the country of origin.

Printed and bound in Great Britain
by CPI Antony Rowe, Chippenham, Wiltshire

His friend sobered. "Amen to that. Heard Waterloo was a dreadful slaughter. But I'm proposing a different sort of contest—and one you definitely will want to see. Trust me, old fellow! Have I ever led you awry?"

Recalling a long line of dubious exploits stretching from childhood to university, Jack smiled. "Frequently."

Grinning back, Aubrey protested, "Well, not this time. If you decide I was wrong, you may afterward exact whatever retribution you like, but I'm sure you will be thoroughly grateful I insisted you come along. 'Tis nearly a…a life-altering experience! Or," he added with a heavy sigh, "so it has proved for many of us. But no more—you must see for yourself. You'll thank me, I promise you!"

"Oh, very well," Jack capitulated, his curiosity by now thoroughly piqued. Abandoning the shirts, he shrugged on his uniform jacket. "In compensation for making me leave my kit in such disorder, you may buy me breakfast."

"Immediately after the match," Aubrey promised. "Only hurry! I've a hackney waiting."

With the speed of long practice, Jack looped the fasteners as he followed Aubrey into the hall.

"Why are you staying here at Albany anyway?" Aubrey asked as he hustled Jack down the stairs. "Dorrie's making her come-out, isn't she? Why not move into the family manse?"

"Mama and Dorothy won't be coming to London for another month. You know old Quisford won't stir from Carrington Grove until the family leaves, nor would he trust an underling to properly open the house here. When

I mentioned I intended to put up at Grillon's until they arrive, a fellow officer whose regiment hasn't yet been ordered home from Paris offered me the use of his rooms at Albany."

"You'll stay in London until the family comes?" Aubrey asked as they boarded the waiting hackney.

"I'll remain just long enough to sell out, purchase new garments and consult our solicitors. Then I'm off to breathe country air and let Mama and Dorrie fuss over me."

"If they can spare you the time," Aubrey replied, signaling the driver to start. "When Mama fired off my sister, 'twas such a frenzy of preparations you'd think they were mustering an army. You'll return with them for the Season, of course?"

"Yes, after I get the spring planting sorted out with Ericson. I promised Dorrie I'd escort her to parties, introduce her to any army chums who happen to be in town and see that only eligible gentlemen are encouraged to call. Which leaves you out," he added with a grin.

"As if she'd look at me anyway, when we've known each other since we were in leading strings," Aubrey retorted. "Besides, I've no desire yet to become a tenant-for-life."

"Since as Dorrie's equerry I shall be obliged to go about in society, I plan to keep my eyes open. Perhaps I'll discover a little charmer who persuades me to settle down."

When Aubrey chortled in disbelief, Jack continued, "No, I'm serious. There's something about finding oneself intact, after riding through a hail of musketry and artillery shot, that makes one contemplate one's own mortality. Perhaps it's time I do my duty to marry."

Aubrey stared at him. "I believe you mean it. Thank heaven I'm a younger son! No duties of procreation for me—not of the legitimate variety anyway," he amended.

"So what *illegitimate* activity are we pursuing this morning? Must be of some great moment, to get you up at such an hour. Or have you merely not been to bed yet?"

"Got a few hours' sleep," Aubrey replied. "Man needs his wits about him for this endeavor."

"Which is precisely...what?" Jack pressed.

"You'll see for yourself soon enough."

And with that, Jack had to be content. During the rest of the drive, Aubrey refused to be coaxed, tricked or bullied into revealing anything further. Mystified and a bit annoyed, Jack was more than happy when his friend had the carriage stop at a modest town house in Soho Square.

They followed several other gentlemen up the stairs to the main floor where Aubrey, after tossing coins into a box beside the door, led him into what appeared to be a converted ballroom. The area by the door was thronged with groups of chatting gentlemen; beyond them was arranged an assortment of chairs, all occupied.

"Blast, I knew we'd tarried too long," Aubrey grumbled. "Now we shall have to stand."

After scanning the crowd, Aubrey elbowed a path to

a space against the left wall. "This will have to do. Ah, they're beginning. Is that not magnificent?"

In the sudden hush, Jack heard the clang of steel on steel. Turning his attention to the floor, he noted facing them an older man clad in breeches and shirtsleeves. His opponent, posing *en garde* with his back to them, appeared to be a mere stripling, but before Jack could glean any further impression, the young man went on the attack.

Although the older gentleman, clearly the instructor, was taller and heavier, the young student seemed nearly his match. The flashing blades struck sparks as the boy thrust and counterthrust, offsetting the master's advantage in size and experience with superior agility and audacious, risky changes of direction that allowed him to steadily drive the man back.

His distaste for combat forgotten, Jack's attention riveted on the interplay of blade with blade. When, after checking an advance intended to throw him off balance, the boy countered with a thrust so swift and unexpected Jack barely saw the weapon move, he joined the gallery in a roar of approval as the master's sword went flying.

"Brilliant!" he said to Aubrey while the student trotted to retrieve the errant foil. "How long has he…"

As the boy untied his mask and turned to face them, the rest of Jack's sentence went unuttered. Walking toward them, the master's sword in hand, was not a young lad, but a girl.

A woman, rather, Jack amended, noting with appreciation the curves suggested beneath the loose-fitting linen shirt and breeches. Though with those rounded hips, that delicious curve of bottom, how could he have believed for a moment the student was a boy?

And her face—Jack literally caught his breath as his gaze rose to what must rank as one of the Almighty's supremest acts of creation. Its shape a perfect oval, the skin luminescent as a China pearl, her countenance was animated by large eyes of deep gentian blue set under arched brows. Though the full, petal-pink lips were unsmiling, the newly minted gold hair pulled severely back and tucked into a knotted queue, she was without question the most beautiful woman he'd ever beheld.

Aubrey's low chuckle pulled him from his rapt contemplation. "Did I not tell you?"

Realizing from the amusement on his friend's face that his mouth must be hanging open, Jack shut it with a snap. "Who is she?"

"Lady Belle—or at least, that's what the ton calls her, after her long-time protector, Lord Bellingham."

"An actress?"

"No, a courtesan—and since Bellingham's death a month ago, the most sought-after woman in London. Every unattached gentleman in the city has been pressing her to consider his offer, though Lord Rupert—" Aubrey gestured to a tall, thin man in black, his expression as somber as his garb "—has the blunt to outbid all comers. Rumor says he once offered Bellingham two thousand guineas to relinquish his claims to Belle—and doubled the offer to the lady privately, though she never left Bellingham, so it might be all a hum. Thought you might want to enter the running."

"At a starting bid of four thousand guineas?" Jack laughed. "I haven't that sort of blunt! She's ravishing indeed, but—alas," he said, surprised to feel a genuine pang of regret, "I could never afford her."

"If 'tis true that she's turned down Rupert on several occasions, she might be angling for more than just money. You're a well-favored gent, war hero and all. Might have a chance with her. And if successful, you would upon occasion allow your best friend to worship at her feet."

Something in Aubrey's tone made Jack transfer his gaze from Belle back to his friend. "You have a tendre there?"

Aubrey sighed. "She'd never look twice at me—an undistinguished younger son of modest appearance and fortune. But wait—the most amusing part is beginning. Once Wroxham discovered she was taking lessons—wearing breeches—the news raced through the ton and a crowd began gathering to watch. Hoping to discourage it, I suppose, she told Armaldi to charge admission, but that only seemed to bolster attendance."

"If she makes enough from that, she'll not need a new protector."

"Oh, she don't keep it—gives it to Armaldi, to reimburse him for his trouble in having such a crowd foisted upon him, she told Montclare. But Ansley—the young cub who's been dangling after her since last Season—protested that her admirers deserved a boon for their devotion. He induced her to agree that after the lesson, she'll meet one challenger. Anyone who manages to best her wins a kiss."

Indeed, as Aubrey spoke, Jack noticed several young men talking with the fencing master, their voices raised as they evidently pressed rival claims to that honor.

While the dispute continued, Lady Belle stood unmoving, the tip of her foil resting on the floor. Jack felt his gaze pulled inexorably back to her—indeed, he expected she would immediately command the attention of all the men and most of the women in any room she occupied.

After subjecting her to a searching second inspection, he found his initial awe magnified. Truly, in appearance she seemed perfection, as if the most skilled of Greek sculptors had crafted the very image of a goddess and then breathed life into it. Though the scandalous man's attire she wore fitted her loosely, there was no mistaking the amplitude of the curves tantalizingly concealed beneath that excess of cloth.

Jack found himself imagining her garbed in classical draperies, her slender arms and toes bare, the fine linen of the chemise outlining, rather than concealing, the shape of her breasts and thighs. Desire tightened his body, rose in a flush of heat to clog his throat.

Idiot, he chastised, making himself look away. The last thing he needed was to fall under the spell of this courtesan, who probably made demands as limitless as her beauty and possessed a heart as warm as the marble from which that Grecian sculptor would have crafted her.

"She doesn't appear to be worried," he said, his tone

sharper than he'd intended. "Has anyone ever bested her?"

"Not yet," Aubrey admitted. "But that doesn't stop men from fighting for a chance to try. Now, they're beginning."

At that moment, the fencing master pointed an imperious thumb at one of the men. Muttering their disappointment, the other contenders quit the floor.

The fencers took their places. In a few moments, with considerably more ease—and decidedly more disdain—than she'd displayed against her instructor, Lady Belle disarmed the challenger and knocked him to the floor.

She looked up from her vanquished opponent, her face expressionless, her intense blue eyes scanning the crowd. By chance, her gaze crossed Jack's. Connected. Held.

The force of it sent a vibration through Jack, raised the tiny hairs at the back of his neck. For a long moment they simply stared at each other, until abruptly, Lady Belle jerked her gaze away.

Ignoring the babble of masculine voices calling out to her, she stepped around her humbled opponent, bowed to the fencing master and strode from the room.

SUPPRESSING A SHIVER, Belle forced herself to walk with calm, even strides to the door. A bold fellow, that tall, thin, dark-haired officer whose scarlet regimentals had drawn her eye—and whose gaze had commanded hers, as if by right. She didn't recognize him, which meant he must be newly come to London.

Probably another bored hanger-on, amusing himself by

watching the latest show. Botheration, how she wished those useless fribbles would leave her in peace!

She'd already refused Lord Rupert half a dozen times and turned down a score of other offers in extremely blunt terms. How could she make it any plainer that she had no intention of accepting carte blanche from any of them?

Not now that she was free. *Free!* Even after a month, the realization still sent her spirits soaring. After six and a half long, painful, humiliating years, the shreds of what remained of her life now belonged solely to her. Even if she had no clear idea as of yet what she meant to do with it. Except, she thought, smiling with grim satisfaction as she recalled her challenger facedown on the floor, train herself so that she was never again at any man's mercy.

Her companion, Mae, a plump older woman with faded blond ringlets, cheerful blue eyes and a gown whose scandalously low cut clearly proclaimed her former occupation, waited in the anteroom to help her change. "Good lesson?" Mae asked.

"Yes," Belle answered as she stripped off her men's garments. "Armaldi made some suggestions about adjusting my stance that improved my thrust nicely."

"Must have made quick work of your challenger," Mae replied, handing Belle her gown. "Who was it this time?"

"Wexley. The man fences like a turnip. Wooden wrists, poor form, no grasp of strategy. Fortunately for the security of England, he was never in the army."

That comment called up the image of the dark-eyed captain and something stirred in her chest. No, she told herself, pushing the vision away, she was not curious.

"Oh, I nearly forgot," Mae said, pulling a sealed note from her reticule. "A boy brought this for you."

While Mae fastened the buttons down her back, Belle scanned the missive. "It's from Smithers, my solicitor, requesting that I call at my earliest convenience." She frowned, wondering what had prompted the unusual summons. "I suppose I can stop on my way home."

"Whatever do you think he wants, Belle?" Mae asked a bit anxiously. "He handles your finances, don't he? I hope…I hope there's nothing amiss."

"You needn't worry. I reviewed the accounts with him just last month, and the investments are performing well."

"You're so clever, I expect you're right. Funds and investments!" The older lady shook her head. "In my day, we dealt in jewels, gowns and carriages. Are you sure it wouldn't be safer to accept another offer? So many you've had this month! And some of the gentlemen quite charming."

Having already responded to this question on numerous occasions, Belle had to struggle to keep a sharp edge out of her voice. "For years I've saved every penny and had Smithers place the funds in the most reliable of investments. We shall not run out of blunt, and the house and its furnishings are deeded to me outright. I don't need another protector."

"I know you weren't too happy with Lord B, but surely

you could find one more to your liking. You can't really mean to live without a man."

Her patience wearing thin, Belle snapped back, "Why do you continue urging me to take a lover? You should know how unreliable are their vows of devotion!"

"Oh, in my youth, 'twas me what was fickle, leaving one for another when I had a better offer. But toward the last…" Mae sighed. "You mustn't fault Darlington for his lack of constancy. I was getting older, and 'tis the way of the world for men to prefer a younger woman."

A world I need no longer inhabit, Belle thought defiantly. But contrite now over her loss of temper, she said, "Pray forgive me for chiding you! 'Twas truly Darlington's loss, for he could have found no one to replace you with so sweet a temper or generous a heart."

Mae smiled at Belle, her eyes misty. "You're a dear child, and I don't know what I should have done, had you not taken me in when he cast me off. I wasn't as wise as you over the years, and after I'd sold all my jewels…"

"You were the only woman who treated me kindly, that first year Bellingham brought me to town, when I thought I should die of loneliness." And shame, she added silently. "And have ever been a true friend. Besides, who advised me to make the best of my lot and accept all the gifts Bellingham showered on me, stashing them away for later use? We owe our wealth today to that wise counsel."

"Well, 'tis good of you to say so," Mae replied, "but I wouldn't know a fund from a trust, and that's a fact."

"Enough of that! Would you like to stop for ices while

I visit the lawyer? I should count it a great favor if you would take the carriage at the front and go to Gunter's while I slip out the back. As soon as I saw the crush in the ballroom today I asked Meadows to summon me a hackney. I'd rather not have a crowd following me."

A great lover of sweets, Mae brightened at the suggestion. "Are you sure you'd not like to meet me there? We could stop by the lawyer's after."

"No, for wherever my carriage goes now, the most annoying throng gathers. Besides, looking as fetching as you do in that new gown, I image some admirers will stop to flirt with you. Darlington will burn with remorse."

"Red always did become me, and if I do say so, I've kept my figure. The most magnificent breasts in London, they used to say, and you're still quite handsome, aren't you, my pretties?" she crooned, patting her ample bosom, the powdered top of which bulged above the low bodice of her scarlet dress. "Seeing how Frederic threw me over for that chit out of the opera—the most grasping, coldhearted little strumpet you could imagine—I like to believe he did come to regret his choice."

Belle gave her companion a hug. "I'm certain of it! Now, off with you and create my diversion."

"You, my dear, have taken on the appearance of a—a veritable *Quaker!*" Mae said frankly, looking Belle up and down as she put on her pelisse. "Not that you ain't still a beauty, whatever you wear. But with your looks, to garb yourself in a plain gray gown with nary a ribbon, cut so high there's not a bit of flesh showing!" Mae shook her head, obviously finding Belle's behavior incomprehensible.

Belle shrugged. "I can dress to please myself now."

Mae looked at Belle thoughtfully. "Will you please yourself? I don't mean to vex you by saying it again, and you may call me a foolish old romantic, which I'm sure I am, but I cannot see how you mean to exist without a man in your life, and you so young! It's…it's not *natural*."

Belle walked to the door, her smile brittle. "You've not been listening to my detractors. Have you not heard that I'm the most unnatural woman in England?"

CHAPTER TWO

As soon as Mae left, Belle headed for the servants' stairs. Enjoying her role, Mae would bandy comments with the gentlemen waiting to accost Belle when she departed, basking in their compliments—and doubtless receiving a coin or two discreetly slipped into the notes she would promise to deliver to her companion. By the time the loitering men realized she was not joining Mae, Belle would be well away.

After tying in place the scarf that masked her gold hair, Belle donned her charcoal traveling cloak and paced to the back gate, where the hackney she'd requested waited. While the vehicle traversed the distance from Soho into the City, she wondered again what business could be so pressing her solicitor believed it required her immediate attention.

Had he encountered some difficulties in changing the terms of Kitty's trust? Hoping any problems could be speedily resolved, she stepped down at her destination.

As she walked to the door, two clerks in conversation and a tradesman with his cart passed by, ignoring her. She paused, drinking in the wonder of it. Though, toward the end, she'd insisted on wearing gowns even less revealing than those favored by ladies of the ton, in the bright colors Bellingham preferred and that garish blue coach—the first thing she'd replaced after his death, with a new equipage all in black—she could go nowhere unremarked. It was still the sweetest of pleasures to walk down a street outside of Mayfair and attract no more notice than any other Londoner going about her business.

Just what business that was, she would soon discover.

Within a few moments of her arrival, Mr. Smithers's clerk ushered her into his office, where the solicitor thanked her for answering his summons so promptly.

"My companion fears I must have suffered some grievous financial reverses," Belle said as she took the seat he indicated. "I hope you are not about to inform me that my investments have taken a sudden fall on the 'Change."

Returning her smile, the lawyer shook his head. "Quite the contrary, actually. I have the pleasure of informing you that you have been named chief beneficiary in the will of the late Richard Maxwell, Viscount Bellingham. The estate itself, of course, is entailed upon a cousin. However, except for small bequests to his wife and daughter, Lord Bellingham left the whole of his cash assets, the value of which is still being calculated, as well as all his unentailed property—a Suffolk manor, a Lincolnshire hunting box and a London town house—to you."

Belle stared at the solicitor, unable to credit what she'd just heard. "There must be some mistake!"

"'Tis irregular, given that you had no link by blood or

law to the deceased, but nonetheless quite legal. And no mistake. His late lordship's solicitor spent most of yesterday afternoon with me, expounding on the details."

"But...why?" Belle asked, more than half to herself. "He knew I had sufficient means to support myself, should anything happen to him." Her brow knit in perplexity, her shock turned to suspicion as she tried to puzzle out Bellingham's reasoning. "How much did he leave his wife and daughter?"

"Two hundred pounds each. Whereas his overall cash assets are estimated to be about twenty thousand pounds."

"Twenty thousand—" Belle echoed. "Why, 'tis infamous!" As an explanation for Bellingham's extraordinary bequest flashed into her head, irritation gave way to sheer, mindless rage. Jumping to her feet, she began to pace the office, too furious to speak.

"Apparently," Smithers said blandly, "Lord Bellingham wished to guarantee that you had more than 'sufficient' support. You are now an extremely wealthy woman."

"Who," Belle said, pausing long enough to glare back at the solicitor, "is therefore much less likely to take a new protector to supplant him."

As Mr. Smithers prudently refrained from comment, a vivid memory of an angry scene recurred to her. Belle, incensed and guilty at the thought of a sixteen-year-old daughter abandoned by her father, threatening to leave Bellingham if he did not honor his responsibilities to his kin by returning to reside, at least outwardly, with his family. Bellingham countering that if Belle ran away, he would neglect his relations entirely to search for her. They'd reached a stalemate of sorts, Bellingham refusing to give up living with her but agreeing to visit his wife and daughter more regularly.

This, then, was her late protector's attempt at checkmate—a permanent, legal spurning of his despised wife in preference to her, done in such a manner that she could neither dispute with him over it nor refuse it.

Once again he was trying to take over her life, mark her as his own, and force her to dance by the strings he controlled—even from beyond the grave.

She could almost hear the vicious whispers circulating through the ton when the terms of his will became known.

The sense of lightness that had buoyed her after Bellingham's death melted away and her chest began to tighten with the same crushing weight of enforced obligation that she'd endured for almost seven years.

Even as she felt she must scream in vexation, an inspiration occurred. Perhaps there *was* a way to evade checkmate. She whirled to face Mr. Smithers.

"The bequest is legally mine—funds, property, all?"

"Yes. In an effort to protect the widow and daughter, Bellingham's solicitors spent several weeks trying to find a way around the will's terms, to no avail. The legacy is definitely legal, and indisputably yours."

"And 'tis mine to handle as I choose?"

"Yes, though I would recommend, with such a vast sum and numerous properties, that you retain an agent to advise you on the management of it." Smithers lifted a brow, curiosity in his expression. "Have you something in mind?"

"My own accounts are in good order, as we discussed last month? You did not then foresee any difficulties in my being able to live modestly for the rest of my days."

The solicitor inclined his head. "You would have been able to live comfortably, but in nothing like the style to which this inheritance will enable you."

"Kitty's trust is fully funded until she marries?"

"Your finances remain as I detailed them last month."

"Very well. Once the estate has been settled and the total assets determined, I wish you to set up a new trust."

The solicitor nodded. "A wise choice. You may choose to leave some of the cash on deposit—"

"A trust," she interrupted, "for the benefit of Lady Bellingham and Miss Bellingham, with a portion set aside for Miss Bellingham's dowry. Consult his lordship's solicitors on the precise terms—they will doubtless be more cognizant of the family's needs. And I should like to offer all the properties for sale to the rightful heirs—at the price of one shilling each."

The solicitor's eyes widened in surprise. "Are you sure, Lady Belle? 'Tis a very great deal of wealth."

"What was his should go to his family. I don't want it, nor is it right that I receive it." With a touch of defiance she added, "He shall brand me no more."

The solicitor gave her a smile of genuine warmth. "I

shall set about arranging it. His lordship's solicitors are going to be shocked—and extremely relieved!"

"Make sure you charge them a hefty fee!" Belle recommended with a grin, filled with the euphoria of a great burden lifted. "Send for me when the necessary papers are prepared. And now, if there is nothing else?"

Mr. Smithers's smile broadened. "I should think inheriting—and giving away—a fortune should be business enough for one day."

"I shall take my leave, then." Satisfied to have evaded Bellingham's last ploy, Belle walked to the door, then paused on the threshold. "I want to thank you for your expertise and counsel over the years, Mr. Smithers. Few men would have agreed to take on so…disreputable a client. I am very grateful you did."

Mr. Smithers bowed. "'Tis I who have learned from you, lady—that appearances are not always what they seem, and that there is honor to be found in persons of every degree. What you are doing is truly noble."

"What I am doing is merely proper," Belle countered. "Which reminds me… If the family has not yet been apprised of the terms of the will, I should prefer that the particulars remain between you and the Bellingham solicitors. Let his family believe Lord Bellingham set up the trust. As he should have done," she added acerbically.

"Given the, ah, sensitive nature of the bequest, I'm sure his lordship's solicitors will be happy to honor that request." Smithers bowed to her. "Good day, Lady Belle."

"Mr. Smithers." With a curtsy, feeling once more in control of her fate, Belle swept from the room.

AFTER DAWDLING, at Aubrey's insistence, at the fencing master's house with the expectation of catching another glimpse of Aubrey's goddess, Jack was as famished as Aubrey was disappointed when they at last arrived at White's. Once Lady Belle's carriage—containing the lady's companion but not the lady herself—finally departed, there was such a mob of gentlemen seeking vehicles that Jack had to use his most commanding cavalry officer's voice to snag a hackney.

Having commandeered one of the first vehicles to appear, the friends found the club relatively deserted. After ordering breakfast, they took their seats.

"Well," Aubrey demanded, smiling broadly, "are you not pleased I insisted you accompany me?"

A vision of vivid blue eyes and a restless, almost feral gaze invaded Jack's mind, sent a reminiscent shiver over his skin.

He shrugged it off. "Not that I can or will do anything about it but...yes, I suppose I am."

"You 'suppose,'" Aubrey echoed. "You only *suppose* you are happy to have discovered the most unusual and exquisite woman in London—and quite possibly the world! Damn, Jack, what an odd fellow the war's turned you into!"

"Sorry to be so disappointingly dull," Jack replied with a grin. "I grant you, Lady Belle is everything you claim. Were I disposed to indulge myself in carnal delights—and had I a bankload of guineas to bolster that aim—I might be tempted to enter the lists. But as I told you earlier, I'm of a mind to settle down."

Aubrey made a disgusted noise and rolled his eyes.

Chuckling, Jack continued, "Even if I weren't, there's Dorrie's Season to be considered. She'd never forgive me for embarrassing her during the most important time of her life by dangling after a notorious lightskirt."

"There is that," Aubrey agreed, somewhat mollified. "You could be discreet, though. Men do it all the time— pay court to the ladies at Almack's, then stop by the Green Room to meet their favorite actress. Besides, what about calling on her for the benefit of your best, most loyal friend? You can't convince me you are indifferent, despite that hen-hearted drivel about getting leg-shack-led!"

Jack took a sip of his ale. He really did mean to look for a wife. And he really couldn't afford to contend for the favors of the intriguing Lady Belle. Still…the powerful attraction of that compelling blue gaze called out to him, in defiance of logic, prudence and good sense.

"I suppose it wouldn't hurt to call," he conceded.

Aubrey slammed his mug down and gave a crow of triumph. "I knew no man could resist her!"

"Lady Belle?" asked one of a group of gentlemen just entering the room. "Indeed not! You saw her fence, didn't you? Magnificent! Totally flummoxed poor Wexley."

"Jack, you'll remember Montclare," Aubrey said as they rose to greet the newcomers. "Farnsworth, Higgins—and this young cub is Ansley—too far behind us at Oxford for you to know him."

After an exchange of greetings, Aubrey said, "Come, gentlemen, help me toast my good friend's safe return."

"With pleasure," Montclare replied. "Far too many of our Oxford mates didn't come back after Waterloo."

After drinks all around, Aubrey turned back to Montclare. "Will Wexley make an appearance, or did he slink home after that disgraceful performance?"

"Oh, I expect he'll turn up to drown his sorrows. Ham-handed clothhead actually thought he had a chance of winning a kiss," Montclare said with a wry grimace.

"Taking on Lady Belle, he's lucky he didn't end up skewered, trussed and ready to roast like a Christmas goose," Farnsworth observed.

"You'd not seen her before, had you, Carrington?" Higgins asked.

"No, he couldn't have," Montclare answered for him. "Went out to the army in—'08, wasn't it, Jack?"

"Yes. I took leave after Corunna and then between Toulouse and Waterloo, but spent my limited time at Carrington Grove, not in London," Jack confirmed.

"As I recall, it wasn't until 1811 that Bellingham brought Belle to town," Farnsworth said.

"Spring of 1811," Aubrey said reverently. "The Cyprian's Ball. Dressed all in virginal white, she was the most beautiful thing I'd ever beheld. Still is."

"Beautiful, yes, but hardly 'virginal,'" Farnsworth said with a laugh. "She's got an avaricious heart as hard as the guineas that golden hair rivals in brightness."

"You only say that because she's just turned down your offer," Ansley responded hotly. "She's as kind as she is lovely. Knowing I could never afford to possess her, when I begged her to allow us to challenge her for the chance of winning a kiss, she graciously granted my request."

"Probably because she knew *you'd* never fence well enough to claim one," Farnsworth answered. "Although you certainly could never afford her. The fortune Bellingham spent on her over the years! Gowns fit for a queen, jewels as impressive as the collection in the Tower, horses, carriages, a house in town as well as a country manor." Farnsworth shook his head. "The man was besotted."

"Given the funds and attention he lavished on her, you'd think she would have been content," Montclare observed. "Yet what must she do two years ago but coax Bellingham to live openly with her! There had long been enmity between Bellingham and his wife, but he owed his family better than so humiliating and public a slight."

"Can't expect a creature like Belle to know or care about proper conduct," Higgins responded. "Besides, we've all felt the force that kept Bellingham with her so many years." With a lascivious look, he added, "You've heard about that interlude in Vauxhall, haven't you?"

At that moment, the waiter arrived with their orders, halting the conversation and giving Jack time to reflect.

Though he knew better than to put much credence in common gossip, he'd felt an irrational disappointment in having his supposition of Belle's expensive, grasping nature confirmed by Farnsworth. Ansley's spirited defense of her had inexplicably lightened his heart. Though he was an idiot to expend any emotion on a woman who would never be more to him than a dazzling, seldom-glimpsed stranger.

Before he'd finished berating himself for a fool, his attention was drawn to an approaching figure and he jumped up with a smile. "Edmund! How good to see you!"

Edmund, Lord Darnley, one of Jack's closest friends from Eton and Oxford, reached out to clasp his hand. "Jack. Praise God, it's good to have you home."

"Ah, Darnley, what a magnificent match you missed this morning!" Montclare said. "After actually disarming Armaldi—hard to imagine anyone accomplishing that feat, I know—Belle had poor Wexley facedown on the floor before a cat could lick its ear. Where were you, by the by?"

"While the rest of you fribbles may have nothing better to do than hang about watching Wexley create the newest on-dit, some of us actually work," Darnley said with a grin, taking the chair Aubrey fetched for him.

"Work—bah!" Higgins dismissed Edmund's reply with a disdainful wave. "Ever since Lord Riverton appointed him as Cabinet assistant, he's been promenading about as if he were as crucial to the government as Wellington."

"The envy of the indolent and incompetent," Edmund said with a drawl, winking at Jack.

"Never mind Darnley's baiting," Farnsworth said. "You were about to tell us about Lady Belle and Vauxhall?"

His quarrel forgotten, Higgins's eyes took on a prurient gleam. "Ah, yes! I'll never forget it, though 'twas nearly four years ago. A group of us went to the gardens and spied Bellingham with Belle and some friends, all well in their cups. Belle was sporting a gown fashioned from some sheer material, the bodice so low cut it revealed nearly the whole of those delicious breasts. Indeed," he continued, his voice thickening, "Bellingham said he would rather savor *her,* for her plump, pebbled strawberries were sweeter than any Vauxhall had to offer."

By now, Jack's entire group—and all the gentlemen sitting within earshot of it—had fallen silent, giving Higgins their undivided attention.

Seeming pleased by his large audience, Higgins continued, "Bellingham leaned over to Belle, and with men and woman of all stations in booths but a few yards away, started suckling her tits—right through her gown!"

After a chorus of indrawn breaths and assorted exclamations, Higgins continued. "When he finished, the bodice was entirely transparent—leaving those strawberries clearly visible for us all to feast our eyes upon—and, ah, how worthy they were of feasting! Before we could look our fill—though I doubt one ever could—Belle suggested a stroll. I felt sure Bellingham would hustle her down one of the dark walks and finish what he'd started, but he invited a group of us to accompany him. Hardly able to imagine what might transpire next, we accepted."

Though shocked by the idea of so intimate an act being performed in public, within view of decent men and women, Jack was ashamed to admit that he was as titillated as he was revolted. An honorable man, he told himself sternly, would walk away, leaving the rest of Higgins's ribald story unheard. Jack tried to tell himself to do just that—but his legs didn't seem to be obeying his brain.

"Bellingham did head for one of the darker paths," Higgins was continuing, "announcing that he felt the need to dispense with some of the wine he'd drunk. That business concluded, instead of sheathing his standard—its condition already, as you can imagine, at better than half-mast—he bade Belle walk on with him. Advising her to hang on to something *firm,* he wrapped her hand around his shaft and set off—her fingers caressing him at every step."

While Higgins paused to take a sip, the entire company sat in a breath-suspended hush. Get up *now,* Jack instructed. His limbs continued to defy him.

Gaze abstracted, as if focused on the memories he was describing, Higgins resumed, "By the time we reached his carriage, Bellingham wasn't the only one gasping for breath. The moment the footman opened the door, Bellingham hustled her back against the squabs—and with all of us, including the footman, still looking on, yanked her skirts up to her waist and thrust her legs apart. Such a vision of creamy white thighs and sweet nether lips in a nest of golden curls, I shall never forget! Then Bellingham lifted her breasts out of that excuse of a bodice and mounted her. The footman, too shocked to move, I suppose, never closed the carriage door, so we saw the whole. Belle's eyes glassy and her mouth open as Bellingham pounded into her—those luscious naked breasts bouncing, barely a handspan away… I must admit, the footman wasn't the only onlooker who discharged his weapon that night!" Higgins exhaled heavily. "'Twas the most erotic experience of my life."

In the midst of the groans, sighs and ribald comments, Jack heard young Ansley mutter, "I don't believe it."

Though with the cynicism of age, he realized that the broad outlines, if not the coarse details, of Higgins's tale were probably true, he found himself sympathizing with the infatuated youth's disinclination to accept that the beautiful creature he obviously worshiped could have been involved in so crude and carnal an episode. Before Jack could decide whether he was more disgusted with Higgins for telling the tale or himself for listening to it, another man entered the room.

"Ah—Lord Rupert!" Higgins exclaimed, gesturing to the newcomer. "Another spellbound witness to the extraordinary events I've just described. Indeed, my lord was so enraptured by the, ah, sights and sounds that evening, he has been mad for the wench ever since, eh, Wendell?"

Ignoring him, Lord Rupert walked calmly onward. Turning back to the group, Higgins continued, "Bellingham removed her from town for a time immediately afterward, some alleged because he feared Rupert would try to bribe her away from him. Though, given the sums you're reputed to have offered and had turned down," Higgins said, addressing the baron, "it don't seem she favors you."

"If Bellingham were still alive," Rupert said, fixing a chilly silver-eyed gaze on Higgins, "you wouldn't have dared recite that story, you miserable muckworm. You, I, the others—we all swore to remain silent."

Higgins's face colored. "B-but that was only—"

"I think, in honor of his memory, I should take care of you for him," Rupert interrupted, giving Higgins a thin smile. "Perhaps it might be...healthier if you left town. Now."

Under Rupert's unnerving scrutiny, Higgins turned pale, then red again. After a moment's hesitation, while Rupert continued staring silently at him, Higgins rose and walked out.

"As for the lovely Lady Belle," Rupert continued, his voice calm as if nothing unusual had transpired, "I have every expectation of her eventually accepting my carte blanche. Make no mistake—sooner or later, that lady will be mine."

"She is not, however, yours *yet*," Ansley reminded doggedly. "Any one of us has the right to approach her."

"Anyone?" Rupert gave a disparaging bark of laughter. "I'd hardly count on winning yourself a kiss, young pup. 'Twould require a swordsman of far more skill than you're ever likely to possess."

"I daresay Carrington might do it," Aubrey said, startling Jack. "He's been the best fencer of us all since Eton."

"So he has," Montclare agreed. "What do you say, Jack? Shall you have a go at it?"

Recovering from his initial shock, Jack knew he

should put an immediate end to the discussion. After all, Higgins's tawdry story should have inspired him with a firm disinclination to have anything further to do with a woman who had allowed herself to be displayed more crudely than the cheapest prostitute out of Seven Dials.

Except he couldn't quite reconcile that vision of offensive carnality with the fierce gaze and intense, focused concentration of the woman who had disarmed her fencing instructor, demolished her subsequent opponent and left the room without responding to any of the offers shouted at her by a gallery full of eager supplicants.

Base voluptuary. Scheming, money-hungry jade. A woman of kind heart. Which of those descriptions—if any—reflected the true Lady Belle?

"Of course he'll do it—won't you?" Aubrey's reply pulled Jack's attention back to the present.

Without having made any conscious decision, Jack heard himself say, "I suppose so."

"Famous!" Aubrey said. "That kiss is as good as won."

Jack laughed, but before he could respond, he felt a prickling between his shoulder blades that had, during his years as a soldier, often been a presage of danger. He turned to find Lord Rupert's gaze on him.

"You might win a kiss," Rupert conceded after studying him. "But you will never win Belle to your bed."

"I say, is that a threat?" Aubrey demanded.

"Nay, 'tis more like a dare," Montclare opined.

"Indeed not, 'tis a wager!" another man cried.

"So it is," several others agreed. And before Jack could

utter another word, calls went out for a waiter to bring the betting book.

Though Jack disavowed interest in anything beyond a contest of blades, the other men, after informing him his participation was unnecessary, duly recorded the wager.

That done, with a cold nod to Jack, Rupert departed. As the other men drifted away, Jack declined Aubrey's invitation to a hand of whist and accepted Edmund's offer of a lift back to his rooms. After bidding Aubrey good-bye, the two friends set out.

After tooling his high-perch phaeton down several streets, Edmund turned his attention to Jack. "Do you really intend to challenge Lady Belle?"

"It should prove...interesting. She is quite proficient— amazingly so for a woman." Jack hesitated. Edmund had always been a steady sort, more detached and observant than the volatile Aubrey. Knowing he could trust his level-headed friend's opinion, he felt compelled to ask, "What do *you* think of Lady Belle?"

"Do I believe she actually took part in Higgins's frolic? Or do I suppose his tale to be a drunkard's embellishment of a more innocent incident?"

Jack shrugged. "The account was a bit...shocking."

"I'm afraid I don't know the truth. Lady Belle has always seemed to me to possess too much...dignity to have participated in such a display. Either way, I doubt it has any bearing on her skill with a foil."

"I suppose not."

"If you wish to get a better sense of the woman, you

might stop by Drury Lane tonight. Lady Belle keeps a box there. When do you mean to challenge her?"

"Aubrey committed me for tomorrow morning."

Having reached Albany, Edmund pulled up his horses. "I shall have to delay going to the office until after the match, then. May I wish you good luck."

"Thank you," Jack said, accepting his friend's hand down. "For the ride—and the opinion, as well."

Edmund nodded. "Drury Lane, upper right. I must work tonight, or I'd be tempted to join you. In any event, I hope Rupert, that slimy bastard, doesn't end up with her." Flicking the reins, Edmund set his horses in motion.

Jack watched as his friend drove off, then took the stairs with a purposeful stride. He had his rooms to put to rights, his solicitor to consult, a valet to hire, new garments to order and Horse Guards to visit.

And he didn't want to be late to the theater.

CHAPTER THREE

ALREADY QUESTIONING her wisdom in letting Mae persuade her to attend the theater, Belle asked her companion to precede her out of the carriage. In a bright purple gown of extremely low cut, her cloak left open to display her famous attributes, Mae set off, cutting a path through the throng like the bow of a frigate through dark water.

Thankfully, Mae would distract some of the gawkers—and enjoy every minute of the attention as fiercely as Belle despised it. But if Bellingham's death was to free her, she couldn't remain behind the walls of her house in Mount Street. Nor was it fair to continue depriving Mae of the excitement and activities of the London she so enjoyed.

Besides, Kean was to play one of his best roles tonight. Now that she was her own—and only her own—mistress, she could bar the door to her box and with the intense concentration she'd honed over the years, shut out the crowd, the chatter—everything but the action onstage.

Closing her ears and her mind to the shouts and whistles that had begun the moment her coach was recognized, she followed Mae into the theater. Her regal posture and icy dignity, reinforced by the presence beside her of Watson, former bouncer at the bordello where Mae had once worked and now Belle's bodyguard-cum-butler, served to keep the curious from crowding her as she crossed the lobby and climbed the stairs to her box.

A mercifully brief time later, Belle took her seat beside Mae, Watson behind them to guard the door. Mae looked about avidly, plying her fan as she nodded and smiled to acknowledge the greetings called out to them.

Her companion was so obviously in her element that Belle had to smile. She was going to have difficulty embarking on a more retired life with Mae at her side, the woman's flamboyant presence better than a handbill as an advertisement for the world's oldest profession. Though her companion had, amazingly, retained a child's delight in the world and a sunny nature as transparent as clear springwater, there was no disputing the fact that Mae Woods, a whore's daughter who'd followed in her mother's footsteps when she was twelve years old, was hopelessly vulgar.

Still, this aging courtesan had been as much mother as friend to Belle in some of her direst hours. She couldn't imagine dismissing her—even had Mae somewhere other than the streets to go, which she didn't.

Teach Mae to be more discreet, Belle mentally added to the list she'd begun of Things To Do With My Life Now, and then chuckled at the incongruity of that notion.

A slight diminution in the noise level signaled that the players were about to begin. But as Belle transferred her attention to the stage, her eye was drawn to the glitter of gold on a red uniform tunic. Her gaze rose to the sunburned face above the jacket—the face of the dark-haired, dark-eyed soldier who'd studied her this morning.

He was watching her now, his regard so intense her skin prickled and a shock skittered to the pit of her stomach. She swallowed a gasp, taken aback at the power of that wordless connection. As if he somehow knew the effect he'd caused, the soldier smiled as he bowed to her.

Feeling heat flush her face, Belle looked away without acknowledging him. Mae, ever alert, leaned over to whisper, "Who was that?"

"I have no idea," Belle replied, pressing a hand over her stomach to quell the flutters and resolutely fixing her eyes on the actor now entering from the wings.

With Kean in excellent form, the supporting cast equally competent and the play engrossing, Belle should have lost herself in the world the players were creating. But to her annoyance, she found the red-coated officer was seated at the periphery of her vision, always just within sight as she followed the events taking place onstage.

Worse, though she never glanced at him to confirm it, somehow she could *feel* his gaze on her, further eroding her concentration. By the time the interval arrived, she was irritated, restless, and tempted to simply go home.

As the audience began milling about, she turned back to Watson. "Remember, I wish to admit no one."

Mae put a hand on her arm. "Please, Belle, Lord M and Sidmouth just waved. Can we not let them in?" She added in a low voice, "Darlington and some gents are in the box opposite. I'd hate for 'em to see me here all alone."

With a sigh, Belle capitulated. "Of course you may receive your friends."

"Thank you!" Mae said, beaming at her.

But even as Belle resigned herself to an interlude filled with noisy chatter, she felt unaccountably more relaxed. As she suspected, when she cautiously looked in his direction, the soldier was no longer in his seat.

Mae's two gentlemen appeared promptly and Belle moved to let the men take the seats nearest her. As she settled into a chair near the back rail, she heard a deep, unfamiliar voice addressing Watson.

Once again, sparks sputtered along her nerves, and somehow she knew the speaker must be her soldier. Sternly repressing the impulse to sneak a closer look at the man, she kept her attention on the stage.

Watson's gravelly reply was followed by another exchange, after which he called to her, "Lady Belle, be ye wishful of receiving a Captain Carrington?"

She felt at once an inexplicable need to flee and a strong desire to tell Watson to let the caller enter. Instead, she said, "I don't know a Captain Carrington."

"But she does know me," a familiar voice interjected. "Will you not allow me in, *mon ange?*"

"Egremont!" Belle exclaimed with delight, turning instinctively toward the sound of his voice. "I thought you were still in the country. Please, do join me."

As Watson stepped aside to admit the earl, Belle caught a glimpse of the dark-haired captain behind him.

In those few seconds before the door closed, she got an impression of broad shoulders, an intelligent face—and a gaze even more compelling over the short distance now separating them.

With a little shiver, she turned her attention to the gentleman, his dark hair silvered at the temples, taking the chair beside her. "When did you return?"

"Just this morning. You look ravishing, as always, *mon ange*," he said, bringing her hand up to kiss. Retaining her fingers in a light grasp, he studied her face. "How are you faring? I didn't hear of Richard's death until two weeks ago. I wish I had been here to help."

"I fare quite well, thank you. And there wasn't much to do as I was not, of course, involved in the funeral arrangements." She took a deep breath. "Having been his friend long before you were mine, you may think it despicable of me, but I'm glad he suffered the fatal attack at his club, rather than in Mount Street."

Egremont squeezed her fingers. "Not despicable at all, my dear. Given how things stood with his family, it would have been most awkward and unpleasant for you, had he breathed his last under your roof. And I hope I've always been a good friend to you both."

Belle's eyes stung with tears. "Indeed you were. I don't know what I should have done, had I not had you to discuss literature and art and politics with me, to escort me to the galleries and concerts in which Bellingham had no interest. To laugh with me." Her throat tight, she added, "You treated me as 'Belle's lady' from the first time we met. I can't tell you how much that meant."

"How could I do otherwise? You are elegance and gentility down to your bones, *mon ange*." After a moment, he added, "I see you are not wearing black."

She gave a bitter laugh. "No. I suspect half those watching will censure me for not displaying a proper respect at the death of my protector. Whereas the other half would condemn me for effrontery, did I dare to wear mourning."

"Would you wear it, could you do as you wish?" he asked, once again studying her face.

"No," she said bluntly. "Our relationship, as you surely observed, was...complex and often acrimonious." Lifting her chin, determined to tell the truth even if it lowered her in his regard, she continued, "Though I would not have wished his death, I am not sorry to be free."

He nodded, apparently pondering that comment. "What do you intend to do now?"

"I'm not certain yet."

"You have adequate funds?"

"I'm quite comfortable, thank you."

"So you don't intend to—"

"No," she said quickly. "Not again. Not ever."

Massaging the hand he still held, he cleared his throat. Something about his hesitancy, the pressure of his fingers on hers, filled Belle with the dismaying suspicion that this man who had been her one friend among Bellingham's cronies, the only man who'd not, openly or by innuendo, treated her as Bellingham's whore, was about to ruin that friendship by offering her carte blanche.

"My wife and I have long had an arrangement," he

began softly. "She despises London. Over the years, she has been content to remain at our country estate, tending to the house and the children, allowing me to go my own way as long as, eventually, I return to her. For an arranged marriage, it hasn't worked out too badly, and for most of those years, I was content. Until I met you."

"Please, don't," she begged, trying to pull her fingers free, dreading to hear the words.

He let them go. "I don't mean to distress you, my sweet. I'm not immune to your attraction, despite being several years your senior, and if I thought I could persuade you to become my mistress and make you happy, I should beg you to do me that honor. But I know how much you hated the notoriety Richard thrust upon you."

He gave her a wry smile. "We have rubbed along comfortably, my wife and I, these many years, and even had I grounds for a divorce, which I do not, I would not do that to her. Since I cannot offer you what you desire most—a legitimate relationship—I beg only that you will allow me to remain your friend."

He did understand. The poignancy of that affirmation helped to mitigate her discomfort at discovering that even Egremont, whom she'd considered more in the light of an elder brother, felt a carnal attraction to her.

At least he did not intend to act upon his desire, indifferent to her preferences.

"I have few enough friends that I want to lose one— especially not one as dear to me as you," she replied.

"Good, that's settled. You will let me know if I can help you in any way? With no obligation, of course."

"I will, and thank you again."

"Then I am forgiven?"

Tilting her head in inquiry, she said, "For what?"

He drew one hand back and kissed it. "For not cherishing you with a purely platonic affection. You are so heartbreakingly lovely, a man cannot help but yearn, you know. Now, how are you finding the play?"

Though his avowal left her still a bit uncomfortable, she was addressing herself to his question when raucous laughter from Mae's group drowned out her words.

Whether because she wished to impress her former lover with her gaiety or because she was in unusually high spirits, Mae, it seemed to Belle, was behaving more outrageously than usual. Giggling at Sidmouth's extravagant compliments, she allowed him to remove her glove and kiss her wrist, while Lord Mannington, who'd stolen her fan, drew the ivory sticks down over the heavy swell of one breast and was now toying with the nipple. Given the loudness of their laughter and the lewdness of Mannington's gesture, Belle knew their box was certain to draw the attention of everyone in the theater.

Her cheeks heating to consider what the stern-faced captain would surely be thinking, were he once again watching them from his seat, Belle made another entry to her mental list: *When in public, screen Mae's companions.*

Then the actors returned to the stage and Belle directed her attention to the play.

JACK STOOD FOR SOME TIME, observing with distaste the antics of the group along the rail of Lady Belle's box while trying to glimpse the couple behind them. Having little success, he gave up and stalked out of the theater.

Just as well that he returned to his rooms, he told himself. Tomorrow would begin early. Although it would be wiser, he thought as he hailed a hackney, to dispense with this ridiculous plan of challenging Lady Belle.

He'd been disappointed, but not surprised when, unable to resist approaching Belle, he'd been refused entry to her box. He was, after all, a stranger. When the man she'd hailed so warmly was admitted, however, he *was* surprised—and considerably disturbed—to discover that he was jealous.

Not just a little jealous, but suddenly, furiously, pistols-for-breakfast jealous of a man he'd never met, for sitting beside a woman he didn't really know. A woman he couldn't and shouldn't possess.

Faith, he was becoming more of a moonling than Aubrey!

Except he knew himself too well. Unlike Aubrey, when he wanted something, he would never be content to simply gaze at it from afar.

And that just wouldn't do. Despite her breath-stopping beauty of form and face, Lady Belle was nothing but an expensive harlot, perhaps a bit more refined in manner but with morals no better than those of her companion, whose suggestive dress and vulgar behavior in the theater box tonight clearly proclaimed her profession.

Only an idiot would actively seek out such a

woman—and chance letting a tart like Belle, who was alleged to have indulged in public lewdness and fornicated for the titillation of leering onlookers, get her harpy's claws embedded any further into his mind and senses.

In the morning, he decided as he arrived back at his rooms, he would tell Aubrey that he'd changed his mind.

But after he'd drunk a glass of brandy and retired for the night, he could not sleep. An indeterminate amount of tossing and turning later, he crawled back out of bed.

Cursing himself for a fool, he dredged his supplies from a saddlebag and began polishing his sword.

AS SOON AS the final lines were spoken, Belle left Mae with her friends, who'd persuaded her to attend an after-theater party, and proceeded down the stairs, hoping to cross the lobby before the bulk of the audience exited.

She'd just refused Egremont's offer to escort her home when a young lady in a fashionable evening gown hurried toward them—and halted abruptly, directly in front of Belle.

Stopping short to avoid colliding with the girl, Belle was about to edge around her when she felt Egremont stiffen.

"Helena, what are you doing here all alone?" he said.

"I wanted to look into her eyes when I confronted her," the girl replied, sending Belle a glance so full of loathing that Belle's breath caught in her throat. "And why are you with *her?*" Helena asked, transferring her furious gaze to the earl. "Papa's been dead barely a month. I thought you were his friend!"

Bellingham's daughter, Belle realized, dread knotting her stomach.

Egremont took the girl's arm. "You're upset—and no wonder, after such a shocking loss! Let me see you home."

Twisting free of Egremont's grip, the girl turned back to Belle. "Is there no man you do not try to bewitch?"

"Helena, 'tis highly improper for you to be here unescorted," Egremont said softly, "or to speak with—"

"My father's *whore?*" the girl shrilled.

Out of the corner of her eye, Belle noted the lobby filling with people—people who slowed, stopped, gazed with openmouthed fascination at the new scene being enacted before them. Nausea growing in her gut, Belle's mind fled to the mental fortress from which she could watch events unfolding around her, her sense and spirit detached from whatever indignities might be inflicted on her body.

"Given my new expectations, Lord Egremont," Miss Bellingham said, "'tis unnecessary to be concerned for my reputation. I doubt I shall receive any respectable offers of marriage, no matter how blameless my conduct."

"Excuse me," Belle murmured, edging away.

"I'm not done with you!" the girl cried, seizing Belle's wrist and yanking her close.

Belle flinched, half expecting a blow. Instead, Miss Bellingham continued hotly, "Was it not enough that you lured my father from his hearth and family, embarrassed my mother before the ton and her friends? That we had barely enough to maintain a household while you were lavished with gowns and jewels? Is your greed so vast that you must bewitch father into bequeathing you the very bread out of our mouths and the roof from over our heads?"

She's heard about the will, Belle realized.

As if from a distance, Belle watched herself calmly wrest her arm free. "Miss Bellingham, I appreciate how grief disorders the spirit, but you are mistaken."

"About what?" the girl demanded. "The extent of your avarice? The fact that you—"

"I advise you to consult your solicitors," Belle interrupted. "Lord Egremont will see you home." She stepped around the girl, Watson advancing to take a protective position at her elbow.

Ignoring the amused and accusing and censorious faces, Belle walked out of the theater and down the steps to her waiting carriage. Not until the door closed behind her, shutting out the murmurs and the avid gazes, did she relax, sagging against the cushions while nausea roiled in her belly and her heart thundered.

She didn't blame Miss Bellingham. Indeed, the girl had shown considerable spirit in confronting her father's harlot in public, knowing news of the scandalous meeting would surely become the ton's latest on-dit. Perhaps she hoped that publicizing the provisions of Bellingham's will would make it more difficult for Belle to entice a new protector, ruining Belle's future as she perceived Belle's supposed greed had destroyed her own.

Or perhaps Miss Bellingham was so filled with rage over the injustice of her situation that she no longer cared that addressing a courtesan would soil her own reputation. That Belle could understand even more readily.

Though she tried to dismiss the disturbing confrontation, the emotions she'd repressed while the incident was taking place refused to be banished. A familiar sense of anguished humiliation made her stomach churn, heated her face, summoned tears that trembled at the corners of her eyes.

Enough! she told herself, struggling to rein in her disorderly feelings. 'Twas just that Miss Bellingham's unexpected attack had caught her off guard, leaving her prey to this atypical excess of sensibility.

She had just about succeeded in squelching the reaction when, with a jerk that nearly unseated her, the carriage squealed to a halt.

CHAPTER FOUR

LAUGHTER AND A BABBLE of loud voices wafted toward Belle as she raised the window shade and looked out, trying to determine the cause of the delay.

Light blazed from the doorway of a house she recognized as one of the more exclusive brothels in the theater district. Highlighted by its glare, several provocatively dressed women had just emerged with a number of fashionably garbed Corinthians, the couples proceeding toward a large barouche whose position in the middle of the street prevented Belle's carriage from advancing.

Another Corinthian stood on the steps conversing with a sharp-eyed woman Belle took to be the brothel's owner.

"Hurry up, Fen," a young buck called to him. "Don't want our lovelies—" he ran his fingers over the bare shoulders of the wench he held "—to catch their deaths."

The gentleman on the steps waved a languid hand. "Just settle our, ah, ladies into the coach while I conclude the negotiations with their charming employer."

"It'll be fifty pounds and not a tuppence less," the older woman was saying. "Not with ye taking off the best of me girls at the very start of the evening."

"A vast sum, ma'am," the gentleman said, extracting coins from his purse. "But how can I quibble when the company is so lovely? Now, my sweet, don't be bashful."

With that, he pulled from the shadows a slender lass who seemed, to Belle's eye, to be scarcely in her teens. Shrinking from the light, the girl raised a hand, trying to cover the bare skin revealed by her skimpy bodice.

"Please don't, sir," she protested when the man, laughing, brushed her hand away and bent to kiss one nipple, clearly visible beneath the gown's thin material.

Instantly Belle was transported to another time and place, when another young girl had vainly tried to hang on to the last shreds of her modesty.

A wave of heat swept through her, intensifying the lingering nausea in her gut, and for a moment, she feared she might faint. An inexorable need for cool air to clear her head of the memories and her stomach of the queasiness set her feet in motion. Several moments later, she stood at the top of the stairs beside the madam without any recollection of having traveled there.

But she was utterly sure of her purpose. "I, too, require a lady this evening," she told the woman. "This one—" she pointed to the cowering girl "—will be perfect. Whatever the gentleman is offering, I'll double it."

For a moment, the man on the steps sputtered a protest. Then his eyes widened and his indignation faded to a smile. "Lady Belle, a pleasure! We should be delighted to invite you to join our humble gathering."

"Regretfully, that is not possible, sir. Watson," she

called to the bodyguard who'd trotted up in her wake, "escort the girl to my coach."

"Right ye be, Lady Belle."

The gentleman on the steps opened his lips as if to object, but after glancing at Watson's impressive bulk, he must have realized that, alone, he could not hope to prevail. His smile more forced now, he bowed. "I must cede to your wishes, Lady Belle. But I consider that you owe me a favor—which I hope to redeem later." He ran a hot, speculative glance over her cloaked figure.

Dismissing him with a noncommittal nod, Belle turned back to the madam. "My man will return to pay you. Good evening, ma'am," she said and paced back to her coach.

She found the girl huddled at the far corner, arms wrapped around her torso as if trying to take up as little space as possible. The flickering carriage lamp revealed her small, pinched face and large, fearful eyes.

"What…what be ye wanting with me, ma'am?" she asked.

What reprobate would trifle with this child? Belle wondered. But the girl's wary pose and the arms braced defensively over her body told Belle more eloquently than words how life had treated the lass, despite the her fragile air and apparent youth.

"What is your name, child?"

"J-Jane Parsons, ma'am," the girl replied.

"Don't be afraid. I require no, ah, personal, services from you, nor am I taking you to a gathering at which you will be forced to entertain. You know who I am?"

"Oh, yes, ma'am. Everyone knows the beautiful Lady Belle." Looking wary, uncertain but resigned, the girl watched her.

Belle smiled wryly. What *did* she intend to do with this child whose services she had purchased on a whim for an outrageously inflated price?

See to her needs first, she supposed. "Have you supped yet, Jane?"

The girl's large eyes widened further. "N-no, ma'am. Mrs. Jarvis don't feed us nothing 'til morning—and then, only if we...we pleased the customers."

The fierce anger that always smoldered deep within Belle fired up again. Swallowing the curse that sprang to her lips, she silently damned all licentious men and the women who pandered to them.

After signaling the coachman to depart, Belle turned back to the girl. "Then first, you shall eat. After that, you may rest, if you like. My companion, Mae, has gone to a party, so my house will be quiet."

Though the girl's disbelief was patent in the dubious nod she returned, she said nothing more. The rest of the short drive was accomplished in silence.

Upon their arrival, Belle ordered food and bore Jane up to her chamber. Meekly the girl followed Belle's bidding that she wash, seat herself near the fire and wrap up in the thick woolen shawl Belle gave her. Her impassive countenance registered no emotion until Watson bore in a tray laden with cold meats, cheeses and fruit.

A gasp escaping her, she turned to Belle and asked if the meal was meant for her. Upon Belle's confirmation, she applied herself to the food with the fervor of one kept for too long on near-starvation rations.

Occasionally the girl directed a sidelong glance at Belle, as if she feared at any moment she might change her mind and have the tray removed.

By the time Jane consumed the last crumb, her wariness had vanished. "Thank you, Lady Belle," she said, her dark eyes glowing with gratitude. "I disremember when I last ate so fine!"

Carefully Jane removed the shawl and handed it back to Belle. "Thank you, too, for the loan of the wrap. Now, whatever it is ye wish me to do, I reckon I'm ready." Taking a deep breath, she squared her thin shoulders.

The forlorn valor of the gesture went straight to Belle's heart. "Truly, Jane, I have no other task for you."

For a long moment the girl stared at her. "No gentleman be waiting to…to sport with me, or with us both?"

Belle couldn't repress her grimace of distaste. "Certainly not!"

Before Belle could divine her intentions, Jane burst into tears and threw herself at Belle's feet.

Belle reached down to pull the weeping girl up. "Hush, my dear. Sit down and calm yourself."

By the time Belle had soothed Jane, the conviction had settled bone deep.

Under no circumstances was Belle going to send this child back to a brothel. Not tonight.

Not ever.

"I'm sorry to weep all over you, ma'am! But…it's been

so long since someone treated me like…like an honest lass."

"How did you come to be at Mrs. Jarvis's house?" Belle asked.

"I never looked to do such a shameful thing, I promise you! Last fall, a stranger come to market day in our village, saying he was a London merchant looking for girls wishful of working in the city. I'm right good with a needle, and clever at dressing hair and such. Weren't much for me at home, so me and two other girls, we signed up. Mr. Harris paid for our tickets and bundled us off on the next mail coach to the City."

All too conscious of the fate that could befall a young girl stranded alone, Belle asked, "Were you separated from your group on the road?"

Jane shook her head. "No, ma'am, Mr. Harris watched us real careful all the way to London, then turned us over to a lady—the hiring director, he said. She brought us tea and asked us what work we was wanting. I got powerful sleepy then, but I thought 'twas just the trip being so tiring and all…"

Though Belle felt certain she knew what came next, she prodded gently. "And then?"

Jane gave a shuddering sigh. "I woke up later in a strange room with naught of my own but my shift! Afore I could figure out where I was, Mrs. Jarvis come in. She said she would treat me nice, because there's men what will pay a lot for girls that look as young as me. Well, I was right horrified and told her straight out that I wouldn't never do such a thing! I begged her to let me work anywhere else, even in the scullery. She just shook her head and had her servant Waldo come in. A big, evil-looking man, he is. She told me if I didn't agree to do what she wanted, she'd have Waldo…persuade me. She said that, he being one what likes 'em young, with a fancy for rough sport, she don't let him use her own girls."

A shudder ran through Jane's thin frame. "The way he *looked* at me, Lady Belle! I thought there couldn't be nothing worse than Waldo. So—" her voice dropped to a whisper "—I…I agreed."

"Oh, Jane," Belle murmured, heart aching for her. "Did the other girls suffer the same fate?"

"I dunno, ma'am. They're not at Mrs. Jarvis's house, so maybe not all the girls brought to London end up there."

"Someone should look into this. Whoever is perpetrating this fraud should be transported!"

Jane shook her head doubtfully. "Mrs. Jarvis said if I ever thought to go to a constable, I'd be wasting my breath. I came to London willing enough, and staying at her house were my own choice."

"Only because you were threatened! I cannot believe such a scheme could be legal. But no more on that now. Do you want to return to Mrs. Jarvis?"

Jane shrugged. "What respectable household or shop would hire me now, however good I be with my needle?"

Belle smiled wryly. "I can't claim to be a 'respectable' household, but the task itself will be honest enough.

Would you like to work for me? I have a great many gowns I should like to have remade and 'tis a project beyond my skills. If you have the talent to do so, you would be rendering me a very great service."

"I should be honored, ma'am!" Jane exclaimed. A moment later, her excited glow faded. "But…I don't expect Mrs. Jarvis would let me. I bring in a lot of business."

Belle lifted her brows. "She can hardly *force* you to stay—unless she wishes to face prosecution. This is still England, and even women such as we cannot be held against our will."

"Then you think…you think I can stay?"

"Jane Parsons, do you wish to work for me?"

"Oh, yes, ma'am!"

"Then consider yourself hired. However, since it is quite probable that Mrs. Jarvis will not rejoice over your decision to pursue a new profession, let me inform her by message."

Jane paled. "I expect she'll be fiercesome angry."

"Never you worry about it! Now, let's find you some proper clothing and get you settled."

But once again Jane hesitated. "The rest of your household…they may not much like having a girl such as me thrust among 'em."

Recalling the range of checkered pasts among her employees, Belle laughed. "'Tis unlikely anyone taking service in the house of the infamous Lady Belle would stand in judgment of a fellow creature—nor would I permit it. Come along now. In the morning, you can begin on those gowns."

Though Jane rose, she didn't follow. "What if Mrs. Jarvis sends somebody to…to fetch me back?"

Behind the question, Belle sensed the girl's fear of the infamous Waldo. "I assure you, even if she dispatches her henchman, Watson is fully capable of handling him. He was once the best prize-fighter in England."

At that, Jane cast herself once again at Belle's feet. "Oh, my lady, I shall be forever grateful! And my skill with a needle ain't empty boasting, neither, you'll see! Show me any style you favor in a magazine or shop window, and I can make you the very thing!"

"I see we shall deal very well together," Belle replied, smiling as she shepherded Jane from the room.

After turning her new charge over to her housekeeper, Belle returned to pen the note informing Mrs. Jarvis of her employee's defection. By the time she'd finished crafting that missive, Belle's satisfaction at liberating Jane had faded.

Though she knew she'd done all she could, she found herself pacing her chamber, the glass of wine she'd sipped while composing her note unable to quell the agitation she'd felt ever since Miss Bellingham had accosted her at the theater.

Also simmering in her veins was the familiar desire to lash out at the world for the outrages it permitted—and particularly at the villains who preyed on innocents.

It was some time before she tired enough to seek her bed.

How fortunate, she thought as she plumped up her pillow, picturing with sardonic anticipation the arrogant,

lustful male faces watching—and then challenging—
her from the gallery, that tomorrow she had another
fencing lesson.

CHAPTER FIVE

AUBREY MUST HAVE suspected Jack might have second thoughts about challenging Belle, for shortly after Jack rose the following morning, he answered a rap on his door to discover his friend standing in the hallway. "Help yourself to some ale," Jack invited, suppressing a smile.

"Much obliged," Aubrey said as he seated himself. "Wanted to arrive early and make sure you were prepared."

"Or to make sure I went through with it?"

"No question about that," Aubrey responded as he poured a glass. "Gave your word. Just thought I'd escort you over, me being your second of sorts."

"Not a second—a principal," Jack retorted wryly. "You being the one who volunteered me."

"Could have refused if you'd wanted. But what man could resist the opportunity to win a kiss from Belle—especially one who has an excellent chance of succeeding?"

Jack wanted to protest, but honesty kept him silent. It would be gratifying to succeed where other men had failed, but Jack knew that deep down, what he sought most was a taste of the woman who so intrigued and attracted him. He had tossed restlessly most of the night, sleep eluding him as his mind kept conjuring vivid images of taking her in his arms, her mouth yielding, opening under his. In lieu of replying, he took a long draught of ale.

"I tipped the hackney driver to wait," Aubrey said after draining his mug. "Given your reputation for swordplay, the gallery should be crowded. We must depart immediately if we wish to secure chairs."

"I would rather stand at the side, where I can observe the lesson without it being obvious."

"Search out her weaknesses," Aubrey agreed, "though not being a fencer of your rank, I've yet to note any. You'll not want to miss even the smallest opening that could allow you to win the wager—and perhaps persuade her that further intimacy would be even more enjoyable, eh?"

Jack laughed. "There's little chance of that. I can't meet her price, and I doubt my lovemaking skill is sufficient to impress a woman of Belle's vast experience."

"Did those French and Spanish ladies not teach you a trick or two?"

Jack shook his head. "Your vivid imagination again, Aubrey. Soldiers spend much more time slogging through dust, mud and rain to bed down on damp ground or in flea-infested hovels than romping with foreign beauties."

Aubrey picked up Jack's uniform jacket. "Please, don't shatter my boyhood illusions. Your coat, sir. If Belle *should* take a liking to you, promise you'll not forget the part I had in bringing you together."

"I'm unlikely ever to forget," Jack replied dryly as he fastened the jacket and buckled on his sword. He would not, he told himself as they proceeded to the waiting hackney, let his imagination play with the intoxicating notion of luring Belle into more than a simple kiss.

She's a wanton who would bed any man for a price, his righteous mind protested. But such a wanton! the part of his brain devoted to pleasure replied. Hadn't she kept Bellingham's desire aflame for years? His whole body tightened at the notion of the love tricks *she* must know… He dare not allow himself to imagine those smooth white hands, those plump pink lips performing their magic on him.

Enough, he brought his thoughts up sternly. Let lust rule his head and, talented fencer that she was, she'd insure he didn't win so much as one kiss.

As they approached the hackney, Edmund Darnley walked up. "Thought I'd come lend my support."

"Come along," Aubrey said. "But if Jack does succeed in winning Belle, he's promised me the first introduction."

"Winning Belle?" Edmund echoed with a puzzled look.

"Just Aubrey leaping to unsupported conclusions, as usual," Jack replied. "There's no question of anything but a kiss—which, I may add, I've yet to win."

"Then let us take our places so you have maximum time in which to determine how to do so," Aubrey said.

The three friends piled into the coach. A short time later, they entered the fencing room to find it, as Aubrey had predicted, already crowded. Jack nodded to Montclare and several others, while Rupert gave Jack a glacial glance as he passed to take up a place along the left wall.

A short time later, master and pupil walked in. Belle, dressed again in breeches and shirt, her golden hair pulled tightly back, ignored the assembly, focusing instead on inspecting her sword and testing its balance.

Releasing the breath he'd not realized he'd been holding, Jack wasn't sure whether to be relieved or vexed that this time he hadn't drawn to himself that compelling, focus-shattering gaze. Though she did not deign to look at him, he was acutely aware of her every movement.

He mustn't, he reminded himself, become distracted by the shapely derriere hugged by her doeskin breeches as she bent to adjust her foil or the arresting curves outlined beneath the shirt as she raised her arm, lest he be trounced as ignominiously as Wexley.

And Lord help him, he wanted that kiss.

That kiss and more.

Alarmed by the insidious observation that sprang, as powerful as it was unwanted, from somewhere deep within him, Jack turned his attention to the fencing master.

After a brisk review of stance and positioning, master and pupil assumed their places. During the lesson, Belle displayed the same quickness of foot and ingenuity of movement Jack had noted in her previous bout with Armaldi.

She maneuvered the foil as if it were a natural extension of her arm, her hands light and quick, her stance well balanced and her intense concentration evident in the swift countering moves with which she met each of Armaldi's advances. Though this time she did not disarm him, the match concluded with neither scoring a decisive advantage.

"Buono, mia bella," Armaldi said. "You fence again?"

"Perhaps not," Belle said. "I am a bit winded today."

Already stepping toward the fencing floor, Jack halted, surprised by the refusal. Quelling a ridiculously keen sense of disappointment, he had to compress his lips to keep from adding his objection to the shouts of protest.

"But you must accept a challenge," Ansley cried, dropping on one knee before her. "You gave your word!"

"Besides, someone particular has pledged to meet you today." Jack heard Aubrey's voice and sighed. "A soldier and veteran of Waterloo. Surely you won't deny this heroic defender of England a chance to win a victory far sweeter than the one he wrested from the brutal fields of battle?"

Belle's gaze swept the room and found Jack. For a long moment those intense blue eyes focused on his, sending a wave of shivers over his skin.

"You," she said at last.

Jack bowed. "Captain Jack Carrington, ma'am, at your service. And perhaps later, if you are skillful enough, at your mercy."

Her lips twitched at that, but in the next moment a man from the gallery strode forward, stripped to his shirt-sleeves and obviously intending his own challenge.

As Jack watched the other man approach, the unexpected and disturbingly intense conviction seized him that the chance to fence with her, best her—kiss her—belonged to him and him alone. He had to squelch a strong, primal desire to draw his sword and repel any other contenders.

The other man frowned at Jack. "'Tis not fair for Belle to be challenged by a military man, a professional!" he protested to Armaldi.

"Do you imply 'tis impossible she could match him, Waterfield?" Aubrey shot back. "That's presumptuous as well as ungentlemanly!"

While Waterfield sputtered that he'd not meant to disparage Belle's skill, Lord Rupert raised his voice above the clamor of disputing opinions. "Mr. Waterfield speaks the truth, Captain. You have, by your friend's admission, fought recently and in deadly earnest. To challenge Lady Belle, who fences upon occasion and for sport, would be to take unfair advantage of the terms of Ansley's wager. I must ask you to decline."

"You only wish him to step down because you fear he might actually win," Aubrey inserted hotly.

Rupert ignored him, his gaze fixed on Jack. "Lady Belle, unusual though she be, is still but a woman. Though she has achieved a remarkable level of proficiency, it is hardly possible for one of her sex to acquire the strength and skill necessary to best an accomplished gentleman."

Belle had been looking into the distance, seemingly oblivious to the argument around her, but at that, she snapped her gaze back. "You think me so paltry an opponent, my lord? 'Tis time, then, that I faced someone of unquestioned skill. Captain, I accept your challenge."

Exclamations erupted from around the gallery, some protesting against Belle meeting a soldier, some calling for the match to begin. His pulse having leapt in anticipation as soon as Belle accepted the challenge, Jack ignored them all, striding instead to an exuberant Aubrey, who stripped off his jacket and handed him his sword.

Lord Rupert followed, still arguing as Jack readied himself, until at last Armaldi waved his arms and stamped his feet to command the group to silence.

"The lady has spoken," he pronounced. "So be it."

After attempting without success to stare down Armaldi, Lord Rupert at last reluctantly took his seat. "We shall have a reckoning over this," he muttered to Jack.

Every nerve tightened by excitement and the tantalizing prospect of victory, Jack did not reply.

A moment later, he bowed again to Belle. "As eager as these gentlemen are to watch, so am I to test your skill."

Lady Belle fixed him with a look whose icy coldness surprised him. "I daresay you are. *En guarde,* Captain!"

So CARRINGTON'S FIRST name was Jack, Belle thought as she slowly circled him, looking for the opportunity to strike. She'd spotted him immediately, watching her, disturbing her concentration during her lesson as he'd disturbed her during the play last night.

Good that he had challenged her. In her current angry, restless mood, she welcomed the opportunity to strike out with the full fury that raged within her, a fury she always held in check when fencing with Armaldi.

So he wanted to "test her skill"? She could just imagine what sort of expertise he wanted to plumb.

She'd show him the edge of her blade, drive him back… Better yet, she decided, she'd feign the amateur and lure him to a humiliating defeat. Then he would leave her in peace and she could put him and his unsettling effect on her out of mind for good.

But though she tried to play on the disdain she suspected he harbored for her skill, attempted with weak and clumsy thrusts to make him commit to a lunge that would allow her to deliver a blow that knocked him off balance and perhaps off his feet, he refused to comply.

With a dawning respect for his perspicacity, Belle discarded that tactic and reverted to fencing him properly. Within a very few minutes, she began to wonder wryly whether she'd truly wanted this demanding a challenge.

Unlike her opponents thus far, Carrington was a fencer who truly knew the art, handling his blade with more finesse than anyone she'd yet faced, save Armaldi himself.

To have survived the slaughter of Waterloo, he must possess skill as well as luck. But she'd not expected a cavalryman, accustomed to brute slashing with a heavy saber, to be a master of subtle moves and shrewd strategy.

Just then he paused, and seizing that chance, Belle lunged. Their blades caught, forcing Armaldi to step in and untangle them.

Belle went immediately on the offensive again. Though the captain fell back, he never allowed her another opening. Seeming content to counter her moves with only an occasional strike back, he simply did not make any mistakes she could use to deliver the decisive hit.

Back and forth across the floor they continued. Belle's hands grew sweaty, her breathing labored. Already tired by her lesson, she knew she was flagging. She would have to redouble her efforts before the captain could turn her growing fatigue to his advantage.

Breaking away to gather her breath, Belle caught sight of the gallery. Men stood beside their chairs, waving their fists and shouting, their eyes feverish, their faces distorted by an excitement very much like lust.

The captain paused also, watching her with those bold dark eyes, a slight smile on his face. Aside from the sheen of sweat on his face, he appeared not at all fatigued. Not at all *challenged*.

The humiliating, infuriating suspicion swept through Belle that the captain was not truly engaging her at all. No, he was merely playing with her, checking her moves to keep from being pricked, but not using his full abilities.

Once again, a man was toying with her—while other men watched and cheered him on.

Frustration, fatigue and anger ignited into a fireball of fury that, intensified by remembered shame and pain, blazed out of control. Her eyes narrowed, her head and body felt suddenly light and her breast filled with a single, murderous desire for vengeance.

On the fencer now taunting her. On all of them.

Teeth clenched in a snarl, she attacked.

PAUSING HIMSELF as Lady Belle paused for a respite, Jack assessed his opponent. She was amazingly good, and he'd been hard-pressed to protect himself without resorting to the dragoon's killing slash that might have injured her, despite the protective bit of cork attached to their foils.

But not having the stamina he had developed after years of performing this deadly game, she was tiring. A few more turns about the room, he judged, and her arms would weaken, her steps start to falter. Then, he would wait for an opportunity to disarm her...and win that kiss.

His whole body stirring at the notion, he smiled slightly. And then suddenly she sprang at him.

Whipping up his blade to protect his face, he was forced to concentrate all his energies on defending himself as, in a frenzy of thrusts and parries, she drove him hard.

Even as sweat began dripping from his face and

soaking his gloves, he wondered what had happened. Between one instant and the next, this match had ceased to be a test of skill. He'd fought in enough battles to recognize in the ferocity of Lady Belle's attack the blood lust of an adversary bent not on simple victory—but on murder.

As he parried one furious slash, the momentum of her lunge carried the deflected blade to the floor, embedding the tip into the wood. With a growl, Belle yanked the blade free—leaving behind the cork protector.

He should call the match to a halt, he thought as she drove him into a corner and tried to pin him. But before he could bring himself to end this curious, exhilarating contest, he gazed down into her eyes.

And encountered a look of such complete, blind hatred that it shocked him to the soul. Unable to imagine what he could possibly have done to have inspired so venomous an expression, for an instant he stood motionless.

In the next instant, he saw light dancing off a flash of blade, felt a blow to the chest followed by a searing, white-hot pain. As he looked down in bemusement, blood began seeping from a hole beneath his left shoulder.

For a long moment, he watched the pulsating flow while the voices from the gallery faded to a hum. His head grew light, his limbs clumsy. Dimly he noted the sword falling from his nerveless fingers.

As the room flickered and dissolved into black, he realized that he wasn't going to win that kiss after all.

CHAPTER SIX

DEAR LORD in heaven, she'd just killed her soldier.

Her fury washed away with the flow of blood trickling down Jack Carrington's chest, Belle dropped her foil and tried to brace him as he swayed. Then his eyes rolled back and he collapsed, taking her to the floor with him.

She scrambled out from under him to rip open his shirt. "Someone get a physician," she cried, dimly aware of a chaos of shouts, overturned chairs and running feet.

Hands shaking with dread, she ripped the cuffs off her shirt and clamped them over the neat hole she had punched into Jack Carrington's chest. Willing away the nausea brought on by fatigue and the scent of blood, she leaned her full weight against him.

Sweat dripped down her forehead and marred her view of Carrington's face, now drained of all color. "Hold on, Captain!" she urged. "You didn't survive Waterloo to die on a fencing-room floor."

A hand closed over hers and she glanced up, startled.

"Edmund Darnley, Lady Belle—a friend of Jack's. If you will allow me to hold the pads in place? I've several stone more than you to bear against them."

"But I must do something," she cried, needing some distraction from the horror that had just transpired.

Darnley's lips curved into a grim smile. "I'd say you've done quite enough. But if you can find something to put under his head, 'twill ease his breathing, I think."

Reluctantly Belle ceded him her place and scurried to grab a cushion from one of the overturned chairs. Dropping on her knees beside Darnley, she wedged the pillow under the captain. "I'm sorry," she whispered to Darnley.

The captain's friend gave her a short nod.

Then another gentleman—blond, exquisitely dressed, a bit stout, whom Belle recognized as one of the crowd that usually attended her lessons—knelt beside them.

"Aubrey Ludlowe, ma'am. How does he, Edmund?"

"Jack's a tough old trooper. Is a doctor on the way?" Despite the calm words, Darnley looked grim and his gaze remained riveted on the still, white-faced figure whose chest rose and fell almost imperceptibly under his palms.

"Armaldi dispatched his assistant to fetch him," Ludlowe said. "Damned if I want to see my best friend stick his spoon in the wall right in front of me when he's scarce returned from battle!" Ludlowe inhaled abruptly, his eyes widening. "Besides, should he…not recover, Lady Belle might be forced to flee to the continent!"

"Unless she had the protection of someone very well connected," Darnley agreed and then frowned. "Is Rupert still here?"

"The whole crowd is milling about."

"If you wish to be useful, ma'am," Darnley said to Belle, "escort Lord Rupert out. I fear he'd snuff Jack in a heartbeat if he thought it would give him an advantage."

The truth of Darnley's words made her shudder, but the last person she wished to entice was the persistent baron. "They should all go," she countered. "The captain needs air and the doctor will need space to work. Armaldi!" she called. "Clear the room, please!"

The wiry Italian nodded. *"Subito, Bella. Signore!"* Clapping his hands to draw their attention, he waved the crowd toward the door. "You also, my lord Rupert," he added when that gentleman looked as if he meant to linger.

"I will await the lady, who should be escorted from this distressing scene as soon as possible," Rupert said.

"I'm not leaving until the captain has been treated," Belle replied.

"Ah, he arrives, *il dottore!*" Armaldi cried.

"The doctor had a colleague visiting, a military physician, Major Thompson," the fencing master's assistant called to them as he entered. "Thought it might be best to bring him."

"Oh, yes, Dr. Thompson, we'll be glad of your experience!" Ludlowe said, relief in his voice.

After having to push his way past several groups of bystanders, the doctor ordered, "Out with you all, now!" Setting down his bag, he knelt beside the captain while Darnley described the injury and Armaldi shepherded out the remaining lingerers. Even Rupert, with a disdainful glance at the physician, walked toward the door. "I shall wait outside to escort you home, Lady Belle."

"I may be here some time," Belle warned.

"Nonetheless, I shall wait," he said, and to her vast relief, finally exited. When she returned her attention to the captain, the doctor had begun examining the wound.

"Why don't you go change, ma'am?" Darnley asked, glancing at her. "I'm sure you'll want to…freshen up."

Only then, following his gaze, did Belle notice the blood spattering her breeches and shirtfront, soaking the ragged edges of her torn sleeves.

Carrington's blood. Blood, welling still around the doctor's probing fingers, from a wound her carelessness had caused. A wound that might yet cost Carrington his life.

Despite a sudden dizziness that made her faint, she shook her head. "I can't leave. Not until we know…" She couldn't bring herself to finish the sentence.

"Remain if you wish, ma'am," the doctor said, "but no attack of the vapors, if you please! There's a frightful lot of blood, but his pulse is steady. If he'd severed an artery, he'd have bled to death already. Much will depend on how seriously the lung is affected."

With that not-so-comforting assessment, the doctor continued probing. And so Belle remained in her gore-spattered garments, gaze fixed on the captain's too-pale face, trying to form a prayer for his recovery out of the tumult of anxious thoughts tumbling about in her head.

She had almost killed a man. Whatever had possessed her to attack him so? The protector must have become dislodged from her blade. She should have noticed it, would have noticed, had she not been in such a rage.

Remembering the ferocity of that anger chilled her. For years she'd felt herself the victim of another's unfeeling, heedless action. It dismayed her to find within herself a similar strain of thoughtless single-mindedness.

Her mind recoiled from the possibility that Carrington might die. The captain would recover. He must.

His probing apparently complete, the doctor sprinkled a powder over the wound, drew a roll of cotton from his bag and began binding up the wound.

Though she knew the doctor could make no promises, Belle couldn't prevent herself asking, "Will he recover?"

"Though the lungs appear intact, he will have some difficulty breathing, and I can't tell yet whether the blade touched anything vital. Of course, there's always the danger from fever, but he will do for the present."

The captain wasn't going to die—yet. Belle almost sagged in relief. "Thanks be to God," she murmured.

"I've bound up the shoulder to keep it immobile. I trust you have lodgings nearby? You'll need to move him carefully to avoid disturbing the wound. Don't worry if he takes a while coming to himself. I'll leave you some laudanum, but on no account administer any until you are sure he is clearheaded. Watch for fever, and if the lungs were damaged, a pleurisy might settle in."

Belle must have paled, for the doctor patted her hand. "Don't distress yourself, my dear. Your husband appears to be a strong fellow, and from the looks of that scar on his shoulder, has weathered worse. Send a servant to fetch me in Curzon Street and I'll check him again this afternoon."

Belle opened her mouth to deny the relationship, then closed it. There seemed no reason to correct the doctor's misapprehension and make this incident more embarrassing for the captain than it was already bound to be.

"Thank you very much, Doctor," she said instead.

Hauling himself to his feet, Thompson laughed and shook his head. "Pricked in a fencing match! You'd think he would have gotten his fill of that in Belgium. Doubtless he'll soon recover and go haring off on some other fool stunt, causing you to doubt your joy at his deliverance. I shall see you this afternoon, ma'am."

With Ludlowe and Darnley echoing Belle's thanks, the doctor departed. "Signore Armaldi, have you anything that can be fashioned into a litter?" Belle asked.

"*Sì, mia Bella*, I go prepare it," the fencing master said. Gathering his assistant, he walked out, leaving Belle alone with the injured captain and his friends.

"Where should he be conveyed?" she asked them.

Darnley and Ludlowe exchanged glances. "I'm afraid that's a bit of a problem, ma'am," Darnley replied. "Jack just arrived back in England and is staying in borrowed rooms. His family is still at their country home, and at present, he hasn't even a valet to attend him."

"I suppose my valet could undertake Jack's care," Ludlowe said, "though he has no experience in a sick-room."

"I've nothing better to offer," Darnley said with a

frown. "My mother would gladly take up the task, but she, too, is not yet in London. I suppose we could ask the physician to recommend a competent nurse, but…"

Both men stared at her. A panicky foreboding added to the mix of fear, regret and worry churning in her gut.

Though she would be more than willing to pay for the services of a competent nurse, it would be unconscionable to send the captain back with only a hired stranger to watch over him. 'Twould be best for his own family to supervise his care. But in the absence of his relations, his friends clearly expected her to volunteer for the task.

"I…I have some sickroom experience," she admitted. "However, I am sure that his family, who will be most distressed to learn of his injuries, would be even more upset to find he was being tended by one of my…reputation."

"They'd be more upset to find he'd died from lack of care," Darnley said bluntly.

It isn't fair, she thought despairingly, torn by guilt and anxiety. Not now, when she could at last begin searching for something that might lay to rest the torments of the past and offer her peace—or absolution. She'd rather introduce a viper into her house than invite the disturbing captain to reside within her walls.

At present, though, his ability to disturb her would be limited. Besides, she could not escape the fact that, having been the cause of his injury, she must do whatever she could to assist in his recovery. Though she dreaded what she must say next, she knew there was no alternative.

"Transport him to my house. I shall manage the captain's care until the doctor declares him well enough to be moved to a more…suitable location."

"Thank you, ma'am," Darnley said quietly. "I know how great an imposition this will be, and if there were any other practical alternative, I should embrace it. You will be doing Captain Carrington a very great kindness."

"I sincerely doubt, when they hear of it, that the ladies of his family will agree," Belle replied grimly.

To her surprise, Darnley smiled. "His mother, Lady Anne, is a fair and reasonable lady who will feel only appreciation for the kind woman who assisted her son."

Even the infamous Lady Belle? Belle shook her head. "Let us hope the captain's sojourn in my care will be brief enough to escape general notice."

Darnley made no reply, but Belle knew, as his friends must also, that such a hope was vain. The titillating news that Lady Belle had wounded a soldier in a fencing match would by midday have become the ton's latest on-dit. The information concerning that soldier's current location probably wouldn't remain secret much longer.

Captain Carrington would just have to deal with the problem later, Belle thought with a sigh. One could only hope that his mother had the strength of mind Lord Darnley claimed—and that he didn't have a fiancée waiting somewhere with a tendency to be missish.

Grimacing at the sticky residue of blood on her hands, Belle wiped them on her ruined trousers. "Gentlemen, with your leave, I will go make myself presentable. Ask

Armaldi's staff to have my coach made ready. I'll return shortly to help you transport Captain Carrington. Thank you again for your prompt assistance."

Darnley and Ludlowe bowed. "Jack is one of my oldest friends. I would do anything for him," Darnley affirmed.

Including never forgiving someone who'd done him an injury, Belle thought as she walked out.

Pensively Belle paced back to the small room Armaldi allotted her as a dressing chamber, thankful that an errand had prevented Mae from accompanying her this morning. As she rang for a maid to assist her, another sigh escaped as she considered what her excitable companion would have to say once she learned of this morning's work.

A few moments later, suitably dressed and outwardly composed, Belle returned to help Armaldi and the captain's friends carefully convey his still-unconscious body into Belle's waiting carriage. Settling herself beside him, she ordered the coachman to drive them slowly home.

Though she tried to close her mind to the possible consequences of having the captain under her roof, as she gazed at Carrington's pale expressionless face, Belle knew the queasiness in her gut was only partly due to the shock of the morning's events and the stench of blood lingering in her nostrils.

CHAPTER SEVEN

AWAKING GROGGILY to the sensation of his chest aflame, as he struggled to consciousness Jack tried to summon the words to rebuke whichever trooper had been clumsy enough to knock a flaming brand out of the campfire and nearly incinerate his officer.

As he instinctively turned from the heat, a blast of pain engulfed him, so searing that it drove every vestige of sleepiness from his head. His eyes flew open, the half-formed words tumbling out in an unintelligible gasp.

"Awake at last!" said a cool, soft voice. "I was beginning to fear you would never come back to yourself."

Narrowing his focus against the agony radiating downward from his shoulder, Jack halted his gaze at a candlelit face haloed against the room's darkness. A face of such perfect, classical beauty he was momentarily distracted from his pain. Then memory flooded back.

Lady Belle. His challenge. The protector on her blade coming loose.

Lady Belle trying to kill him.

As he gritted his teeth and cautiously shifted to see her better, he noted that she had very nearly succeeded.

"You must be thirsty. At least, the doctor said you would be when you finally reached consciousness."

He *was* thirsty, he discovered. His tongue seeming too thick for speech, he nodded. As Belle put a glass to his lips, he leaned forward and drank greedily, ignoring the immediate protest from his shoulder. Before he'd barely slaked his thirst, dizziness assailed him and he sagged back against his pillows, his eyes fluttering shut.

Damn and blast, he thought in disgust. He had about as much strength as a newborn kitten.

"Dr. Thompson said I could give you laudanum for pain, once you were fully conscious. You…are conscious?"

He opened his eyes, as much to prove it to himself as to reassure her. "Yes."

Picking up a spoon and a small brown bottle from a tray beside the bed, she asked, "Do you want—?"

"No," he said, recalling the nightmarish narcotic-induced sleep he'd endured after being wounded at Corunna. "Pain is…tolerable. Don't like being cloth-headed."

"As you wish. The doctor also said you might have difficulty breathing, if the injury affected the lung."

"Hard to tell," he said with a grimace, "but I can breathe." Inhaling deeply enough to utter more than a few words at a time, however, was a different matter.

"Praise heaven!" She opened her mouth as if to say something else, then hesitated.

Jack might be in a sorry state, but he wasn't half-dead enough not to feel a spark of masculine response as she ran the tip of her tongue over those plump lips. "Do you remember…how you became injured?" she said at last.

Why she had tried to kill him? he asked himself. A disturbing vision of her lovely face contorted with hate flickered through his mind and he inhaled sharply, then gasped as another surge of pain seared his chest.

He struggled to regain his concentration. If he could induce her to describe what had happened, maybe he could find out what had prompted her violent response.

"It's all…rather hazy."

"It cannot possibly be sufficient, given the injuries you've suffered, but I owe you an enormous apology. You had challenged me to a fencing match—you remember that?"

He nodded, prompting her to continue.

"Sometime during the match," she said, moistening her lips again, "the protector on my blade became dislodged. Being unaware of this, when you chanced to drop your guard and I saw a chance to score a hit, I took it. I never dreamed…!" She stopped again, her eyes and expression mirroring a clear distress. "The fault is entirely mine."

"Had I done you some injury," he asked, gritting his teeth against the increasing pain of each inhaled breath, "that you felt moved to attack?"

Her face coloring, she didn't immediately reply. So she knew her response had been disproportionate. Why? he wondered anew.

"Of course you had done me no injury," she said after a moment. "I—I merely wished to test my skill against one who was accounted a superb swordsman."

"Our relative positions now…argue against that," he observed wryly.

"There is no way I can make restitution for all you have suffered, but I have arranged to oversee your care until you are sufficiently recovered to be transported to your family's estate, which Lord Darnley assured me you would wish as soon as possible. At the moment, you are lodged in my house on Mount Street. Not a very… respectable arrangement, I realize, but there seemed no other recourse, you being far too ill to be left—"

"Nay, madam, don't apologize! I should be…in bad case indeed had you returned me to Albany. Only hope I've not been…too much of a charge." He attempted a smile. "Many a gentleman would consider…a sword wound a trifling cost…to lie where I do now."

"Not if theirs were the chest pierced by the blade," she retorted, ignoring his attempt at gallantry. "In any event, I shall arrange for your journey as soon as the physician allows. Though I fear," she added with a sigh, "that shall not be soon enough to prevent the troubling news of your present…situation from reaching your family."

"My family will thank you," Jack replied, surprised that Lady Belle seemed aware of the distress his mother might well experience upon hearing her only son was being nursed by the ton's most celebrated Fashionable Impure. Odd, he thought, that a woman who had embraced a calling like Belle's would spare a thought over how an association with her would be viewed by respectable people.

"Do you feel up to drinking some broth?"

At her question, he realized he was indeed hungry, though broth didn't appeal. "Feel like having the steak...I didn't finish for breakfast."

"Beefsteak might be a tad ambitious," she replied with a smile.

Despite the pain, Jack's breath caught at how the sudden warmth of that expression, seen for the first time up close, magnified the natural beauty of her face. Though she was garbed in a high-necked, plain gray gown, her hair once again pulled severely back, the Quaker austerity of dress and coiffure seemed to emphasize rather than detract from the perfection of her features.

A smiling Botticelli angel, bending over his sickbed.

Extraordinary that a woman of her profession could exude such an aura of innocence. He felt that he might be content to spend the rest of his days simply gazing at her.

No wonder Bellingham had been so besotted.

And you, Carrington, had best keep a tight hold over your senses during the time you spend under her roof.

"Besides, that would have been breakfast yesterday," she continued while he remained speechless, staring like a lackwit. "'Tis evening now, so you were unconscious nearly a day and a half. Indeed, I was beginning to feel I must call Dr. Thompson back to check you again."

"That long?" Jack asked, shocked. As he studied her, recovering now from his bedazzlement, he noticed shadows beneath her eyes...and pulled up by the bed, a chair

with a shawl draped over its back. "You tended me…
all that time?"

"My companion Mae, though she possesses the kind-
est heart imaginable, turned queasy at the sight of you,
the footman was little better, and I feared that my butler, a former prize-fighter, might not be gentle enough.
But now that you are awake, I shall send Watson in and
rest."

"Please do! I apologize for being…such a burden."

"Having been the instrument of your injury, 'twas only
right that I do everything possible to assist you. In any
case, I should not have been able to sleep until you regained your senses, giving me more confidence in your
eventual recovery. Now, the doctor tells me rest and quiet
are essential for healing, and I know you—and your family—will wish to have you on your way as quickly as
possible."

With that, she offered him another sip of water, bracing his shoulder as he leaned forward to drink. This
time, Jack found his meager strength fading even more
quickly—and now that he'd had time to sort out the gra-
dations of pain and pressure in his chest, he discovered
that breathing was becoming more difficult, as well.

He couldn't stifle a groan as she eased him back against
his pillows. There was so much more he wanted to ask
her, but the words seemed to elude his grasp. "Sleep…
might be…wise," he admitted.

"You're sure about the laudanum? Sleep, then."

For the few moments before the vortex of pain and fatigue sucked him down to oblivion, he savored the feel of her fingers, gently stroking his face.

FOR THE NEXT TWO DAYS, Jack dozed and woke and dozed again, except when roused for the doctor's periodic visits, experiences uncomfortable enough that afterward he several times accepted Belle's offer for a bit of laudanum. Mercifully, a small dose dulled the agony enough for him to sleep without filling his dreams with nightmarish visions.

Or perhaps being wounded in the safety of London, rather than in the middle of a grim winter retreat through the wilderness, allowed him to rest undisturbed. Whatever the reason, he awoke on the fifth day to find his mind and senses had at last escaped the haze of pain and laudanum.

Except for an itchy tickle of beard, he was reasonably comfortable, his soiled garments having been removed at some point in favor of a plain nightshirt, and his body washed. He gazed about him, able now that a tepid daylight illuminated the room and he was finally lucid to take stock of his surroundings.

He lay in a handsomely carved canopy bed, its hangings and the curtains at the windows a rich blue damask, a hue mirrored in the Turkish carpet upon the floor. The room itself, its walls painted a pale blue, boasted a fine plastered cornice, classical broken pediments over the windows and a doorway flanked by inset pilasters.

'Twas a bedchamber such as one might find in the home of any ton aristocrat of superior taste and unlimited funds. Lady Belle's late protector had obviously been endowed with both, Jack decided.

Though the constant pain had eased, he still possessed very little strength, and moving even a small distance remained a teeth-gritting endeavor.

His vain effort to reach his water glass was interrupted by the entrance of a tall, hulking man whose dark livery proclaimed his status even as his crooked nose and huge fists spoke of a previous occupation. This must be Belle's former prize-fighter-turned-butler.

"The maid what built up the fire said you was awake," the man said. "Lady Belle sent me to ask iff'n you was wishful of having a shave. She done washed you off some when you first come, but she didn't trifle none with them whiskers. I'm Watson, by the way, Lady Belle's butler."

"Jaimie Watson?" Jack said, a memory beginning to surface. "Defeated Molynieu back in '09, in one of the best bouts of fisticuffs ever seen?"

The big man's face brightened. "You saw the match?"

"No, I was on the Peninsula at the time, but troopers who witnessed the event talked of it for months."

Watson smiled. "'Twas my best fight."

"Don't start him talking about the Fancy, or you'll never get your shave," Lady Belle said as she entered.

Conversation ceased as Jack let the beauty of her wash over his senses. She was garbed today in a plain, high-necked gown of a medium blue that underscored the brilliance of her deep blue eyes. With her golden hair pulled back in a simple chignon, her cheeks and lips devoid of artificial enhancement and her rigidly upright stance, she might be taken for a governess. Yet the sheer loveliness of her unadorned beauty still caused him to suck in a painful breath.

"Good morning, ma'am. How charming you look!" Jack said—and immediately regretted it, for at the banal compliment, he saw her almost physically withdraw.

"You seem better, Captain," she said coolly.

Forewarned now, he copied her matter-of-fact demeanor. "Much better, thank you."

"Should you like a shave before breakfast?"

Jack had never considered himself vain, but in the face of her luminous beauty he was feeling decidedly unkempt. Bad enough, he thought, to have practically cocked up your toes in front of a lady you hoped to impress without looking like a hooligan who'd ended up on the wrong side of an altercation with the Watch.

"That would be wonderful. I understand I have you to thank for making me more presentable."

She shrugged. "You needed to be stripped out of those bloody garments—which are ruined, I'm afraid, so that I insist you allow me to replace them. It seemed best to do so while you were still unconscious."

The idea of her stripping him down, laying hands on his naked skin, even for the prosaic purpose of cleansing it, sent a ripple of arousal through him. After spending several days in an enfeebled state, he thanked his body for this hard evidence that he was finally on the mend.

"Watson, you have the shaving utensils ready?" Belle interrupted his wandering thoughts.

"Aye, Lady Belle." While Belle helped Jack to a sip of water, the butler brought in water, soap and razor.

While Watson shaved him, Belle recounted the doctor's findings and informed him that both Darnley and Ludlowe had called to check on him and would return in the afternoon.

After Watson finished, a boy trotted in carrying a covered dish. "Mornin', Miss Belle, Cap'n," he said, fixing a curious and entirely undeferential gaze on Jack.

Scrawny and obviously undernourished, the child had hair that stuck up at odd angles, as if barbered by a blind man. With his narrow face, sharp nose and small, gleaming eyes that reminded Jack of a rodent, the child was one of the ugliest specimens of boyhood Jack had ever beheld. Where, Jack wondered, had this little street rat come from?

"Thank you for bringing up the tray so quickly, Jem. You may return to assist Watson—in the kitchen."

The boy groaned. "Be I still in the kitchen?"

"For another week, Jem."

"But Miss Belle—"

"No arguing, Jem," Belle cut him off.

If the child weren't too old—and far too unattractive—to make such a relationship possible, Jack could almost suspect the boy was Belle's son rather than her servant. Though from what he'd seen, while Lady Belle's *house* was similar to those of London's ton, the appearance of her staff and the familiarity of their behavior was decidedly not.

"Enjoy your breakfast, Cap'n," the boy said. His

face mournful, he walked with dragging steps toward the door.

On impulse Jack called out, "Wait, Jem." To Lady Belle's sharp look, he said blandly, "If the boy isn't needed now, perhaps he can keep me company while I eat."

The lad hastened back, his thin, homely face turned toward Belle. "Couldn't I, Miss Belle? I be very good company when I wants to."

Belle bent her penetrating regard on the boy for a long moment before sighing. "I have some work that really needs attention. I suppose you can remain, if the captain will allow you to assist him with his breakfast."

"I won't hurt him none, ma'am! And I'll get his gruel into him faster'n a fly lighting on a sticky bun."

"Is that arrangement agreeable to you, Captain?"

Jack would much prefer Belle's to be the hands that assisted him, but since so far he'd learned little about Belle from the lady herself, maybe he could discover more from the boy—especially if Belle were not present. "If it will not inconvenience the household, ma'am."

She lifted an eyebrow at that and turned to the boy. "Don't tease him with too much chatter, Jem. He should rest and converse as little as possible."

Jack watched her graceful glide of a walk as she exited. Meanwhile Jem removed the cover from the tray, unveiling a pot that wafted the siren scent of fresh coffee and a surprisingly appealing bowl of gruel.

"Don't you stir them nabsters, Cap'n," Jem advised as

Jack tried to lift a hand to reach the spoon. "Jem'll feed you right and proper."

Surmising that Jem meant he was good with his hands, Jack subsided back against the pillows. He'd best hope the boy didn't spill his breakfast all over him, since his own feeble attempt to feed himself had failed dismally. Silently cursing his recurrent weakness and the pain that skewered him every time he moved, Jack said, "I'd be much obliged for your help, Jem."

"Don't wonder you need it, Lady Belle sticking you like she done. Watson says your togs was soaked right through in blood. Here's your broth, now."

For a few minutes Jack contented himself with slurping down all the soup that Jem spooned in as handily as promised. His immediate hunger subsiding, Jack decided to see what information he could eke from the boy.

Before his stint in the army, where men from all ranks and walks of life were obligated to work together, Jack might have felt awkward, attempting to converse with a servant. Having long since mastered any such discomfort—and certainly the erstwhile servant seemed to feel none, Jack said, "You don't like working in the kitchen, Jem?"

"It ain't my usual lay, helping old Watson. I'd rather be back at the mews, learning to tend the bits of blood and hoof and swabbing the tinkle and jangle."

"You prefer working with horses and tack?" Jack guessed.

Jem paused for a minute and gave Jack a gap-toothed grin. "You be right smart, for a toff."

Jack felt the urge to chuckle and, mindful of his chest, restrained it. "I am moved by your accolade."

"Watson says you was in the cavalry. Did you have a bloody great horse? Did you slash the Frogs to bits with your sword?"

Jack's smile turned grim as he suppressed the memories. "Yes, I had a fine, big horse. I'd rather not talk about the slashing, if you please. How did you—"

"But that be the best part!" Jem interrupted, clearly disappointed. "Here's your last sip, anyways."

As Jem spoke, Lady Belle entered. Though she moved silently, the almost palpable change in the air telegraphed her presence to him instantly, even before Jack caught her faint scent of lavender.

If being in the same room with her disturbed him so profoundly, how might his body react to greater intimacy?

"Bloodthirsty whelp," Belle murmured. "That will be enough, Jem. I'm sure the captain is tired."

"Can I come back later, after he's rested, Miss Belle? We ain't hardly talked yet. It musta been powerful exciting, killing Frenchies over in them foreign parts. Was you ever wounded afore Miss Belle sliced you, Cap'n? Would you show me your scars? Your sword, maybe—"

"Jem!" Belle interrupted. "Watson needs your assistance in the kitchen."

"All right, I be going," the boy said, picking up the tray. "But iff'n I was a soldier, I'd want to show off my scars. Impresses the females, I'll wager," he added, his dark eyes mischievous.

"One more minute, Jem," Belle said. "Put down the tray and let me see your hands."

"Aw, Miss Belle!" the boy protested.

"Now, if you please, Jem."

Reluctantly the boy set down his burden and opened his hands. "See—bare as a baby's bottom."

"Turn out your pockets."

For a moment Jem eyed Belle resentfully. Then he heaved a sigh, slid Jack's pocket watch from under his sleeve and laid it back on the table. "Don't let a man have no fun," he muttered.

"You ought to be ashamed," Belle reproved, "stealing from the captain when he is ill!"

Jem shrugged. "Best time to snarf him, I'd say. Weren't as if I was going to keep it. Not with him being a soldier 'n all. Just exercising the twiddlies."

"More 'exercise' like that and you'll serve another week in the kitchen. I cannot have you picking the pocket of everyone who enters this house! Besides, ply those tricks on the street again and the magistrate will be happy to stretch your neck—over a penny or a pocket watch. Now, get on with you."

"Thank you for your help, Jem," Jack said, not sure whether to be amused or outraged.

"You're welcome, Cap'n. No hard feelings about the watch?"

"Not if you heed Lady Belle's orders."

Seeming to ponder that, the boy went out. Once the door closed behind him, Jack asked, "Wherever did you find him? On his way to the gallows?"

Belle returned a faint smile, even that slight response warming him. "Jem has a rather...storied past."

As do you, I'll wager, Jack thought. And how he would like to discover more about both!

"Rest now, Captain. Your friends will be calling later."

To his annoyance, the cursed weakness was overcoming him again. Though he'd hoped to try to lure Belle to linger, the effort of conversing had set his chest to throbbing and brought back that damnable shortness of breath. He barely managed to croak out a thank-you.

As she exited the room, a vision of golden hair and light blue merino wrapped in the summer-rich scent of lavender, Jack eased back against the pillows. How, he wondered groggily, had a courtesan come to be attended by a not-quite-reformed thief and a retired prize-fighter?

Sometime before he left the shelter of her roof, he promised himself before sleep claimed him, he would find out about them—and their mistress.

CHAPTER EIGHT

AFTERNOON SUNLIGHT warmed the room when next Jack woke. As he stirred, hunger roiling in his innards, he suddenly realized he was not alone.

His pulse leapt, then slowed as he recognized his attendant—not Lady Belle, but the woman who had shared Belle's theater box. Though it was still daylight, she wore face paint and a gown cut so low that her jutting breasts looked likely at any moment to tumble free.

"Afternoon, Captain. I be Mae, Belle's companion—and relieved I am to see you looking so much better! You must be fair starving, you having eaten next to nothing for nigh on five days. I've brought soup." With that, the lady lifted the cover from a tray on the bedside table.

"Thank you, Mrs...." he said, easing himself upright.

"Mae be good enough, Captain. Now eat up," she admonished, putting a spoon to his lips. "Belle said you was to swallow every last bit."

"Lady Belle is resting?" he asked between spoonfuls.

"No, she be working on her account books. 'Tis an amazement to me, being as I could never add two figures together, but she's fearsome clever. I should have helped her care for you much sooner, for which I do apologize, but such a sight you was at first, blood all over and looking like a corpse! I nearly swooned dead away. Even tidied up, you looked as if you was about to stick your spoon in the wall at any moment. Belle hardly left your side that first night, bless her, what with her feeling so guilty, though why she should blame herself I don't know, for it stands to reason in a fencing match there'd be blades a'crossing. It worries me fierce, her taking them lessons—and why should she, when so many gents would fight the devil himself for her if only she asked 'em. Though she won't look at none of 'em, more's the pity. But here I am rattling on, which Belle told me most particular not to."

Obligingly eating his soup during this monologue, Jack felt his spirits rise. The woman Mae might be as vulgar as she could stare, but in a few short minutes she'd already offered more information about Belle than he'd been able to discover from the lady herself in several meetings. With a little encouragement, Jack hoped, her "companion" might be induced to relate the history of everyone in the house.

"Nay, madam, I enjoy conversation."

"None for you," Mae said, presenting him another spoonful. "The doctor says you mustn't strain yourself talking. Just swallow down this good broth Cook made you and keep that wound healing."

Either he was more famished than he'd thought, or the soup was particularly delicious. Realizing his chances of questioning Mae were slim while the woman, with an amusingly serious expression, continued to shovel in broth, he settled for finishing every drop.

"Excellent," he pronounced, liberated at last by the empty bowl. "I am much obliged, Mae, for your kindness."

"'Twas a pleasure to serve a fine young gent like you, Captain." Picking up the tray, the lady rose.

"Stay, please?" Jack begged. "I shall remain silent. I find your company charming, and a fellow can't help but recover faster, attended by such beauty."

A natural blush darkened her rouged cheeks. "Ain't you the gallant one? If Belle wasn't my dearest friend and me too old besides, I might have a mind to offer you more than soup! But Belle says you was to rest now, being as how your friends and the doctor be expected later. I'd be happy to come back later while Belle tends her business."

He wanted to ask what business that was. But simply sitting upright and sipping soup had sapped his tiny store of strength. His chest aching again, he hadn't the energy to force the words through his lips. For now he would have to be content at having discovered that the loquacious Mae might prove a font of useful information—once he had the stamina to chat with her.

"Th-thank you—" he struggled.

"Nay, don't speak," Mae said. "Just rest some now." Her smile as open and friendly as a child's, she tucked the coverlet under his chin.

With a sigh, Jack subsided into the pillows. Mae might be a stranger to gentility and his mother truly would have palpitations if she knew he was encouraging this aging harlot to visit. But aside from the behavior he'd witnessed in the opera box, Jack did find her charming.

Her sunny disposition glowed in her clear blue eyes and artless chatter, despite the garish dress and nearly bare bosom. His soldier's knack for quickly evaluating character told him that whatever she said would be the truth as she knew it. The only artifice about her was the paint on her face.

Apparently the discreet Lady Belle had warned her voluble companion as well as her servants not to converse with him—for more than just a desire to spare his recovering lungs, he suspected. But if plumbing Mae's knowledge would bring him closer to the lady who was fast coming to fascinate him, he thought as he drifted to sleep, he was quite willing to encourage this much older woman who'd virtually propositioned him in his sickbed.

A short time later he roused from his nap to see Watson escorting in the doctor.

"You're much more alert than when last I checked you," the military physician said approvingly as Watson helped him remove the bandages around Jack's shoulder.

"I've not yet thanked you sufficiently," Jack said, trying to gird himself for the discomfort sure to follow.

"Thank your strong constitution as much as my efforts, and the care your friends gave you," the doctor replied as he examined Jack's wound. "Still red and swollen, which is to be expected," he pronounced, "but no signs of putrefaction. By the looks of that shoulder, you've had need of a strong constitution in the past. Saber?"

Though the doctor's ministrations weren't as agonizing as during his previous visits, sweat had broken out on Jack's brow and he had to use all his meager strength to keep from crying out. "Yes. At Corunna," he managed through gritted teeth.

"'Twas a fearsome time, I hear," Dr. Thompson replied as he applied a clean pad over the wound and began re-wrapping the bandages. "I was in the Americas with 29th Foot myself. Didn't return until just before Waterloo." He laughed and shook his head. "How quixotic is life, eh? A man survives a saber blow at Corunna and the killing fields of Waterloo, only to nearly cock up his toes at a London fencing match! Well, let's have a listen."

After putting his ear to Jack's chest for a few minutes, the physician said, "Still a hint of a whistle, but less than before. Thank you, Watson," he said, turning to the butler. "I can find my own way out."

Watson hesitated before bowing. "If you say so, sir."

The doctor waited until Watson had closed the door. "Captain, I now know that this is…not your house. You are doubtless wishing to return home as soon as possible. If you have lodgings here in the city and someone to tend you, I believe you could remove there now, at an easy pace. If not, I suggest that you beg your…hostess to allow you to remain here a few more days. You can expect the weakness to continue, and both your wound and your lungs still bear watching. In any event, I'll check you again tomorrow."

"I'm greatly in your debt, Doctor. Let me give you my banker's direction so that you may forward your bill."

With a slight smile, Dr. Thompson shook his head. "The, ah, lady has already settled it. Stunning, isn't she? At first I thought she was your wife, but…" The doctor bent an inquiring look on him.

Clearly the man was hoping for an explanation. Nonsensical as it was, for no man breathing could look at Lady Belle without desiring her, Jack felt an immediate rush of possessive jealousy. He could not, in truth, state there was an understanding between them, but if the doctor were trying to size up the nature of their relationship so he might make an overture to Lady Belle himself, neither did Jack wish to deny a connection. He settled for meeting the doctor's eyes with a cold, unblinking stare.

Coloring, the doctor cleared his throat. "A lovely lady. One would never suspect she was…well, you know."

More illogically still, Jack found himself resenting the doctor's implication—though he couldn't argue with the truth of it. "Lady Belle has been a gracious, kind and devoted hostess," he replied stiffly.

"Yes, indeed," the doctor replied, his flush deepening. "I didn't meant to insinuate—"

"Then don't," Jack snapped.

"May I come in?" Aubrey peeped in at the doorway. "Watson said the doctor was finished."

"I'm just leaving," Dr. Thompson replied. "I shall see you—where tomorrow, Captain?"

"Here, for the present. Good day, Doctor."

With a bow, tinges of redness still in his cheeks, the

doctor left the room. His eyes following the physician's speedy exit, Aubrey said, "Sawbones put you through torture again? You were rather short with him. Give you agonies or no, you ought to be grateful. Probably wouldn't still be among us, had we not secured his timely assistance."

Guilt nibbling at him, Jack managed a rueful smile. "You're right, and I shall apologize later." Not wishing to detail what he needed to apologize for, Jack continued, "But where is Edmund?"

Aubrey shook his head. "Another interminable meeting, his note said. He'll be by later—and will be delighted to see how much better you look. Gave us quite a scare, you did!"

"I am better," Jack said, noting that the pressure in his chest had eased and speaking was no longer as taxing.

"Must be Lady Belle's tender touch. I hear she's hardly left your side since you arrived."

"So I understand. I've been mostly unconscious until this morning. I do know I owe her a great debt."

"Aside from the fact that she wounded you—though I still don't understand how, superb fencer that you are, you could have given her such an opening! But no matter. I don't envy you the ordeal you've suffered, but now, what an opportunity is yours! Here in Belle's own home, the focus of her solicitous attention. You're a fool if you don't use this chance to fix her interest."

Jack was surprised into a laugh, which immediately changed to a groan as pain knifed through him. "I'm not a very commanding figure at present," he replied when he could catch his breath.

"Find an excuse to linger. She's already admitted feeling guilty over wounding you. Play on that until you're recovered enough to charm her with your manliness."

"Play on the lady's guilt over what was my own damn fault in order to somehow winkle my way into her affections? Such artifice and trickery appalls!"

"Oh, Jack, don't be so particular," Aubrey advised. "What's wrong with a little artifice, with a prize as luscious as Belle for the winning?"

"When," Jack demanded, eyeing Aubrey narrowly, "did you become such a rogue?"

"Call me what you will, but *I* say you're attics-to-let if you allow yourself to be hurried into exchanging Lady Belle's sweet hands soothing your fevered brow for those of your mama or sister—meaning no disrespect to either lady."

Jack's lips twitched at the thought of having the ministrations of his mother, an earl's daughter of impeccable reputation, or his virginal sister, declared wanting when compared to those of a practiced courtesan.

But perhaps Aubrey did have a point.

"The doctor informs me I've not yet healed sufficiently to be able to jolt halfway across England. If neither you nor Edmund wishes to take over nursing me, I must perforce remain where I am."

Aubrey grinned. "That's the spirit! I knew you couldn't let this chance pass you by!"

Jack shook his head. "I believe you're the one who's attics-to-let. You know I can't afford Belle, even if I should recover enough to 'charm her with my manliness.'"

Aubrey gave an impatient wave. "If money were all she cared about, she would have snapped up Rupert's offer long ago. Given the consideration with which she treats that idealistic cub, Ansley, I'm convinced she's attracted to men of a nobler sort. And here you are, positioned conveniently right in her own house. I'll wager 'tis but a short leap from this bed to hers."

"And I'm in such prime condition for leaping," Jack retorted. But despite his protests to the contrary, the scheme Aubrey proposed was insidiously tempting.

Maybe Jack could afford her. Or maybe she would respond to the admiration and attention of a gentleman who treated her with the respect due a lady. Given the strength of the wordless connection that arced between them, maybe she could be enticed to yield to him.…

But enough heated imagining. 'Twas pointless to speculate over capturing Lady Belle's fancy with Dorrie's Season about to begin. He should be turning his thoughts to the wooing of a well-bred virgin, not contemplating a scandalous long-term liaison with a concubine—no matter how much she fascinated him.

And long-term it would be, for if Aubrey's far-fetched scenario were to become a reality, he knew instinctively that a few weeks or months would not be enough for him to penetrate the mystery of—or slake his desire for—the beautiful Lady Belle.

Jack looked up to find Aubrey grinning at him. "I see you're thinking on it. Reflect well, my friend. I won't stay longer and tire you, but I'll be back tomorrow. Perhaps then your comely hostess will grace us—"

Aubrey's eyes widened and his lips paused in mid-phrase. But even before his friend's reaction, before the slight stir of air from the silently opened door wafted to him the faint scent of lavender, an instinctive awareness had already informed Jack of Lady Belle's arrival.

BELLE PAUSED on the threshold, her smile fading as her eyes took in and then skittered away from the expression on Ludlowe's face. Despite the passage of years that should have inured her to it, she still recoiled inwardly at a man's avid appraisal with as much ferocity as she had the first time Bellingham had paraded her in public.

Some, like Ansley, dazzled by the beauty nature had bestowed on her, believed her the repository of all virtue, a veritable angel come to earth—in spite of obvious evidence to the contrary. Some, like the captain's friend watching her, mixed a healthy dose of lust with the awe.

And then there were the worst, the Lord Ruperts. Privileged by birth or wealth, accustomed to having the world rearrange itself to suit them, they felt entitled to take whatever they wanted, regardless of the wishes or feelings of those they considered lesser beings.

Would that it had been the baron at the point of her sword! She'd not have regretted thrusting home the blade.

Suppressing a sigh, she forced herself to pick up the thread of the conversation, which currently consisted of some stilted compliments by Ludlowe on her hospitality.

"Kind of you, Mr. Ludlowe," she interrupted, "but I did only what any person of sensibility would have done. I'm just happy to learn from Dr. Thompson that he considers Captain Carrington well on his way to recovery."

"How could he not be, with such an angel of mercy attending him?" Ludlowe said, his eyes still fixed on her with uncomfortable fervency.

"I came to congratulate you on the doctor's encouraging opinion, Captain, but I don't wish to intrude." Belle turned, ready to make good her escape.

A rapid patter of footsteps distracted her from Ludlowe's gallant reply. A moment later, Jem burst into the room.

Panting, a panicked look on his face and his hair even wilder than usual, he cried, "Miss Belle, you gotta come now. Someone done tried to carry off Jane!"

CHAPTER NINE

Begging the gentlemen to excuse her, Belle hurried Jem down the stairs. "Is Jane all right? What happened?"

"Dunno, Miss Belle. I were in the kitchen when we heared shouting and John Coachman come running, saying some villain had tried to nab Jane and for me to fetch you."

Watson met them in the hallway and bid them follow him to the bookroom. There Belle found Mae, a groom and the housekeeper clustered around Jane, who was seated on the small sofa, weeping, her gown muddy and torn, a cloth held to a cut over one eye.

Outrage swelled in Belle's breast at the audacity of someone invading her home and attacking one of her own. Taking a deep breath to calm herself, she sat beside Jane.

When the girl saw her, she burst into a fresh round of weeping. "My...lady...so...sorry," was all Belle could make out.

"Jane, you are safe now," Belle soothed. "Calm yourself and take a bit of this wine." Accepting a glass from Mae, Belle urged the girl to drink.

Making a visible effort to swallow her sobs, Jane consented to take a sip. By the time Belle had coaxed her into consuming half the glass, she was breathing normally, though tears still sheened her eyes.

"I be right sorry, Lady Belle," she said.

"Whatever for? You've done nothing wrong."

"I knew I shouldn't have stayed here! But you was so kind, and I just didn't want to go back. Now I brung this trouble on you—"

"Nonsense! If there is trouble, it will fall upon the man who tried to kidnap you. Was it Waldo?"

Jane shuddered. "Yes, ma'am. I been cooped up in the house nigh on a week, no one knowing what to do with me while you was occupied nursing the injured gentleman. I thought it wouldn't do no harm to take a turn about the garden. But…but he done snuck in somehow and took me by surprise. He brung a pistol and he told me he'd blow my head off iff'n I didn't come quiet. Then, when he put the popper down to drag me into the carriage, I seen my chance. Bit his hand and screeched to wake the dead. Jacobs here heard and come to help me, kind soul that he be."

"Bravo!" Belle said. "How brave of you both!"

"But ma'am, he said afore his coach drove off that he wouldn't never let me leave Mrs. Jarvis," Jane continued, her dark eyes stark. "That when he caught me good 'n proper, he'd make me pay, me and all them what helped me."

"'Tis rather Waldo who will pay," Belle retorted. "The

man trespassed on my property and assaulted a member of my household, and so I shall inform the constable."

Jane paled. "No, ma'am, you mustn't! Waldo said if you sent the law after him, he had friends in Seven Dials who'd make you wish you was never born."

Rage eddied through Belle again and she thought longingly of her slim, sharp fencing sword. "That ignorant bully dares to threaten me?"

"I couldn't bear knowing I'd caused you hurt, after you been so good to me." Jane drained the wine and set the glass down. "Better I go back to Mrs. Jarvis."

"You will do nothing of the sort!" Belle retorted.

As if her remaining reserves of strength and courage were finally exhausted, Jane slumped back against the sofa cushions. "I dunno know what to do," she whispered.

"For now, you shall go rest—with a stout footman to guard the door. Madame Duchamps, help Jane upstairs and brew her a tisane, please."

"Come, *ma petite*. Madame will plaster the cut so it leaves no scar on that pretty *visage*, eh?" the housekeeper said as she assisted Jane to her feet and led her away.

After thanking the groom for his aid and promising him a bonus for his bravery, Belle paced to the window, frowning. Along with her note informing Mrs. Jarvis that Jane would not be returning, she'd sent a handsome sum, though she'd not told Jane about it. Belle was angry but not surprised the bawd hadn't accepted the peace offering. Mrs. Jarvis obviously did not intend to relinquish Jane willingly.

Nor did the loathsome Waldo.

She turned to find Mae and Watson watching her.

"Daisie, who run the house I was with before Darlington set me up, told us that Mrs. Jarvis was a bad woman," Mae said. "Rules her girls with an iron fist—don't never let them out of her house—and that Waldo is a truly fearsome bloke. All the girls roundabout were afraid of him. They won't neither of them give up."

"Watson, what do you know of them?" Belle asked.

"The same about Mrs. Jarvis. As for Waldo, he's the worst sort of bragging bully boy, who don't pick on none but them what's smaller and weaker." Watson gave a derisive sniff. "He made sure never to tangle with me."

Mae unfurled a small ivory fan and began plying it vigorously. "All this botheration is giving me palpitations. Could we not just send the girl back?"

The look Belle sent her drove the color even higher into her rouged cheeks. "Didn't think so," Mae muttered. "Send her away, then. There's going to be trouble with that Jarvis woman if we keep one of her girls."

"I shall turn the matter over to the magistrate," Belle countered. "This is England, after all! The girl can't be held against her will."

To Belle's surprise, Watson shook his head. "I wouldn't do that, ma'am. If Waldo'd tried to snabble some gentry-mort, that would be different, but what do the law care about the likes of a dab like Jane? And 'tis true enough he's got friends in bad places, men who'd grab you as you walked in the Park and slit your throat in some back alley for no more than a glass of blue ruin."

"S-slit your throat?" Mae echoed, her rouged cheeks paling. "I—I feel a swoon coming on," she whispered.

While Watson soothed Mae with a glass of wine, Belle dropped back into a chair. 'Twas disconcerting to learn that her retainers, having lived all their lives well below the salt, had no great opinion of the usefulness of English law in protecting Jane—or Belle. Though she was still outraged that a ruffian like Waldo thought he could invade her home with impunity, Watson's description of how easily she herself might be dispatched made her pause.

She might be good with her blade, but men such as that would not observe the gentleman's rules governing combat.

Still, she would at least consult Egremont before she gave up entirely on the idea of a legal solution. But what to do with Jane in the interim? "Help from the law or not, Jane must be protected," Belle said after a moment.

"Send her away," Mae urged again. "It be too easy for some whoreson like Waldo to snatch her—or any of us here."

"Where, Mae? Even if her family would take her back, which I doubt, Mrs. Jarvis knows where she comes from and could send Waldo after her. Nor, inexperienced and defenseless as she is, could we secretly remove her from London and leave her all alone in some other town."

"She'd end up in a house as bad or worse as the one she sprung from," Watson agreed.

"We shall have to think of something else." Belle rose to pace the room, cuddling her brain for alternatives.

In the end, there seemed only one acceptable solution. "I have ever intended to leave for my country house before the Season starts. I shall just advance those plans."

"Leave London?" Mae gasped. "I know you told me you meant to, but I thought 'twas just the shock of Lord B's passing. You truly mean to...to *live* in the country?"

At Mae's tone, one would think Belle had proposed removing to some savage tropic island and dressing in skins. Suppressing a smile, she said, "I know how much you love London. But I have...pressing reasons to be away this Season. I know 'tis selfish of me to ask you to accompany me, but with Jane's situation, it seems the best plan. I doubt Waldo could buy himself accomplices willing to venture beyond the city, and with Watson guarding us, he won't dare pursue us alone."

"But what of the captain?" Belle asked. "You can't mean to just put him out in the street."

The captain. In the agitation of the moment, Belle had completely forgotten the uninvited guest in her front bedchamber. "I shall have to consider what to do about him. But one way or another, we shall leave London soon. Watson, have the staff begin making preparations."

"As ye wish, Lady Belle." With a bow, Watson left.

Belle turned to her companion, who was still looking agitated. "Mae, my dear friend," she said, taking the woman's hand, "if you simply can't bear the thought of exile to the country, take the next few days to look for another friend with whom to stay in London."

With a sniff, Mae withdrew her hand. "Why you need

to go haring off, I can't imagine, but I see that's none of my affair. We must protect Jane, I suppose. Now I believe I'll lie down for a spell."

Belle watched her companion exit the room, that lady's back ramrod straight and her carriage eloquent of disgruntlement. Was Mae jealous of Jane's presence, or was she merely hurt that Belle had not confided the reasons which compelled her to quit London this Season?

Whatever had upset her, Belle hoped her companion would soon recover her usual good humor. Sighing, she bent her thoughts to her next problem—Captain Jack Carrington.

Like his friend Lord Darnley, the captain didn't fit into any of three categories into which she normally divided men. His demeanor toward her wasn't adoring, nor did she sense admiration mixed with lust or naked lust alone. Though she certainly felt *some* strong force spark between them.

Perhaps that was why she seemed always more aware of him than she was of admirers like Ansley who shadowed her footsteps—and more disturbed by him than by Lord Rupert. Something about the man's mere presence seemed able to pierce the protective barrier of disinterest she had erected around her heart and mind, forcing her to acknowledge him, compelling a reaction.

She didn't understand how she could be conscious of him the instant he entered a room. Why she was so nervous and on edge when he was near—even immobilized in a sickbed.

Whatever the reason, he cut up her peace and she didn't like it.

And yet, she had no instinctive fear of him, as she did of Rupert. Indeed, she had the oddest sense that he would never harm her. An absurd feeling, given how effectively he rattled her calm, and ludicrous to put any faith in, given her experience with men.

Though getting him out of her house and out of her life held strong appeal, she felt responsible for assuring his recovery. With the Carrington estate, Darnley had told her, located several hard days' journey north, no amount of wishful thinking could delude her into believing the captain was yet up to a journey of that magnitude.

However, since he was no longer so dangerously ill as to require round-the-clock attention, perhaps she could see him returned to his rooms at Albany. With his friends to check on him and a nurse engaged to wait upon him, he could safely remain there until he was fit enough to make the long trip home. At his next visit, she'd ask the doctor whether such an arrangement would be suitable.

After all, the captain had friends who could oversee his recovery—whereas Jane was alone in the world. If the decision came down to which one needed her assistance most, the answer was clear.

For Jane's sake, Belle saw no alternative to leaving the metropolis—thereby sending the unsettling Captain Jack Carrington out of her house, her thoughts and her life.

Her decision made, Belle headed for the door. She'd go immediately to inform the captain of the prospective change in his circumstances.

ENTERING UPON HER KNOCK, Belle halted at the doorway. Expecting to deliver her news to the captain alone, she'd forgotten that Mr. Ludlowe had been visiting when Jem bore her off to check on Jane.

But perhaps it would be well to inform Ludlowe and solicit his assistance from the outset. Telling herself again that both men were sure to quickly acquiesce with her reasonable proposal, Belle continued into the room.

"I hope nothing serious is amiss," the captain said.

"Indeed, ma'am. Can I assist?" Ludlowe echoed.

"A small matter which has been dealt with, thank you, gentlemen. But it does…somewhat alter my immediate plans. I'm afraid I must leave London as soon as the arrangements can be made. I'm sorry I shall not be in town long enough to oversee your complete return to health, Captain, but if the physician believes it will not adversely affect your recovery, I propose to have you moved back to Albany sometime in the next few days."

"Moved!" Ludlowe repeated. "So soon? Surely Captain Carrington isn't stout enough yet to risk moving him! Nor could he possibly manage his own care."

"Indeed not," Belle agreed. "I mean to engage whichever competent nurses Dr. Thompson recommends until the captain has recovered sufficiently to journey home. Mr. Ludlowe, I would ask that you and Lord Darnley assist by insuring the nurses are properly attentive."

"I'm afraid Edmund's schedule doesn't allow for daily checks on a regular basis. And I fear I haven't the expertise to judge a nurse's care. Surely you don't mean to leave the captain in his enfeebled state—"

"Blast, Aubrey, I'm not completely helpless!" the captain interjected.

"—all alone for hours with no recourse, should the nurse turn out to be incompetent!" Ludlowe finished.

"I should hope Dr. Thompson would not recommend anyone incompetent," Belle protested, her tentative decision shaken by Ludlowe's unexpected opposition.

"One hopes not, though a physician hardly spends enough time at the bedside to know for sure, eh? But then, this is really a matter between you and Jack. I'll let you two discuss it—if he's up to the conversation now. Lady Belle, 'tis always a pleasure. Until later, Jack."

With that, Ludlowe walked toward the door, pausing on the threshold to give the captain a pointed glance. "Remember my advice, now," he admonished, and went out.

Left alone with her patient, who was regarding her with a rather reproachful look, Belle took a deep breath and prepared a bit desperately to deliver all the arguments she could summon to convince her troubling guest of the merits of a speedy departure from her house.

CHAPTER TEN

AFTER LADY BELLE'S unexpected announcement, Jack was irritated to find his reasoning abilities as slow to react as his injured body. Damping down a sense of hurt and disappointment far keener than it should have been, he struggled to evaluate his hostess's plans to evict him.

Lady Belle still stood silently before him, uncertainty and more than a trace of guilt on her face. "I am sincerely sorry to—to issue so ungenteel an ultimatum. And I do wish it were possible for me to remain in town until you were safely on your way to your family."

It was quite reasonable that she wished to be relieved of the inconvenience of his care. She had already been more than hospitable. Still, he couldn't help saying rather stiffly, "I regret having been such an imposition."

"You were not!" she answered too quickly, the fair skin of her face flushing. "Having wounded you in the first place, 'twas only right that I—"

"Please, ma'am, you said that before, but as I was barely conscious, I didn't respond properly. You must not consider the accident in any way your fault. I saw the protector come loose. I should have signaled the match to an immediate halt. I did not. The consequences for that omission rest on my head entirely."

She stared at him. "Why did you not stop it?"

He looked up into her vivid blue eyes and the intensity of the connection between them crackled in the air. "I don't know," he admitted.

For a long moment their gazes held, as if fused by some invisible bond. Then, with a little shudder, she turned away. "Still, I should have noticed the blade was unprotected. It was unconscionable—"

"Enough recrimination," Jack interrupted. "Shall we agree to share the blame?"

She glanced at him warily, as if surprised by the offer. "If…if you wish, sir. Returning you to Albany isn't the best of solutions, I know, but would you be amenable to that?"

Since she seemed so set upon ridding herself of him, he ought to agree. He could tolerate the unpleasantness of being tended by a stranger for the few days necessary until he could manage the journey to Carrington Grove.

Except that he found himself wanting with unexpected fervor to remain in Belle's company. Though thus far he'd had tantalizing glimpses of the woman behind the elusive beauty, he'd not yet learned nearly as much as he wanted about her curious staff or the lady herself.

Prudence advised that the sooner he departed, the better. She was much too beautiful—and affected him much too strongly. His incapacity had protected him so far, but as he recovered, his fascination with her would draw him ever more squarely into harm's way—as the intensity of his resistance to leave already attested.

Then another possibility occurred to him, sending his flagging spirits soaring. "Your country house is to the north?" he asked.

"Yes, about a day's journey up the Great North Road."

"Then if it does not inconvenience you extremely, might I travel north with your party? If you can grant me the privilege of resting overnight at your manor, I should be able to reach home within another two or three days."

The look of dismay that crossed her face before she could school her features far exceeded the mild annoyance the idea of carrying along an invalid should have generated. "Would that be wise? I thought the doctor said you should not travel such a distance yet."

So he was right about her reluctance to remain near him—a reluctance, he felt, that stemmed from more than the desire to divest herself of the burden of nursing him. She felt the force that pulsed between them as strongly as he. Though, more sensibly, she was trying to run from it.

A gentleman, after confirming the lady's unspoken desire not to acknowledge that attraction, would acquiesce. A prudent gentleman, knowing how susceptible he was to her, would seize the opportunity to escape his unsuitable attraction.

But whether inspired by Aubrey's suggestion or not, Jack found he could not. Somehow he knew that until he explored the force that drew them together, he would never be free of her spell, never be able to resume with a clear and unencumbered spirit the sensible course of his life.

So, how to persuade her to change her mind?

Shamed to realize, when it came down to it, he possessed no more scruples than Aubrey, he said, "You are right, of course. I've already imposed on your hospitality for far too long. I apologize if it seemed I was trying to foist on you company you are clearly unwilling to accept. I shall make other arrangements for leaving town."

Her eyes searched his face. "You mean immediately?"

He nodded.

Her brow creased in a frown. "Would it not be more prudent for you to recuperate in London for another few weeks before undertaking such a journey?"

"Perhaps. But I've been abroad for more than a year and I'm anxious to return home. The notion of traveling immediately has far more appeal than the idea of being banished to my rooms. However, you needn't worry—I shall manage the journey one way or another. I'm almost ready to quit my bed in any event."

"You are not ready to do any such thing!"

"If the wound troubles me on the road I shall be in a bit of a bother, but I traveled in far worse state after Corunna, I can assure you! And I don't want to inconvenience you any further than I already have."

She worried her bottom lip between her teeth. He should be ashamed, playing on her guilt in so brazen a manner, but he'd make it up to her later. As for physical pain, being able to journey in her company would be worth it, if he had to grit his teeth every mile of the way.

For a long moment she was silent, clearly considering. Jack sensed her trembling on the edge of acquiescence, but he'd pressed as much as his newly flexible conscience could tolerate. If she did ask him to join her, the final invitation must come from her alone.

Even if Aubrey would berate him as an idiot for being too squeamish to push her the last step of the way.

Holding his breath, he prayed to whichever guardian angel had protected him through the carnage of the Peninsula and Waterloo that she would agree.

"If you cannot be persuaded to remain awhile longer in the City," Belle said at last, "I should feel better if you journeyed in company. As long as Dr. Thompson agrees that traveling with my party will not place your overall recovery in jeopardy, you are welcome to join us. And, of course, to rest at Bellehaven as long as you require."

Clever lady, she'd tendered her reluctant invitation with a loophole attached, but 'twas an invitation nonetheless. It remained only to persuade Dr. Thompson to pronounce him fit to travel and he would have a few more days with her after all. Relief, gladness and a surge of anticipation flooded him.

Even as he rejoiced, a whisper of the prudence he'd exiled to the back of his brain warned that proceeding down this road could have far-ranging and unforeseen results. Though, gazing on the loveliness of her face, it was easy to ignore that Cassandra's call, he wasn't too dazzled to acknowledge that at some later date, he might well come to believe demons rather than angels had answered his prayer.

THREE DAYS LATER, Jack waited in his bedchamber for Belle's party to depart, enjoying after over a week of enforced bed rest the welcome feeling of being fully clothed. Fortunately, his body had continued to make steady progress toward recovery, enough that, with a cogent reminder of how he'd managed the retreat from Corunna under much more dire circumstances, Jack induced Dr. Thompson to reluctantly approve Jack's removal from the City.

He had seen little of his hostess over those days, Belle warning early on that preparing for the move would likely occupy all her time. Watson had tended his needs, Belle had sent to Hatchards for some books, and a gleeful Aubrey had visited each afternoon, but after several days in the lady's house without the benefit of the lady's presence, he was anxious for the journey to begin.

His only regret was that for the trip itself, Lady Belle had announced her intention to ride, relegating him to the company of her companion Mae, who, she assured him, would see to his comfort. When he protested, pronouncing himself capable of sitting upright so both ladies could travel inside and pointing out the possibility of inclement weather, she had merely given him a smile and assured him she much preferred fresh air, regardless of the weather.

He would have to content himself with making the most of the opportunities for conversation that would be presented when they stopped for meals and to change horses. If the roads were not too muddy, Belle informed him, they should reach Bellehaven in time for the late dinner.

What couldn't be changed might as well be turned to advantage, so during the trip he intended to subtly cull as much information as possible from the loquacious Mae. If his luck held, after their arrival at Bellehaven he'd be able to linger in Lady Belle's company long enough to profit from whatever he'd learned.

As the door opened, Jack looked up, the automatic leap in his pulse slowing as Watson walked in.

"All yer gear from Albany be stowed, Captain, and there's a groom to lead yer horse. Lady Belle sent me to tell you 'tis time to load the coach."

"Thank you, Watson. I'm ready."

Having practiced walking the last few days, Jack managed to shrug on his greatcoat, lever himself to his feet and proceed toward the door with a minimum of light-headedness, though he was still damnably weak. He was more than ready, he acknowledged, not only to travel with Lady Belle, but to shake off the last vestiges of illness and feel himself again.

Still, he was decidedly woozy by the time he reached the carriage. Watson stepped before him to open the door—and doubtless insure he managed to haul himself into the vehicle. "Settle yerself in, Captain," the butler said. "There be a hot brick for yer feet and a hamper from Cook with victuals for the journey."

Though he felt better now that he was seated, his exertions in descending the stairs had set his chest to aching again. The pillows tucked in the corner beckoned invitingly, as did the carriage blanket and the warmed brick at his feet. He eased himself into a semireclining position and closed his eyes, appreciating anew Belle's thoughtfulness in giving him the entire seat to himself.

A moment later, Watson handed Mae into the coach. Though her traveling cloak of red satin—which, for a change, fully covered her famous attributes—and the matching chip bonnet looked cheery, her compressed lips and mournful expression were in such marked contrast to the animated demeanor she'd exhibited on the other occasions Jack had met her that he felt immediately moved to apologize.

"'Tis a dismal prospect, I fear, being shut up with an invalid. I promise you, ma'am, I'll cause you no bother."

That won him a smile. "Lands, Captain, you be fine company for the eyes, even without you conversing, which Belle says you still ought not to do overmuch. 'Tis leaving London that has me so down-pin. My old friend Polly, whose new protector is a regular Golden Ball, said I could stay with her in her town house—which has everything bang up to the mark, the furniture with carved feet and dogs' heads everywhere! Though good English oak be fine enough for me, but I suppose I know my duty clear as anyone. Couldn't let Belle go tearing off to the wilderness with That Person and none but Watson to tend her, the chit being too young and helpless to be of use."

Before he could comment, she sighed and continued, "Even if I don't know how I can stand it. A few cows in a London park be well enough, but…but to actually *live* in a place with nothing for miles around but trees and fields and wild animals?"

Jack had to grin. "You are not country-born, then?"

Mae shuddered. "No, sir. Give me shops on every corner, lamps to light up the night, carriages rattling by at all hours and neighbors who don't live ten miles off, like Belle says they do at this manor of hers. But it's going I am, so I'd best resign myself and not fill your ears with my complaining. Just hope we make it there unharmed," she finished darkly.

Did Mae worry about footpads? "Incomprehensibly enough, I've lived most of my life in the country north of Lady Belle's manor. Let me assure you, ma'am, the area is very civilized. I've ridden from my home to London many times the last ten years without so much as a glimpse of a highwayman. In fact," he added, hoping to cheer her, "we'll pass some superior inns with very skillful cooks."

Mae brightened slightly. "Well, that's something. Indeed, I'm feeling a bit peckish. Should you like a mug of ale and a bit of bread before the coach sets off?"

At that moment, the carriage door opened and Lady Belle's presence wafted to him on a wave of scent and sight. As usual, she was plainly garbed in a gray habit under a matching wool cloak. A veiled hat masked her hair and left only the pale skin of her face uncovered.

But she had no need of intricate designs or fancy trim to draw the eye. The simple cut and sober hue of her clothing served only to make her skin more luminous, the blue eyes more arresting.

By the time he'd pulled his senses free of the spell she seemed to cast over him whenever she came near, she had already bid him good day and expressed her hope that he had everything necessary to make his journey comfortable.

"Everything, ma'am, a kind hostess could provide, save her charming presence to brighten the journey."

"Gallantly spoken, Captain, but I'm sure you will both be more comfortable without a third person inside."

"Why not heed the captain and join us?" Mae urged. "You're so slender, you'll scarce take up any room."

"Thank you, Mae, but I've had few opportunities of late to enjoy a long ride though the countryside. I've been looking forward to one today."

"Won't you have tea first?" Mae asked. "The wind be fearful sharp. I worry you'll be frozen to the bone."

Belle cast an affectionate glance at her companion. "My gown being a good deal warmer than the charming ensemble you've chosen, I shall be fine. If we wish to reach Bellehaven by nightfall, we should be on our way. I promise to share a cup with you later."

"We shall look forward to your company," Jack said.

She nodded in acknowledgment and then, to his surprise, pulled a pistol from the pocket of her cape. "I know you worry about leaving London, Mae. Though it is highly unlikely we shall encounter trouble, I thought you might feel better having this at your feet."

Paling, Mae stared at the weapon. "It won't go off… all on its own, will it?"

"No, you must cock it first—which I did not mean for you to do. If there should be some disturbance, simply point it out the window. That should be enough to give pause to any ruffian who considers approaching."

From the fearful gaze Mae had fixed on the pistol, Jack wasn't sure she found its presence reassuring. "Shall I take charge of it, ma'am? I'm fully trained in its use."

"Please do, Captain!" Mae said at once. "Iff'n a highwayman did appear, I'd more'n likely blow off my own foot than manage to scare him away."

"Nay, Captain, you needn't exert yourself," Belle said, waving him away as he reached for the weapon. By chance, their fingers touched, sparking a shock he felt all the way to his toes. From her ragged gasp and the jerk with which she drew back her hand, she had felt it, too.

Avoiding his glance, Belle set the weapon down in the corner. "The pistol will be fine here. 'Tis only to make Mae feel safer."

"Then she should feel perfectly at ease, knowing I can fire it, if necessary. It does have shot and powder?"

"Y-yes, but it cannot be good for you to—"

"We've both just assured this lady I shall not need to," Jack retorted, a bit exasperated at being treated as if he would collapse at the slightest exertion. "Now, can we not coax you to a cup of something warm before we go?"

Looking as if she were considering arguing further, Belle shook her head. "No, I'd rather mount up and depart. Please, do have something yourself, though."

She turned from him to give Mae an encouraging smile. "We shall be all right," she said softly, patting the woman's hand before drawing the carriage door closed behind her.

Mae busied herself pouring ale and tea. Soon after, in a jingle of harness, the carriage jerked to a start.

Mindful of his goal and trying to set his companion, who still appeared nervous, more at ease, after they'd finished their refreshments, Jack asked, "Do you usually stay with friends when Lady Belle visits the country?"

"No, for I've only been with her a month, though we've been friends this age. When Lord B died, Belle's maid and butler both left. Not that she couldn't afford them, for Lord B left her pretty well set, but they was hired by Bellingham himself and always thought themselves too high in the instep to be serving the likes of Belle. As if she don't act more the lady than most of them society beldames what won't walk on the same side of the street as her! Anyways, I come round soon's I heard about Lord B and found everything at sixes and sevens, the butler having walked out the minute he knew Lord B'd cocked up his toes."

"You stayed to help her put the household back in order?" Jack prompted when Mae stopped for breath.

"So I did. Always giving himself airs, Randall was, as if he didn't button up his trousers like any other man! And that dresser, Winset, was just as bad, though Belle got back her own on that one. The downstairs maid told me Winset asked Belle right off for a raise, saying she'd need to make up for the big comedown in the world of tending Belle now that Lord B weren't there. Belle told her cool as you please that she was free to go—but since she were Lord B's employee, not Belle's, she'd need to see Lady Bellingham for her references."

Mae went off in a peal of laughter. "Wish I'd been a fly on the wall to watch the old prune-face's lips turn blue! I've never, before or since, seen Belle be anything but kind to any soul, but Winset deserved that!"

Knowing on what poor terms Lord Bellingham had stood with his legal wife—and surmising how that wife must have resented the mistress whom her husband had preferred to her—Jack had to smile at how neatly Belle had cut the dresser out. "And so Belle asked you to stay on?"

"At first, for just a few days 'til she found a new maid, me being good at making a woman look her best, if I do say so. Then I come to find myself…between engagements, so to speak, and Belle asked me to stay on permanent. We've always gotten on famous, and I just wish…but here I go, rambling again. You mustn't talk long, Belle reminded me, but won't you tell me something about you, Captain? Do all your people live up north?"

Turning out not to be as malleable as Jack had hoped, Mae brushed off Jack's subsequent inquiries, saying she'd jawed on enough. Not wishing to alienate this amiable source of information, Jack knew he mustn't press her too hard.

Somewhat to his surprise, after turning the talk to him, Mae showed herself to be a skillful conversationalist, drawing him out about his family, his army days and his plans for a future at Carrington Grove.

By the time they'd reached the countryside beyond London, however, the bounce and jolting of the vehicle had set Jack's chest and shoulder to throbbing, prompting him to bring the chat to a temporary halt. Instantly solicitous, Mae advised him to get a few winks, there being nothing of interest to see now that they'd left the City.

Mae settled herself in her corner, obviously ready to take her own advice. However, Jack's discomfort was by now sufficiently acute that he knew sleep was not a possibility. Wryly concluding that it was fortunate he'd vowed to make the journey regardless of the pain, he had just decided to try dulling it with a second mug of ale when, after a shout followed by the unmistakable explosion of a discharging musket, the carriage squealed to a halt.

CHAPTER ELEVEN

IN THE SILENCE that followed Mae's shriek and the report of the musket, Jack heard the carriage door rattle. In
one practiced motion he seized the pistol at Mae's feet,
cocked it and fired at the hand clawing open the latch.
Beneath the shrill of Mae's second scream came a lower,
hoarser cry and the hand fell away. The pain in his chest
forgotten, Jack struggled to his feet and launched himself
through the now-open door.

Landing hard, he saw a man on the ground, clutching
his arm…Watson struggling with a masked ruffian at the
door of the baggage carriage behind them…and Belle
bringing her whip down on the head of a masked man
trying to grab the reins of her sidling, rearing horse.

Rage seized him, a desire to rip the arms off the miscre-
ant who dared threaten her. Cursing the now-empty pistol,
Jack thrust it in his coat pocket and looked about wildly
for something, anything he might use as a weapon.

His gaze caught on the dancing end of the whip dangling from the hand of the coachman struggling to control the plunging horses. Grabbing it, Jack loped off to
where Belle still grappled with her attacker.

He arrived just as Belle managed to strike a blow hard

enough to set her attacker back on his heels. Using his good arm, Jack lashed out at him with the heavy coach whip.

He watched with savage satisfaction as the trailing thong coiled like a noose about the man's upper torso, pinning his arms to his chest. Jack then ripped the whip free, spinning the attacker onto the ground. Seizing the empty pistol, he struck the man a blow to the head that left the attacker facedown and motionless in the dirt.

He turned to Belle, his relief that she had escaped her attacker changing to alarm when he saw she was urging her horse toward the coach where Watson still struggled…a raised pistol in her hand.

Before he could shout a warning, he realized that, fully aware of the danger of shooting at the attacker with the two men so close together, she was controlling her mount with one hand, gun leveled in the other, waiting for a clear line of fire.

Then, in a move that would have won him roars from the crowd during his days in the ring, Watson managed to rip free of his assailant and deliver a full roundhouse punch to the man's ear. Jack heard the crack of shattering bone before the ruffian dropped like a log to the ground.

Belle thrust the pistol into her cape pocket and leapt free of the sidesaddle. "Watson, Jane, are you all right?" she cried as she ran to the coach.

"I be good, Lady Belle, and Jane, too, though she done fainted straight off. This gallows-bait didn't never get more'n his hand on the door."

"Are *you* all right?" Jack gasped, halting behind her.

"I'm fine," she tossed over her shoulder. An instant later she turned back, as if only just realizing who'd called to her. "What are you doing out of the coach?"

Watson glanced from Jack to the unconscious man on the roadway to the one whimpering beside the carriage. "Been doing a right good bit of soldiering, looks like."

Jack shrugged—and immediately regretted it, as fire shot through his chest and shoulder. "Couldn't expect me to cower inside while we were being attacked."

But with the end of the encounter, his strength seemed to ebb away. He had the dismaying sensation that he was starting to sway on his feet.

From the concerned expression on Belle's face, he must not be looking very well. "Captain, that was incredibly brave, but you should never have stirred from your seat! Watson, get Thomas and John Coachman to help you tie up these fellows while I walk Captain Carrington back."

"I can lend a hand, Watson," Jack said, not sure whether he could in fact make good on that offer. "The coachman is still busy with the horses."

"At least two of them fellows—" Watson indicated the man Jack had bashed with the pistol and the one he himself had felled "—ain't goin' nowheres, and it appears you shot the fight out of the other when you winged his arm. I can handle 'em for now, Captain. You go rest."

Belle handed Watson her pistol. "Thank you, Watson."

Watson took the weapon and trained it on the one still-conscious bandit. "They was so anxious to catch us, let's see how them prison rats like traveling with us—trotting behind the coach 'til we turn 'em over to a magistrate. Appreciated your help, too, Captain," Watson added. "Not sure I coulda gotten to the other two in time, what with having to take care of this one here."

"Your assistance was timely indeed—if most reckless!" Belle agreed. "You're hardly ready to run a race with footpads. Please, let us return to the coach at once."

In truth, Jack was feeling the imprudence of his intervention in every limb and with every painful breath. His chest was on fire, beads of sweat had popped out on his brow and a wave of nausea was threatening to swamp him.

"Perhaps I should return," he admitted, hoping he managed it before he disgraced himself by getting sick in front of her. Fine soldier you are, he thought in disgust.

His disgruntlement was tempered when a moment later she took his hand and wrapped her other arm about his waist. "Lean on me, Captain. You're pale as Mae's face powder, and if you fall, I may not get you upright again."

He wanted to say something gallant, but he couldn't summon words or breath. Still, despite his afflictions, he felt the burn of her arm touching his body even through the thickness of his coat. Would the lavender scent filling his nostrils, the brush of her cape against his chin, help clear his head or make him dizzier? he wondered.

The idea of her almost in his arms hardened other parts of his body in a slow rush of sensation that, for the moment, triumphed over the nausea, reassuring him that he must not have reinjured himself too badly.

All too soon they reached the coach. While they stopped for him to rest, Watson loped over.

"Left the coachman guarding them Newgate nasties. Let me help, Captain. Don't want that chest wound opening up."

Realizing he would only look more foolish if he refused Watson's assistance and ended up falling, Jack allowed the big man to half lift him into the vehicle.

While he settled gratefully into the cushions, Belle dispensed a dose of hartshorn and some soothing words to a still-agitated Mae, who alternated between exclamations at Jack's bravery and claims of having been frightened out of ten years of her life. Not until Belle, after complimenting Mae on her fortitude, said that she was depending on Mae to tend the heroic captain once they resumed their journey did that lady calm herself.

Pausing on the carriage step, Belle said to Jack, "Though I still wish you hadn't left the coach, I know I owe you a tremendous debt for your assistance. Those ruffians might have injured some of my household, had you not so gallantly come to our aid. I only hope you have not aggravated your injury or set back your recovery."

Then her lovely face warmed in a half rueful, half appreciative smile whose brilliance sparked that now-familiar shock to run along his nerves. "This has not been the 'easy' journey into the country we both hoped for."

"A journey in your company is a pleasure, whatever befalls us."

The compliment seemed to bubble out before he could stop it, and he cursed himself as a shuttered look replaced the warmth in her face. She obviously thought his words mere practiced flattery—although, he realized with some dismay, the sentiment had been impelled by an emotion stronger and more instinctive than judgment or prudence.

"Perhaps you should have some ale before we set out again," she said, once again the concerned but remote hostess. "Mae, would you pour some while I check on the others?"

Annoyed with himself, he watched her walk away.

"Ah, Captain, you be wondrous brave!" Mae exclaimed. "When that man started climbing into the coach, I thought my heart would bust right out of my chest! But Belle be right, you ought not to have strained yourself. Here you be now, looking about as healthy as the corpse at an Irish wake! Sip some of this ale. Don't need you coming down with an inflammation of the lungs."

Jack took the ale, but though his dizziness abated, the pain in his chest continued to intensify. Worse still, he now sensed wetness in the linen padding his wound.

A carriage rumbling through the chilly English countryside was hardly a suitable place to redo bandages, however. Easing deeper into the pillows, he told himself it would keep until they reached their destination.

A moment later, a draft of cool air wafted Belle's lavender scent to him as she entered the carriage and seated herself beside Mae and unstoppered a bottle that released the pungent tang of brandy.

"I thought you might wish for a restorative," she said, pouring a glass.

"You are prescient, ma'am," he replied, accepting the cup and gratefully throwing down its fiery contents.

"I also brought this," she said, holding up a small bottle of laudanum. "I advise you to take some. We've a long journey still, and some of the roads are rough."

Little as Jack liked the idea of dosing himself with the drug, he knew the jolting he'd endure for the rest of the carriage ride was bound to make his chest worse. It would only be prudent to medicate himself.

Though he'd prefer to keep his mind clear. Now that he'd had time to consider it, the attack on them did not seem the work of common highwaymen. There had been no demand to "stand and deliver," nor would highwaymen have troubled their baggage coach, knowing a wealthy traveler would normally keep his coin and valuables in his own vehicle.

But the sharp pain throbbing in his chest was already making coherent thought difficult. Wiser, perhaps, to leave analysis of the incident for later and accept a small dose of the drug. "Thank you, ma'am," he said at last, reaching for the bottle.

After several days seeing her only briefly, it was almost worth feeling so wretched to have her near him again. Despite his throbbing chest and recurrent nausea, he found himself focusing on her every movement: the slender fingers in their gray kid gloves gripping the bottle...the classic loveliness of her downcast profile...the rosy blush with which wind and exertion had painted her cheeks...the impossibly blue eyes gazing at him with concern. Bracing himself for it, welcoming it, he savored the sharp thrill of contact when he deliberately let his hand graze her fingertips as he took the bottle from her.

Though the impact of that touch registered in her eyes, this time she did not jerk her hand away. As if she, too, had known to expect it.

"Take good care of the captain, Mae," Belle said as she exited the carriage. "We'll be starting again soon."

Wistfully Jack watched Belle leave, feeling the loss of her presence as if a chill wind had blown through the coach at her departure.

Jack my lad, he warned himself as he settled painfully against the cushions, *you're a fair way to being lost....*

Though he would have sworn it impossible, the exhaustion brought on by his unexpected exertions compounded by brandy, laudanum and the warmth of blanket Mae swaddled him in, managed for a time to lull him to sleep. That period of relative easiness ended when he woke at their next stop. By lunchtime, he gave up trying to mask a misery that, despite more brandy and another dose of laudanum, had increased to the point of nullifying even the pleasure of Belle's company during a meal he couldn't pretend to eat.

By the time well after dark when Watson, with relief in his voice, stopped by to announce that they had just turned onto the drive leading to Belle's manor, Jack was wishing he had stayed in London. Not since the retreat to Corunna when weak, bleeding and half-frozen, he'd lashed himself to his horse, knowing if he fell off, he'd be left behind to die, had he felt so wretched.

Although, he thought, stifling a cry as the carriage took a particularly hard jolt, the idea of dying was beginning to seem rather attractive.

BELLE FELT FEAR stab through the uneasy mix of anxiety and guilt weighing her chest when the white-faced captain, without a murmur of protest, allowed Watson to virtually carry him from the coach into her house. Captain Carrington must be in bad straits indeed to not even attempt to move unassisted.

She trailed Watson up the stairs and into a guest bedroom, wincing in sympathy when Carrington groaned as Watson eased him onto the bed. Where, she noted with deepening concern, he simply lay unmoving, his eyes closed.

She should have insisted he remain in London. Still, she'd never imagined Waldo would be persistent enough to track them out of the City. Assuming the attack on them *had* been the work of Mrs. Jarvis and her henchman, at this far distance from the metropolis they were probably safe, Belle thought as she watched Watson gently ease the captain out of his greatcoat. If the woman had a steady supply of new innocents from the country, she would probably content herself with the money Belle had sent and simply replace Jane. Her chief worry, then, was that the captain might have a relapse here in the country, far from his London doctor.

Her concern deepened as, his face gone from pale to gray, Carrington's eyes flickered open briefly and he uttered a stifled cry. He'd been foolhardy to risk himself as he had, but wondrous brave, as well. No thought of self-preservation had stayed him when he'd abandoned the relative safety of the coach to confront their attackers, despite his still much-weakened condition. She had hardly been able to credit her eyes when she'd turned and saw him, the ruffian he'd downed lying in the mud beside the coach.

He had fortitude, as well. At their luncheon stop, Belle had read pain in the white line about his tightly compressed lips, the creases in his forehead, yet throughout what must have seemed an endless day of jolting discomfort, he had uttered not a word of complaint.

As she stood watching his still figure, she suddenly realized that to recuperate from his participation in today's events, Captain Carrington would likely have to remain at Bellehaven, not for the simple overnight stay she had envisioned, but for several days at least.

What worried her most was that the prospect of him tarrying didn't alarm her nearly as much as it should.

Watson's next words, however, wiped from her mind the speculation about what sort of hold the captain seemed to exert on her.

"Lady Belle," Watson said grimly, looking down at the red stain on the captain's waistcoat, "his wound be bleeding again."

CHAPTER TWELVE

FIGHTING DOWN PANIC, Belle scanned her memory for every treatment the doctor had administered to the captain. "Reynolds," she called to the housekeeper who had followed in their wake, "I'll need my medicine bag, brandy and hot water at once, please."

As the woman bobbed a curtsy and hurried off, Belle bent to assist Watson. "Captain, can you hear me? We're at Bellehaven now. We must get your jacket off and change your bandages. I'm afraid your wound has reopened."

With a visible effort, Carrington managed to open his eyes. "Sorry...to be such a bother," he whispered.

"Nonsense! But no talking now—you must rest."

For the next several minutes, Belle blessed Watson's strength as the prize-fighter held the captain suspended off the bed so she could strip his garments free with a minimum of disturbance. Noting with relief the housekeeper bringing in her supplies, she said to her patient, who had maintained a grim-lipped silence through the disrobing process, "I must cleanse the wound, then rebandage it."

The captain nodded. Closing her ears to his occasional grunt of pain, Belle set to work.

"Doesn't look so bad," Watson said, inspecting the wound she'd washed free of blood. "Flesh isn't red nor hot to the touch and the blood be seeping just from this one corner. With all ye done today, Captain, you be lucky."

"He would have been luckier had he remained in London," Belle noted, guilt coloring her concern.

"So he would," Watson agreed, "but we'd 'a been a far sight worse off without him. Let's hope the Lord blesses them what helps the needy and sends him a quick healing."

"Amen to that," the captain inserted in a breath of a voice, surprising her. Admiration entered the mix of emotions pulling at her, that instead of utilizing his slight strength to request something or complain, Carrington had tried to lighten the moment.

With Watson's help, Belle rebandaged the wound, the captain's arms and neck going rigid as she pulled the bindings as tight as she could. They all released a sigh of relief when at last she motioned Watson to lay the captain back against his pillows.

A maid arrived with bread and soup. Forestalling Carrington's feeble attempt to reach for the spoon, Belle said, "Please, Captain, let me. Save your energy for mending that wound."

Mechanically he swallowed down the hearty chicken stew, though he shook his head at the bread. "Rest... now."

Watson approached with a nightshirt the housekeeper

had produced. "I'll help you into this, unless you brung one of your own?"

A twinkle flickered in the captain's eyes as he angled a glance at Belle. "Never wear 'em."

Suppressing a chuckle, Belle hoped his good humor indicated the captain was beginning to recover from his exertions—permanently this time. But too worried about the possibility of his developing fever to relax, she said to Watson, "Stay with the captain while I change, please. I'm having a tray sent here."

The butler nodded. Belle touched the captain's forehead, reassured to find the skin, as Watson had said, warm but not hot. Then Carrington startled her by moving his hand to cover hers.

"You will...come back?" he whispered.

Something sharp and aching stirred in Belle's chest. Pushing the feeling aside to be dealt with later, she squeezed his limp fingers. "Yes, of course."

"Good," he said, the word a bare exhale of breath before he closed his eyes again.

After changing out of her traveling clothes, Belle took up her vigil beside the captain's bed. Watson stopped in several times, offering to relieve her while she rested, but Belle couldn't bring herself to leave. Heavy on her chest weighed the fear that the captain's heroic defense of them—a defense her lack of foresight had made necessary—would lead to a relapse that could kill him yet.

And so she sat though the long night, chair pulled close to the bed, ears alert for any change in his breathing. To her relief as the hours passed, her frequent, anxious checks of his forehead revealed no hint of a burgeoning inflammation. Several times she succumbed to the urge to let her fingers linger, brushing the dark hair off his brow or stroking the smoothness of his temples. Once, she thought he murmured, "good," but she was so weary herself that she might only have dreamed it.

She was not dreaming, however, when she woke the next morning, neck cramped from dozing on the arm of her chair, to find dawn light illumining the room—and her hand on the captain's shoulder, tucked under his own.

She stared, torn by twin desires to snatch her hand free and let it remain. On some private, soul-deep level his peacefully sleeping figure drew her, a reaction as powerful and even more alarming than the shocklike tingle that leapt between them when he was awake.

It must be excessive worry and lack of sleep, she told herself, for there was no place in either his world or hers where any mutually acceptable relationship could develop between them. She ought to remove her fingers, steal silently out, perhaps get a bit of sleep herself. But she couldn't seem to make herself draw away.

Instead, with her free hand, she gently stroked the captain's forehead. An instant later, he stirred and the dark eyes opened.

His gaze darted about the room, as if he did not remember where he was. Before she could remind him, his eyes returned to focus on hers with an intensity that trapped the words in her throat.

Something stirred again deep within her chest when

his lips curved into a smile. "You're still here," he murmured, his voice a gravelly whisper. "I'm glad."

She forced herself to look away. "And I am delighted to report that you have not developed fever, which makes it a very good morning indeed." Only then did she recall he still held her fingers and tried to pull them free.

He resisted, retaining them a moment before letting go. "Did I keep you awake all of the night?"

"I dozed quite a bit of it. How are you feeling?"

Cautiously he eased to a sitting position. "Much improved, it appears. Takes more than a three-man skirmish to put a tough old soldier permanently out of action."

"Thank heaven for that!"

"I fear you suffered more than I last night," he said, indicating her armchair and the shawl that still covered her knees. "That can't have been very comfortable."

"'Tis little enough, after all you did yesterday."

"As for yesterday, though I'm glad to have been of service, I should like to know more about the ambush. I wasn't thinking too clearly afterward, but it did seen odd that highwaymen would attack as they did."

She felt the heat as remorse and guilt washed color into her face. "I fear you are correct. We didn't tarry after turning the men over to a magistrate, but I suspect he'll discover that robbery wasn't their intent. I suppose you deserve an explanation as well as my apologies for once again putting you in harm's way."

"I'd like the explanation."

"And some breakfast, too, I imagine. Are you hungry?"

"Famished," he admitted with a smile.

Relief eased the ache in her chest. "An excellent sign! I'll send for something at once."

After ringing the bellpull, she returned to face him. "Now, your explanation. Do you remember that afternoon Jem came running to fetch me? I expect by now you've noticed my staff are rather…unconventional. I'd given shelter to a young girl who'd been tricked into service at one of the brothels in the theater district. Although I sent a rather large sum to pay off the madam, she was not satisfied."

Belle felt color rising again in her cheeks. "Excuse me for putting it so crudely, but certain men prefer a virginal-looking girl like Jane and will pay handsomely for her. The madam sent a henchman to try to remove Jane from my house by force. After the attempt, I decided to leave London so as to take Jane out of danger."

The captain frowned. "Should you not rather have turned the matter over to the authorities?"

"Both Mae and Watson counseled against it, feeling the law wouldn't be overly concerned about the fate of a prostitute, no matter how young. I consulted a friend with connections in the government, but he agreed that without proof from more…credible witnesses, probably nothing would be done. Since it appeared that any redress under law would be slow to obtain at best, I decided to bring Jane to Bellehaven. And I—" she faltered "—I was so certain that the miscreants would no longer be a problem once we left London, I did not bother to inform you of the possible danger. For that, I am profoundly sorry."

"If we were attacked by villains such as that, I can only be happy I was able to assist. However, I am afraid I shall have to impose upon your hospitality for longer than the overnight I'd initially requested."

"Of course. You do…you do see how necessary it was that I protect Jane?" she asked, wanting, for no good reason she could think of, his approval.

"Certainly, and it was admirable of you to do so, especially when it did in fact place you at risk."

"Not that admirable," Belle said in a low voice. "Such as Jane and I must help each other, for few others would trouble to assist us."

"I'm not of as much use yet, but while I'm under your roof, I'll aid in any way I can. Perhaps I could help Watson plan a strategy of defense to foil any attempts at Bellehaven, should the miscreants be so unwise as to pursue you here. If that would set your fears at rest?"

Though she told herself not to put too much credence in his unexpected offer, nonetheless Belle felt her worry over the household's welfare lessen. "I hesitate to call upon you any further, but…yes," she admitted, "I should feel better knowing we had a system of protection devised by someone of your military experience. But you must promise to do nothing more strenuous than plan—I'll hire some local youths to assist Watson with the rest."

A knock at the door was followed by the entrance of the butler, bearing a heavy tray. "Morning, Miss Belle. Captain, what a sight better you look!"

"Thank you, Watson. I'm feeling much better."

"Will you assist the captain while I get myself present-able?" Belle asked.

"You could never be less than beautiful," the captain replied, the quiet fervency of his voice making her suddenly uncomfortable. Retreating from the bed, she said, "I'll leave you in Watson's able hands."

She felt his gaze follow her all the way out the door. Oh, please, she thought as she left, let him not spoil the fragile accord that seemed to be developing between them by beginning to pursue her.

And please, let him heal soon and leave—before it became too tempting to lean upon the strong shoulder he seemed to be offering.

JACK MENTALLY KICKED himself as he watched Belle wrap herself in that cloak of cool dignity and walk out. Would he ever learn to check the admiring comments that rose naturally to his lips—and that she saw as empty gallantry?

Despite that faux pas, his spirits were high, for he felt infinitely better this morning, his chest less tight, the tenderness of his wound at a manageable level. Apparently, thank God, his heroics of the previous afternoon had not drastically compromised his recovery.

Nor did he mind having to linger a few days longer than anticipated at Belle's. Would that his healing proceeded apace, that he might put them to good advantage!

Since Watson seemed determined to remain at his side, he might as well make a virtue out of the annoyance of his infirmity, Jack decided as the butler began spooning in his broth. Once Watson finished, Jack could solicit the man's view of yesterday's events—and the girl Jane.

Though it seemed unlikely, he wasn't so jaded as to dismiss the possibility that she might have been an innocent somehow entrapped into life as a bawd. He had to suppress a smile, however, as he imagined his mama's reaction, should she learn he now resided under a roof that sheltered no less than three of the Fashionable Impure.

But someone had pursued Belle's party with evil intent. Speculation about who might have done so and why banished the smile from his lips.

At Jack's insistence, Watson allowed his patient to manage his own coffee cup. But as he turned to leave, Jack said, "Stay, please. I should like to learn more about Jane and her connection to the attack on us yesterday."

Watson frowned. "I can't rightly say if the two be connected, but it looks suspicious. Miss Belle brought Jane outta Mrs. Jarvis's fancy house—a mean old witch, that one is. Pays a bully boy named Waldo to keep her girls and her customers in line. Appears Waldo fancied Jane, too. Though to my mind," he added, scowling, "any bloke who'd touch a little slip of a thing like her needs a home lesson at the end of man's knuckles."

"This Waldo tried to steal her from Belle's house?"

"Yes. Miss Belle was all for going to the magistrate, but Jane begged her not to, saying Waldo told her he'd have revenge on Belle and anyone who helped her if she did."

"Did he, by God?" Jack said, incensed that someone

would threaten Belle—a detail that the lady had neglected to mention.

"Aye," Watson confirmed. "She done talked to some toff about getting the law into it, but in the end we convinced her 'twas best that we all leave the City."

"So the men who attacked us meant to capture Jane?"

Watson nodded. "I think it likely."

"You think they might try again here?"

Watson thought a moment. "I'd not expect them to come this far, but best to be cautious-like."

That decided the matter. Though Jack had mentioned almost idly to Belle the idea of organizing a system of defense at her manor, now that he knew she'd been actually threatened, he would definitely make such plans—and perhaps linger as long as possible to be able to assist, should it become necessary to implement them.

"Lady Belle mentioned engaging some extra footmen, which would be wise, as well as sending back to the magistrate to see what he discovered about the attackers. Perhaps, with your expertise in the ring and mine in the army, we can devise some plans for the household's protection. Just, as you said, to be cautious."

Watson nodded. "My lady's a gallant lass, but I'd not like to see her tangle with the likes of the men who come at us yesterday. Won't none of them fight like gentlemen."

He paused for a moment and then looked down at Jack. "Did she really best you with a sword?"

Jack gestured with his good hand. "You see me here."

Watson chuckled. "How I'd like to have cast my peepers on that match! She asked me once if I would train her in the Fancy. I turned her down, of course, but damn, I was tempted. Imagine the fortune a man could earn off all who'd come to see her fight!"

"She is most…unusual. Speaking of unusual, how did you come to be a butler?" Jack asked, seizing the opportunity to satisfy this point of curiosity. Though his ton acquaintances, he thought wryly, would doubtless find his engaging in such a discussion with a servant far odder than Watson's change of occupation.

Watson said nothing for a moment. Jack was on the point of apologizing for making so personal an inquiry when the butler replied, "Might as well admit it, I took a fearsome pounding my last few matches. Fighting was all I'd ever done since I growed to be such a block of a man, but I knew after that last time, when I couldn't rightly see or hear for near a week afterward, that if I didn't stop, it would be the end of me. Still, with the war over, jobs was scarce, especially for a bloke who knew nothing but using his fists. So I took a position at a fancy house, protecting the ladies and escorting out any gents that got too liquored up or quarrelsome. Met Mae there, afore she went off with Darlington. But I had…spells. One night, a customer hit me on my bad side and by the time I come to, he'd torn up the place pretty good. The madam was fit to spit nails and sacked me on the spot. Mae sent me to Lady Belle, and she took me on.

Then, when that high-and-mighty butler quit after Lord B cocked up his toes, she offered me his job. Me—a butler!" He shook his head wonderingly. "I'm trying not to disappoint her."

"I'm sure you won't," Jack said.

"After yesterday," Watson continued, "I'm glad you'll be staying awhile, Captain, though I be sorry about your wound. I—I still have…spells," he admitted, and Jack could sense what it cost the big man to confess that weakness. "I'd shoot myself, did something happen to Lady Belle 'cause I weren't myself to protect her. She's hardly bigger than Jane, but there's a warm heart in her what looks kindly on even the raff and scaff."

"Like Jem?" Jack suggested.

"Jem!" Watson sighed. "Lawton thinks to make a groom of him yet, if he can ever break him of thieving. He's quick to learn, but so troublesome, his thiefmaster sold him as a climbing boy. Wasn't but a blackened scrap when Lady Belle found him stuck in the chimney last winter, hands and feet all over burns and him too weak and cold to get himself out. 'Course our Miss Belle, she couldn't abide sending him back, so she bought him from the sweep."

"Rescued him, too? Like Jane."

Watson nodded. "Took in Mae, too. And me." His smile faded and he fixed a hard look on Jack. "Every one of us would do anything for her, nor would we take kindly to any what might do her an insult."

Was that a not-so-subtle threat about his potential dishonorable intentions? Jack wondered. "I shall keep that in mind," he responded gravely. "But certainly you don't think I mean to cause her harm."

Watson studied Jack. "Mayhap you could do her more harm than you think. Or more good. Who's to know?"

After that enigmatic pronouncement, his belligerence faded. "I best let you rest. I'll be waiting to hear more about them defense plans." Giving Jack a short bow, he gathered up the tray and left the room.

Watson, Mae, the pickpocket Jem and now this Jane. It seemed Lady Belle had a habit of taking in strays and unfortunates. He tried to examine the implications of it—a courtesan who ran her home like a Methodist mission.

But more fatigued than he wanted to admit after breakfast, Jack found sleep claiming him again. He awoke hours later, ravenous, his room bathed in a gilding of what looked to be late-afternoon sunlight.

From some nearby room drifted in the lilting sound of what could only be a Mozart concerto, being masterly performed on a pianoforte. He was trying to puzzle out which piece it was when Mae walked in.

"Awake at last! You must be fair starving, since Belle told the maid not to rouse you for nuncheon."

"I would appreciate something more substantial than gruel, this time, if you please! And whom should I thank for the lovely serenade?"

"That be Belle, of course. She does love her music and so she should, so well she plays. 'Tis beyond me, for I'm sure I couldn't get my fingers to hit three right notes together. Plays like a wonder, don't she?"

"A wonder indeed," he murmured, enchanted by the beauty of the concerto and surprised by the excellence of her rendering. Beyond the obvious, a courtesan of Belle's repute would doubtless be skilled at repartee, practiced in presiding over a man's drawing room and table, perhaps clever at cards or other games of chance.

But he'd never heard of a courtesan who played Mozart.

"Watson says you've recovered right well since yesterday," Mae's voice recalled him. "You look better, your eyes clear and some healthy color to your face."

"I am much better, thank you. Indeed, I hope tonight to present myself at dinner. In the interim, I should be glad of some company."

"Let me send for food. Can't play pianoforte or read to you, but I'd be happy to sit here awhile. Belle and Lord Egremont like a hand of piquet, but I've no head for cards neither."

"You'll converse with me, I hope. 'Tis something at which you are very good indeed!"

Mae chuckled. "I expect, even if you was in more strenuous frame, you'd not be interested in what I do best. But no matter. Of course, we can talk. Though to my way of thinking, you'd best keep to your room another day or so and let that wound heal over good. No point traipsing about too soon just to land yourself back in bed again."

Knowing how little time he had left to penetrate the mystery of Lady Belle, Jack was far too impatient to be up and about to heed Mae's advice. Not wishing to argue the point, however, he simply nodded. "I appreciate your concern, but enough about me. How do you fare today, ma'am? Have you recovered from yesterday's fright?"

Mae shuddered. "La, best not to think on it! Belle, bless her, thought to beg a bit of the coachman's restorative to help calm my nerves."

The coachman's "restorative" being strong spirits, no doubt, Jack thought, suppressing a smile. "And the maid Jane? Watson said she'd fainted away after the attack."

"I wouldn't doubt it, what with pistols firing and flash-coves banging on doors! Though she be so grateful for her rescue, she can't do enough to show it. Brung me chocolate and built up my fire with her own hands this morning, all the while thanking me for being so kind! Fair made me blush for shame, for I have to admit, I weren't too happy about Belle agreeing to take on all her troubles."

If the girl's gratitude led her to willingly perform tasks generally relegated to the lowliest servant in the house-hold, perhaps she was the innocent Belle had claimed. "Sounds like she is a good lass at heart."

Mae nodded vigorously. "What did she do this noon but bring back a gown I'd given my maid, for I'd trodden on the hem and torn the satin beyond repair. Somehow Jane managed to fix it—and added a trimming of silk roses she'd fashioned herself that makes the gown look better than new. 'Tis a marvel she is with her needle."

Mae angled a glance at Jack and chuckled. "Best pre-pare yourself, Captain. Once Jane learns what a hand you had in her rescue, I expect she'll be wanting to stitch you up a whole new wardrobe!"

Jack laughed as well—and was heartened to discover the effort cost him only a mild pull of discomfort. "Since I'm soon to turn in my uniform for a gentleman's coats, perhaps I should take advantage. Jane wishes to be a seamstress?"

"A lady's maid was what she always wanted to be, Belle told me. No real lady'd take her now, but she might do as a seamstress. Sure as sure, she dare not work in London, but I expect she'd prefer the country anyways. The way she went on this morning—" Mae gave a disbelieving shake of her head "—praising the birds and trees and sweet fresh air, you'd think she'd been transported to Paradise."

Mae paused and frowned slightly, then looked back at him, her eyes brightening. "You've got a big estate up north, don't you? Far enough away for Jane to be safe. The females in your household would love to have such a seamstress as Jane. Might be you could hire her?"

Jack had a swift mental picture of trying to explain to his disapproving mother how he had arrived at the familial doorstep with a young, probably lovely, definitely unchaperoned girl. That lady's reaction when he informed her of Jane's previous occupation would likely be worse. He hesitated, at a loss to explain to Mae the myriad social violations that made her well-intentioned suggestion impossible.

But before he could think of a reply that turned aside the proposal without insulting Jane or Mae, that lady drew herself up, coloring. "Begging your pardon, Captain!" she said a bit stiffly. "I forgot how Watson told me your lady mother lives there, and your sister, too. I expect the pair of 'em would faint dead away, was you to bring someone like Jane to their door. What with you talking to everyone as if you was no more than an ordinary bloke, sometimes I forget that you be a gentleman. Excuse me for speaking outta place, milord."

Jack stared at Mae with regret and a bit of dismay. Both his army experience, when he'd lived and fought and had his life saved on more than one occasion by troopers from all stations of life, and the special camaraderie in this household, so different from the rigid hierarchical organization generally found in ton establishments—compelled him to try to heal the breach. "Please, Mae, my mother may be an earl's daughter, but I'm plain 'Mr.' Carrington, and I hope you'll always consider me so."

Mae returned a slight smile. "You may not have a fancy handle afore your name, but you're a gentleman for all that. And your mama be a regular nob."

"'Captain' I will answer to, but no more. Or else I shall have to assume the lordly airs you say I lack and command you to treat me in the same charming manner you have thus far!"

Mae gave him a reproving look and shook her head. "You be a silver-tongued rascal, and that's the truth. 'Captain' it be, then. But you better rest if you're determined to drag yourself to the dinner table." She rose and gave him an exaggerated curtsy. "Until later—your *lordship*," she added with a wink.

So, what had he gleaned from the day's exchanges?

Jack asked himself as Mae, in a provocative swing of hip, swayed out the door.

That Lady Belle presided over an odd amalgam of staff who interacted more like a family than a hierarchy of servants. Individuals who displayed a fierce loyalty and protective concern toward their mistress, who treated them in turn more like relations than paid staff. Indeed, Jack thought, he could hardly come under more critical scrutiny than that to which Watson had subjected him this morning when, perhaps later this Season, he stood before the father of an aristocratic lady whose hand he sought in marriage.

Though his mental image of that scene was growing dimmer by the day.

And Lady Belle herself? By now he was certain that she was far more than a clever woman who had used her stunning beauty to lever herself into the ranks of the most sought-after of courtesans. Whatever her parentage, she must have been gentry-raised.

Speech and mannerisms could be copied, skill at games of chance and witty conversation acquired by one astute enough to learn them, but her mastery of music and the concepts of honor, loyalty and fairness that colored all her actions…these were qualities that must have been acquired during years of growing up in a genteel home.

Besides, he thought, suddenly struck by the notion, unlike her companion who flaunted her sensuality, Belle deliberately downplayed her beauty. He had never seen her, even at the opera, garbed in a gown that featured more than a modest décolletage. For the most part, she kept her burnished hair pulled severely back or hidden, her figure masked in the sober sort of gowns he remembered his sister's governess had been wont to wear.

He chuckled, finding it rather easy to imagine her as an earnest young lady trying to stuff French grammar and Mozart into the heads of her unappreciative charges. Hiding her comeliness under gowns chosen to mask her beauty from the notice of an employer's randy husband or son.

Could that have been her fate? he wondered with a sudden burst of furious insight. Daughter of impoverished gentry who'd been sent out to earn her bread and victimized by the idle lechery of some amoral employer? Had Bellingham discovered her at a country-house party and lured her to ruin? Or persuaded an already fallen maiden about to lose her situation to accept his protection?

The fact that taking up Bellingham's offer would have been better for Belle than being thrown defenseless into the street did not lessen the white-hot heat of his anger.

If such had been her fate, small wonder that she had with cool calculation amassed enough assets to allow her to spurn the aristocrats now vying to become her next protector—even one as wealthy as Lord Rupert.

Or that she had such sympathy for Jane and others trampled upon by those of greater wealth and power.

Damn, he thought with a wry grin. He was beginning to sound like a flaming Republican.

Regardless, he simply couldn't leave her now. Lady Belle was drawn to him—he was certain of that. Somehow he must build on that foundation, persuade her to trust him and confide in him the truth of her story.

So he could…what? Far too late, in their society, to ride like a White Knight to the rescue of a wronged demoiselle, if such she turned out to be.

Whatever he did, he would have to proceed cautiously, he concluded, remembering Watson's thinly veiled warning. Though he couldn't blame the butler. It was hardly surprising that Watson, recognizing Quality when he met it, considered the mistress he served so loyally deserving of only the most honorable of attentions.

The implications of that realization rocked him to his core. Just what was Jack Carrington prepared to offer this woman who had slowly come to take possession of his mind, his thoughts, his senses?

And how was he going to make the lady he was quickly coming to feel he could never permanently leave behind a part of his future?

CHAPTER THIRTEEN

EARLY THAT EVENING, WATSON stopped by Belle's room to inform her that Captain Carrington had rung requesting Watson's help in dressing for dinner.

"Dressing for dinner," Belle echoed, aghast. "Surely he can't mean to attempt anything so foolhardy, when only last night he could scarcely walk or take a deep breath!"

"He's much heartier now, though I have my doubts about him managing them stairs—or sitting up the length of a dinner. Anyways, I figured you'd want to know afore I answered his bell."

"Thank you, Watson. Tell Cook the captain will dine in his room as previously instructed. I'll talk to him."

Could Carrington have recovered that quickly in a single day? Though she doubted anything that miraculous, Belle could only hope he was making rapid progress, since his return to health would signal his ability to remove his disturbing presence from her household.

All day long, she'd deliberately kept herself occupied with the myriad details of opening the house, consulting the stable staff and talking with her bailiff about the tenants and the spring planting. All day long, she'd resisted the temptation constantly teasing at the back of her mind to check on the captain.

Though she told herself she did not wish to disturb his rest, she knew the real reason she'd forced herself to stay away was because the pull to be with him was far too strong. It did little for her peace of mind to recognize how effectively he could diffuse her usually strong focus. She absolutely must stifle the foolish impulse to talk with him, solicit his advice...trust him.

Which meant she must cordially countermand his desire to dine outside his room. She couldn't afford to let him overexert himself, setting back his recovery any further.

Though as she walked to his room, she had to squash a treacherous whisper of hope that he might have to linger.

After rapping briefly, she entered. "Good evening, Captain. What's this I hear from Watson about you intending to go downstairs for dinner?"

Though she'd braced herself for the rush of awareness that struck her when she came near him, still her foolish nerves tingled anew as his eyes brightened and a smile leapt to his lips when he saw her.

"Indeed, ma'am, 'tis time I stopped malingering."

"An admirable ambition," she said, trying to ignore the potent charm of that smile. "Happy as I am that you feel like making the attempt, after yesterday I dare not permit you to risk another setback."

"Having had a near corpse foisted upon you twice now, I understand your concern. But truly, I am much improved. I practiced walking in my room this afternoon and feel stronger even than I did before we left London. Did I not warn you old soldiers are hard to vanquish?"

In truth, he did look much better. Gone was the listless demeanor, the grim set of the mouth, the sense of suffering. Instead, healthy color lit his cheeks, keen awareness burned in the dark eyes, and he emanated an aura of strength, confidence—and a virile masculinity that sent another jolt to her senses.

She took a deep breath to steady her shaky breathing. Except for when they had faced off with swords, when her perceptions of the captain as a man had been overridden by concentration on him as opponent, 'twas the first time they had been in close proximity when he was not injured and near helpless.

The captain injured was attractive enough. The captain recovering, she decided as she took an involuntary step backward, was far too compelling.

"Would you not humor my anxiety and agree to remain at least one more day in your chamber?"

"Should I not rather dispel that anxiety by showing I can dine without suffering dire consequences?"

Belle hesitated. Rather than relieving anxiety, the idea of facing all that charm over the close confines of her small dinner table was almost as alarming as the thought of him suffering a relapse.

Yet, he was a soldier accustomed to action—and her guest, as well. She could hardly *order* him to stay put, like a sick child in the nursery.

"Of course, you may take your meal in the dining room

if you feel up to it. Although I fear I should scarcely eat a bite for worrying about you," she added a bit smugly. A guest who had already pronounced himself beholding to his hostess would hardly wish to cause her additional distress.

The captain bent on her a look of such clear comprehension that she felt compelled to drop her eyes. No lackwit, this one. He knew exactly what she was doing.

"I should be loath to spoil your digestion," he replied. "If dining with me is so worrisome, I shall ask Watson if he could set a place for me in the kitchen."

Though Carrington's pleasant expression didn't alter, Belle realized he meant what he said. After having dealt with the invalid for more than a week, she found it disconcerting to suddenly confront the firm resolve and quick-witted response of the battle-tested soldier.

Impressed despite herself at how neatly he'd countered her move, Belle replied dryly, "I believe I recognize bargaining when I hear it. What will it take to keep you above stairs, Captain?"

"Let me sit in a chair at a real table," he replied promptly. "And you must come and dine with me."

With difficulty, Belle kept her face from mirroring her dismay. If supping with him in the dining room had seemed disturbingly intimate, sharing a meal in his bedchamber was even more so. Yet he looked and sounded capable of carrying out his threat to descend all the way to the kitchen. Where, if he did not collapse in the attempt, her staff, who since the captain's assistance during the rescue spoke of him in worshipful tones, would be much more likely to do whatever he bid than urge him back to bed.

"Since I cannot feel easy at having you exert yourself to that extent, I suppose I must bow to your wishes." With a touch of asperity, she added, "You've humbugged me as neatly as Boney did Wellington before Waterloo."

"Ah, but Wellington won the day in the end."

"Only because of a lethargic Ney and a loyal Blucher. I've no such reinforcements. Put to the test, I fear my staff would abandon me and flock to your banner, as the Royalist troops did to Boney after he escaped from Elba."

Carrington raised his eyebrows. "You are a student of the late war?"

"I read the newspaper accounts like everyone else," she replied, not wanting to appear knowledgeable enough to pique his interest. "And I have a friend in government who used to rattle on about it. But enough of that. Please, *my lord,*" she asked with exaggerated courtesy, "since it appears we will be having dinner, would an hour hence be acceptable?"

With a grin, he inclined his head. "Most acceptable, my lady."

"I shall go prepare, then." Dropping a curtsy deep enough to honor a royal Drawing Room, Belle withdrew.

Precisely an hour later, dressed in the plainest gown that could be considered suitable, Belle had Watson announce her as she entered the captain's chamber, only to check three steps later.

From his seat at the linen-draped table set before the fireplace, the china and silver upon it reflecting the flicker of candlelight, the captain rose and bowed to her.

She had seen Carrington in his regimentals across the expanse of a theater and the width of Armaldi's ballroom. She had adjusted to seeing him closer up while he slept or tossed about, half-conscious and glassy-eyed with pain. She'd even managed to settle herself after the shock of seeing him earlier tonight, sharp-eyed and clear-witted.

None of those meetings prepared her for the commanding presence the captain presented as he towered over her, garbed in the shining array of a full-dress uniform, his penetrating gaze exerting a near-hypnotic pull. Her knees went shaky and for a moment she forgot to breathe.

"Won't you join me?" he asked, gesturing to a chair.

Idiot! she rebuked herself, trying to stiffen her knees and get her lungs functioning as Watson seated her. She'd dined with handsome, commanding men before, was still being pursued by a number of powerful London gentlemen.

But none who affected her like Captain Carrington.

"Madam, you look lovely," Carrington said. Her lips might have twitched in amusement at the compliment offered to so dull a gown, had not the captain at that moment brought the hand she reluctantly offered to his lips.

She felt that polite salute all the way up her arm. As soon as decorum allowed, she withdrew her fingers, rubbing them on her gown to quell the residual tingling.

"Nay, Captain, tonight you far outshine me," she replied, relieved that her voice wasn't betraying her inner agitation. "No wonder young maidens lose their hearts over soldiers. You should post a warning for ton mamas to guard their daughters when you return for the Season."

"'Tis not young maidens a man wishes to impress."

Was he trying to flirt with her? Deciding to ignore the remark, Belle motioned for Watson to serve the first course. One thing she'd learned well over the years: men liked to talk about themselves. It would be worth risking a demonstration of her intellect if she could focus their conversation on Carrington's experiences—and forestall any more gallant remarks.

"You mentioned you'd been injured at Corunna. I understand the retreat was dreadful—icy rain and snow. How did you manage with a saber wound to the shoulder?"

He grimaced, as if the memory were not pleasant. No matter, as long as it kept his thoughts away from her.

"I lashed myself to my horse, a surefooted beast, thank the Lord." He shook his head as if to dispel the memory. "So you can understand why I am able to recover so much faster here. In fact, I am feeling so much improved tonight despite my exertions yesterday that I begin to think the original wound must have been less serious than the physician thought."

"That would be excellent news," Belle said.

"Yes, for if my recovery continues apace, I shall be able to take a more active part setting up those defensive arrangements we mentioned. I've already discussed the matter with Watson. With your permission, I should like to remain at Bellehaven long enough to insure the measures put in place have rendered you entirely safe."

Belle found his words at once reassuring and disturbing. Much as she did not want to rely on him, it felt like a burden lifted to know he intended to guarantee they were protected from any recurrence of the trouble that had found them on the road. Having the captain delay his departure, however, stirred that familiar mix of alarm, anticipation and an unsettled *something* akin to yearning.

She knew it would be much better for her senses and her sanity to bid goodbye to him as soon as possible.

Why did that prospect hold less and less appeal?

Restraining her muddled reactions to be dealt with later, she tried to steer the conversation back to him.

"Did you take part in all the Peninsular campaign?"

"First Regiment was involved in most of it."

"Ah, the 'Gentlemen's Sons'! I understand General Moore himself complimented the Guards for being nearly the only unit which did not turn the retreat at Corunna into a rout. Did you see action with them later?"

"After being invalided home awhile, I made most of the engagements, from Barrosa to Bayonne to Belgium."

After pausing to let Watson serve the second course, she continued, "You were with Maitland at Waterloo?"

"Yes, we gave the Coldstream Guards an assist at Hougoumont earlier in the day, but were recalled to the regiment before the main attack on Wellington's lines."

"I must immediately withdraw my objections to any activity you wish to undertake. A soldier who survived not only Corunna, but the advance of Napoleon's Imperial Guard must be nearly invincible!"

He smiled. "This invincible soldier preferred watching their *retreat*—thanks to a timely intervention by the lads in Sir John Colborne's 52nd."

"You did not wish to remain on occupation duty in Paris with the Duke? See some of the rest of Europe?"

"Paris is lovely as always, but I have little desire to visit a countryside which has been stricken by war for nearly twenty years. I've seen enough of the devastation wreaked by armies on the march. Give me the quiet green fields of England."

"You mean to settle on your estate, then?"

"Yes, after squiring my sister through her Season. Although I have an excellent bailiff, I'm eager to take back the reins. I may even pay a visit to Coke at Holkham and study the latest in agricultural techniques." He laughed. "Although I would lose whatever esteem I may have won in Mae's eyes by admitting such a goal."

Belle smiled. "She would find it incomprehensible."

"Do you prefer town, as well?"

"No, Bellehaven—" she refrained from adding "alone" "—is exactly where I wish to be. Except for occasional visits to London for shopping or the theater, I intend to establish myself here."

"You grew up in the country?"

He posed the question so casually that had cautious prudence not insisted she maintain her guard, she might have been lulled into returning a detailed answer. Checking that impulse, she said simply, "Yes."

A small silence ensued while he waited, probably expecting her to amplify that response. Instead, Belle called Watson to remove the covers and bring in tea.

Apparently accepting her reticence, while Watson served them, he continued, "I must compliment you on your musical talent. Mae told me it was you I heard earlier playing the pianoforte—a Mozart concerto, I believe."

"Yes," she answered, surprised and impressed by his knowledge of music. "I'm afraid I'm much out of practice."

"What I heard sounded masterful. You must have begun lessons at a very early age."

Her wariness had not been amiss. The captain was definitely trolling for information—as he had done already with Mae and Watson, from what those two had recounted of their conversations with him. Unusual as it was for a man of his rank to express interest in individuals society considered so very far beneath him, Belle had no objection to her servants relating to the captain as much about their lives as they chose to tell or he wished to hear.

Fortunately, not even Mae knew enough about Belle's background to pose a danger. Having no intention of augmenting what little he might have already gleaned, she said, "I do enjoy Mozart. There's such order and symmetry to his music, I find it…soothing."

A bittersweet sadness coiled within her. How many times, when the role forced upon her became too much to bear, had she escaped into those calming cadences?

"My sister enjoys the harp, which showcases her lovely voice. Do you subscribe to the Philharmonic Society?"

"Yes. One can actually hear the music there, which is not always the case at the opera."

He opened his mouth, then closed it. Probably, Belle thought, he had been about to remark that private musicals sponsored by the ton offered even better listening experiences—until he recalled that she would not have entrée to such evenings.

Still, she liked him all the better for initiating a conversation so free of flirtation and innuendo. She had feared as he recovered his health, he might decide to pursue her, out of boredom if not desire.

Save Egremont, none of Bellingham's friends had ever expressed an interest in her beyond the perfect face and body they schemed to possess. Their conversation consisted of recitations of current gossip interspersed with overblown gallantries and attempts to impress her with their wealth, power or desirability as potential lovers.

She must be doubly on guard against the insidious appeal of a man who appeared more interested in knowing about her than winning her, who solicited her opinions rather than just her favors.

Wiser, then, that she bring this evening to a close before she ended up any more eager for his company.

"I should go now," she said, putting down her cup. "'Tis your first dinner out of bed and you must be tired."

"Not at all! I've felt increasingly stronger all day and I am certainly enjoying the company. Would you not stay a bit longer? Perhaps indulge me in a hand of piquet? I understand you often play with Egremont."

Was there an edge of jealousy in his voice? she wondered, surprised. More disconcerting, she realized that on some deeply feminine level, she was *pleased* that the captain might be jealous. An odd reaction, since normally she found the rival claims men pressed on her annoying.

And yet another signal that it was definitely time to go. "Perhaps another evening, Captain. With all the details of opening up the house, I am rather tired myself."

He held out a hand before she could rise. "A glass of port, then? To ease my discomfort and help me sleep."

It seemed such a blatant attempt to forestall her departure that she had to smile. "Captain, you use your afflictions most conveniently."

He shrugged, an unrepentant twinkle in his eye. "As I earned them, I might as well use them. Just one glass?"

He was so transparent about his manipulation, so clearly hopeful of beguiling her to stay, that she couldn't help being amused.

Why not remain? In a few short days he would leave Bellehaven and she was unlikely ever to see him again. What harm would there be in indulging in the company of a man who treated her with intelligence and respect... as if she were still a lady born?

That she was as loath as he to have the evening end should have been reason enough to speed her out the door. Instead, she heard herself say, "Just one glass, then."

"So you enjoy the theater?" he asked as she poured them each a small portion of the rich cherry liquid.

"Very much. Kean of Drury Lane is marvelous. Have you seen his Shylock?"

"No, I've spent little of my adulthood in London."

"Since you are to be there for the Season, you must take your sister to see Kean—and Kemble at Covent Garden."

"I shall keep that in mind. I'm a great admirer of Shakespeare's works."

"I love them, as well."

"Perhaps we might attend the theater together when you are next in London."

She looked up sharply, but his eyes held no suggestive gleam, nor did innuendo shade his voice. He looked and sounded more like...like a friend discussing with another friend a subject of interest to them both.

She could almost feel the warmth of his camaraderie beginning to melt the layers of ice behind which she concealed her true self. Confused, she looked away, torn between relief that his remark had not been a prelude to another sort of suggestion and a rush of delight at apparently discovering a kindred spirit.

She shook her head, trying to damp down the elation. That she had discovered someone with whom she could speak freely of the things she loved—or had used to love, before her life had taken so drastic a turn—was a dangerous illusion. She must not permit some chimera of friendship to breach her defenses. At this critical moment, with fulfillment almost within her grasp, she dare not risk losing everything she had sacrificed so much and endured so long to achieve.

It was definitely time to retire—before she allowed this foolish sense of connection to deepen any further. Finishing the port, she set down her glass and rose.

"I've enjoyed our conversation, Captain. Until tomorrow, then? When I hope you will discover this late evening has not caused you any harm."

He rose, as well. "The evening has been a delight. And I assure you, ma'am, I've suffered no *physical* harm."

His emphasis on the word making her immediately suspicious, she shot him another sharp glance. But she could read nothing suggestive into his tone or expression. Relief greater than she ought to feel swept through her.

With a curtsy to his bow, she left him.

Slowly she walked back to her room, mulling over the evening they'd just shared. He was…restful, she decided, lulling her fear that he might try to lead her into a dalliance so effectively that she had ended up treating him with almost none of her usual reserve, though the attraction between them still hummed in the air. Except for that single, quite proper kiss to her fingertips, he had not attempted to touch her again, nor had his eyes played over her with lascivious admiration, as even that young cub Ansley's did.

Longing and a sadness long suppressed rose in her.

Aside from time spent in Egremont's company, she had not felt so at ease with a man since the days she had studied with her father in their library, reading and conversing with him about literature, art, politics. Listening raptly, as she'd listened tonight to the captain, to Papa's tales of John Company and India.

He'd hoped to make there the fortune that would enable his young family to once again command the elegancies of life. How different would her life had been, had Mama's health allowed them to all go together? Or if Papa had not contracted a fever so soon after his arrival, turning all his dreams for their future to the dust of the Indian plains that had received his last remains?

She shook her head, forcing the questions back to the depths of memory where she usually locked them away. Dwelling on what might have been never did anything save make her weep. Her life had become something very different from what her papa would have hoped, and there was nothing now to be done about it.

Dwelling on the possibility of friendship with the all-too-attractive Jack Carrington was equally fruitless. Whatever the future held for Lady Belle, former courtesan extraordinaire, the respectable eldest son of an earl's daughter who planned to marry off his sister and then retire to tend his acreage would play no part in it.

CHAPTER FOURTEEN

AFTER A REVIVING CUP of ale the following morning, Jack felt well enough to tell Watson that he would breakfast downstairs. The small tear in his wound appeared to have healed nicely, he noted when they changed the bandages, and the whole area was only mildly sensitive.

The rebinding of his wound completed, Watson helped him dress and supervised his descent to the breakfast parlor, a maneuver he managed, to his jubilant relief, without incurring either severe pain or dizziness. Though his elation over this evidence of his continuing recovery dimmed somewhat when Watson informed him he would be breakfasting alone, as Mae took her chocolate in her room and Lady Belle had gone out early to visit the tenants.

Yet another indication of her upbringing, Jack concluded. Just so would his mother ride out after returning to Carrington Grove, to see how their land and the dependents who farmed it had fared in her absence.

After Watson directed the footman to set before him a hearty helping of steak and ale, opining that one couldn't expect a man to recover his strength on naught but a bit of toast and tea, Jack said, "If you would join me after breakfast, I should like to start on the defense plans we discussed. I'll need a list of all the able-bodied men employed on the estate, their duties and whether any have had training with the army or the militia. Or the Fancy."

"Aye—having some what be handy with their fives would come a blessing. I'll do that list for you, Captain, and meet you in the library after your meal." With a bow, Watson left the room.

Jack occupied himself while he ate with sketching in his mind the arrangements he would discuss with Watson, then proceeded to the library, where the butler met him with the requested list and assisted him in drawing up a general plan of defense. Telling the butler he would re-fine his instructions after he'd had a chance to inspect the property personally, he recommended putting out inquiries to hire some additional men.

Since at the conclusion of their discussion, Lady Belle had still not returned, Jack decided to test his strength with a walk about the lawns. He must look better, he thought, for without protest, Watson led him to a study whose French doors led onto a small terrace overlooking a well-tended lawn bright with the pale green of newly emerging grass.

He breathed deeply of the sweet fresh air, grateful to be able to do so with a minimum of discomfort, and seated himself on an inviting bench. After a week of minute gains, the rapid increase in strength and endurance he'd experienced over the last two days seemed to confirm, as he'd speculated to Belle the previous evening, that his initial wound had not been as severe as originally feared. His spirits rose at the prospect of soon recovering his health and vigor.

With that improvement came a growing impatience to have done with the sickroom. The only factors restraining him from launching back into his normal activities were the prudence that warned against overexerting himself prematurely—and a desire to remain Lady Belle's guest.

What a magical evening last night had been! Happenstance had not trained that mind to appreciate music and politics, those hands to perform at the keyboard and in the drawing room. He was now firmly convinced that she was gentry born—and more eager than ever to discover what catastrophe had catapulted her out of the position in society which should have been hers by right.

But beyond the curiosity to discover her circumstances, he had reveled in the simple pleasure of conversing with a woman who showed herself to be as intelligent and talented as she was lovely.

Now that he knew his recovery had not been placed in jeopardy, Jack was almost grateful to the ruffians who had attacked them, making necessary the development of a defensive plan for Bellehaven and giving him an excuse to linger longer than the additional day or two required for his wound to finish mending.

Perhaps by tomorrow, he'd be fit enough to have Belle drive him about her property so he could gain firsthand knowledge of the land's features.

The idea of having her all to himself for a several-hour drive filled him with eager anticipation. While assessing the estate's defensive strengths and weaknesses, he could prompt her to talk about the land she loved, perhaps lead her to tell him more about her past.

Though traveling beside her in a small conveyance would pose its own problems. He'd done better of late at avoiding the compliments she perceived to be empty flattery. Her haste to remove her fingers from his grip and the step backward she'd taken to maintain a distance between them at dinner, however, told him she was still wary of the physical pull between them. As he had last night, he must continue to be careful not to crowd her.

Something that would not be possible when they traveled by gig or phaeton—the small open vehicles which would give him the best view of Bellehaven's land. He would have to remember to keep to himself—no matter how tempted he was to sit close beside her, or let his fingers linger when he helped her in or out of the vehicle.

Still, the reward for the restraint he'd shown last night had been a dramatic lessening of her reserve. She'd become almost animated during their conversation, several times treating him to a glimpse of her enchanting smile.

Gladness filled him and his own lips curved just remembering it. He would hold himself under rigid control for a millennium if it would bring that charming twinkle into those deep blue eyes or prompt the lilting music of her laughter.

To make her look so happy and carefree.

Damn, but he couldn't wait to be with her again!

Ah, Jack, you are well on your way to being lost indeed. But he pushed to the back of his mind the problem of what to do about his deepening fascination with Lady Belle. For now, he meant to simply enjoy for as long as he could contrive to remain at Bellehaven the wonder of her nearness and her friendship.

Enough woolgathering, he told himself. Time to begin refining those defensive plans.

Slowly he paced the terrace, noting that the manor house crowned a small rise and was flanked by tall oaks, which also bordered the curving drive leading from the entrance down across a scythed meadow to a gatehouse set in a copse of the same oak. The trees beside the house and stone wall flanking the lane beyond the gatehouse would be excellent positions in which to station watchmen without them being seen by approaching vehicles or horsemen, while their commanding the higher ground would allow them to spot anyone who tried to draw near the manor while they were still at a distance.

Whoever had designed Bellehaven, which appeared to date from late Elizabethan times, had known the importance of being able to secure his land, Jack thought approvingly.

The terrace was equally well planned, featuring a screen of hawthorn which blocked the wind and accented the warmth of the pale, early spring sunshine. Returning to the stone bench within the curve of the shrubbery, Jack sat down and lifted his face to the sun.

He was celebrating the blessing of being here with Lady

Belle, rather than in some overheated Paris ballroom, a smoke-filled London club—or a chilly grave, when the close of a door followed by a rustle of skirt roused him.

He looked up to see Mae advancing toward him with a smile, a slim, mobcapped maid following behind her.

"I near accused Watson of funning me when he said you was out on the terrace," she said as she reached him. "How glad I am to find it true!"

"Won't you join me?" he asked, motioning to the bench.

"La, I came out without a parasol, but I suppose a minute of sun won't ruin my complexion."

"I'll fetch your parasol, ma'am," the maid said.

"Why, thank you, Jane, that be right kind of you."

Jack arced a swift look at the girl now rising from her curtsy. Slender almost to the point of emaciation, with her small frame, heart-shaped face dominated by large dark eyes and the quantity of soft brown curls escaping her mobcap, she appeared to be a junior housemaid—the youngest of servants, a child barely in her teens.

Pure outrage bubbled up in his blood and for a moment he couldn't speak.

"Such a good child she is," Mae was saying as she watched the slim figure retreat. "I was vastly suspicious of her at first, thinking she might be trying to take advantage of Belle, but she's won me over."

"Th-that is Jane?" Jack finally got out.

"The 'Jane' Belle brought out of a fancy house?" Mae asked, her gaze still on the retreating girl. "Yes."

Jack spit out an oath so vicious Mae gasped in surprise.

"My pardon for such language, ma'am, but 'tis an abomination! Someone forcing that innocent to become…" He couldn't bring himself to utter the ugly word.

"A harlot? A drab?" Mae filled in the lapse dispassionately, in her eyes a sad acceptance of the evils of the world. "Aye, she was, for near on a year."

"How could something so despicable come to be?"

"Some houses keep one such as her around to please customers what want their girls virgin-like. Jane told me she were lured to London on promise of becoming a lady's maid, then threatened by Waldo, a brute of a man, if she tried to leave Mrs. Jarvis. No wonder she didn't try to run. Poor mite wouldn't have been no match for Waldo."

"God in heaven."

"Some come to the trade natural—like me. Born in a fancy house, I never knew nothing different. Others be thrown out by their families after being taken in by a man what promises 'em marriage. Some be seduced by one of their own kin, then sent away to hide the shame of it."

A sudden image struck Jack—Belle, cloak wrapped around her as she tramped down a cold country lane, cast out of the only home she'd ever known.

"Is that how Belle—" he blurted out.

Mae stared at him a long moment. Before he could decide whether to apologize for displaying an unseemly curiosity—or press her further, she said, "I don't know how Belle come to it. I never asked, no more than she offered. Though she never took to it any more than Jane did, and anyone with eyes could see she was born to better."

Not knowing how to respond without possibly insulting his companion, Jack groped for a suitable reply.

Before he found one, Mae continued, "I always thought she be some lordling's poor relation, mayhap born on the wrong side of the blanket, making her an easy mark for some man to take advantage of. Or a wealthy tradesman's daughter, educated like gentry and then left to fend for herself when the family lost their money. Not much a girl alone can do, 'specially not one as comely as Belle. Lord B must have discovered her when she weren't hardly older than Jane, for far as I know, she's never been with no one else, many as have tried to woo her!"

"You think...Bellingham seduced her?" Jack said, renewed outrage almost choking him.

Mae shook her head. "Don't rightly know. I do know they didn't always get on well and she sometimes thought of leaving him. Leave the trade, though I tried to tell her once you're in it, there's no going back, so she might as well make the best of it. And she be set up pretty well now, from what I understand."

"She planned to leave Bellingham when she was, ah, 'set up' well enough?" Jack asked, knowing he shouldn't ask, loathing the jealous rage that boiled over within him despite his attempt to remain calm and rational.

Mae looked regretful. "I probably shouldn't 'a told you this much, Captain, for Belle be fearsome private about her life. Hardly speaks even to me of her plans, and far as I know I've been her only friend since Lord B brought her to town. But having said so much, I suppose I might as well tell you the whole of what I know."

Hesitating again, she took a deep breath. Jack clamped his lips together to refrain from urging her to continue, not wanting to risk having her change her mind even as he wondered what further revelation she could be so reluctant to voice.

"There be a child," Mae said at last. "'Twas Bellingham's threat not to provide for it if she left him that kept her with him so long, for they fought fearsome at times."

A child. Belle had a child she'd been forced to hide away, he thought, trying to master his shock.

Not that he should be surprised. Though ladies in the trade strove to avoid it, conceiving children was a natural and sometimes inescapable consequence of the profession.

A new wave of disgust fired his simmering anger. That any man would use a child as a weapon, especially a child of his own flesh, even if that offspring were illegitimate, was abominable.

If Lord Bellingham weren't already dead, Jack would have been hard pressed to restrain himself from assisting the bastard to his grave at the point of his sword or the barrel of his pistol.

But with his fuller knowledge of Belle's past came a better understand of the chilly demeanor that discouraged approach, her cautiousness with and apparent disdain for men. Why she preferred to spurn suitors as wealthy as

Lord Rupert rather than take advantage of her current popularity to amass more riches as a hedge against the future, when age would inevitably bring about a decline in her beauty and desirability.

It even explained, perhaps, the hatred that had driven home her blade.

How had she come to "the trade," as Mae called it? he wondered anew. Had Bellingham wooed her to ruin with the pretty words she now so despised?

Infuriating as that thought was, it hurt less to think of her participating willingly in her fall than to picture her as a defenseless innocent forcibly dishonored by an amoral houseguest or a venal relation.

Before he could master his violent, conflicting emotions, Jane returned, Mae's parasol in hand.

"Here ye be, ma'am," she said and then hesitated, gazing at Mae. When that lady gave the girl an encouraging nod, she turned toward Jack, her cheeks pinking.

"Captain, I wanted to thank you personal for helping me. Watson said they might have made off with me if you hadn't been along. I'm so glad the Lord answered my prayers to make you heal! If ever I can do ought for you, I be more'n willing. I can mend and stitch right well."

"You needn't thank me, Jane. I was happy to assist."

"I be forever grateful nonetheless," the girl said. "Miss Mae, if you be needing anything, just call." After bobbing another curtsy, Jane walked back to the house.

Mae laughed. "Didn't I warn you? Stay long enough, and she'll make you a whole new wardrobe."

Though Jack spent another half hour on the terrace

nodding politely at Mae's inconsequential chatter, his mind seethed with the information he'd just learned—the infamy of Jane's deception, the despicableness of Belle being controlled by a threat to her child, the natural affinity that must have led Belle to rescue Jane.

If Belle had a poor opinion of men in general and aristocrats in particular, he could hardly blame her. The customers whom the Mrs. Jarvises of the world sought to satisfy were drawn from this wealthy, powerful group.

'Twas almost enough to turn any honest man into a flaming revolutionary.

Except such men represented only a fraction, however noxious and visible, of the class into which Jack had been born. Many, most of Jack's peers were honorable men, conscientious landlords, and if some were not always faithful to their ladies, they at least strayed into indiscretion only with willing and experienced partners.

However long fate and Lady Belle granted him to remain her guest, Jack vowed to show his hostess even greater respect and deference. And perhaps demonstrate to her how a true gentleman treated a lady.

CHAPTER FIFTEEN

SHORTLY AFTER BREAKFAST three days later, Mae helped Belle into a carriage dress for her drive with Captain Carrington to inspect the Bellehaven property.

"Such a treat you look, Belle," Mae said approvingly. "If you can't be talked outta wearing gowns cut for a spinster at her last prayers, you could at least have more made up in that pretty blue." Mae gave her a wink. "The captain's going to be that pleased."

Belle felt a spurt of irrational irritation. "I'm not wearing this to please the captain," she said stiffly. Even as an annoying voice in her head questioned the veracity of that statement.

Mae shrugged. "And iff'n you was, would it be so bad? The captain's the finest gentleman I've met this age. If he was to take a fancy to you and you to him, what would be the harm in that?"

"Captain Carrington is about to escort his sister through her first Season—and since he intends to settle on his land, probably will be looking about for a wife. Plans which are not compatible with beginning a liaison with a well-known courtesan. Nor, must I remind you again, do I have the least intention of taking another lover."

"So you've told me," Mae agreed, but with a look on her

face Belle could not like. However, since arguing would only encourage the matchmaking gleam in her friend's eye, Belle let the matter drop.

"I don't know how long the captain will need for his inspection, so I've ordered Cook to prepare us something to take along for nuncheon. I expect to return by afternoon."

"There's no hurry. 'Tis a lovely day—enjoy it." *And the company*, Belle knew Mae refrained from adding.

Mae had justification for that twinkle in her eye, Belle thought grimly as she headed downstairs to meet Carrington. Belle's actions of late virtually shouted her partiality for the captain's company.

'Twas wanton self-indulgence for her to drive him on this inspection tour instead of sending him with Watson, just as it had been two days ago when she personally conducted him through the house, rather than delegating the task to her housekeeper.

She'd told the staff then that she wanted to make sure he did not overexert himself. But deep within, she knew that excuse was just a sham to camouflage her desire to savor his nearness, enjoy the warmth of his camaraderie and the stimulation of his conversation.

It was but a small sop to her conscience that she resisted seeking him out during daylight hours. For in the evenings after Watson removed the tea tray, they sat together later and later after Mae, with an arch look, excused herself—sipping wine, chatting or playing whist, at which the captain posed her a genuine challenge. Knowing that he would fight for every point rather than simply allow her to win, she'd even succumbed to the temptation of challenging him to chess, a game at which she'd not tested her skill since her father's death nearly ten years ago.

And all the while, they talked—ah, how they talked! Politics, literature, art, farming—the captain seemed well informed about almost every topic that interested her.

One evening they had debated the merit of the settlements established at Vienna, Belle questioning whether the German and Italian states would accept being arbitrarily placed back under the Austrian yoke, the captain countering that Castlereagh, the master realist, had exacted the best agreement possible.

Another night they debated the relative merits of Turner's landscapes versus the stylized portraits of Lawrence, another whether Drury Lane's manager was pandering to prurient masculine taste by abandoning Shakespeare for the appeal of plays featuring the lovely Vestris in breeches roles.

'Twas little wonder she'd not been able to keep herself from lingering while the fire burned low and the night stars rotated through the sky outside their window. The captain was the most accomplished and knowledgeable man she had encountered since quitting her father's knee.

And as Mae had pointed out, the nicest.

Which made her predilection for his company all the more dangerous. The thaw in the ice wall behind which she'd hidden herself for so long had increased from a drip, to a trickle, to such a flood that her defenses had all but melted away. She had even grown almost used to the perilous physical attraction between them.

She'd certainly been wary enough of it initially. But as days passed and despite his recovery, the captain made no move to take advantage of that constant pull, she had gradually relaxed to the point that she now felt more comfortable with him than she had with any man in years.

Perversely enough, she thought with a wry grimace as she headed to the stables, even as the captain's proper behavior—excessively proper when he knew he was dealing with a woman who was but high-priced harlot—set her at ease, she found herself wondering *why* he hadn't tried to touch her.

Worst yet, as something dangerously akin to trust blossomed between them, she'd begun experiencing the oddest yearning to touch *him*—to explore the texture of his hair, run her fingertips along the line of his jaw or the muscle of his arms. This, from a woman who'd long viewed with distaste all physical contact between a man and a woman.

Last night she'd awakened from a dream in which he'd been caressing her, and instead of the familiar revulsion, her nerves had been singing with anticipation, her nipples tingling, a warm moist heat building between her thighs.

It was all most unsettling.

Even more unsettling, though, was the idea of having him leave. Much as she loved her country manor, the thought of remaining with only Mae and Watson for company, of losing his stimulating, charming, intelligent presence, caused an immediate pang of protest.

Made her feel empty. Alone.

Yet she must prepare herself for his imminent departure. Once he finished the defensive plans after his inspection of the grounds today, and if their drive proved him able to travel by carriage without any ill effects, she would have no excuse to hold him.

With the Season soon to begin, his family must be expecting him daily. They would be distressed and resentful if they suspected his return was being delayed—especially if they knew who was delaying him.

Although to spare them the dismay such a revelation would certainly cause, the captain had probably not revealed precisely where he had gone after leaving London.

She paused at the turn of the path where he was to meet her. How much longer did she have to savor the delicious anticipation of seeing him again?

An ache squeezed her chest, sharp enough to send a lump into her throat and set her eyes stinging.

Oh, enough of this endless speculation, she told herself, brusquely dashing the moisture from her cheeks. He would leave soon enough and there was nothing to be done about it. 'Twas a glorious spring day and the circuit of her property would keep him in her company for several hours at the least. She would enjoy the day, and him.

He met her with that smile that warmed her from the inside out and helped her into the curricle, his hands at her waist so fleetingly she immediately regretted their removal. And though they conversed as she drove, him asking and her answering questions about the woods and fields they passed, she remained always conscious of him seated just a few inches beyond her elbow.

Though the captain seemed as careful to stay on his side of the carriage as they jostled along as he was to keep his distance in the house.

Toward the end of their tour, Belle succumbed to the temptation to deliberately hit a few ruts, to see if she could throw him against her. Alas, he'd probably weathered much worse roads in the Peninsula, for he managed to maintain his position without bumping her.

It was early afternoon when they finished their circuit and Belle brought the curricle to a halt. "'Tis such a lovely day, I had Cook prepare us some refreshment. I thought we could share it up on the heights. The view is the finest on the property, so you can assess the land one last time and ask any questions that arise."

"Sounds like an excellent suggestion."

He helped her down, his brief touch at her waist again leaving warmth in its wake. Together they walked up a steep rise to where the land leveled out before falling away sharply. In a cleared space at the end of the trail stood a brushwork arbor, under which a felled tree served as a bench and cut rounds of log as makeshift tables.

Beyond the cliff edge before them spread a vista of cultivated fields interspersed with stands of forest. The manor house capped the rise opposite, its oak-bordered carriageway leading to the gatehouse and down the lane until it disappeared in the woods in the distance.

"What a lovely spot!" the captain exclaimed.

"I think so," Belle returned with a smile, "though Mae was not impressed. Just a lot of empty fields and trees, she said, that would be much more jolly with a cluster of inns or shops to liven it up."

As he laughed, Belle indicated the bench. "Please, be seated. 'Tis rather primitive, I'm afraid."

"I've broken bread at many a site more primitive, but few so scenic," he replied. "Let me pour you some wine."

As they ate the bread, cheese and ham, Belle answered the captain's questions about various features of the land they'd traveled through while he consulted his notes.

"I'll have Watson station lookouts along the carriageway behind the gatehouse, there," he said, pointing, "and assign more to patrol the high ground around the manor. One of the men he's hired is a former rifleman, whom I've recommended he place in charge. The man's a crack shot and has a good grasp of tactics. Though with luck, you shall never need your defenders, I believe with this team in place, you can feel safe from further threat."

"How can I thank you?"

"I suppose I should rather thank you by, in the next day or so, ceasing to be a charge upon your household."

So he did mean to leave—and soon! She had to struggle to suppress the cry of protest that sprang to her lips.

"Would it not be prudent," she said, searching for an excuse to induce him to remain, "for you to tarry awhile after the men are in place? To...to make sure the plan functions as you envision it? Besides, you indicated that your home is still several days' journey north. Although you have recovered amazingly, I cannot yet be easy about you attempting a journey of that length."

He hesitated, his sober gaze resting on her. *He's thinking of a polite way to turn aside my concern and reaffirm his departure,* she thought with a frisson of panic. She closed her eyes, waiting for his refusal.

"Perhaps it would be...prudent to stay a bit longer."

At first she thought she must not have heard him correctly. Then a wave of relief swept through her so keen that for a moment she couldn't reply.

"Y-yes, more prudent," she echoed after a moment.

Though she knew, for her, it was not prudent at all.

"Another glass of wine?" she said, loath to return to the house—where in the solitude of her chamber she might have to confront the implications behind the desperate need she seemed to have developed for his company.

"Gladly. Let me offer congratulations. Everything I've seen of the land today speaks of diligent, careful tending."

"I was lucky enough to inherit the estate manager when I acquired Bellehaven. His family has served here for generations."

"He obviously both knows and loves the land."

"As you obviously love your own. Tell me about Carrington Grove, if you would."

Prompted by Belle, the captain described his fields and crops, the improvements he planned to implement once he was able to resume management of the land, how he hoped to win over some of his older tenants to the use of the newest seed drills and threshing machines his agent had been unable to persuade them to try.

Though he spoke only of mundane farming matters, she found herself leaning closer, listening as intently as if each word he spoke were a clue to the purpose of her life.

His lips themselves fascinated her. She felt an inexplicable need to touch them.

Have them touch hers.

Only dimly, at the back of her mind, did she note that this unusual desire did not trigger the automatic distaste that normally filled her at the thought of a man's kiss. She was conscious instead of the breeze on her face, the sun heating her chest, legs, the skin beneath her gown.

Of his hand on the log seat, a few inches from her hip. His mouth just above hers, near enough that she could not tell whether what she felt was the wind—or his soft breath against her cheek.

Mesmerized by the golden flecks dancing in the irises of his dark brown eyes, she didn't immediately notice that his lips had stilled, his voice gone silent. Then those eyes narrowed, darkened with a heat she recognized only too well.

Except this time, she was not revolted. Instead, she waited, scarcely breathing, as his lips descended nearer, nearer, until his sigh mingled with her own.

She closed her eyes, every nerve honed with anticipation. Awareness of him spiraled through her body, down to her toes, her fingertips, tightening her nipples, making the moist center of her throb.

How, she wondered, would he taste?

Hardly had that unprecedented thought registered in her dazed mind than suddenly the warmth vanished. She opened bewildered eyes to discover Captain Carrington drawing away. As she watched, uncomprehending, he sprang up and paced to the edge of the cliff and stood with his back to her, scanning the sky.

"Clouds are gathering," he said, his voice sounding strained. "We'd better get back to the house. I wouldn't want you to…to suffer a drenching."

Disappointment and an overwhelming frustration flooded her. "Of—of course," she stumbled. "With your lungs just recovering, you don't need to get soaked."

Why had he not kissed her? she wondered as they gathered up their belongings and trudged back to the gig. Surely he knew she would not have repulsed him.

Or had she been mistaken about what she thought she saw in his eyes?

Before she could puzzle it out, he was handing her into the carriage. This time, he let his hands linger, even as she left hers on his shoulders, her fingers tingling at the contact. He opened his lips as if to speak, then with a slight shake of his head, closed them.

But though he remained silent, she gazed into his still-smoldering eyes long enough for her to be certain she'd not imagined the desire in them.

Why, then, had he not acted upon it?

Her longing for the kiss they had not shared seemed to

magnify the need pulsing through her to touch him, be touched by him. But as they set off, he remained stubbornly at his side of the carriage, close yet so out of reach that, but for the frenzy of her deprived nerves, she might as well have been in the carriage alone.

The air between them radiating with tension, the drive back passed with scarcely a syllable exchanged. Belle ought to have regretted the sudden loss of the easy camaraderie that had sprung up between them in the last several days.

Instead, all she could think of—all she wanted—was the kiss he'd denied her.

When they reached the stables, the captain left her with a stiff goodbye, saying he wished to rest before dinner. Belle turned the vehicle over to a waiting groom and wandered up to her chamber, the force of their near connection still reverberating through her.

Absently she sat at her dressing table and stared at the bemused face reflected in the mirror.

She might as well admit that she didn't want the captain to leave. Not in a few days. Not for a long time.

She'd seen the expression too often to mistake the desire in his eyes. Was he being reticent out of guilt, not wishing to make advances toward the woman who had nursed and housed him? Or not wishing to take advantage of her guilt in having wounded him?

If that was all that restrained him, she could probably persuade him to become her lover.

He would have to return to his family soon. But if she pleased him—and in the days before Vauxhall revealed

Bellingham's deception, she had dutifully mastered every device known for pleasuring men—she could insure that he would come back to her as often as possible.

She might even return to London—and forestall pursuit by other men by becoming his acknowledged mistress.

His mistress.

As the word echoed in a chest gone suddenly hollow, Belle's mind finally broke free of the sensual spell Carrington had cast over her. Guilt and shame slammed her with a roundhouse punch to the gut.

What in heaven had come over her? Surely she couldn't have been entertaining, even for a moment, the possibility of becoming another man's whore!

Revulsion followed the shame. For years, she'd told herself she'd done what she'd had to survive, had played a role that was forced upon her. That once free from it, she would let nothing and no one ever trap her in it again.

Yet here she was, hardly more than a month after Bellingham's death, actually considering becoming the wanton the lechers of the ton believed her to be. Thereby destroying what little self-respect she still possessed.

Besides, even if she could stomach the role, what did she imagine would become of the cozy friendship that seemed to have blossomed between her and Captain Jack Carrington? Did she truly believe, once he had her in his bed, he would continue to treat her like a lady—instead of the skillful harlot who pleased him between the sheets?

She couldn't bear to spoil what they'd shared by having it end like that.

She gave a bitter laugh. She might as well admit that she would be halfway in love with him, if she still believed in love. She mustn't let his intoxicating presence make her forget the hard lesson that such schoolgirl emotions were but a pretty illusion.

But our friendship is real, her heart protested.

Remember what you've learned, her head replied. Whatever compatibility of spirit and interest she thought existed between them was only on the surface. Fatherly affection excepted, males wanted females for one purpose.

For that, and to get heirs, they married—women of their own station. The only connection possible between a woman like her and a man like Jack Carrington would be a crude exchange of sexual favors for money.

Beside, she mustn't do anything that might place Kitty's future in jeopardy.

If she had become so besotted by her fantasy of a relationship with Carrington that she had forgotten the girl who depended on her, it was past time to send the captain away.

That her heart immediately issued a protest only underlined the need to wean herself from this weakness for Carrington's company. And since that same foolish heart resisted believing what her whole life's experience taught her to be true, there was one simple way to destroy once and for all the myth that Jack Carrington was some godlike paragon, attracted by her interests and intellect.

By proving him to be a man like every other.

Not a kindred spirit whose soul called to hers. Not a friend she needed like the warmth of a fire in winter.

But rather a man who respected her no more than Lord Rupert. One she could live just as well without.

Better to make the break soon, before she wove herself any deeper into the fantasies she'd been spinning. And since Carrington was now well enough to travel, better do it immediately before the opiumlike effect he seemed to exert over her mind and senses dulled that clear purpose.

The joy she'd felt in the day drained away, leaving a gritty residue of certainty. She took a deep breath and tried to armor herself against the pain of it. Tonight she would insure that tomorrow, Jack Carrington would ride out of her life and her heart for good.

CHAPTER SIXTEEN

EARLY THAT EVENING, Belle stood choosing a gown for the *intimate* dinner she'd told Mae she hoped to share with the captain. That comment had been enough to prompt a beaming Mae to reply that, as she feared she might have a cold coming on, she'd take a tray in her room.

Given her expectations of how Belle meant the night to end, Mae would probably applaud the gown Belle selected. Made of deep blue satin that matched her eyes and cut extremely low, it had been Bellingham's favorite. So pretty was it, she'd considered having Jane remake it in a more modest style—but for now, it would serve the courtesan one last time.

The sapphire and diamond set Bellingham had given her to set off the dress now reposed in a London banker's vault. Without the necklace and long dangling earrings, the gown would be even more scandalously bare, but Belle resisted the impulse to select some other jewelry to cover what would be a flagrant display of flesh.

Jane had come to help her dress and now waited quietly for her direction. Swallowing her distaste, Belle handed the shimmering blue gown over to the maid.

The effect, as she beheld her image in the glass after

Jane had fastened her into it, was all she could have hoped. The vast expanse of naked skin provoked a startled gasp even from the far-from-innocent Jane.

"Shall you be wanting your jewel case now?" Jane asked, giving her a troubled look.

"No, that will be all. I can finish on my own."

"As you wish, my lady." With another dubious glance, Jane curtsied and withdrew.

After applying some borrowed rouge to her cheeks and lips, she patted Mae's powder on her face and chest, added a double dose of lavender scent, then turned to her mirror.

In place of the modest young woman who'd stared back at her this past month was an elegant stranger with gold hair pinned high upon her head, a single curl falling to her bared shoulder. Her powdered skin emphasized the blue of her eyes; the rouge made her mouth appear fuller, moister, as if she'd just been thoroughly kissed. The deep V of the décolletage led the eye to a swell of full breasts restrained beneath a bodice so brief it appeared her next breath might treat the viewer to a glimpse of her barely concealed nipples.

Voila Lady Belle, courtesan extraordinaire.

A wave of self-loathing shook her.

Resisting the urge to hide beneath a shawl, despite the chill, she headed for the dining room. To her annoyance, her stomach started churning.

Why she should be nervous she couldn't imagine—unless she were already subconsciously mourning the death of her dream that Jack Carrington might be different. She knew perfectly well what would happen in her chamber after dinner—if in fact they made it out of the dining room. Her late protector had enjoyed sampling her in the public rooms of the house, where at any moment a servant might, and sometimes had, come upon them.

So it wasn't as if she were some terrified virgin, about to be thrust into intimacy for the first time.

And yet, the low vibration humming along her nerves, the sensitivity of her nipples brushing against the satin, the flutter of expectancy in the pit of her stomach—all were sensations she had not experienced before.

She had to admit that, knowing Jack would be the man who would use her, she was not dreading the imminent invasion of her flesh as much as she ordinarily would. She even felt a mild curiosity to see his lean body naked, to caress his hardened shaft, to use her lips and tongue to pleasure him.

A spiral of something hot and dizzying curled from her belly outward, tingling her thighs, her breasts.

Surprised by that unexpected reaction, she halted outside the dining-room door, hand on her stomach.

Add one more to the list of uncomfortable, atypical responses Jack Carrington seemed to provoke in her.

He affected her too strongly in every way. She was too aware of his presence, too appreciative of his wit, too grateful for his kindness and the gentility with which he treated her—and far too complaisant about the idea of being touched by him. All compelling reasons why she must force herself to follow through with her plan and send him away.

Having been so sure the evening would end with Belle taking a new, more amenable lover to satisfy her restlessness, Mae was going to be sorely disappointed, Belle thought, swallowing the lump in her throat.

If only Belle could be satisfied with just that.

Was she so sure she could not? an insidious doubt whispered. Would it not be enough to have Carrington's company as well as his body in her bed morning after morning, to tease over breakfast, to consult about the estate, to discuss the latest plays and politics and ton posturing in London?

Until he left her to marry.

And what would Lady Belle, his former mistress, do then? For even if this most improbable of her fantasies turned out to be true and Jack Carrington really did show himself capable of treating her mind and heart with respect once he'd had the use of her body, somehow she knew that the honor so essentially a part of the man would preclude his keeping a mistress when he married. Especially if Jack Carrington proved to be the paragon she longed for, he would set her aside then.

To forever regret the shame of allowing herself to become his mistress. To suffer a heartbreak far beyond what she'd previously experienced, for this time she'd be relinquishing a man who truly was the embodiment of a dream.

No, far better to plunge the knife in now, excise the feelings cleanly while there was still a chance to bleed and heal. Destroy the dream while it was only a dream, not a reality whose loss would mean slow hemorrhage to emotional death.

Angrily she shook her head to stem the gathering tears. Enough melodrama. Time to get on with it. Taking a deep breath, she opened the door.

Jack turned at her entrance, on his face the smile that made her nerves hum and the hairs at the back of her neck prickle. Then the warmth in his gaze changed to shock and his lips froze, the words he'd been about to say unuttered.

"Good evening, Captain," she said coolly, as if her heart were not hammering and her chest so tight she felt faint. She made herself walk forward with unhurried steps, deliberately taking the deep breaths that would treat him to near glimpses of her nipples.

By the time she reached the table, he had opened and closed his mouth several times without producing any sound.

"Mae, who is slightly indisposed, begs that you will excuse her this evening. Shall we begin?" Pasting on a smile, she motioned Watson to serve the first course, ignoring the look of patent disapproval on his face.

"You look...lovely," the captain managed, sounding oddly breathless. "Different, but very beautiful."

She slid him a sultry look from under a fringe of lashes. "I wanted this evening to be...special."

"Any evening with you is special."

Her heart contracted and the tension in her chest tightened, but she forced herself to continue. "I chose this dress to please you. It does...please you?"

His avid gaze devoured her, from the arrangement of curls atop her head down her face, her neck, the bareness of her shoulders and chest, to linger on her breasts. "Everything about you pleases me," he said hoarsely.

"I hope that will be especially true...tonight."

While he digested that remark, she took a sip of her wine. She'd not been a courtesan for more than six years without learning, however inadvertently, what sparked a man's response. Putting the glass down, she let a single drop of wine bead like a molten ruby on her rouged lips, then slowly licked it away.

As she expected, Carrington's eyes riveted on that gesture, his hands locked on the wineglass suspended halfway to his mouth. Never taking his gaze from her, he set the glass back down abruptly, nearly upsetting it.

Knowing her nerves would be too on edge for her to have any appetite, Belle had ordered a succession of lighter courses—cold fowl, vegetables with removes of beef followed by savories and fruit. A menu which also permitted her to sample most of the offerings with her fingers, allowing her to use up a great deal of time while actually consuming very little as she caressed the foods against her lips, inserted them deeply in her mouth, licked her fingers as she slowly pulled them free.

To her sorrow, the captain appeared as mesmerized by this performance as the most callow of her admirers. Scarcely taking his gaze off her long enough to pick at his own food, he responded in monosyllables as, between taking sensual bites, she maintained a light flow of conversation.

By the time the last course was removed, Belle was having difficulty keeping her lips from trembling and the tears at bay. How different was this awkward charade from the warm, intimate sharing of ideas and opinions that had characterized their other dinners this week!

After motioning a dismissal to a glowering Watson, Belle said, "Neither you nor I appear to have had much appetite tonight...for dinner. Shall we...withdraw?"

Slowly she walked toward him, forcing herself to breathe past the constriction in her chest, shutting her ears to the protests of her heart. She had a dream to kill, and there was no point drawing out its execution.

Sitting still but for the turn of his head as he watched her approach, for a moment after she reached Jack, he simply stared at her. Then, as if comprehending all that bare, freely offered flesh was but a hand span away, he jumped up, nearly knocking over his chair.

Her heart uttered one last, desperate assertion that his abnormal silence and stunned demeanor meant he was confused by her unusual dress and manners—rather than spellbound with lust. Then she took a discreet glance downward and that pathetic hope expired in a wrench of grief and self-mocking triumph.

The bulge straining the front of his trousers confirmed his reaction to her whore's performance was no different than that of Bellingham or that toad Markham or the distasteful, disturbingly persistent Lord Rupert.

Already hating herself and him, she took his limp hand and kissed it, caressing his knuckles with her tongue as well as her lips. Lowering that hand to rest on the swell of her breast so that his fingertips almost, but not quite, touched the nipple, she murmured, "Shall we?"

With a strangled groan, Carrington leaned down, pulled her roughly into his arms and kissed her.

Numbly she parted her lips, sought out his tongue and bid it enter. She would let him devour her mouth for a few moments, then break the kiss, lead him to her room, where he would separate her from her clothes in seam-ripping haste while she undressed him in turn. She would pose on the bed, one hand parting her nether lips invitingly, the other cupping her breast so the nipple beckoned like a signal beacon. He would seize her by the shoulders and thrust himself in, bury and withdraw his shaft in deep, grinding lunges, biting her neck or roaring out as his climax took him. Which, since he'd been too ill to enjoy a woman for several weeks, shouldn't take long.

Then, with his spilled seed within her making the matter easier, she would play with him where they were joined, nibble at his neck, his chin, run the wetness of her tongue over his mouth and down his throat to his chest, nipping and sucking at his nipples until he hardened within her once more. Depending on how fully he'd recovered from his wound, she should be able to bring him to completion several more times this night, send him away in the morning sated, with a teasing promise of meeting again soon.

While her heart strangled within her and the love-words tasted like bile in her mouth.

He was still kissing her, though by now he was far

enough gone in passion that she didn't need to kiss him back. Her mouth under his began to tremble and she felt the hot sting of tears on her cheeks.

Finally he broke the kiss, his breathing ragged. But instead of wrapping a possessive arm around her and hauling her toward the door, he stepped away.

"What the hell is all this about?"

His reaction was so unexpected, at first she wasn't sure she'd heard him correctly. "All…this?" she echoed.

"The gown. The food. The seductive show. You are trying to drive me insane, and succeeding, but why?"

She struggled to make sense of his words. "I…isn't it… obvious? You—you are recovered now. I thought you'd appreciate a…reward."

"Reward? For what?"

"Being so understanding about my wounding you in the first place. Coming to our defense."

He shook his head impatiently. "Belle, you don't need to 'reward' me for any of that."

"But I thought—" she began, stepping toward him.

"Don't!" he said harshly, putting up a hand to halt her as he backed away. "For God's sake, Belle!"

He was retreating from her.

She had never encountered such a reaction from a man before. Embarrassment roared through her, a blaze of heat igniting her skin.

He didn't want her after all. Instead of attracting him with her harlot's behavior, she'd repelled him.

"I'm sorry. I didn't mean…but you…" Confused, humiliated, her thoughts too tangled to summon words of explanation, she pointed to his still-prominent erection.

Only once before in her life had she felt such a sense of total degradation, an overwhelming desire to crawl out of her own skin. Backing away, she turned and ran, desperate to escape the distaste and censure in his eyes.

How could she have so misread him? What did he want from her? But in the midst of her degradation, one small ray of irony penetrated.

She may have repelled him, but her instincts were right.

He was different.

Down the hall she fled, scarcely knowing where she went, except that it must be somewhere dark and alone.

When she halted to catch her breath, she realized she'd ended up on the terrace outside the small study. Gulping in air, she listened for any sign of pursuit.

But by the time her breathing steadied, all she heard were small night noises, the scuffle of some animal in the bushes bordering the terrace, the distant hoot of an owl.

Well, she had indeed ruined everything, though not in the way she'd planned.

She couldn't bear to face him now, a new wave of embarrassment flaming through her at the thought. She'd write him a note. Yes, a proper note, omitting any mention of this evening, thanking him again for his assistance, wishing for his speedy return to full health and bidding him goodbye.

She'd ride out tomorrow early, just in case her fierce

need to be with him managed to triumph over her chagrin. He would be gone by the time she returned.

And she would never see him again.

Shivering now in her skimpy gown, Belle put her face in her hands and wept.

Lost in her anguish, at first she scarcely noticed the hand on her shoulder. "Please, Belle, don't cry."

It sounded like Carrington's voice. But those soft, apologetic tones couldn't be coming from the man who had just backed away from her in horror. When she lifted tear-blurred eyes to discover it was in fact the captain, another wave of misery—part heartache, part embarrassment, part longing—engulfed her.

"I'm so…sorry," she gulped.

And then she was in Jack Carrington's arms, his warmth shielding her from the night's chill, one hand stroking her curls while the other held her close against his chest.

"No, sweeting, 'tis all my fault! Whatever you were trying to do to me in there, I never meant to hurt you."

She could still feel the impressive length and hardness of his erection against her belly. And yet, his touch was as gentle as if he were cradling a child. Consoling, not condemning. Despite the obvious evidence of his desire, she could not, with all her experience, read into his embrace any indication of carnal intent.

Her mind flashed back a dozen years, to when she'd taken a fall from her horse. Just so had her father gathered her up in his arms, soothed her against his chest.

Yes, Captain Jack Carrington was different. Indeed,

he appeared at this moment to be everything her school-girl fancy could have wished for, dreamed of. A man the last painful years of her life had convinced her did not exist.

A man she could never have, not even, it appeared, in lust.

The long day of agonizing and the agony of that dinner had shredded her already tightly wound nerves to the snapping point. Though she told herself she should pull free and walk away with whatever remnants of dignity she could muster, she found her legs too weak to move. Leaning her head against his chest in defeat, she let the sobs she could no longer contain overwhelm her.

At last she managed to halt the flood of tears and push weakly away from his chest.

He let her move back, still keeping her loosely in the circle of his arms.

"Belle, I don't understand what happened tonight, and I want to understand it, rather desperately. I do know that we are both too…overwrought to discuss it now. Go to your bed, sweeting. We'll talk about it tomorrow."

He gave her a little push toward the terrace doors. "Leave now, while I can still make myself let you go."

For a moment she stared up at him, but his face was too dim in the moonlight for her to read his expression. Then, with a whispered, "Thank you," she gathered up her strength and her skirts and stumbled away.

CHAPTER SEVENTEEN

HEART POUNDING and hands shaking as he battled the frenzy of frustrated lust still roaring in his veins, Jack commanded himself to remain motionless as Lady Belle hurried through the terrace doors into the house.

Into safety. After hovering all evening on the razor edge of losing control, he could at last relax.

In a manner of speaking. The outraged protest of his denied body, the almost painfully intense erection, would prevent any real relaxation for hours to come.

He uttered a harsh laugh. Were Aubrey to have witnessed Jack's repulsing Lady Belle tonight, he would have dragged him off to Bedlam.

But whatever Belle had meant to do—and beyond driving him mad with frustrated desire, he still had no idea—she hadn't truly wanted him to act on the invitation she had been conveying by every possible means.

He'd seek her out tomorrow. As awkward as that meeting might be, he had no intention of leaving Bellehaven until she explained what she'd been about tonight.

Why she'd masqueraded as a woman so different from the one he'd grown to know.

Why afterward she'd wept in his arms as if her heart were breaking.

With a sigh, Jack entered his room and headed straight for the brandy decanter. After pouring himself a hefty glass, he sat down and contemplated the deep ruby tones glinting through the sparkle of crystal in the candlelight. Unlike other nights when the fiery liquid had taken the edge off his suffering and helped him find peace, he knew it would be far into morning before his fully aroused senses calmed enough for him to sleep.

HAVING GOTTEN as little slumber as expected, Jack rose the next morning scarcely rested. Still, anticipation filled him at the prospect of seeing Belle—and dread, that the show she'd put on for him might have been her prologue to the final act of their relationship.

Hoping she would be as restless as he, Jack descended to the breakfast room early. Though to his disappointment, Lady Belle was not present when he entered, Watson quickly came forward to offer coffee and beef-steak.

He then surprised Jack by leaning close as he filled Jack's cup, murmuring, "Thank ye for taking care of our lady last night. She…weren't herself."

Bemused, Jack propped an elbow against the mantel and savored the steamy brew. He ought to know by now that little escaped the notice of one's servants.

He wondered if Watson had a better idea than he did of what had motivated his lady to not "be herself." Though even as informally as this household was run, there was no way he could ask the butler such a question.

"Lady Belle be down in a minute, Jane said. Sun's warm on the terrace. Should I bring you a tray there?"

The terrace where Jack had held her weeping in the moonlight. Where the hawthorn would shield them from prying eyes and overhearing ears while they breakfasted.

Jack sent Watson a grateful look. "Yes, thank you."

Before Jack could speculate which Belle would come to breakfast—the seductress of last night or the reserved lady of the previous two weeks, the woman herself walked in.

Dressed, he noted at once, in the most unattractive gown he'd seen her wear yet—a long-sleeved, high-necked dull gray garment with no ornamentation whatsoever which did its utmost to mask Belle's loveliness—though no garment made could truly do that, he thought with a wry smile.

Spying him by the fireplace, she halted, a look almost of panic flaring in her eyes.

He thanked God to the bottom of his soul that his instincts had been right and he'd been given the strength to resist his desire. For the lady poised for flight at the doorway was the woman he'd coaxed to reveal herself layer by layer these past two weeks—modest, sensitive, with a keen intelligence burning like a clear flame within her. A woman he'd grown to appreciate and treasure.

Beautiful. Desirable. But neither the cold, calculating courtesan men had described to him nor the practiced wanton she had appeared to be last night.

He was about to reassure her and beg her to stay when, with a sigh, she lifted her head to meet his gaze.

At that forlorn yet gallant gesture, something charged and intense shot through him, as if in that instant his feelings passed through a refiner's fire and emerged in truer, purer form. Yes, he still craved answers to the mystery of her past, but who she had been, who she later became, no longer seemed important.

All he knew was the fact that *his* shy, diffident lady stood there, gamely trying to mask the discomfort her flaming cheeks broadcast so eloquently, made his chest swell with tenderness and a sheer, unalloyed joy more intense than any he'd previously experienced. He wanted to shout with laughter, whoop with excitement, seize her hands and swing her round and round until they were both dizzy.

And never, never leave her.

Thrusting out of mind the cruel truth that such a future could never be, he set down his cup and walked slowly toward her, as if approaching a skittish, half-wild colt. "Watson is bringing breakfast to the terrace. Will you share it with me?"

She was trembling, he noted, another wave of protective tenderness sweeping through him. He wanted desperately to pull her against his chest as he had last night, but was too afraid of frightening her off.

While he forced himself to stand back, she studied his face intently. Looking for what, he couldn't imagine.

Mercifully, she seemed to have found it, for after a moment she exhaled a shaky breath and returned a tentative smile. "Y-yes, I should like that."

He held out his arm. Warily she placed her hand on it, and he closed his eyes for an instant to savor the immediate sizzle of connection at her touch. Tucking her slender hand in his elbow, he led her out to the terrace.

ALMOST DIZZY with relief to find in the captain's steady gaze no hint of the contemptuous censure his expression had held last night, Belle let him lead her away, intensely aware of the arm beneath her fingertips.

Despite his kindness on the terrace, she had not quite convinced herself he would not turn from her in distaste this morning. Since he hadn't, however, she must now offer him some explanation for her odd behavior. Unfortunately, a night of tossing and turning hadn't turned up any.

Except the truth.

She didn't dare tell him that.

Watson hurried after them with a breakfast tray, and for the next few minutes, the mundane business of fixing cups and plates muted the initial awkwardness.

Once Watson withdrew, Belle took a deep breath. Best address the matter now, before she lost her courage.

"I must apologize again for last night. I didn't mean to make you…uncomfortable." And although she knew she shouldn't, she couldn't help adding, color rising in her face, "I hope I've not given you a…a disgust of me."

"You could never do that!" he exclaimed, easing somewhat the nauseating churn of emotions in her breast.

She managed a smile. "Having made it quite obvious you were not...interested, I promise I'll not throw myself at you again."

"Not interested?" he echoed and uttered a strangled laugh. "No man breathing could help but want a woman as attractive as you! A lady who, for me, is even more compelling since I've discovered her mind to be as lovely as her person, her accomplishments as impressive as the astonishing beauty of her face."

She shook her head, not understanding. "But if you wanted me, and I was offering you—"

"A whore's tricks! I thought we meant more to each other than a mindless exchange of passion. Especially since it appears I was the only one feeling the passion. I have my pride, too, Belle. I refuse to be reduced to simply a...a toy, for you to practice your wiles upon."

He thought she had been *using* him, she realized incredulously. Trying to manipulate him—as Bellingham had manipulated her all those years? "I never meant it like that!" she gasped, horrified.

He scrubbed a hand over his face. "I'm sorry. I know you didn't. But, Belle, I don't want you to offer yourself out of some misplaced sense of gratitude. Much as I yearn for you, I don't want you to kiss me with practiced art or do any of the surely wonderful things you could do to bring me to ecstasy—while all you do is go through the motions. I would have shot myself as an idiot for turning down what you offered, but for the fact that, despite the most arousing show of seduction I've ever had practiced on me—" his voice softened and he gently drew one finger across her cheek, as if wiping away a tear "—other evidence seemed to indicate that seduction wasn't really what you wished."

He'd wanted her, but had not taken her because he sensed *she* had not really wanted *him?* Deep in her chest, she could almost feel the last of the barriers she'd erected to resist him crumbling. Her breath caught in her throat and she fought back the burn of tears.

"Belle," he continued quietly, "when—if—I ever touch you, I want you to desire me as I much as I desire you. I'm willing to wait until you are ready to share with me all the joy and wonder of it."

Joy? Wonder? She shook her head. After the last six and a half years, she could probably compile a dictionary of terms describing the joining of man and woman, but those two words wouldn't be in it.

Somehow it seemed both sweet and achingly sad that he might think otherwise. "If that is what you truly want, I'm afraid you would wait forever."

"Forever?" He studied her for a long moment. "Do you mean to tell me," he said at last, "that in all the time you were with him, Bellingham never gave you pleasure?"

The old anger boiled up and a harsh laugh escaped before she could stop it. How many treacheries and lies had been perpetrated against her for the sake of a man's enjoyment? "Pleasure?" she spat back. "Pleasure is something a man takes from a woman's body, and all he gives back is the seed he spills upon her sheets."

However accurate that assessment, she instantly regretted giving voice to it in such crude terms. "Forgive me," she murmured. "I shouldn't have…"

He was shaking his head, on his face an expression that looked like…amazement? "My poor Belle," he murmured, "that explains so many things. Bellingham should have been shot."

Before she could puzzle out what he meant by that, he continued, "Even so, if you tried to entice me out of gratitude, why the last-minute regrets? Why did you weep into my kiss, Belle? What did you really want?"

She found it impossible to look away from his gaze. *I wanted to prove you as unworthy as every other man, so I could rip you out of my heart and send you away—before I hung on with both fists and begged you never to leave.*

Saying that was unthinkable, but before she could find something plausible, he said, "To satiate me completely so I'd have no strength to resist your sending me away?"

He couldn't possibly guess the whole truth, but hearing him voice that much of it rattled her into blurting, "Y-yes."

Now that her affirmation couldn't be unspoken, she fought back the urge to explain, to try to make him understand. Saying more would just make matters worse.

For a long moment they stared at each other in silence. "Do you want me to leave?" he asked at last.

She tried to look away, but his unyielding gaze held hers captive. What did she want? Or rather, what should she want? "I— Yes! No! Oh, I don't know!"

He closed his eyes and muttered something that

sounded like "Thank God." "'Tis what I should want, too. For us to part now, before parting becomes any more difficult."

A slowly dawning sense of wonder filled her chest. "So…you feel it, too, this…connection between us?"

He nodded with a sigh. "And I've no more notion of what to do about it than you. Right now I'd like nothing better than to stay here forever, but we both know that can't happen. I should do us a favor and leave right now, this morning. But unless you order me to go… Belle, I don't think I can make myself. Could you be wise for us, sweeting? Ask me to leave, Belle. Please."

She tried to make her lips form the words. But the exultation swelling in her heart strangled her voice and refused to let her utter the words.

He cares for you, as you do for him! her heart exulted. This amazing, wonderful, exceptional man who prizes your intellect and respects—*respects*—you, can be yours for a few more days—more than you'll have the rest of your life if you send him away now. And the pain of his leaving cannot be any more intense then than it would be today.

Instead of the prudent dismissal he'd asked for, she found herself saying, "Can you stay just a bit longer? I…I should be more comfortable if you were here to supervise the guards, if trouble develops. And I would worry less about your traveling if you were well enough to ride."

The excuses were thin and both of them knew it.

He looked away. She could feel the tension coiled in him as she waited, barely breathing, knowing it would be better if he refused, desperately hoping he would accept.

At last he looked up. "All right, Belle. 'Tis madness, but I'll stay another week. And then I must—"

"Go," she interrupted quickly, filled with both elation and the dread of knowing she'd just made possibly the most dangerous decision of her life. "I know. In a week, I will not try to stop you. I promise."

The tension seemed to drain from him and he smiled at her, such tenderness in his eyes that her throat ached and once again her eyes stung with tears. "And I promise I will never take from you anything you do not gladly give."

He picked up her hand and kissed it. "Now I'd best get you back in. The sun is warm, but that wind is sharp."

She let him walk her back to the hallway, where the housekeeper met them, requesting Belle's assistance.

Giving her a deep bow, the captain left her to her duties. Belle paused to watch as the captain climbed the stairs to his chamber.

How had he insinuated himself into her heart and life so completely? How had it come to seem so natural for him to be here? She didn't want to contemplate what a void it would leave in her life when he left. In a week.

A week in which he would take nothing she did not wish to give. Unfortunately, she thought, heading for the kitchen, she was already so close to giving him everything that by the time he departed, she might have nothing of her heart and soul left.

CHAPTER EIGHTEEN

TELLING HIMSELF he could afford to be a fool for one more week, Jack went to his chamber to pen a message to Carrington Grove. He'd dispatched a short missive before leaving London to inform his no-doubt anxious relations that he was recovering and would journey home by easy stages. Since they probably had been expecting him for several days, he'd reassure them that he was recuperating at the home of a friend and would set out in a week's time.

Having given himself up to irresponsibility, he refused to think of the speculation or anxiety this additional delay might cause his family with the beginning of the Season rapidly approaching.

Neither would he worry about how he was going to resolve the dilemma posed by his steadily strengthening feelings for Belle.

All he wanted now was to focus on these precious few days. He hoped, rather desperately, that before he had to leave she would once again offer him the heaven he'd glimpsed last night, this time on terms he could accept.

If not, he trusted his iron will and the affection he bore

her would prove equal to resisting the promptings of his body. Especially now that he had a better understanding of what her life must have been.

He'd wondered last night why a woman who'd lived by seduction could have put on such a tempting show while feeling nothing. Now he speculated that she must have been forced into carnal knowledge very young, before the natural urges of her body had prompted such exploration.

If Bellingham had caused Belle's ruin, Jack thought, a murderous rage rising in him, and had kept her all those years with no concern for her pleasure, shooting was too good for him. Praise heaven, the man was already dead, for were he still among the living, Jack wasn't sure he could have kept himself from calling the cad out when he returned to London. And my, what a scandal that would cause at the start of Dorrie's Season!

For an instant, he had a vivid, horrifying image of what might have happened to his high-spirited sister, her letters to him filled with enthusiasm about her Season and the prospect of marriage, had her innocence been stolen from her. The very idea sickened him, prompting him to vow anew that he would expire from unrequited lust before he would touch Belle without her freely given invitation.

He recalled her choice of plain, high-necked gowns and the chilly disinterest with which she'd treated her court of admirers in London. It appeared she'd developed a distaste for the physical and an understandable wariness toward men. Given that heritage, he realized ruefully, he'd best count on enjoying no more than the wonder of her companionship for their stolen week together.

Then he recalled the kiss they'd almost shared. She had wanted that kiss, he was certain. Which meant the attraction that pulled at him, that he'd sensed in her, did in fact exist. There was always a chance that, if he gave her the time and space to respond if and when *she* chose, she might grow comfortable enough—or curious enough—to explore with him the impulses she'd been denying.

Best, however, not to let his mind—or his senses— dwell on delights that might not be. No, the next few days would be for her to direct and him to simply revel in her company. That would be enough for now.

Whether or not it would be enough to last him the rest of his life, he refused to consider.

By the time he met her for nuncheon later, most of the awkwardness between them had dissipated, and the last vestiges vanished during their second tour around Bellehaven later that afternoon. On their initial excursion, Belle had avoided the settled areas, but this time she stopped at each cottage and beside each field where workers toiled, introducing Jack as the soldier who was reorganizing Bellehaven's defenses.

The story of their attack on the road had already spread about the countryside, and several of the men thanked Jack for his assistance to their mistress and pledged their help in defending the manor.

The country folk so obviously liked and respected Belle that Jack realized they must know nothing of her years in London. For them, she was the lady of the manor who looked after them and their welfare.

Indeed, Jack thought as he watched her, was that not who she truly was?

But the respect she enjoyed was fragile. He had only to make a reference to her former life or an over-familiar gesture and the good reputation she'd won among these people would be damaged, perhaps irreparably—a fact she was too intelligent not to recognize. That she trusted him enough to risk driving him about touched and humbled him.

They ended their drive, as they had the previous day, at the arbor on the heights overlooking Bellehaven.

"Your tenants obviously hold you in great esteem—the highest mark of excellence in a landholder, my father used to tell me," Jack said as they shared the wine she'd brought. "You've done a wonderful job at Bellehaven."

"The land was already in good heart when I acquired it. And my father, too, preached the importance of valuing the land and the people who work upon it."

Jack went instantly on the alert. "Your father held property?" he asked cautiously, wanting to encourage her without appearing too curious.

"No, he was a younger son, forced to make his own way in the world. It was his unrealized dream to earn the fortune that would allow him to purchase an estate like this." She smiled wistfully. "I suppose he would be happy knowing I have—little as he'd approve the means."

"He is no longer living?"

"No. He died when I was thirteen."

"I'm sorry." Jack waited, barely breathing. He wanted so badly for her to confide the rest, confirm what he only surmised. But as the silence stretched between them and she sat gazing into the far distance, a look of deep sadness on her face, his thirst for information evaporated.

"You must have loved him very much."

She looked back, tears glimmering on her lashes. "I did. For years, the only thing that made the sorrow bearable was knowing he would never learn what I'd become."

He'd be proud of you, the thought sprang to Jack's mind. Proud of the gallantry with which she'd met an unspeakable fate, the dignity she'd preserved throughout. Proud of how she'd never lost the essence of her true self and had eventually won her way free.

Jack was proud of her and enthralled by her for those reasons and more. But she so obviously saw herself as damaged beyond redemption, would she think he mocked her were he to express his admiration?

While he debated whether or not to speak, she gave him a slight smile. "I suppose you've wondered how I came to be…what I am. And though you've discreetly made inquiries of my staff—" Jack felt his face burn at that all too correct assessment "—you've been too much the gentleman to ask directly. It's not a time I like to remember. Mama died shortly after Papa and there was no money—nothing."

"Did you have no other family?"

She closed her eyes briefly, as if the mere mention of "family" hurt. "There was…no one. I imagine you can guess what followed. In any event, the story is too long and tedious to recount."

No relatives at all? Jack wondered, watching her intently. He couldn't imagine anyone having absolutely no relations, however remote—unless her birth had been illegitimate or the result of a mésalliance so extreme that both families cut all ties to the lovers.

She sat straighter and wrapped her arms tightly around her shoulders, as if fighting off a chill—or withdrawing within herself. Even her voice grew distant. "Despite having no choice, I loathed myself for it. Though I suppose you would expect someone like me to excuse herself thus."

He hesitated, wanting badly to say the right thing, something that would affirm his regard and bring her back. "I think you're the bravest, finest woman I've ever known."

The tribute that sprang so naturally and sincerely to his lips made her look back at him sharply—thinking he mocked her, perhaps?

"Truly, Belle. Have I ever lied to you?"

She studied him until, apparently taking him at his word, her lips curved in a rueful smile. "I trust you'll never let your mother hear you say such a thing. But… but 'twas wondrous gallant and I thank you for it."

Her smile faded and hesitantly she touched Jack's hand. Over the years he'd been touched in many more carnal ways, but nothing had seemed as intimate as that tentative press of her fingers. Euphoric at having headed off her retreat, he impulsively linked his fingers with hers. To his further delight, she did not even try to pull free.

"Until very recently, I disdained the…urges that drive men. I understand them now, a little. I don't find your touch…distasteful."

Jack felt himself grinning. "I am glad of it."

She smiled back. "You have been so good to me, so kind, I wish I could have responded as you'd like."

"Oh, I dream that someday you may kiss me as you did last night and truly mean it."

"You still want me, after the fool I made of myself?"

He looked at her squarely. "I want you with every breath. But I meant what I promised. I will not touch you unless you desire it as much as I do."

Her eyes went blank, as if she were looking into the past. "I don't think I'll ever feel that sort of wanting."

"If, as I suspect, you were forced into intimacy against your will, how could you know how beautiful it can be, a giving as well as a taking? Between two who share affection, a touching of hearts as well as bodies. It will be like that for us—or not at all."

"It sounds beautiful."

"It can be—with the right person."

She was quiet for a moment, staring at their joined hands. "I'd like to experience that."

"I'd love to show you. When you are ready."

She looked back at him. "But how shall I know when I'm ready?"

Jack laughed, a bit unsteadily since merely discussing

the possibility of loving her had his body fully aroused. "You will know."

Abruptly she stretched up toward him, eyes closed and lips pursed. Surprised, Jack leaned away.

She opened her eyes and gazed up at him, her cheeks pinking. "I...I want to kiss you."

"Truly?" he asked, not daring to believe in such good fortune. "Why?"

She stared up at his lips, then raised a finger and brushed it across them. A shiver ran through Jack and he barely suppressed a groan.

"I've never actually *wanted* to kiss a man before, but I want to know what kissing you will make me feel. I trust you to let me stop whenever I wish. So...may I kiss you?"

Swiftly Jack uttered a prayer that he would neither melt nor lose control. "Yes."

He held himself absolutely still, feeling the pulse beat at his wrists, his temple, as she leaned up. The first touch of her lips against his was cautious, tentative, like the whisper of a spring breeze against his cheek, though he felt that gentle brush in every nerve.

It was just a kiss, something he'd previously considered a pleasant preliminary. He hadn't imagined so simple a touch could so utterly rivet the mind and senses.

Then she clutched his shoulders and increased the pressure, exploring the contours of his mouth, her lips nuzzling his from the fullness at the center to the corners, her movements thrilling and touchingly naive.

Heaven, he thought, this is heaven, an erotic pleasure

that transcended lust, one he wanted never to end. Until she shocked him with a flick of her tongue against his closed lips.

He gasped, then called on yet greater reserves of will as he opened his lips and let her slide the plush wetness of her tongue into his mouth.

His heart pounding as if he'd just received the command to charge the enemy lines, he ordered himself to remain motionless, despite the paroxysm of sensation spiraling through him. As agonizing as it was to feel the warmth of her body heating his skin, the pressure of her breasts against his chest, and yet remain motionless, he would not devour her lips as he had the other night nor give her any reason to be frightened or retreat.

I trust you to let me stop.

And so he kept his rigidly fisted hands at his sides and let her kiss him, until finally, when he could stand it no longer, he permitted himself to meet her tongue with his own and gently explore the contours of her mouth. Even then, he let himself touch only her lips.

The piercing sweetness of it wrapped around his heart.

She was a courtesan, one reputed to know every skill imaginable to pleasure a man, a woman who'd been touched intimately in every way a woman could be touched—and yet she had never before, by her own admission, voluntarily kissed a man. Something deep within him ached for the innocence that had been ripped from her and the brutal, loveless knowledge that had been forced upon the unwilling mind and body of a defenseless young girl.

At the same time, he felt a purely masculine triumph that what she shared with him now, felt for him now, she had never shared or felt for any other, despite her years of carnal experience.

Showing her how much pleasure there could be in the touch of two people who treasured each other would be his privilege and his gift, even if he were fated never to share more than this kiss.

When at last she broke away, he wrapped his arms around her and settled her against his shoulder, then brought one of her hands up to rest against his chest. Pressing his fingers over hers, he was gratified to discover her heart drumming as rapidly as his own.

"Do you feel it?" he whispered, "our hearts beating almost as one? This is how intimacy should be, Belle. The only way it will ever be between us."

She looked up at him, wonder in her eyes. "It *is* beautiful. Thank you, Jack."

He pressed a kiss on her hair as she settled back into his arms. For a long time they sat in silence, Jack hardly daring to breathe lest he rupture that fragile moment.

Finally, a sudden gust of afternoon wind made her shiver. "We'd best be getting back," Belle said, pushing away with what he hoped was reluctance.

Lord help him, he wanted to keep her there and kiss her and kiss her and kiss her. Instead, he bit back a protest. "Yes, Mae will be wondering what delayed us. I promised her a round of billiards before dinner."

To his delight she let him keep her hand while they walked back to the curricle. As he started to draw away after helping her in, she stopped him. "I shall never forget this afternoon," she murmured, squeezing his fingers before releasing them.

"Nor will I," he replied. Indeed, he thought as he swung himself into the vehicle, memories of it were likely to haunt his mind and cut up his peace for years to come.

TWO EVENINGS LATER Belle hummed to herself as she dressed for dinner in an elegant gown of aquamarine silk Jane had altered. Ornamented with brilliants on its tiny sleeves and about the neckline of the now modestly cut bodice, she knew it showed her at her most attractive.

It would be another wonderful evening. They would laugh and chat over dinner, perhaps induce Mae to regale them with an anecdote drawn from a trove of stories she told from the vantage of her friends from the stage or the Green Room. Then, after they had tea, Mae would discreetly retire, leaving Belle and the captain to spend the rest of a lazy, firelit evening talking together.

For the first time since her parents' death, Belle was happy, though that word was inadequate to describe what she found in Jack's presence—in life itself with him here. A joy she dare not trust, to be savored only for this moment, and for which she would no doubt pay bitterly later.

A joy she refused to give any other name.

After realizing he would not try to coerce her into intimacy, she had been able to completely relax with Jack,

which immeasurably enhanced her pleasure in the time
they spent together. She found herself not just enjoying,
but even seeking out, opportunities to touch him.

Or kiss him. She had become almost compelled to kiss
him every time they had a few private moments, to see
if the next kiss would be as sweet as that first one.

Thus far, the wonder of it had not abated.

She realized now that the odd sensations she'd experienced after meeting the captain, that had gradually
strengthened during their time together—the fullness
in her breasts, the tingling in her nipples, the warmth
and wetness between her thighs—must result from some
form of the desire men felt. Feelings that drew her to him
and intensified when she kissed him.

Her initial, rather idle speculation about what it might
be like to become Jack Carrington's lover had become a
frequently entertained fantasy. Given the desire the captain had admitted, all that now kept her from trying to
make those vague images a reality was fear.

She didn't want to spoil their friendship or tarnish the
beauty of those kisses. She was afraid if she invited his
hands and mouth upon her, his body into hers, the familiar revulsion would recur. That in order not to cry out or
struggle to get away, she'd have to disengage her mind
from her body and finish the business by rote.

In addition to forever ruining her memories of a sweeter
closeness, that would risk having Jack become aware of
her withdrawal. Whether or not at that extreme point he
was still able to stop, she couldn't possibly lead him into
so unfair and potentially disastrous an encounter.

She already felt guilty enough, that while she greedily savored his kisses, he was battling what the erection she felt straining against his breeches showed to be a continual frustration that the passion her kisses encouraged was never allowed to reach its conclusion.

It wasn't right for her to keep tempting his heroic restraint. She should either stop kissing him, or allow matters to proceed where kisses normally led.

They'd had one minor contretemps over it already. While she'd tasted his mouth on the terrace last night, her fingers crept down his shirtfront toward that familiar bulge in his breeches. Her own blood rushing through her veins at the play of his tongue on hers, she'd wickedly wanted to stroke that most sensitive part of his anatomy, feel him shudder into her kiss.

But before her fingers could reach their destination, he'd seized her hand.

"Sweeting, take your fill of kisses," he'd said, his voice ragged. "But you mustn't touch me."

"You don't want this?" she'd asked, stroking his chest, unhappy at being stopped short of her goal.

"You mean to drive me mad," he'd responded with a groan. "I'm only human, Belle. And I refuse to break my promise."

She'd not tried to touch him there again—though she'd been tempted. Then, as she stared at her reflection in the mirror, it struck her that in two more days, he must leave.

No more magical evenings.

No further chances to find out if heaven could extend to more than a kiss.

And if it did not, did it truly matter if she enjoyed every aspect of intimacy? Knowing it was *Jack* she was inviting into her body, surely she wouldn't be repulsed.

Using the techniques she'd been taught, she could give him all the satisfaction he longed for, repay him for the frustration her kisses had caused and reward the restraint and tender concern he'd shown her.

Besides, though granting him intimacy would be her gift, touching him all over would reward *her* as much as *him*. Since he'd rebuffed her, she'd developed a positive eagerness to unclothe him and explore his body with hands and lips. She quite relished adding the image of him writhing in an ecstasy of her making to the collection of memories she would cherish.

There were already so many. The wry quirk of his smile and the dance of his dark eyes when he teased her. The deep tones of his voice flowing over her, energizing her mind and senses. She loved his wide-ranging knowledge, the way he challenged her to support her views, the gentle press of his fingers on her hand, her arm.

She especially loved the taste of his mouth and how, with a stroke of his tongue, he could send shivers of fire to her breasts, her core, so that she ached with longing.

Perhaps intimacy with Jack would be less unpleasant than she'd feared.

I will never take more than you gladly give.

Her mind made up, she set out for the dining room. Tonight, he would have it all.

CHAPTER NINETEEN

As THE EVENING crept on, Belle waited impatiently for the meal and the ritual of tea to be finished. Although she did not experience the anxiety that had afflicted her a week ago, when she'd schemed to seduce Jack and send him away, still her mind and body hummed with tension.

Her restlessness this time was more anticipation than dread, colored by a mounting eagerness to be able to use skills so bitterly learned to repay with delight the joy Jack had brought into her life.

At last Watson and Mae withdrew. Despite her inner agitation, Belle thought she'd been conducting herself much as usual—until she suddenly noticed the room had grown silent. She looked up at Jack, a guilty flush on her cheeks, and found him smiling.

"I see my comments on Byron's poetry have been less than fascinating."

"It isn't that at all. It's just—I've been waiting and waiting to kiss you again."

His smile deepened and something hot and needy glittered in his eyes. "Then wait no more, my lady."

She walked over and he drew her onto his lap, opened

his mouth willingly to her invasion. Her tongue sought his, that first, glancing contact sending a heady excitement racing through her veins.

As her tongue advanced, his retreated. She sensed him holding back, exercising once again that iron control. Wanting to compel him to a more fevered response, she pursued his tongue, laved it with broad strokes, until she felt him shudder.

Whipping his hands up to grip her shoulders, he went suddenly from quarry to hunter, deepening the contact. Then he captured her tongue, sucked it, sending a scalding wash of sensation to her nipples and between her legs.

Her breasts felt turgid, heavy. She wanted the hands gripping her shoulders to cup them, the thumbs now bracing back to play across her nipples. But when she reached up to tug his hand downward, he broke the kiss.

"I want you to touch me," she protested.

His eyes were dark, his breathing uneven. "Where?"

She guided his hand to her breast. "Here."

Though he left the hand where she'd placed it, his fingers did not move. She gave a whimper of frustration. "Caress me—please."

A sigh escaped as he closed the hand around her breast. Then, keeping his eyes on her face, he traced around it, his thumb moving in smaller and smaller circles until at last it skimmed the nipple just beyond the areola.

Moaning, she leaned into him, kissing him fiercely, her hand urging his to caress her there again and again.

But it was not enough to satisfy the need building

inside her, throbbing between her thighs. Knowing his fingers on her naked skin would intensify the sensations, Belle angled away from him and tugged down the bodice of her gown, then pulled his hand back to the bared nipple.

Ah, the feeling was indeed more intense, so much that she cried out, tried to thank him with lips and tongue for how exquisitely wonderful it was. Yet she knew there might be a way to intensify the sensations even further.

Part of her quailed before the idea that tempted her. Never before had she *wanted* a man to suckle her. Usually that act was the spur that sent her mind and spirit fleeing into its mental refuge while her body continued on by rote.

But tonight she craved the feel of his mouth on her breasts.

Once again she broke the kiss. "Please, I want your lips here," she said hoarsely, pressing the thumb still moving lazily over the tip of her nipple.

He looked at her with those molten eyes, his mouth moist and swollen from the fervor of her kisses. But he did not lower his head.

A fury of frustrated need coursing through her, Belle wondered at his hesitation. She was about to plead again, when he shocked her by pulling her bodice back up.

"Belle, this isn't the place," he said, his fists on her gown trembling. "What if a footman returns to gather up the glasses?"

The unpleasant memory of embarrassments past cleared

some of her passion-induced fog. "Yes. Yes, you're right. We mustn't continue here."

Fortunately, the hard shaft pulsing against her bottom reassured her that concern for privacy hadn't lessened Jack's ardor. She slithered off his lap and took his hand. "Will you come with me?"

He pulled the hand free. "Where, Belle?"

She realized she didn't have a destination in mind. They had already progressed so far, there was no continuation that would be fair to the captain short of finally finishing what she'd begun. Was she truly ready?

She looked at Jack, who continued to sit, his jaw set, his clenched fists at his sides, making no move to persuade her despite the obvious evidence of his desire. Even now, if she said "no more" or "good night," he would let her go.

A wave of tenderness swamped her panic and washed away the last of her doubts. "My chamber."

He looked surprised. "That wouldn't be wise."

"Why? You said you would touch me if I wanted it. And I do!"

"But I also promised to stop, and if we proceed further in the privacy of your chamber, Belle, I don't know that I'll be able to keep that promise."

"You won't have to."

He studied her face. "Are you sure?"

She recalled the dizzying sweetness of his thumb circling her nipple, let herself imagine even more. "Yes."

"Then, my lady, I should be happy to follow you."

Since, in case they chanced to meet some late-working

servant, it was necessary to maintain a proper distance as they walked through the hall and up the stairs, by the time they reached Belle's bedchamber, her eagerness had cooled and some of her doubts returned. Not wishing to pause long enough for the captain to sense her unease, she quickly drew him inside and closed the door.

She should touch him now, try to shatter his control so he would be beyond noticing if, at some critical moment, her usual revulsion occurred. But when she reached for him, once again he parried her hand.

Surprised, she glanced at him. "Why not? There are no restrictions here."

He shook his head, smiling. "I agreed to accompany you. I did not agree to a change in the rules. I will touch you wherever and however you command. But aside from kissing my lips, *you* may not touch *me*." He lowered his gaze to her breasts. "I would suggest you begin by letting me disrobe you."

His steady regard was almost as potent as a touch. Feeling her nipples puckering, she replied, "Very well," surprised to hear her voice had gone breathless.

Instead of tugging down the silk bodice as she had done in the parlor, however, he stepped behind her and began unfastening the garment.

Though "unfastening" was hardly an adequate term for the way he worked each clasp and tape, stroking his fingers along her back and shoulders, brushing his lips along the nape of her neck. "The silk feels luscious beneath my fingers," he breathed into her ear, "but 'tis nothing to the feel of your naked skin."

All her attention riveted on the slow descent of his hands, the gentle nuzzle of his mouth. She bit back a moan as he loosened the final tapes, his hands shaping and fondling her buttocks. Then he slid the gown free, gliding the garment over the back of her thighs, her knees, her ankles, caressing her heels. "You may step free."

All the nerves of her legs tingling, she complied.

He rose and stood before her, avidly examining. Though in her modest chemise, all the private areas of her body still concealed, she felt as naked as if he'd bared her to the skin.

Naked—and wicked. She deliberately lowered her gaze to stare at the taut front of his breeches and was thrilled to see the tented fabric rise.

But once again, he stopped her from reaching for him. "My lady, you are still far too clothed," he murmured, moving once more behind her.

This time as he slowly loosened the undergarment, he followed the stroking of his fingers with that of his lips. First her collarbone, then her shoulders, then the curve of her spine tingled and burned under the gentle, teasing pressure of his lips. By the time he'd pulled the garment down to her bottom and knelt before her, hooking his thumbs over her drawers to remove them along with the chemise, she was trembling all over, every nerve straining.

He smoothed the round of each cheek, nuzzled them with his lips. And her legs nearly gave way at the sudden, shocking, exquisite feel as the wet blade of his tongue, traced the place where buttock met thigh, then traveled inward and up.

But not quite far enough to soothe the ache between her legs before he resumed his leisurely descent, rubbing, nuzzling, tasting the now-bare skin along her legs, knees, to her ankle.

He steadied her after she hobbled out of the chemise and turned her to face him, clad now only in garters and stockings.

Once more, her whole body hummed under his gaze. Then he leaned over to kiss her chastely on the lips.

"It seems almost sacrilege to touch such beauty."

"Be a sinner, I beg you!" she cried, panicky at the thought that he might stop now.

Chuckling, he urged her toward the bed. When she grabbed at his shirt, anxious to begin divesting him of his garments, he pulled her hands to her sides.

"Not yet, my princess. Let me please you first."

"You are pleasing me! I would touch you, too!"

"Later you may touch me as much as you will, but this first time I want to be all for you, sweeting. Please."

Unable to summon enough coherent words to protest, she let him nudge her onto the high bed. He propped pillows behind her and eased her against them, coaxed her to spread her legs as he sat on the edge of the bed and began to draw off one stocking.

The idea that she was exposing her most intimate place to his penetrating gaze, reclining nearly naked before him while he remained completely clothed, both shocked her and amplified the tension coiling deep in her body.

Heat sheened her skin and a single drop of perspiration trickled between her breasts, slid down the slick skin of her abdomen as he drew the stocking off and massaged her bare toes. Then, still watching her face, her body, he lifted her foot and suckled it.

A stab of sensation arced to her center, setting up a curious but intense vibration. She pushed down against the mattress, straining for something to ease the delicious, almost unbearable tightness.

Nibbling lightly on her toes now, he ran one finger from her ankle down her leg to her thigh, his fingers stopping maddeningly short of the pulsing center she now yearned for him to touch.

He released her toes and gently parted her legs farther, watching her. "Yes, my beauty, glisten for me."

Never before had she desired being touched there. But now she thought she would go mad if he did not.

"Please!" she pleaded, grabbing his hand and tugging it closer. "Stroke me here."

"As my lady desires."

He moved closer to her on the bed. She moaned in frustration and delight as, rather than follow her command, he bent his head to her breast. Where instead of easing her torture by drawing an aching nipple into his mouth, stopped a bare inch away to exhale a long, warm breath over the acutely sensitized skin. When at last he closed his lips over the nipple, she cried out at the exquisite pleasure of it.

She was beyond thought, conscious only of sensation after sensation as he suckled her while his fingers glided up her inner thigh to fondle the tight curls between her parted legs.

Suddenly his finger delved into the moist skin of her inner lips to caress the small, rigid nub hidden within, producing a reaction so intense she arched her back and bucked beneath him. He murmured, soothing her, lightening the contact to a feather-soft brushing until, some timeless minutes later, she pushed herself against his hand, craving once more the intensity of a harder stroke.

The tension seemed to build and build, making her frantic as she writhed against his fingers. Then he stopped, and she would have shrieked a protest except that within seconds he exchanged the ministrations of his fingers for that of his tongue.

Her legs went limp and fell apart. Every bit of consciousness in her body concentrated on that tiny ridge of flesh and the power of the feelings he was evoking. Perspiration dripped down her belly, dampened the hands with which she clutched the pillows as she frantically strained toward something, some release—

And then it happened, an explosion originating where his tongue caressed her and erupting in a million scintillating points of light that carried the exquisite sensations to every corner of her body.

Wave after wave pulsed through her, suspending thought and will, until at length they softened, dispersed. Totally spent, Belle slumped back against the pillows.

For some time after she heard only the ragged rush of

her breathing. Jack eased himself onto the pillows beside her, gathered her limp body in his arms and held her.

Awe, wonder and a profound gratitude filled her mind, though it was many minutes before she could gather wits enough to produce speech.

"I never imagined…" she breathed at last.

"'Tis how pleasure should be. How it always will be for us."

"But—you lied to me."

He tensed immediately. "Lied to you? How?"

"You said we should taste pleasure together. This—" though her limbs still seemed boneless, she managed to tap one hand clumsily at the waistcoat concealing his chest "—does not seem like 'together.'"

She felt the rumble of his laughter. "I suppose you are right, but I want you too badly to have risked finding pleasure together the first time. I'd never have lasted long enough."

"I think 'tis time you got your due. And now, if you please, you will do *exactly* as I command."

"I am hereafter always and ever yours, my lady."

And command him she did. Though, as he'd predicted, by the time she had slowly, teasingly, removed his clothing, she had hardly begun sampling his chest and nipples and belly before his corded arms and gusty breathing warned her he was but a few moments from climax. And that, she wished for him to experience in the way she knew would make his pleasure most intense—her hands caressing the plump sacks while she enfolded and tasted his length.

His outcry and his collapse after he reached his peak was gratifyingly dramatic. But after giving him a short period to recover, she chided him that she had been cheated of her turn and commanded him to let her finish her exploration of his body.

A command he appeared entirely amenable to following. Positioned as she directed, in dusky candlelight, she indulged herself by making a reality of all the fantasies she'd dreamed about touching him. A deep feminine satisfaction filled her at using her training and instincts to determine what would please him most, letting the moans and sighs of his response guide her.

Ah, yes, the skin beneath his ears, at the backs of his knees and ankles, responded instantly to her touch. He rewarded with gasps the progress of her tongue along the ridges of his ribs, at the tender skin just beneath his arm. And his hands clutched her hair, pulling it down from its pins as she grazed her teeth lightly across the pebbled tips of his nipples.

She was surprised, however, after kissing her way across the flat planes of his abdomen to discover his cock already stiffening. A thrill darted through her body, hardening her nipples and warming the places his tongue had moistened at this evidence of his unexpected virility.

She immediately rewarded him by stroking and petting his steadily increasing length, then plying her tongue against the skin beneath the shaft where the roughness of those rounded sacks smoothed into the velvet skin of his erection. Far sooner than she'd imagined a man could recover, his fully erect length jutted upward.

The delectable tension that had been building in her body as she ministered to him tightened further. Before she could wonder whether he would satisfy her as he had before, he lifted her and set her astride his legs.

"This time we will go together, my love," he murmured. Kissing her lips lightly as he drew her forward, he positioned her so the broad head of his erection barely parted the skin beneath which her hidden nub throbbed.

"Move as you wish, sweeting, whenever you wish."

That near touch was so titillating, she automatically pushed forward to increase the connection. The slick contact of those two moistened surfaces sent a surge of pleasure through her and tightened still further the tension at her center. Smiling, he cupped her bottom, tilted so that she slid down, taking just a bit of his engorged penis within her.

'Twas different from the feel of his lips there—yet lush, exciting. Whimpering, she urged him a bit deeper, then deeper still. Then, when he bent to suckle one tight nipple, she rocked her hips, wanting all of him inside her.

Instead of what she'd previously experienced as an unpleasant stretching that approached pain, now the smooth, moist glide of his cock within her seemed to spread the pleasure up and down the length of the passage his member stroked. As the piercingly sweet tension coiled tighter, she rode him harder, faster, pressing toward a goal she was not even sure she could, in this fashion, achieve.

The pleasure that followed proved just as intense and

even more satisfying than the first. For this time, Jack reached the pinnacle with her, his release shuddering through her as she collapsed against him, their bodies joined as deeply as flesh could be.

Truly one, just as he had promised.

For a long time they lay motionless. Finally he leaned up to kiss her. "Is it not beautiful?"

Tears started at her eyes for the wonder of a completeness more profound than any she had ever imagined. "Yes."

"Good." She felt his lips curving into a smile against her cheek. "And we've just begun."

As BELLE SAT combing out her hair later that morning, she marveled at how, despite over six years of experience, she had proven to be so ignorant about the responses and the potential for pleasure of her own body.

And of Jack's. They had dozed briefly, but soon after their first coupling, he'd awakened her to demonstrate that the promise she thought had been meant for the days to come, he intended to fulfill that very night. Twice more he brought them together to the shuddering peak of ecstasy before at last they fell into deeper, sated sleep.

For a few more short days, this marvel of loving him could be hers. Thank all the saints in heaven she'd had the courage to reach for it!

After washing her love-dampened body in a ritual of tenderness at dawn, with an equal display of concern for discretion, he'd insisted on returning to his chamber. As if the whole household, in the way servants had of discovering what their employers were up to, would not soon know they'd spent the night together.

Not that anyone in her employ was likely to feel, much less display, any moral indignation. Mae would be over the moon, sure her hopes for Belle's future had been realized.

Belle refused to spoil what she planned to be a glorious day by recalling how soon Mae's hopes would be disappointed.

She couldn't wait to see Jack again. After deciding the days they had left were too valuable to waste a second in mundane household activities—and unwilling to have to mask her delight in him by maintaining a proper decorum before onlookers—Belle decided they would carry their breakfast up to the heights. Being able—between kisses—to take her coffee and toast from Jack's own hands would more than compensate for braving the early morning chill.

Despite her bravura, when Watson answered her call, she felt a guilty blush heating her cheeks. "Ask Cook to prepare a breakfast for myself and Captain Carrington, please. We will be driving out as soon as it is ready."

As Watson rose from his bow, he surprised her by smiling broadly. "I hope you both be happy, my lady," he said before he exited her chamber.

An hour later Belle sat with Jack on the bench under the arbor overlooking the fields of Bellehaven, leaning back against his chest with his arms around her as they sipped coffee from the same cup.

Lazy contentment filled her. "A most excellent day, is it not?"

"Most excellent," he agreed. "Despite those gathering clouds—" he pointed to the western horizon "—that seem to indicate rain may shortly arrive."

"What is a little rain to us on so splendid a day?"

He hugged her closer. "Or after so splendid a night."

That reminder seemed to call for a kiss, which Belle willingly awarded him. A few moments later he broke the kiss, laughing, and leapt up, scattering the remains of the toast and ham and knocking the coffee cup off the bench.

"'Tis much too splendid to sit placidly about," he exclaimed, dragging her up and swinging her in a circle.

"Stop, you'll make me dizzy!" she protested.

"Not as dizzy as you make me. Giddy as a schoolboy on holiday!" he said, swinging her faster still.

"You are mad!" she cried, trying to pull away.

"If this be madness, I hope never again to be sane."

"Enough!" she said, laughing as she broke free and lurched to the bench, one hand pressed against her temple. "My head is spinning so, I don't know when it shall stop."

"I don't think mine ever shall." His lowered tone, the look he fixed on her, turned the frivolous moment suddenly serious.

She already realized the few days they'd stolen would probably cost her years of misery. Did his words mean he, too, felt himself doomed to a life of desolate loneliness?

She didn't dare ask, didn't want to know. Fortunately, he broke the fraught moment by loping off to the wood's edge where the remains of an old cottage stood. Along its broken front wall grew a mass of spring snowflakes, nodding their tiny, green-tipped white bells in the freshening breeze. While she watched in amusement, he picked a handful and trotted back.

"For my lady, sovereign of my heart and mistress of my future," he said, dropping to one knee to extend the bouquet. "A gracious gift of nature's bounty."

"How lovely, Sir Knight," she replied, charmed by his whimsical offering as she had never been by the elegant floral tributes with which Bellingham had presented her.

At that moment the wind picked up and a gust of chilly rain peppered them. Glancing at the clouds scudding overhead, Jack pulled her to her feet.

"Unless my lady wishes to experience a downpour, Sir Knight suggests we make haste to the castle."

Disappointed, for returning to the manor meant she would probably have to share Jack with Mae for the rest of the day until the night—one of their last few nights—freed them to be alone again, nonetheless, for the sake of Jack's recovering chest, she felt forced to comply. "Very well, Sir Knight. Your lady agrees."

FEELING A CLOCK in his head inexorably ticking away the hours they had left, Jack wrapped Belle in his cloak and braced her against him as he drove them back through the steadily increasing rain to Bellehaven.

The lady he sheltered was so precious, the night they'd shared so wondrous beyond anything he'd previously experienced that he refused to let his thoughts leave the perfect, two-person universe they'd created here, far from the world's censorious gaze. Soon enough both his thoughts and his person would be forced to return to that world.

Though his heart would remain behind.

Since the first moment at Armaldi's when a slender youth metamorphosed before his eyes into an enchanting woman, Lady Belle had fascinated him, excited him, surprised him and inspired him with an insatiable lust. But after last night he knew beyond doubt that he'd also fallen in love with her, so deeply he could no longer conceive of insulting her with an offer of carte blanche.

How to reconcile that fact with his duty to his family was a conundrum he would wrestle with for many a weary hour once he left this haven. But for now, he would concentrate only on the joy of having Belle near, his nostrils filled with the scent of rain and lavender, the warmth of her body against his inspiring in him both desire and tenderness.

Ah, that these final two days might last forever!

Half an hour later, they turned the team over to a groom and ran up the entry stairs into the hall, laughing as they dashed the moisture off their dripping cloaks.

Watson appeared to relieve them of their sodden garments. "There's a fire blazing in the parlor. Should I send you in some hot wine?"

"That would be excellent, thank you," Belle said.

"And my lady—" Watson's lowered voice stopped Belle as she was turning away. "You got a—a visitor."

Before Jack could wonder who might have come to call, the parlor door opened and an elegantly dressed gentleman stepped out.

"Lady Belle." Lord Rupert's deep, unwelcome tones assaulted Jack's ears. As Rupert's gaze reached Jack, who was standing behind Belle, his eyebrows lifted. "And—Captain Carrington! How very...interesting."

CHAPTER TWENTY

STIFFENING AUTOMATICALLY as he recognized the baron, Jack returned Rupert's unfriendly gaze.

Before he could speak, Belle said, "The captain accepted my invitation to rest here for a few days on his journey north." Her tone indicated she thought Jack's presence none of Rupert's business. "What are you doing in the country?"

"My dear Lady Belle, your departure from London was so precipitous, I was worried about you. When some matter of business brought me to the vicinity, I felt compelled to call and make sure you were well."

"How…thoughtful," she replied, all traces of warmth and ease vanished from her face and voice. Jack could almost see her retreating within the reserved, wary shell of the Lady Belle he'd known before Bellehaven.

A Lady Belle abused by and mistrustful of men like Rupert. Instinctively Jack stepped closer and put a hand on her shoulder.

His gray eyes narrowing, Rupert fixed his gaze on Jack's hand—as if waiting to see whether Belle would shrug off that possessive gesture. Jack took it as a subtle victory when she did not.

Apparently Rupert did as well, for his jaw tightened and something like anger briefly crossed his face before he composed it back to his usual sardonic expression. "I had heard the captain might still be…in your company. I suppose congratulations are in order, Carrington? Will you return to London to claim your prize before going home?"

"Prize?" Belle angled a questioning glance at Jack.

In the flash of an instant, Jack recalled breakfast at the club after he'd first seen Belle fence. The wager the other men had proposed and he'd disdained, but that they'd nonetheless recorded in the betting book. A wager he'd completely forgotten—but which, the look of satisfaction on Rupert's face warned Jack, the older man now intended to use to his maximum advantage.

Nausea slammed into his gut as he realized how Belle would likely respond to what Rupert was about to convey.

"Surely it's not slipped your mind—the wager concerning you and our lovely Lady Belle?"

His heart and mind were already screaming a protest as he felt Belle tense, then move out from under his hand. Her voice iced even further. "There was a wager?"

Rupert chortled, so clearly enjoying Jack's discomfiture that, praying the catastrophe about to overtake him would be redeemable, Jack had to clench his hands into fists to prevent himself from wrapping them around the baron's neck and choking the life from him.

"I must apologize, my dear," Rupert said with a notable lack of sincerity. "We men are such vulgar creatures. I was singing your praises at the club one morning, saying you were the one true, unattainable Beauty of the ton. The captain's loyal friends took exception, touting his charms as sufficient to breach the stoutest of barricades. After some discussion, most of the men, myself included, wagered that you would remain indifferent to his blandishments." He shook his head and sighed, a malicious grin lighting his features. "How grieved I am to find I underestimated the good captain's resourcefulness."

"They wagered he could…seduce me?" Belle asked stonily, refusing to look at Jack.

"I blush to have the matter stated so…indelicately, but yes. The interest in the affair, I regret to admit, was quite high, so I expect the payout will be substantial, Captain. Though, of course, what is mere money compared to the, ah, person of our incomparable Lady Belle? Still, 'twill be a fine addition to the treasure you bring to the wedding rumor says you are planning."

"Rumor says many things, most of them untrue," Jack shot back, in that moment loathing Rupert more than he'd ever despised anyone. It wasn't like that, he wanted to shout at Belle. But she avoided his imploring glance.

He hated Rupert for trapping him in such a disadvantageous position, knowing that defending himself might make him appear even more guilty. He certainly didn't want to try to explain this tangle in front of the gloating baron. But would it be worse to say nothing?

Unable to bear the thought that his relationship with Belle might be dying before his eyes, he stepped into her line of vision. "I swear to you, Belle," he said urgently, his voice pitched low, "I did not participate in—"

"Is it true?" she interrupted, looking directly at him at last. "Was there a wager?"

Pain stabbed his chest and his heart contracted at the hurt in her eyes. "Having no interest in such a thing, I didn't pay much attention—"

"Was. There. A. Wager?" she interrupted again, enunciating each word.

For a long moment Jack stared at her, willing her to understand, to trust him, to believe he would not be capable of such gross deception. But in the cold, shuttered look that took the place of the pain in her eyes, he saw the extermination of his hopes. "Yes," he admitted.

She wheeled to face Rupert. "Thank you, my lord, for the concern which prompted your call. Regrettably, I have urgent tasks which must be completed today, so I cannot tarry. With the weather coming on, I know you'll want to resume your journey while it is still full daylight. My staff will see you out. Good day."

She curtsied and would have walked away, but Lord Rupert seized her hand and forced her fingers to his lips, kissing them at length before at last releasing them. "I shall leave you, my dear, to indulge in the quarrel that is obviously brewing. The end of an affair is so disillusioning, is it not? But I'll expect to see you in town again shortly. Farewell, my sweet."

She returned a glare in which there was not a trace of even false civility. "I am not your sweet, my lord, nor do I ever intend to be." With a nod, she swept past him.

A triumphant smile on his face, Rupert made Jack a bow. "Sorry to have spoiled your charming idyll, Captain. But Belle will be mine in the end. You can count upon it."

I'll see you dead first, the thought flashed through his head. Controlling with an effort the fury that urged him to mill down the earl in the middle of Belle's entry hall, not bothering to force any hypocritical politenesses through his gritted teeth, Jack set off after Belle.

As soon as she made it out of the hallway, Belle broke into a run, barely conscious of where she was going. Her chest felt as if pierced by a blade, filled with an agony that made her want to beat her fists on the wall and shriek with anguish, each beat of her heart thrumming the re-frain.

Betrayal…betrayal…betrayal.

Jack, the time they'd spent together these last few days, had seemed too good to be true. And so, of course, they were. Having learned from cruel experience, shouldn't she have remembered not to trust in a man's sweet words?

Still, knowing this fiasco was her own stupid, blind, self-deceiving fault didn't ease the agony.

Dimly she heard footsteps behind her. "Belle—wait!"

Jack's voice.

Nausea stirred in her stomach and her vision clouded with tears. Picking up her skirts, she hurried faster.

But with his longer legs unencumbered by petticoats, he soon caught up to her. "Please, Belle," he said, seizing her shoulder. "At least give me a chance to explain without that viper Rupert distorting every word."

Now that he'd caught her, she wouldn't make this ignoble moment any more humiliating by struggling. Trying to summon the glacial calm that had sustained her through tragedies past, she let him turn her around.

Though she couldn't yet bear to look at him. She knew if she gazed on his beloved, treacherous face and saw guilt—or worse, continued protestations of innocence despite the glaring evidence of his duplicity, her tenuous control would falter and what was left of her heart and self-respect would explode in all directions like one of Congreve's faulty rockets.

"I don't see what else there is to say. Please be gone by tomorrow morning."

"I won't go until you hear me out."

She glanced pointedly at his hand restraining her shoulder, and after a moment, he removed it.

"Very well. Give me your speech and go."

"The bare facts of what Rupert reported were true. We were at the club, the members discussing your trouncing of poor Wexley. My erstwhile friends, proud of my prowess with a sword, proposed me as the challenger most likely to best you. Rupert, made jealous, I expect, by the thought of any man claiming the victor's prize, stated that I might win a kiss, but I'd...I'd never win you to my bed. Although I refused to have anything to do with the matter, some of the so-called 'gentlemen' present recorded the statement as a wager. I never told you because it meant nothing to me. I had truly forgotten about it."

"But you did challenge me to fence."

"Yes. I was too intrigued by you to resist that. But you can't believe I got myself injured to play upon your sensibilities, insinuated myself into your household and your affections simply to win a bet!"

"In my experience, men will do almost anything to win a wager. They put great credence in some ridiculous code which requires them to honor scraps of paper won in games of chance or to duel to the death over some perceived insult, yet see nothing amiss in casually ruining any parlor maid or servant girl who takes their fancy."

"Gentlemen worthy of the name do no such thing," he countered. "Belle, I know you're angry over what you see as my deception and I don't blame you. But if you will put aside your outrage and calmly consider the time we've spent together, you must know Rupert's allegations are untrue. Can you truly believe what we've shared, what we've felt for each other, was false?"

He was so smooth, so persuasive, so seemingly sincere. Just as Bellingham had been after Vauxhall. But when her former protector's protestations of devotion had failed to move her, he'd found a new way to bend her to his will.

How could she trust this man she'd known for less than a month to be any better?

Don't be twice a fool, her head urged her.

"I've heard you out. Now, you will be gone by morning, please."

For a long moment he stared at her. Then he nodded. "I'll not harangue you any longer," he said quietly. "I love you, Belle. If you can't believe that, if you think the joy we found together was just a sham, then no words of mine will make any difference."

Oh, he was so convincing, she was almost tempted to waver. Until another thought occurred, sending revitalizing anger through her.

"So, even if I accept your explanation, how did you think this charming interlude was to end? Did you expect to persuade me to become your mistress?"

She waited, ready to counter the admission she expected with an acid refusal to ever again become any man's whore.

"I was coming to think I must marry you."

She was about to deliver her scathing rejoinder when his words penetrated, stealing the breath from her lungs. And then anger fiercer than any she'd felt for a very long time flamed through her.

How dare he mock her so!

She confined herself to a single, bitter laugh. "Oh yes, I'm sure you were. Let me inform you, then, that I have even less desire to give to anyone the control over my person, wealth and future a legal husband would gain than I have to become some man's harlot!"

"Belle, that's not what—"

"Please," she interrupted, tears brimming in her eyes, dangerously close to spilling over. "I believe we've truly said enough now. Let us not further sully the end of what was an...agreeable interlude with any more brangling. As I shall doubtless be occupied when you leave, I'll wish you a safe journey now."

He held her eyes for a long time, his face unreadable. Belle damned herself again for the hope her weak, foolish heart still harbored that he would fall at her feet, beg forgiveness, refuse to leave her. Like a dying woman's wishes for her daughter's happiness, that hope was futile.

Instead, his face as shuttered as she hoped hers now was, he made her a bow. "I promised I would never force you to something you did not wish. But remember, my leaving like this was your desire—not mine."

Standing motionless and resolute while she hemorrhaged within from ruined dreams and shattered hope, she watched him go. Leaving might not have been his wish at the moment, but now that she knew the truth, he would have departed soon enough. Once he discovered sweet words and falsely penitent apologies would not win him forgiveness, any more than they'd helped Bellingham after Vauxhall.

'Twas ironic, though, after more than six years among the gentlemen of the ton, she'd allowed herself once again to be so deceived. She swallowed a short, half-hysterical laugh. Who would have believed the notorious Lady Belle still had such innocence left to lose?

The false offer of marriage had been the cruelest blow of all. As if a respected member of the aristocracy would actually offer marriage to a woman known throughout the ton as another man's whore! She wanted to skewer him with her sword, just recalling it.

So she would put it out of mind. Sometime later, when she could stand it, she would review what had happened and try to figure out just how she'd allowed herself to be so taken in—by the captain and the last remnants of her old childhood dreams.

Jack Carrington would be gone tomorrow. Since she intended to remain at Bellehaven indefinitely, she was, mercifully, unlikely ever to see him again.

She had more than enough work to occupy her here. Giving her eyes one last angry swipe, Belle set off for the kitchen.

CHAPTER TWENTY-ONE

A MONTH LATER, Belle sat in the bookroom, gazing over her account books. Harold, the farm manager, had just finished reporting on the progress of the spring crops.

The meadows had been pale green with newly sprouted grain when last she'd driven to inspect them, Jack by her side. Both passing Bellehaven's fields and surveying her land from the heights were now so entangled with memories of Jack that, except for a daily ride along a path they'd never taken, she avoided going farther than the gardens.

Her irrational fury, flamed by hurt and a raw sense of betrayal, had lasted barely into the evening after Jack's departure. Upon the sober reflection he'd begged her to grant him, she'd had to acquit him of trying to deceive her. 'Twas nonsensical to think he'd have deliberately courted death by allowing her to wound him so he might have enough time to insinuate himself into her good graces.

She had even cautiously come to believe his claims of having grown attached to her. If merely bedding her to win a wager had been his goal, he could easily have done so the night she'd tried to seduce him.

Instead of taking what she offered and setting off to

collect his winnings, he'd set her at arm's length and vowed never to touch her unless she desired it. And during the halcyon week he'd remained—as cynically as she'd tried to reevaluate it afterward in the heat of her anger—she'd not been able to read into his many acts of tenderness any meaning but that he'd developed for her a sincere affection.

She probably owed him an apology for doubting his word and his honor, not that she was likely ever to have a chance to tender it.

Perhaps the greatest of his gifts had been showing her the bliss and closeness possible in the physical union of a man and a woman. A bliss he'd staved off his own pleasure to let her savor. A closeness she would ache for the rest of her life.

Still, he might admire and respect her with all the fervor the British public felt for Lord Wellington, but that didn't change the fact that a man like Captain Carrington could not marry a woman like Lady Belle. That he had even considered such a thing was proof of the power of what they'd shared, isolated in their cocoon of enchantment at Bellehaven. An escape from the harsh realities of their world as fragile and ephemeral as any caterpillar's web.

An enchantment which could not have survived Jack's return to his family and his proper place in life. Since even the sincerest of attachments would not be enough to create a legitimate future for them, 'twas probably best that the vile Lord Rupert had shattered their idyll.

Before she grew so dependent upon Jack's presence that

she abandoned all her scruples and begged him to keep her as his mistress. Hidden away, waiting for the bits of time he could steal, she would eventually have ended by hating them both for agreeing to it.

And even if by some miracle the impossible happened and Jack actually offered to marry her, she'd not been making idle claims when she said she had no wish to marry. Though Jack might not have participated in that tawdry wager, he had not seemed much disturbed by it. With even Jack, the best of men, adhering to a code of honor she neither trusted nor understood, now that she possessed the means to survive on her own, she wasn't sure she could have been able to yield even to Jack the power over her life and future a legitimate husband would wield.

Fortunately, she'd not had to make so terrifying a choice. Instead, he had left her with memories of passion and tenderness she could cherish forever.

Through all the long, lonely years ahead.

A rap on the door called her out of her gloomy thoughts, followed a moment later by Mae's entrance.

"You're up early this morning," Belle observed.

"With my chocolate came some news so important, I had to find you at once."

Something had happened to Jack? the thought flew into her head. She shook the silly idea free. Should anything befall Captain Carrington, Mae was even more unlikely than she to be informed of it.

"Have the allied sovereigns returned to set London celebrating again?" she asked, trying for a light tone.

"And how would I know, little as we hear about the City? No, 'tis only that Jane told me Sergeant Jackman said today's Market Day in the village, which don't happen but once every few months. We've both been trapped here like mice in a barrel this past age. Do say we can go!"

Belle frowned. "I'm not sure that would be wise."

"But there's not been a bit of trouble since we arrived, near on seven weeks ago! Sergeant Jackman agrees. See, I brung him with me to tell you so himself." At that, Mae opened the door and beckoned.

His thin frame garbed in the worn Rifleman's jacket, the tall soldier limped in. "Morning, Lady Belle."

"And to you, Sergeant. Mae says you've told her you think an excursion to Market Day would not pose a risk?"

"No, ma'am. My men haven't seen any strangers in the towns hereabouts and they been watching close. Market Day brings in mostly the country people, and the men will know all of them. I think you'll be safe enough, but just in case, we'll keep a close guard. If some London toughs make an appearance, we can handle 'em."

The sergeant might have returned from Waterloo with a scarred face and a pronounced limp, but he had a keen intelligence and a sharp eye, and she trusted his judgment.

"See?" Mae replied triumphantly. "Reynolds says there be some tolerable shops in the village and the inn has a very good cook. If I don't soon see something besides trees and fields and cows, I'm going to go madder than the old king! Besides, Belle, you've been as snappish as a dog with a sore paw since…since a certain gentleman left. Getting out would do you good."

Guilt washed through Belle. She *had* been drifting along in a private fog of grief since Jack Carrington drove away, selfishly leaving Mae on her own to find amusement. "You're right, and I do beg your pardon. Since the sergeant approves the excursion, we shall go."

A sudden worry occurred and she looked at Jackman. "Only I cannot feel comfortable leaving Jane behind."

"We'll take her with us," he replied. "Don't you worry none, ma'am. I won't let nothing harm Miss Jane."

Belle smiled. Even as distracted as she'd been this last month, she'd noticed the friendship developing between the shy Jane and the reticent young soldier.

She'd known the members of her own household were unlikely to disdain the girl for her sullied past. She'd not been so sure about Jackman.

Though the story she'd put round the countryside blamed the attack on them on highwaymen intent on stealing her jewels, Jack—she still could not recall his name without a pang—had felt it necessary to inform the man he'd placed in charge of protecting them of the true circumstances. Belle had worried he might look upon Jane with contempt. But from the first, the sergeant had treated her with the same respect he accorded the rest of her household. A fact which raised him considerably in Belle's good opinion.

"Sergeant, would you ask Jane? If she wishes to go, we shall all do so."

After the soldier went out, Belle turned to Mae. "If Jane does not feel comfortable going out, I shall stay behind with her. Watson and some of the other staff can accompany you. I'm sure they would all enjoy a holiday."

Mae's smile wavered. "I'm so desperate to see a real street with shops and houses, I'm fair tempted to agree. But I don't know this place or these people. Without you to watch so I knows how to act, I…I might say or do something that would set folks to talking about you."

Belle looked at her with surprise. Perhaps her friend was more aware of how her flamboyant manner of dress and behavior might be perceived than Belle had credited. In any event, Belle was touched that Mae would worry about how her actions might harm Belle's standing in the community.

Before she could ponder alternative arrangements for the girl's protection, though, Sergeant Jackman returned to report that Jane was quite willing to go on an excursion.

Scarcely more than an hour later, Belle's carriage and a wagonload of Bellehaven staff arrived in the village, Mae so excited she could scarcely wait for the steps to be set down. Even Jane, as she alighted from the vehicle, said shyly how much she was looking forward to the outing.

"Thank you, ma'am, for bringing me. I can't rightly remember when I last walked down a street in daylight, nothing on my mind but looking at the shops and stalls."

"Relax and enjoy yourself, Jane. Sergeant Jackman assured me he would watch over you all day."

A blush tinted the girl's cheeks. "The sergeant's been ever so kind. I won't be afraid, not with him staying right by me the whole time—as if he were my beau. Not that he would ever think of me like that! But…but a girl likes to dream," Jane said, her voice wistful.

Would she not feel invincible herself, were Jack at her side? Belle thought, her heart embracing the image before it faded on a tremor of longing. Jane was right, she thought with a sigh. A girl couldn't help but dream. Though, she noted, watching as the sergeant presented Jane with a posy he'd purchased from a flower vendor, in Jane's case, dreams might become something more substantial.

Not knowing most of the residents thronging the streets and marketplace, Belle found she could not completely relax. In addition, after they left the open-air market and strolled through town, encountering in person for the first time the shop owners from whom she ordered Bellehaven's provisions made her doubly uneasy.

But the merchants treated Belle and her party with smiling deference, and Mae was so clearly enjoying herself as she bargained over lengths of cloths, discovered a fetching bonnet and called upon Jane to inspect it, that Belle was glad she'd permitted the excursion.

After partaking of a dinner at the local inn which, to Mae's delight, proved as excellent as their housekeeper had promised, they were walking toward their carriage when Jane halted abruptly. She darted behind Belle, frightened eyes fixed on something at the far side of the crowded market.

Sergeant Jackman fell in beside her, hand on the rifle he'd kept slung over his shoulder. Belle and Mae halted as well, with Watson taking Jane's other side so that she was completely surrounded.

"What is it, Miss Jane?" Jackman asked.

"Over there," she whispered, "beside the fruit seller's stall. That man talking to those girls. It's Mr. Harris, the man what talked me into coming to London. Oh, don't let him see me!"

"Don't you worry. We'll protect you," Jackman said.

"You're sure, Jane?" Belle asked. Though she had always believed the girl's story, until this moment the idea of someone trying to lure country girls to ruin had seemed more the stuff of a Minerva Press novel than something that would actually occur in present-day England.

"After two days and nights traveling with him, you think I could forget? See—he's smiling at that girl, just as he smiled at us. Oh, someone must warn them!"

"Sergeant, please dispatch one of your men to listen to him and draw away the girls, if necessary," Belle said. "We must know what Mr. Harris is telling them."

Before leaving London, Belle had spoken with Egremont. Though sympathetic to Jane's plight, he'd indicated that without sufficient proof to buttress the girl's tale, he saw little likelihood of the government pursuing the matter. If Harris was in fact dangling offers of employment to try to lure these girls to London, their signed statements to that effect might be enough to persuade Egremont's friends to initiate an inquiry.

After exchanging a few words with the assistant,

Jackman said, "Davie will handle it, ma'am. One of them girls growed up with his sister. If they get any silly ideas of taking off, he'll tease 'em back home quick enough. Let's get you ladies into the carriage."

After securing them in their vehicle with Watson and two other men on guard, the sergeant left to meet his assistant. Belle waited tensely, planning what she would do next if Jackman confirmed what they suspected. A short time later, the sergeant returned to the carriage and bid the coachman set off.

"The man's name is Harris, like Miss Jane said. He was filling them girls full of tales about the fine jobs awaiting 'em as ladies' maids and shopgirls, did they come down to London. Said they could have their brothers or da travel on the stage with 'em, if they was fearful of setting out with just him for escort." The sergeant sniffed scornfully. "As if a farmer had time to traipse down to London, with the growing season full on!"

"I hope your man dissuaded them," Belle said.

The sergeant grinned. "Oh, he did. The gent was none too happy about him interfering, but he didn't try to keep the girls from leaving."

"He only wants to bring along girls who are willing, so they can't later claim they was forced," Jane said.

"Have a man follow him, Sergeant," Belle said. "For several weeks, if necessary. I must know where he takes any girls he recruits and to whom he reports."

"Davie's started on it, ma'am. We'll watch that gent from now until he goes to ground, wherever that be. You been paying us right handsome to sit around. We be only too happy to start earning those shillings. Besides," he added, his scarred face hardening, "any man what would lure an innocent lass into Satan's web ought to hang, I think."

The Rifleman rapped on the carriage wall, signaling the vehicle to halt. "We're out of the village now, so I'll ride the rest of the way outside. And I'll let you know as soon as Davie learns anything."

Belle felt a quiet satisfaction—the first glimmer of emotion she'd felt since Jack's departure. Soon, she might have some evidence to offer Egremont and vindicate Jane.

If Jackman's assistants could testify that Harris operated out of London in connivance with Mrs. Jarvis or some other bawd, surely the government would take action. But though the farm girls and the former soldiers should make credible witnesses, no one knew the whole story, save Belle and Jane.

She could write Egremont the details, but explaining it to him in person would be more effective. Besides, she couldn't possibly send Jane alone to testify. Belle would have to go to London, as well.

Where, now that the Season was approaching its height, Jack would surely be.

She wouldn't seek him out, of course. In fact, for the same pressing reason that had sent her from town in the first place, she'd have to take care to be seen by as few acquaintances as possible.

But—she might catch a glimpse of him driving down some street or riding in the park. There would doubtless be news about him, his mother or his sister in the society pages. She could let her heart splinter all over again as she read about the ladies he had danced with or called upon, or whom gossip said he was considering as a bride.

Such slow torture might be just the thing to rip him out of her heart and head for good.

Heaven knows, country isolation had done a poor enough job of it this past month.

That settled it, then. If Sergeant Jackman's spies brought back proof of Harris's involvement in the scheme that had ensnared Jane, Belle would return to London.

TWO WEEKS LATER, Jack sat with a party of guests at his mother's table in their London town house, nodding to the expensively gowned, pretty little thing who was his dinner partner. The chit, some acquaintance of Dorrie's also being presented this Season, was embarrassingly eager to catch his interest, forever flapping her fan to attract his attention.

Unfortunately, Miss-Whatever-Her-Name-Was possessed no attributes beyond her lovely face and an impressively jutting bosom, which, though attractive enough, barely tempted his carnal appetites. He recalled how Belle, in that ugly gray gown buttoned up to her chin, had kept his senses as roused and alert through dinner as a soldier on patrol while he imagined removing it.

The young lady sighed and fanned her ample chest. Averting his eyes, he was tempted to sigh himself.

Conversation thus far had consisted of polite monologues on his part punctuated by her "oh, la!'s." He wasn't sure he had the fortitude to make another attempt.

His mind slipped away to the candlelit evening he'd spent with Belle discussing the accords reached by the Congress of Vienna. His lips curved in a smile as he pictured her, garbed in a gown far more conservative than the peek-down-my-décolletage garment of the chit beside him, her eyes sparkling, one pointing finger punctuating her argument.

The pang of loss pierced him like a saber slash, keen enough to bring moisture to his eyes. Lord, how he missed her.

Though he'd still like to spit Lord Rupert on his sword and roast him over a Spanish campfire, the baron had probably done them both a favor. His feelings for Belle had deepened to such a point that he'd actually contemplated trying to talk her into marrying him. Had he coerced her to accept, society would have deemed it the most shocking mésalliance to titillate the ton since the elder Burney girl snabbled herself a duke.

Not only would their marriage bring Belle, instead of the acceptance that should be hers, almost certain contempt and social isolation, such a union would embarrass his mother, Lady Anne, quite possibly causing her to be cut by the highest sticklers among the ton. And it would likely cripple the chances for his innocent sister to marry well. Even if the young gallant now courting her had the backbone to wed her despite the infamy of that connection, the misery would widen as his family in turn was exposed to snide whispers and pointing fingers.

No, marrying Belle would be an act of selfish irresponsibility so vast he ought to be grateful Lord Rupert had made resisting the temptation unnecessary.

Prevented in spite of himself from doing the wrong thing, he could now get on with the business of doing what was proper with his life.

His achingly empty, unsatisfying life.

He knew his mother worried about him. She'd accepted his edited version of his accident, recovery and progress home without inquisitive comment. After several times introducing the matter and receiving only stony silence in reply, she'd asked nothing further about the intentions he'd expressed in his letters home of seeking a wife. And while she continued to invite a variety of eligible ladies to dine—respectable widows and maidens a few seasons beyond their come-outs as well as the buds of youth unfolding their beauty in the Marriage Mart for the first time—he would sometimes find her reproachful gaze resting on him from the other end of the dinner table. And realize with a start that he must once more be gazing off into the distance instead of helping to entertain their guests.

He didn't mean to appear rude. But even given that his still-sharp longing for Belle might have gilded his memories of her and their time together with too bright a luster, he could find nothing about any of the attractive, well-born maidens being trooped before him that struck a responsive chord or excited his interest.

Nor could he seem to prevent the momentary racing of his pulse as he drove down Bond Street or St. James or in the park and chanced to glimpse a tall, golden-haired lady. A spurt of excitement followed by disappointment and a short lecture to himself on the idiocy of subconsciously seeing Belle everywhere, when he knew quite well that she was permanently established at Bellehaven.

He would do his duty—eventually, he told himself. After a year or two, when Belle's presence in his thoughts and senses started to fade, he might be able to stomach looking for someone to replace her in his heart.

If anyone ever could, he thought wistfully.

A sharp kick to his shin recalled him to the present. "Jack, the ladies are retiring," his sister said in an urgent undertone, glaring at him from her side of the table.

Feeling himself color, he jumped belatedly to his feet. He didn't need to glance in his mother's direction to know her exasperated gaze was fixed upon him, as well.

The young lady recently seated beside him shot him an injured look before curtsying to leave with the others.

"I'll do better in future," he silently promised his mother as she led her guests out.

Now for the brandy and cigars, he thought glumly. All he had to do was keep the liquor flowing and let the ton gentlemen present, most of them friends of his late father or fathers of Dorrie's friends, natter on about horses, hounds and husband-hunting until they rejoined the ladies.

He took a deep drink from his own wineglass. This part of being a good host, at least, he could handle.

MUCH LATER, after they returned from the ball they'd attended after dinner and bade their mother good-night, Dorrie came over to take his hand.

"Would you sit up with me, Jack?" she begged, her bright blue eyes imploring. "I'm too excited to sleep, and I know you stay up half the night anyway."

She looked so grown-up and lovely in the gown of white satin that set off her fair skin and dark hair, his aching heart eased. "Very well, little sister," he agreed, twisting one of her silky curls around his finger. "But don't even think of asking me for a glass of my brandy."

"As if I'd want such nasty stuff," she said scornfully as she bade him follow her to the library. "James says champagne is the proper drink for a lady."

"So now it's 'James,' is it?" Jack asked with mock severity. "If that young cub is bandying your name about as freely you are his, he'd better be coming to me with an offer for your hand! And it's ratafia for you, minx."

His sister accepted the glass and waited until Jack was seated beside her. "I think he will. I do like him ever so much. He speaks intelligently of important things, like Parliament and tending the land and the tenants, instead of prosing on about the cut of a coat or the latest gossip. Would you approve, were he to call on you?"

"I should send him packing with his head under his arm!" he replied, and laughed as Dorrie punched him. "Though no one could be good enough for my baby sister, if you truly care for him, poppet, I'll steel myself to let you go. But enjoy a whole Season first, eh?"

"I am enjoying it. But I do not think you are," she added, her face sobering. "You always look so—serious. So 'doing-your-duty' that sometimes I wonder what became of the darling brother who used to tease me and cheat at cards—"

"I would never have won, else, you Captain Sharp—" he interrupted, trying to deflect her.

"And put me on my first pony," she continued, undeterred. "Whose eyes were always laughing. They're not anymore, Jack. Please, don't tell me to hush! Mama said I shouldn't tax you about it, that you would tell us what was wrong in your own time, if you spoke of it at all, but I hate seeing you so—so tense and unhappy! Was it the war, Jack? Everyone says Waterloo was horrible."

He wanted to command her to heed their mother's advice, but the pleading, tear-glazed eyes Dorrie raised to him made him bite back his first, angry response.

This was Dorrie, not some inquisitive dowager looking for gossip, and she loved him as much as he loved her.

"The horrors of Waterloo aren't something I intend to share, poppet," he said at last. "But I'm not suffering from nightmares of battle."

"Then is it that woman?"

"That—" he echoed, breaking off in astonishment as he realized to whom she referred. God in heaven, gossip had grown to a fine art if tales of his stay with Belle had reached even his innocent sister. He felt the flush rising in his face, but before he could respond, Dorrie stamped her foot and shook a finger in his face.

"Don't even try to give me that rubbish about how a gently born maiden shouldn't acknowledge the existence of such a creature! Though I may have to sustain in public the tiresome pretense of knowing nothing of what transpires between men and women, I'm not a nodcock. We hadn't been in London an afternoon before Lydia Lampton and Lady Ashcroft were sitting in Mama's parlor, asking the most obnoxious questions concerning your accident and the 'lady' who had tended you during your recovery. Fishing for information, though Mama gave them none. She's told me nothing either, so I don't know whether she knows more or not. But Jack, I don't want to be shut out of something that concerns you so nearly! And if this…this Jezebel broke your heart then I should like to shoot her!"

"Such intemperance, little girl," he said, staving off a reply while he tried to determine what he ought to say. "Take care you don't scare away your proper young suitor."

He should probably turn aside her questions as best he could and send her to bed. But he hated to have her believe the distorted, inaccurate picture of Belle ton gossip would doubtless have given her.

And it was far too sweet to speak her name.

"Mama would doubtless blister my ears for discussing this with you, and if you repeat to a soul anything of what I'm about to say, I shall banish you from London before that obliging gentleman makes you his offer. But I can't have you thinking ill of Lady Belle. She's a beautiful, accomplished woman who showed the utmost kindness in nursing me after my injury. I did form an attachment, ill advised as that was. But nothing will come of it. I'm as cognizant of my duty to marry well as you are, poppet."

Dorrie was silent for a moment, apparently weighing his comments. "And what of your heart, Jack?"

What of it indeed? he wondered, all too conscious of its constant ache. "Hearts heal, Dorrie."

"On a diet of duty?" she said dubiously. "My dearest Jack, I so want you to be happy!"

"I'm sure I shall be, eventually. You're a darling to be concerned for me, but you mustn't trouble your pretty head over it. I shall come about."

She studied him, as if not believing his claim.

Which was understandable, since he scarcely believed it himself.

"I hope so. Especially now that I've found James, the notion of embracing duty for the rest of one's life seems repugnant. Will you not consider your choices again?"

"Perhaps you just need to introduce me to more of your charming friends."

She grinned. "An excellent notion! In fact, that was the other thing I wanted to talk with you about. There's a young lady only lately come to town, but so witty and intelligent, she's quickly become the best of my friends. I do so want you to meet her! We're going riding in Hyde Park tomorrow morning. You'll come, won't you?"

"You will wake early enough to ride?"

"She's country-bred like me, so the Season has yet to turn either of us into slugabeds," Dorrie replied. "Proceeding at a walk during the promenade hour is so annoying, 'tis more than worth rising early to be able to indulge in a gallop! Though I do enjoy London, I shall still be ever so glad to leave it at the Season's end."

"To go to Carrington Grove—or with your James?"

She smiled. "We shall see, won't we? You will ride with us tomorrow?"

"Yes, I will come do the pretty to your new friend."

"Excellent! Then I shall tease you no more—for now."

As his sister walked away, Jack's smile faded. Next to her youth and enthusiasm, he felt ancient—and jaded.

He hoped with all his battered soul that she never had to learn about duty and the small place the desires of one's heart played in it.

The smoldering embers in the hearth, the late hour, the warmth of the liqueur heating a path from his lips down his chest, all brought back to him their time together so vividly, he could almost feel Belle's presence.

When even the smallest details of life recalled her so strongly, how would he ever get her out of his head?

CHAPTER TWENTY-TWO

THE FOLLOWING MORNING, Belle stood at her window surveying her mist-shrouded garden in Mount Street. After a long journey, she and Mae had arrived late yesterday, Mae exclaiming with delight at each familiar street.

Just a few nights ago they'd sat with Sergeant Jackman in the firelit parlor at Bellehaven while his assistant disclosed that Mr. Harris, after attempting to entice girls at another Market Day in a town closer to London, had returned to rooms in Chelsea—and then passed the night at Mrs. Jarvis's establishment. 'Twas proof enough of the link between the recruiter and the bawd, Belle felt, that she could bring the evidence to Egremont.

She'd decided to ask Mae to accompany her back to London. Her old friend had been a cheerful presence during her exile to the country, but Belle knew how much the woman missed the theaters, inns and shops of the capital city. Telling Mae that she intended to return to Bellehaven as soon as the business with Jane was completed, she offered to let her friend stay on at the town house.

Implying she did not wish to suffer the attentions of

the gentlemen who would doubtless hound her if her presence became known, Belle had asked Mae not to tell anyone she'd returned to the city. She'd already warned Mae she would not accompany her on any outings. Only one pleasure would Belle indulge—her usual morning gallop.

At this hour, the fashionables of the ton would have just found their beds, particularly the gentlemen who made up her usual court. And given the grayness of the day, she thought, looking at the clouds of swirling mist, even should any of them chance to be abroad, in her gray habit with her bright hair concealed under a hat, she would have to practically collide with one in order to be recognized.

A short time later, she rode through the park gates. She found the cool morning air refreshing despite the lingering fog, though prudence dictated she refrain, with visibility so poor, from indulging in a gallop. Nonetheless, she was enjoying pushing her mare to a brisk trot, when the muffled sound of approaching hoofbeats reached her ears.

Deciding 'twould be wiser to turn aside and wait for them to pass, rather than risk having the unknown riders overtake her, Belle guided her horse onto a side trail.

When out of the mist, two figures riding sidesaddle emerged, the tension she'd not realized had been gripping her eased. She relaxed further when they drew close enough for her to tell, from the cut of their habits and the groom trailing behind, that the riders must be young ladies.

To be in the park so early, they must be chits in their first Season, not yet aware that 'twas the mode to sleep until noon, Belle thought with a smile. Or perhaps they, too, were country-bred and fond of a morning ride.

Then something about one of the riders caught her attention. She stiffened in the saddle, her heartbeat accelerating as the girls approached, until at last, through the thinning fog, she could discern their faces.

Heat, then cold flashed through her and for a moment she thought she might faint. Her hands clenched on the reins, her knee on the pommel as she fought to stay in the saddle.

Her instincts had been correct. The slender, chestnut-haired girl riding nearest her had to be Kitty.

The sister she'd not seen in almost seven years.

The sister who believed Belle dead.

Her pulse pounding at her temples, she silently backed her mount away. Though 'twas nearly impossible Kitty might recognize her, Belle didn't wish to take any chances.

Straining to see as the two figures neared the crossroad, Belle drank in the sight of her sister's face.

Kitty had been not quite twelve, a sweet and lively girl bidding fair to become a lovely woman the last time Belle had seen her. Though the habit revealed little of her sister's figure, Belle had a clear enough view of her face to realize that promise had been fulfilled.

Fortunately, Kitty's oval face and even features were pretty rather than stunning, her eyes a paler blue than Belle's, her hair their mother's chestnut rather than their father's gold. Armed with the dowry Belle had carefully accumulated, her loveliness would attract respectable offers, yet she was not so conspicuously beautiful as to draw to herself the attention—or inspire the lust—of the more bored and venal of the ton.

If Kitty could find a fine man to marry, protect and cherish her, Belle thought, an ache in her throat, all her bitter years of sacrifice would be worth the cost.

All too soon this unexpected, unrepeatable glimpse into her sister's life came to an end. The girls passed her hiding spot and continued on without a backward glance.

She'd almost quelled the fluttering of her heart when she heard another horse approaching, followed a second later by a female voice calling, "Hurry up, Jack! You've fallen too far behind."

Though, concealed in the misty shadows, she had an imperfect view of the main trail, still Belle had no difficulty recognizing the profile or the upright, military bearing of the rider just coming into sight.

A profile moonlight had outlined against her pillows as he slept. A broad-shouldered figure who had sheltered her within his arms as he drove her though the rain.

But why was Captain Jack Carrington riding in the park with Belle's sister?

She sat for a moment, stunned, before panic sent her stomach plunging. Not until he'd passed the side trail, his attention fixed on the riders ahead of him, the steady clip-clop of his horse's hooves unfaltering, did her stomach begin to settle.

Concentrating on drawing in even, steady breaths, Belle waited for the group to ride on. Finally judging it safe, she urged her mount back to the main trail.

As she left the side path, the feeble sun, struggling to penetrate the clouds and fog, made a glowing curtain of the swirling mist, like smoke illumed by lamplight.

How fitting an end to this clandestine glimpse of her sister, Belle thought as she kicked her mare to a trot. Shadow and sunlight, mist and fog, deception and heartache.

HEARING UNEXPECTED hoofbeats behind them, Jack whirled in the saddle. After watching the potential threat resolve itself into a lady on a sidesaddle, he was chuckling over the enduring strength of his soldier's protective instincts nearly a year after his last battle, when a shaft of sunlight briefly illumed the rider. A woman whose tall figure and graceful carriage looked strikingly familiar.

His hands locked on the reins and the breath caught in his throat. But after that one glimpse, mist once more closed over the retreating figure, which was soon lost in the distance.

For an instant he almost succumbed to the impulse to gallop after her. But 'twas nearly impossible the gray-garbed horsewoman could have been Lady Belle. He simply must stop seeing her in every tall woman he passed, every arrangement of golden curls that caught his eye across a crowded street or theater lobby.

Sighing, he shook his head. Lady Belle still haunted him so much that when he first met Dorrie's friend Catherine this morning, some indefinable something about her had reminded him of Belle. And now he was once again hallucinating about seeing the lady herself. He really must do something to put an end to this obsession, he thought as he spurred his mount to catch up with his sister.

Dorrie greeted his return with a smile. "Catherine and I have just decided this ride has been so delightful, we shall play truant the rest of the day. Could we take a picnic and go visit Hampton Court this afternoon?"

Though his sister's words were light, the quick frown she sent him conveyed her annoyance that, with an unchivalrous lack of attention, he'd lagged behind. "If you wish," he replied placatingly. "But do you really want to miss being home when your *friends* call?"

She wrinkled her nose at him. "If you are referring to James, he has to accompany his father on some matter of business today. I don't relish staying at home, knowing he won't be calling. Especially since that annoying Lady Ashcroft would probably take advantage of his absence to tease me about not having yet brought my 'highly eligible suitor' up to scratch."

"I don't mean to be uncivil," Catherine said, "but 'tis just that her own daughter is so shy and plain, you quite cast her in the shade."

"See, Jack? You must rescue me from Lady Ashcroft's malice. Do say you'll take us to Hampton Court, please! Besides, I'd like my best friend to have a better chance to become acquainted with my best brother."

A warning pinged in Jack's head. He'd agreed to ride with Dorrie this morning since, as restless as he'd been since returning to London, he could use the distraction. And he appreciated the frustration his sister, a skilled equestrienne, felt at the decorous pace dictated by the crush of fashionables during promenade hour. He'd been quite willing to include her new bosom-bow in their plans.

Unless Dorrie had taken a bit too seriously his casual comment that she find him an attractive lady to court.

Not amenable even to her well-intentioned matchmaking, Jack returned a quick frown, to which Dorrie replied by darting her tongue out at him. The gesture was so typical of the scamp he remembered growing up that his ill humor evaporated.

Very well, he'd entertain his sister and her new friend with a picnic to Hampton Court.

But after he deposited them back in London, just to be certain, he'd pay a call at Belle's town house.

THE JOURNEY BY WATER up the Thames, the girls' delight at exploring the castle and maze and the excellent repast their cook had prepared, along with finding Miss Catherine Germayne to be as intelligent and amusing as Dorrie had claimed, should have made the afternoon one of unalloyed enjoyment.

Except that Jack was beginning to wonder at his sanity, for as he watched the girls talk and laugh and explore, he couldn't seem to stop finding in Miss Germayne's profile, the timbre of her voice, the way she carried herself, echoes of Lady Belle. Telling himself if he got to know the young lady better, he would be able to see her for herself and banish the nonsensical illusion that she resembled a famous courtesan, he decided on the journey back to engage her in conversation.

The camaraderie of the afternoon having allayed his fears that either Dorrie or her friend were bent on encouraging a match between them, he felt comfortable venturing remarks of a more personal nature than the rather general comments to which he'd confined himself thus far.

So, after they'd settled in the boat, Jack said, "You ride very well, Miss Germayne. You must have had an excellent horseman as your instructor."

"Thank you, Captain, and I did—my uncle Thaddeus. Although he's not really my uncle, but rather a very distant cousin I came to live with after my parents died."

At that remark, Jack's interest rocketed from casual to acute. Though he told himself it was absurd even to imagine there might be a link between Catherine Germayne, making her debut under the patronage of the respected society matron Lady Abrams, and the courtesan Lady Belle, he had difficulty keeping the urgency out of his voice as he continued, "My condolences on such a grievous loss. Did your brothers and sisters go live with your cousin also?"

She shook her head, sadness in her eyes. "No. My only sibling, my older sister, died shortly after Mama."

"How awful!" Dorrie exclaimed. "You must have felt so alone!"

"Terribly. And guilty, too. You see, we were traveling from our old home to Uncle Thaddeus's when Mama fell ill. She and Constance insisted that I continue on with our abigail, so as not to be exposed to the infection, while Constance stayed behind to nurse Mama. But after we left, she took sick, too. Snow delayed our journey for several days, and by the time we reached Uncle Thaddeus and he could return to the inn, they...they were both dead."

While he and Dorrie made sympathetic murmurs, Miss Germayne shook her head. "I've always wondered, if I had stayed to help, whether they might have survived."

"You only did what your mama and sister asked of you—perhaps saving your own life in the bargain," Dorrie protested. "'Tis very unlikely your presence could have altered the course of their illness."

"I'm sorry, I should not have responded to your kind inquiry with such a tale of woe," Catherine said to Jack.

"Don't be a goose!" Dorrie replied fondly, squeezing the girl's hand. "Friends rely on their friends, do they not, Jack? We are honored to be in your confidence."

"Thank you," Miss Germayne replied, giving Jack a shy smile. "Though Uncle Thaddeus and Aunt Mary were as kind as anyone could wish, I missed my own family dreadfully. It...it is good to be able to speak of them again."

Since politeness would have compelled Jack to refrain from further questioning, he was delighted to be offered this excuse to continue. "How old were you then?"

"Ten, when Papa died, the winter of 1808. Although we did not get word of it until the following spring. He'd gone to India, you see, to earn his fortune, for as a younger son of a younger son, he had no land to inherit."

It was his unrealized dream to earn the fortune that would allow him to purchase an estate like this. The echo of Belle's words raised the hair at the back of his neck.

Trying to keep his voice even despite a rising excitement, he said, "And your sister?"

"Constance was three years older, so she would have been thirteen when Papa died…and just fourteen when she…left us. The sweetest and best of sisters as well as the most beautiful, it was truly a tragedy to lose her."

He died when I was thirteen.

While Jack struggled to draw breath, Dorrie continued, "Lovelier than you? I find that hard to believe!"

"Oh, much prettier. While I hope to be a modest success, she would have truly been a Diamond, with her hair the color of spun gold and her eyes so deep a blue." Miss Germayne chuckled. "How we could have annoyed Lady Ashcroft, were Constance making her debut with us!"

Jack felt dizzy, a fact for which the motion of the river craft was in no way responsible. Hair like spun gold… eyes of deep blue… Surely there could not be so incredible a coincidence.

Yet Miss Germayne claimed her sister had died. And Belle had told him she had no near relations, which certainly did not match Miss Germayne's depiction of the kind cousin who had taken her in, then battled through winter storms to try to aid his afflicted relatives.

Besides, Belle had told him there was no money after her father's death, and he knew from Dorrie that her new friend possessed a respectable dowry. Which might, of course, have been provided by the cousin.

Unfortunately, good breeding absolutely forbade Jack to ask her about that.

He desperately wanted to know more, so he could dismiss as odd coincidence the parallels between Belle and Miss Germayne—or confirm them. But how to find out?

Then an idea occurred. "What town did you stop in when your mama became ill?"

"Eastwold. I thought when we first arrived what a lovely little village it was. Now it is forever emblazoned in my memory as a place of sorrow."

"Do you recall at which inn you stayed?" Jack asked, ignoring the questioning look Dorrie shot him.

"I don't recall. 'Twas almost seven years ago."

"What was on the sign in front?" he persisted.

Miss Germayne's eyes lit. "Now that, I do remember! A rooster within a golden crown."

"The Cock and Crown, probably. Is it not remarkable how well we recall small details long after larger events have faded?" he observed, hoping to deflect his sister's curiosity about his unusually insistent questioning. "From Yorkshire to Eastwold was quite a journey in winter."

"Indeed it was," Dorrie agreed, her frown smoothing. "Your uncle Thaddeus sounds like a wonderful man, to have traveled so far to try to rescue them."

"Oh, he is! He and Aunt Mary had no children, and treated me from the first as if I were their own daughter. Not that I wasn't desperately lonely at first, but I soon grew to love them and my new surroundings. Although I've never stopped missing my family, of course."

"Of course," Dorrie echoed. "Your aunt and uncle were not able to come to London this Season, you told me?"

"Regrettably, Aunt Mary's health has declined, and she so dreaded the long, jolting journey by carriage that I did not wish to beg her to come. Especially as Lady Abrams, a neighbor and good friend, invited me to accompany her. She made a very good match for her own daughter two Seasons ago and told me she relished the task of doing the same for me. Though I suspect it will challenge all her skill!"

"I doubt that," Dorrie countered. "For you are accomplished as well as lovely. Jack, you should hear her play the pianoforte. She is quite brilliant! I am certain you shall capture the affections of a most eligible parti."

The soft notes of a Mozart concerto drifted out of memory, tightening Jack's chest.

"No, 'tis you, my future viscountess," Miss Germayne replied, "who are about to make the brilliant match. One has only to see the expression on Lord Winston's face when he gazes at you to know you have entirely captured his heart. Oh!" she exclaimed, her eyes widening, "Perhaps *you* are the 'business' he and his father are discussing today!"

Though Dorrie, blushing herself now, exclaimed in surprise, Jack thought her friend might well have the right of it. Leaving the girls to an animated discussion of when and how Dorrie's James might tender his proposal, Jack turned his attention to examining what he'd just learned.

If there *were* some connection between Miss Germayne and Lady Belle, the link joining them must have been broken—or irrevocably altered—at the inn where Miss Germayne's mama died.

Where, Jack was more than half convinced, her sister had not. But there was only one way to know for sure.

As soon as he could make the arrangements, Jack meant to visit the Cock and Crown.

CHAPTER TWENTY-THREE

LATER THAT AFTERNOON, Belle restlessly paced her chamber, awaiting the arrival of Lord Egremont. To the note she'd dispatched when they arrived, asking that he wait upon her at his earliest convenience, he'd returned a message promising to call today.

Important as the information was that she wished to convey, she was finding it impossible to keep her mind from returning to the shocking sight of her sister—riding in Jack Carrington's company.

The other young lady might have been Jack's sister, though Belle had been so wholly focused on Kitty she could not now recall if there'd been some familial resemblance. Happy as she was at this evidence that her sister was mingling with the best of society, she had to admit that, after the panic of almost meeting Jack faded, her next reaction had been an ignoble and intense jealousy.

It was one thing to wish for Captain Carrington to discover a pretty, charming young lady to make his wife. Yet another to think it might be her own sister who ended up wedding the man Belle might as well admit she loved.

Was this to be fate's final, ultimate jest?

Still, she had persevered all these years to provide her

sister precisely this chance to take her place in the ton and secure her future. And though no man could ever be completely trusted, Jack Carrington was the most worthy Belle had yet encountered. If he and her sister should develop a mutual affection, she should be glad for them.

She supposed she had always clung to the hope that someday, when Kitty was safe and settled, Belle might try contacting her. Though she'd risk discovering that her sister, after learning what Belle had become, had no desire to acknowledge the connection between them.

But it would be a risk well worth the taking as long as a chance remained that Kitty still harbored for her a glimmer of the same deep affection she bore her sister.

Belle might become part of a family again.

Such an eventuality would be impossible, however, should Kitty contract an alliance with Jack Carrington.

It would be of some comfort to know the two people she cared most for in the world had found happiness together.

Lonely as that comfort might be.

A knock sounded at the door. Shaking off her increasingly painful thoughts, she bade the caller enter.

Jem bounced in and gave her his jagged-toothed smile. "Watson says there's a gent waiting below to see you."

"Thank you, Jem. Tell him I'll be down directly."

"No need to hurry—it ain't the captain, though I thought I seen him by the mews."

Longing and consternation flooded her. "When?"

"'Bout long enough ago for a cat to wash her ear. I thought sure it must be him calling, but I flashed my peepers into the parlor and 'twas just some old gent in a frock coat," Jem noted. "Mayhap he'll call later."

"You were probably mistaken about seeing him," she replied, as much for her own sake as for his. "Now that he has recovered, he doubtless has pressing business."

"Man ought not to forgit his friends," the boy said. "Didn't we keep him body and soul for nigh on a month?"

"The captain…occupies a different place in the world."

"Well, he mighta been a nob born, but he didn't act the nob whiles he was here," Jem countered stubbornly. "I'll be right disappointed if he don't come calling. I'll tell the other gent you be coming down."

Jack, here? Belle couldn't let herself consider the possibility, alarmed by the wild hope the mere thought of it sent soaring within her.

Belle shook her head as Jem walked out. He'd been severely let down when they'd gone to Bellehaven, leaving him in London to continue his training and depriving him of the company of the soldier he so admired. Watson reported he'd about driven poor Lawton to distraction with his antics. Since she returned, he'd shadowed Belle as she went through her daily activities.

Out of gratitude for her kindness—or because he hoped to inveigle his way into any visit his idol might pay her?

Though Jem was likely to be disappointed. Belle could think of few things less likely, after their bitter parting, than Jack Carrington voluntarily calling on her.

And 'twas better that way, no matter how much it hurt. Or so she told herself as she tried to focus on the information she was to deliver to Egremont.

"MON ANGE," *Egremont said as she entered the parlor. "London has been a wasteland without you."*

She stiffened slightly, recalling what she'd lately learned of his true feelings toward her, but he saluted her hand with quite proper brevity and released it. Thank heavens, she thought, relaxing, that he'd meant his vow to treat her only with friendship. Here, too, was a man who had proved himself faithful and stalwart.

"With all London's amusements?" she parried, smiling.

"Amusements lose their power without an agreeable companion to share them. But your note surprised me. I thought you intended to remain longer in the country."

"I did," she replied, gesturing him to a chair. "But there were developments which I felt merited your immediate attention."

She proceeded to tell him everything that had occurred since she'd left London. Except for a muttered curse when she described the attack on them outside the City, he listened without interruption.

"You've done excellent work," Egremont said as he looked over the statements she'd collected from Sergeant Jackman, his associates and several of the girls whom the recruiter had harangued. "Shall I ask the Home Office to find you a position in their organization?"

"I shall have my reward if someone there believes the

situation serious enough to pursue. Though Jackman was willing, I did not wish him to approach Mr. Harris, thinking it would be better to let your contacts handle that. They will take action now, don't you think?"

Egremont nodded. "The testimony of a single young girl of…shall we say, limited credibility, might be discounted, but these—" he indicated the statements she'd handed him "—will not. There will be an inquiry."

Relief flooded Belle. "That's all I hoped for—and that they act swiftly, before any more girls are harmed."

His face thoughtful, Egremont continued, "If this scheme is as far-reaching as it appears, there must be considerable capital in it. After you left, I did a bit of investigating myself. A number of the men who patronize Mrs. Jarvis are quite wealthy, some of them highly placed. The inquiry will have to proceed…delicately."

"To avoid embarrassing certain noblemen of means?"

Egremont raised an eyebrow. "You wound me, *mon ange*. Surely you know that if there is wrongdoing afoot, I shall see it revealed, however noble the persons involved."

Chagrined, for she knew Egremont had never indulged in any of the excesses practiced by some of his peers, she murmured, "Forgive me."

He gave her a wry smile. "You have reason enough to doubt the motives of men, I suppose. But what I meant was, if this enterprise is as profitable as it is extensive, the men funding it would likely take strong measures to prevent its discovery. As the investigation goes forward, it might become dangerous if someone were to trace any of the responsibility for it back to Jane—or you. We shall have to move carefully to avoid that."

Belle nodded. "Although Sergeant Jackman felt the risks now are probably small, I didn't wish to take chances either. I've had him quietly remove Jane from Bellehaven. My household there believes she accompanied me; Mae and Watson think she stayed behind. In actuality, Jackman took her to stay with his family near Brighton. With," Belle added with a smile, "a trunk of my gowns to alter to keep her occupied until the investigation is concluded."

"Good. If for any reason she must leave Brighton, I'll see her safely settled on one of my properties."

"Thank you! That is most kind."

Frowning, Egremont pressed Belle's hand. "That attack on you troubles me. I would offer to settle *you* on one of my properties for safekeeping, if I thought you'd accept."

"Which you know I cannot, much as I appreciate the offer." Though Belle trusted Egremont's honorable intentions, she did not want to enter into any arrangement, however innocent, which might be misunderstood by that gentleman's wife. "Two of the sergeant's assistants are still here in London. Their continued presence in my house shall ward off any trouble."

"'Tis a good first step, but I'd as lief you have them accompany you whenever you go about the City. And no solitary morning rides," he added.

Her mind immediately recalled the image of Jack

trotting by in the fog, oblivious to her presence. Sorrow squeezed her chest and she had to struggle to keep her expression neutral and the tears at bay.

"Now that I've conveyed to you what I know, I don't mean to tarry in London. You will send me word of how the investigation proceeds?"

"Of course. Although I should feel more comfortable if you would remain for a time in the City, where I can watch after your safety. At least until I know where the investigation might lead. Will you consider it?"

"I will," she agreed. Was it gratitude for his concern, or the gnawing desire to catch another glimpse of Kitty—or Jack—that led her to acquiesce so quickly? "I'll not be going out, though."

"Ah, yes. You don't wish to have Rupert or the rest of his rabble discover you've returned. I do hope you'll allow me to call on you—discreetly, of course."

"Of course. I am always glad of your company."

"I am very glad to hear it," he replied. "Now, what else is troubling you, *mon ange?*"

Surprised, Belle shot a glance back at Egremont, to find in his eyes a sympathetic—and uncomfortably perceptive—concern. She felt her face coloring.

"The captain, I suppose." Egremont sighed. "Would that I had the right to be jealous. Should I be happy for you, my dear, or sad?"

She didn't pretend to misunderstand. "Happy and sad," she said after considering the question.

"You know I would do anything to spare you pain. If I can help in any way, call on me."

Belle felt the burn of tears beneath her eyelids. "You are too kind, but there is…nothing."

While she struggled to regain the self-control thoughts of Jack seemed to jeopardize so easily, Egremont said, "And Mae? Can she keep your presence a secret?"

Grateful he'd moved the conversation to a less distressing topic, Belle smiled wryly. "She did promise not to breathe a word of it, but I doubt she can remain silent long. She hasn't the least talent for deception."

"Yes, but she possesses so kind a heart, one cannot hold her indiscretion against her. Since in that case, your sojourn here may be briefer than I'd like, will you dine with me tonight?"

She angled a glance at him. "I cannot believe in doing so that you would not be disappointing several hostesses to whom you are already promised."

He shrugged. "London will be available to me all Season. As I recall, I was two games ahead at whist?"

Her evenings had seemed particularly long and empty since Jack went away. Egremont's intelligent, witty conversation and his flattering predilection for her company were a balm her troubled soul found hard to resist.

"Very well. But if the hostesses you disappoint give you the cut direct the next time you encounter them, I refuse to accept any of the blame!"

TWO DAYS LATER, after riding at the most grueling pace he'd sustained since on one of Wellington's forced marches, Jack at last entered the village of Eastwold. Set upon a small rise and backed by a pretty wood, with its thatch-roofed, half-timbered dwellings he found it as charming as Miss Germayne had reported.

The Cock and Crown was housed in one of the larger of such buildings, adjacent to the main road. He decided to bespeak a room and dinner so that he might observe the inn, its owners and its clientele at his leisure.

After lifting a few tankards of home-brewed with the local farmers, he learned that the innkeepers had owned the establishment for the last twenty years. Surely they would remember an event as singular as having two guests die under their roof—though they might be loath to speak of it. As soon as a suitable opening arose, Jack would inquire.

Unfortunately, the taproom was bustling all evening, keeping the innkeeper too busy for Jack to engage him in conversation. Not until he took his breakfast in the relatively deserted dining room the next morning did Jack judge the time propitious to question the man.

Laying some coins on the table, he said, "I'll be on my way shortly. I do thank you for your hospitality. Your establishment came highly recommended, and I'm happy to find the reputation well deserved."

The innkeeper straightened, preening a little. "Glad to hear it, m'lord. We have a fine snug place here, if I do say so, and my wife be the best cook in two counties."

"Indeed she is," Jack said, winking at the lady in question, who blushed as she cleared his table.

"Who was it recommended us?" the innkeeper said.

"A friend of my sister's. The story my sister passed on to me was unusual enough that I've always remembered the name, vowing I should stop here if I ever passed this way."

"Gratified you thought of us, m'lord, and hope you'll pass along the good word to your friends."

Jack added a few extra coins to the stack. "My sister said her friend's mother fell ill and they took shelter here, but despite the efforts of everyone involved, the mother died. This happened, oh, seven or so years ago."

The innkeeper exchanged an uneasy glance with his wife. "Aye, m'lord, though my recollections are a bit hazy after so long. Sorry we was, though it weren't none of our fault."

"I'm sure it wasn't," Jack agreed, watching the innkeeper visibly relax. "My sister said she remarked how kind and helpful you and your wife had been."

"I'm gratified she thought so, for a big storm having blown up, we was full of guests right up to the rafters!"

"I seem to recall the older sister staying behind to nurse her mother," Jack continued, trying to keep his voice light, despite the excitement pulsing in his veins. "But I do not perfectly recall the rest. Did she do so?"

The innkeeper darted a glance at his wife, then cleared his throat. "Aye, she did—and died, too. A perfect shame it was, she being so young and pretty."

That flat avowal struck a blow through the fragile web of speculations Jack had painstakingly constructed. But perhaps the man was mistaken. He'd admitted his inn was full and his recollections hazy.

"Are you quite sure? I rather thought that a party of friends happened by and bore the sister off with them."

"Don't I wish they had," the innkeeper said. "But sorry as I am to say it, m'lord, the girl died but a few days after her mother. They's buried in the churchyard just outside town, if you'd like to pay your respects."

Disappointment scoured him. A man's memory might be faulty, but there could be no disputing with a tombstone. "Perhaps I will."

As much as he didn't want to believe the innkeeper, when Jack made his way to the cemetery, the evidence seemed incontrovertible. The graves sat side by side, each marked with a pretty, carved stone tablet. *Constance Germayne, departed this earth in the fourteenth year of her life...*

So it was coincidence after all, Jack thought, the crushing of his hopes making his steps drag as he returned to the inn. What a fool he was, chasing after improbable rainbows, trying to create an identity for Belle that might enable him, without abandoning the duty he owed his family, to pursue the woman he loved.

As he entered the now-deserted taproom, the innkeeper's wife peeped out from the kitchen. When he waved a goodbye, she motioned him to wait, then rapidly crossed the room.

After glancing over her shoulder as if to confirm they were alone, she said in a low voice, "My husband's a good man who doesn't want no trouble with anyone. Still, I weren't never happy about what happened with that poor girl. Something in your eyes made me think you was more interested than you tried to let on."

"What do you know?" Jack asked, pulling out a coin.

"I don't want your money, m'lord. Did you come on behalf of her family?"

"Yes."

"Then let me tell you what really happened."

Two MORNINGS LATER, Belle sipped her chocolate, debating whether or not she would ride. Thus far, each morning she'd succumbed to the temptation, though she had not, since that first day, had a glimpse of either her sister or Jack.

But this morning, except for the sooty haze that always wrapped about London's rooftops like a gauzy shawl, it appeared the day would be clear. Sunny weather would make everything in the park brighter and more visible.

Though Kitty, not expecting to see Belle, might happen upon her from a very short distance and not recognize her, the same could not be said for Captain Carrington. Belle had little doubt he would be able to discern her identity a considerable ways off, as she could his.

She wasn't sure whether it would be sweet torture or the worst of folly to deliberately chance meeting him.

She was still mulling over the question when her door burst open and Jem erupted into the room.

"He's here! Down in the parlor right this minute! Didn't

I tell you he'd call! C'mon, my lady," Jem admonished as she sat there, shocked into immobility. "Git yer togs on. The Captain be waiting for you!"

CHAPTER TWENTY-FOUR

DESPITE JEM'S EUPHORIC welcome, Jack found himself nervously pacing Belle's parlor while his enthusiastic emissary went to fetch his mistress. Would she receive him? Or send Jem back with a message that they had nothing further to say to each other?

He was formulating the outlines of a counterattack, should the latter prove true, when the parlor door opened. Even before he turned toward it, he sensed her presence.

In the next instant, the sight of her filled his eyes, the beauty and dearness of her washing over him with the force of a Channel tide breaking onto a Dover beach. For a few seconds he was beyond speech, content to breathe in the air that carried her distinctive lavender scent.

She stood watching him, her calm eyes and expressionless face giving him no clue to her feelings. Then, belatedly remembering his manners, he swept her a bow. "Lady Belle, 'tis a pleasure to see you again."

"Captain Carrington," she said, extending her hand and allowing him, to his delight, to kiss her fingers. He had to struggle to make himself let them go.

She must not hate him completely if she'd agreed to

receive him, but he couldn't bear to begin without discovering exactly where he stood with her.

"I wasn't sure you would come down. Does this mean you've considered forgiving me?"

A slight smile curving her lips, she motioned him to a chair. "It would be a great deal easier to believe you a villain, but after examining events in a calmer frame of mind, I found there was nothing to forgive. Lord Rupert had every reason to twist the truth. And…and you were correct. To believe that you deceived me, that what we shared was only a sham, would be a sin against both your honor and my heart. I expect I owe *you* an apology."

As those sweet words filled his ears, relief and gladness welled up from deep within him. 'Twas better, far better than he'd dared hope. He wanted to fall to his knees and beg for her hand that very moment. Reining in that desire, he replied, "Having you believe me is enough."

"That what we had was true and honest does not change the fact that our…interlude had to end. Nor can it be repeated, as you must realize. So—why did you come?"

She might believe him, but she still meant to send him away. Begging all the angels of heaven to lend him their most persuasive words, he said, "To tell you a story. About two sisters and their mother, forced after the death of the father to give up their home and travel to the distant cousins who promised to take them in."

Though her calm expression did not change, he heard her quick intake of breath, saw her hands clench the fabric of her skirts. "Should I go on?" he asked.

She hesitated, not meeting his eyes. "If you must."

"During the trip, the mother fell gravely ill. The elder sister sent the younger one to the cousins' house with their maid and remained to tend her mother, who died a week later, leaving her virtually penniless and alone—except for a gentleman who had broken his journey at the inn to escape a winter storm."

He paused, but Belle said nothing. Her gaze fixed on the window, she sat perfectly still—except for the thumbs rhythmically stroking the muslin of her skirts.

"Helpful throughout the mother's illness," Jack continued, "this gentleman insisted on paying the girl's expenses at the inn and the costs of the mother's burial. He then convinced her that it would be better for her to accompany him home and wait there while he contacted her family and requested that someone come fetch her."

He paused again, but still Belle remained silent. Finally he said softly, "How long was it after Bellingham took you from the inn before you realized he had no intention of restoring you to your family?"

For a few heartbeats longer, Belle sat as immobile as the Three Graces carved into the marble of the mantel. Then she closed her eyes, a single tear slipping down her cheek.

Unable to stand it any longer, Jack went to her and drew her into his arms.

He held her while her shoulders shook with silent sobs, his heart pierced by anguish at her grief and fury for the vile deception that had been perpetrated upon her. Finally she took a shuddering breath and pushed away.

"I should not have gone with him, I suppose. But he

seemed so sincere, and truly I was destitute. I'd spoken to the landlord about serving in the taproom, but...but the way the men looked at me after Mama died made me uneasy."

She knuckled the last of the tears from her eyes. "Bellingham did contact my cousins. They told him that, having lived with him at his hunting box for several weeks by then without a chaperon, my reputation was ruined. As I had disgraced my name, they...they no longer wanted me. I was dead to them, and they would tell my sister I'd succumbed to the same illness that took Mama. So I stayed with Bellingham because I had no place else to go."

She exhaled a gusty breath. "Would you fetch me a glass of wine, please?"

"Of course." Jack went to the side table, frowning as he poured them each a glass. The innkeeper's wife told him a gentleman had come back later to commission a tombstone for Belle's mother, offering a hefty extra sum if they would set one up nearby with the daughter's name. The man had left another sack of coins with instructions to tell anyone who might inquire that both women had died.

He'd believed that gentleman to be Bellingham. But might it have been Belle's cousin instead? Before he mentioned anything to her, he would need to find out.

After taking a sip, Belle said, "I suppose I might as well tell you the rest. After I discovered that my...my family no longer wanted me, I begged Bellingham to let me go into service. He refused, saying that a girl as lovely as I, unprotected by family and friends, would soon be preyed upon by some lecherous man, and this his conscience simply couldn't allow. Remembering the way the men had looked at me at the inn, I believed him."

"Conveniently for Bellingham," Jack said, though he had to acknowledge the truth of her protector's warning.

"He told me some other solution would present itself. Meanwhile, his attentions became more and more marked, until one day he declared he had fallen in love with me the moment he saw me at the inn. Since he was already married, he could not offer me his name, but I would make him the happiest man on earth if I would consent to become his...paramour."

Belle took another sip, her eyes once more focused on the far distance. "I resisted, of course, begging him to let me serve his household in some other fashion. But he said his wife, who detested him, would eventually hear of it and seize the first opportunity to get rid of me behind his back. Every day he swore his love anew, vowing to cherish and protect me until the end of his days, if I would just grant his most fervent desire. As time passed, he began saying that, unless I came under his protection, there would be no place for me in his house and he would be forced to send me away. Finally, in despair at losing my family and rationalizing that if Bellingham loved me, it would be less a sin, I...I agreed."

"What else could you have done?" Jack asked.

She raised haunted eyes to him. "Something. Anything. For a time, I tried to convince myself that I'd come to love him, too—perhaps to justify to myself complying with all he taught me to do to serve his pleasure. Until one night, he used me so publicly, so shamefully, that I could no longer blind myself to the fact that he cared only for the lust I could satisfy."

"At Vauxhall," Jack said.

Her gaze sharpened. "So you know of it, too?" When he nodded, she gave a bitter laugh. "I ran away that night. Mae happened by me at the river, about to cast myself in, and persuaded me to come with her. Bellingham didn't locate me until several days later. Claiming he'd been too foxed to realize what he was doing, he begged my forgiveness, said no one but the handful of witnesses would ever learn what had happened that night. Promised he would never do such a thing again."

"And you believed him?"

"No. I suppose I'd known from the first that his pretty words were a lie, but couldn't bring myself to face the truth. Vauxhall forced me to confront what I'd become. A whore—just a whore, no better than the harlots plying the Covent Garden street corners. I hated us both for it."

"Yet you went back to him. Because by then, you truly had no other choice?"

"So Mae tried to tell me, in addition to urging me to take advantage of his penitence to extract the maximum benefit in gold and jewels. But I'd have thrown it all in his face—except that he found another, better way to force my compliance. In my darling, innocent sister."

"How could he affect her life?" Jack demanded.

"My cousins had accepted her on sufferance, he said, intending to make her their unpaid drab. To prevent that, he'd been sending them money—blood money for having seduced me, I suppose—to guarantee she would be treated as a daughter of the house. He threatened to cut off funding her if I did not return and resume our…relationship."

So Bellingham *had* used a child to control her—just not his own, though that didn't much mitigate the infamy of the act. Not until his first rush of rage faded did it occur to Jack that this description of her sister's position in her cousins' house did not match what Catherine Germayne had told him of her uncle Thaddeus and aunt Mary.

Or had the arms with which they'd welcomed her been eased open by a judicious application of Bellingham's coin? After all, her relations had recently managed to fob off the inconvenience and expense of presenting her onto an obliging neighbor.

'Twas another mystery he must solve before discussing the matter with Belle.

"Once again, you were forced to remain," he summed up.

"Yes. Though this time, I made demands of my own. I promised myself I would connive until I accumulated wealth enough to support Kitty myself, and then I would leave him and never look back."

"But Bellingham made sure that never happened?"

"Not exactly. A year ago, my solicitor advised me my financial reserves were now sufficient for me to maintain both myself and Kitty. When Bellingham realized he could no longer use her to hold me, he threatened to shoot himself if I left. After I laughed in his face, he seized a pistol, though his valet deflected the shot so it merely grazed his shoulder."

"Good Lord!" Jack exclaimed. Was the man mad? Or had he become so obsessed by Belle he could not contemplate living without her? Despite his contempt for Bellingham, Jack couldn't help feeling a reluctant sympathy.

"Whether he would truly have killed himself," Belle continued, "I was never sure. If he did, though, I would be implicated, and for Kitty's sake, I couldn't risk that. But from that moment, I forbade him to touch me."

"And he agreed?"

Belle shrugged. "I gave him no choice. I hoped he would quickly tire of the arrangement and set about replacing me. Instead, it seemed to make him even more anxious to keep me under his control. In any event, he scarcely allowed me out of his sight. May heaven forgive the blasphemy, but his death was a blessed relief. After almost seven years, I was at last free. And Kitty, having grown into the young woman I'd prayed she'd become, is now in London, taking her rightful place in the world. She is lovely, isn't she?"

Jack started. "Why do you ask me?"

Belle smiled, her expression this time wistful. "I saw you riding with her in the park."

"I thought 'twas you I'd glimpsed in the fog! But I'd been missing you so, I told myself I'd only imagined it.

Only imagined the resemblances I saw in the face of Catherine Germayne."

"So you do know her."

"She seems to have become my sister's best friend. As I learned more about her, the similarities in your appearance and mannerisms—there are many, you know—combined with the parallels between what she relayed about her life and the bits and pieces you had told me, convinced me there must be a link. So I rode to the inn to find out."

Belle's eyes widened. "You will not expose the connection, surely! 'Twould ruin—"

"No, I shall say nothing unless—until—you wish it."

"Thank you. I hope one day to be able to reveal myself to her, though 'tis unlikely she will wish to acknowledge me. You have spoken with her at length?"

"Yes. I've accompanied her and my sister, Dorrie, on several excursions."

"Oh, do tell me about her! What she speaks about, her interests and her accomplishments. Please!"

Though Jack was much more interested in discussing what the knowledge he'd pieced together and Belle had just confirmed meant for the two of them, he was not proof against the longing in her eyes. Having finally penetrated the mystery that had driven him practically from the moment he'd met her, he could wait a bit longer. Until he'd offered her the few observations he'd garnered and that she so clearly craved to hear about the sister she'd sacrificed so much to protect.

"She's an excellent horsewoman. Soft of voice, keen of

mind, and witty—much like you. An excellent performer on the pianoforte, too, my sister says."

"Her dowry is handsome, as I have reason to know." Belle lowered her eyes, her tone diffident. "She will make some fortunate gentleman an excellent wife, will she not?"

It took him but an instant to catch the implication. "So she shall. Some *other* gentleman, Belle. There is only one woman I wish to marry, and it is not your sister, pretty and accomplished though she be."

Her chin jerked up, her eyes searching his. "You cannot mean…"

"'Tis exactly what I mean. When I left you at Bellehaven, I'd resigned myself to do what duty and my intention, before I met you, indicated—to look for a well-bred, intelligent, compatible lady to make my wife. Over the past weeks, I have met dozens who fit that description. But none who warms my heart like you do or—" he paused, brushing his finger over her lips, that simple action sending a shudder through her frame and his "—who awakens my senses simply by walking into a room. No other lady inspires me with the desire to swing her in circles or denude the landscape of wildflowers to make her a bouquet. I love you, Belle. *You* are the only well-bred, intelligent, compatible lady I want." He pushed off the sofa to go down on one knee before her. "Would you do me the honor of becoming my wife?"

She stared at him, her eyes wide. "You are serious."

"I've never been more serious in my life."

"But…but you can't have considered! 'Twould be disastrous—"

He put a finger to her lips. "I have considered. The lady I love at my side, or a marriage of convenience to a woman to whom I could never pledge more than respect. My happiness versus the superficiality of social acceptance."

"Do not despise what has always been yours."

"I don't discount it—but neither do I prize it above all else. Once what happened to you becomes known, you may find that social acceptance is not beyond the realm of possibility for you, either. But whether that proves true or not, I'm no more a creature of London than you, Belle. I mean to live at Carrington Grove. We could be happy there. Please, say you will let us try."

"And are you willing to gamble your family's position on the unlikely possibility that society might forgive me my past? The future of your innocent sister?"

She had struck the one weak link in his argument. "No," he admitted with a sigh. "Though I intend to do my utmost to persuade you to marry me, I do not propose for us to wed until Dorrie is safely settled. I know you prize your independence. Life has given you little reason to place any trust or confidence in men of our rank. But for the few months until Dorrie marries, will you promise to at least consider my proposal, Belle?"

She gazed at him, regret, exasperation—and longing—in her eyes. "'Tis preposterous."

"Indeed."

"I ought to refuse you outright."

"Perhaps you should. After all, I'm not of whole mind. You now occupy too much of it for me ever to be whole again—without you at my side. Have pity on this poor, doomed sufferer…and say yes."

She was wavering, he could tell. And so in one swift movement he reached to cup her face and kissed her.

He remembered the times—too many times—on campaign when the supply wagons had fallen behind the troops, when they'd hunted hares and foraged for roots and berries to sustain them. But in his leanest days, he had never hungered for anything as much as he had for this kiss.

He'd meant it to be a gentle, respectful salute. But apparently she'd missed him, too, for almost immediately her arms came up to encircle his neck, her nails biting into his back, her mouth opening to his and her tongue plunging in, as if she could not taste him deeply enough.

Her unexpectedly passionate response instantly overwhelmed the tight rein he'd been maintaining over his simmering senses. After weeks without her, it took every ounce of his soldier's control to keep himself from laying her back on the sofa, popping open his trouser buttons and thrusting them into the intimate contact she seemed to crave as much as he did. Arms wrapped around her, his hard length sheathed within her, making them both complete.

Hands fisted and neck corded with the strain of caging the desire roaring through him, he broke the kiss, shaking as he pushed her away and waited for his voice to steady enough for speech. "P-promise me."

He felt gratified that her breathing took just as long to control. "I…I'll consider it. But only after your sister is married. And only if your family agrees."

That was enough, more than he'd dared hope for. "So be it." He gave a ragged laugh. "Given how anxious I am to claim you as my bride, I shall have to hurry Dorrie's young man to the sticking point. And once her engagement is announced, I shall haunt your door until you accept me just to clear your entryway of my carcass."

"Perhaps it is just as well that I shall soon be returning to Bellehaven."

His enthusiasm dimmed. "When? And why must you go?"

"I always meant to spend this Season at Bellehaven. I've worked for too many years to insure Kitty's success to risk having some sharp-eyed, scandal-minded ton gossip tumble to the resemblance between us, as you did."

"But I noticed only because I was looking for it."

"Nonetheless, 'tis a chance I'm not prepared to take."

Disappointed though he was, Jack could understand her caution. "Leave if you must. But you should expect me at Bellehaven soon, prepared to be my most persuasive!"

Her eyes held a tenderness that made his heartbeat speed like drums beating the advance. "But now you must go before someone sees you and realizes I am in London."

He captured her hand and kissed it. "I shall go because

you ask it—and because I can now look forward to the day when I shall never have to leave you again."

She smiled, but did not reply in kind. He told himself not to be disappointed, that what she'd said to him thus far was more than sufficient.

"Goodbye, Captain Carrington," she said as he bowed himself to the door. "My dearest Jack."

His heart warmed with delight at that addendum. But as he reached the threshold, he couldn't help pausing to pose one last question. "Do you love me, Belle?"

Surprise flashed in her eyes and she hesitated. He damned the yearning that had compelled him to ask, pushing her to a declaration she might not yet be ready to make.

He should give her time, let her adjust to the idea of wedding him. Keep her secrets, prove himself worthy of her trust and confidence. He was about to tell her to disregard the question when she softly said, "Yes."

Dizzy euphoria made his ears ring, as if a battery of nine-pounders had fired right behind him.

"Then anything is possible." Bowing once more, he walked out.

CHAPTER TWENTY-FIVE

HIS HEART INFUSED with hope, Jack arrived home to discover he would not have to make the rounds of the clubs, searching out Dorrie's James. As he walked in, the butler informed him that Lord Winston awaited him in the study.

His sister's ardent suitor speedily confirmed he had come on precisely the errand Jack suspected. After agreeing to have their solicitors hammer out the details of the settlements and sharing a celebratory glass of port, Jack sent the young man off to find Dorrie.

Smiling, Jack warmed the glass in his hands. First Belle's agreement to consider his suit, then Winston coming up to scratch. It apparently being an auspicious day for matrimony, perhaps he should begin the siege to conquer the last bastion that would likely oppose his own.

Time to seek out Mama.

First, he'd weaken her defenses with a barrage of good news about Lord Winston's proposal. Then he'd lob the bombshell about his own plans.

The housekeeper told him Lady Anne was in the back parlor, going over the day's menus. She looked up when he entered, fixing on him eyes as dark as his own, then smiled a welcome as he crossed the room to plant a kiss atop her glossy chestnut curls.

"I missed you at breakfast, Jack. You must have had an appointment very early. Something to do with that business that took you from town so unexpectedly?"

"Yes, although more of that later. First, I must tell you I've just approved James Winston's suit. He's gone to propose to Dorrie."

"Wonderful!" mother exclaimed. "He is an excellent young man, do you not think, Jack? I believe he and Dorrie shall make a very happy match of it."

Jack agreed, then let his mother run on for a few minutes expounding with delight on the character of her prospective son-in-law and the tasks to be accomplished in preparing for the wedding.

When at last her observations slowed, he said, "I believe they will be happy. Certainly they both seem set on the match. As it happens, I am set on one of my own."

That volley effectively silenced all her chatter about wedding details. "You sly thing!" she exclaimed. "You developed a tendre for some young lady right under my nose, and I never noticed?"

"It didn't precisely happen under your nose."

Her smile of delight faded a bit. "Someone you met outside of London? Oh, not some Parisian lady, I do pray! Come now, don't make me guess! Who is she?"

"Someone of whom, initially, you may not approve, although I hope to convince you otherwise. A wonderful, intelligent lady. The ton knows her as Lady Belle."

Shock flared in her eyes before she gave him a reproving look. "Jack, if you mean that as a jest, I do not find it funny."

"Nor do I, Mama. I'm entirely serious."

He heard her tiny gasp of dismay when she realized he meant exactly what he'd said. She remained silent a long time—probably searching for diplomatic words in which to inform her only son he'd run mad.

"When you returned to us after your accident," she began at last, "I suspected you had conceived a...a tendre for the woman. But the sort of passion she inspires, intensified I do not doubt by the rivalry among the men over who will next possess her—"

"Stop, Mama!" Jack interrupted, his tone harsher than he'd intended. "Never speak of her in such terms."

Her mouth still open after being halted in midspeech, his mother stared at him. "You truly are in thrall to her," she said a moment later. "Oh, Jack, my darling son, I do not mean to disparage her attractions. Only please, for my sake, do not rush into something you would then have a lifetime to regret!"

"I appreciate that you did not immediately point out the disadvantages attaching to such a match for you and Dorrie. And they are many. But before you convict me of having lost my wits, my sense of what is due the family, and my honor, will you hear what I have to say?"

"Of course."

In a few succinct sentences, he conveyed to her all he had learned about the death of Belle's parents, Bellingham's deception and her subsequent life. "She is not some urchin off the streets who used her wits and beauty to claw herself to a select position among the muslin company, Mama. But a lady born and raised. What if it had been Dorrie stranded alone, frightened, destitute in some rural inn far from home?"

His mother shuddered. "I don't wish to consider it."

"I assure you I have," he replied grimly. "And I cannot find it in my heart to condemn Belle for what happened afterward. Her real name is Constance, Mama—and 'steadfast' she was. Despite the appalling situation in which she found herself, she stayed true to the values of her youth, endured years of isolation and shame to protect her sister—Dorrie's friend, Catherine. I believe she has been punished enough for a disaster not of her making."

After giving his mother another moment to ponder all he'd said, he continued, "Since Belle is probably correct in assuming that marrying her will mean we will both be cut by society, I shall not pursue her until Dorrie is safely leg-shackled. I don't want to spoil the end of her Season or her wedding with scandal. Then, however, if I can persuade Belle to have me, I mean to marry her. Would you accept her as the choice of my heart?"

He knew his mother to be honest and fair, a lady who appreciated but did not boast about or overvalue the high estate to which she'd been born. Even so, requesting that she approve Belle, a woman whom Lady Anne's friends and peers would probably always associate with sophisticated vice, was asking a great deal.

"What happened to her was despicable," she said after pondering for a few minutes. "For all my privileged po-

sition, I know the evils of which the world—and men—
are capable. We women have so little power or control
over our lives, I would be a traitor to my sex if I were to
condemn Belle for what befell her when she was young
and defenseless. If she truly is who you claim her to be
and not some vile adventuress, I will accept her."

Jack exhaled a sigh of relief. "Thank you, Mama. Your
blessing is all I seek. You mustn't think that, once I convince her to marry me, I shall expect you to include us
in your social gatherings. My only regret in loving Belle
is knowing our marriage shall very likely cause you and
Dorrie embarrassment, regardless of how much we distance ourselves from you."

Lady Anne sniffed. "If it comes to that, the happiness I have in the company of my son and the woman
he loves will be more than sufficient compensation for
any decrease in invitations to balls and parties—which
are generally a dead bore anyway. But it may not have
to come to that. Lady Belle is actually Catherine's elder
sister?"

"Yes."

"Germayne…" his mother said. "The family name
is unfamiliar. Do you know to whom they may be related?"

"Both Belle and Catherine said their father was a
younger son of a younger son. And they indicated the
cousins who took Catherine in were distant relations."

"I shall have to make some discreet inquiries of Lady
Abrams. You know how much ton families are intercon-
nected. 'Tis likely the Germaynes are related to someone

more noble and influential, however remotely. Perhaps I shall be able to garner more support for your lady than you think."

"Your blessing is all that matters to me."

His mother smiled. "You shall always have that. Now, I shall send you off to exert your persuasive powers. I'm anxious to meet the lady who has stolen my son's heart—and soon, not some months hence, after Dorrie's wedding."

"I shall do my best, Mama. And thank you."

He bent to kiss her cheek. His confidence and enthusiasm soaring at her approval and with the knowledge that, in claiming the woman he loved, he would not have to sacrifice the family he loved as well, he walked out.

Now to convince that lady to let him claim her.

SEVERAL DAYS LATER, Belle gazed out the window as her carriage turned into the drive at Bellehaven. Despite her confused and restless state, she felt her spirits lift with the sense of belonging that had filled her from the first day she'd viewed the property that was now her home.

Jack's unexpected proposal had left her so unsettled she'd decided to return to the country immediately. Pausing only long enough to pen him a note informing him of her departure, she'd packed a few necessities and been on the road by the afternoon after his morning call.

Though the long journey without Mae's company left her plenty of time for reflection, she'd not managed to sort out her turmoil of emotions. Elation that he truly loved her and awe at his proposal warred with the old anger at having been stripped of the position in life that would have made her an acceptable bride for him. Despair at having to live the rest of her days without him mocked the tenuous but unquenchable hope that somehow, he might find a way for them to be together. Beneath all was an exasperation with her wild swings of mood and the muddle into which they'd cast her normal clear thinking.

Doubting both her judgment and her ability to resist seeing Jack or trying to contact her sister had made leaving London doubly urgent, for if Jack missed her half as much as she missed him, the temptation to call on her again—and for her to receive him—would be nearly overwhelming. Better, safer for herself and her sister, that she be here at Bellehaven, where she had the house, garden and farms to tend, work that would prevent her from drifting aimlessly from room to room, as she had much of her time in London, half listening for the knock on the door that would signal a visitor's arrival.

Mindful of Egremont's warning, she had left Watson to watch over Mae, carrying with her instead two of Jackman's former soldiers. Though she doubted she would need protecting, their presence would satisfy Egremont's concern for her safety.

She'd also brought Jem. Supervising the boy, whose high spirits were matched only by a near-complete lack of moral scruples, had been exhausting poor Lawton. Catapulted into the unfamiliar world of the English countryside, perhaps Jem would be less inclined to wander about exercising his skills at petty thievery. The soldiers could earn their keep instilling a bit of discipline in him while they assisted the grooms in continuing his training with the horses.

To her relief, unlike the town-bred Mae, the town-bred youth had found everything about their journey and the scenery through which they traveled interesting. John Coachman had been mercifully patient, answering the rapid battery of questions Jem continually fired from his position on the bench beside him.

As if her thoughts had conjured him, Jem startled her by appearing outside her window, dangling by one arm from his perch on the box. "Would that big mansion up on the hill there be ourn?" he asked.

"It is," she confirmed with a smile. "But please, Jem, get back up on the seat! I don't want to end our journey by having you trampled under the carriage wheels."

His low whistle reached her ears as he obligingly clambered back up. "Cor!" she heard him exclaim to the coachman. "Jem be coming up in the world now!"

Chuckling, she settled back in her seat, glad she'd decided to bring the boy along. His fresh viewpoint and the mischief he would certainly kick up might distract and entertain her, keep her from dwelling on the uncertainties that continued to plague her.

THREE DAYS LATER, trapped indoors by a heavy rain, Belle found herself pacing the parlor. Her household chores were already done, her account books up to date, and neither the novel she'd begun nor the desultory game of billiards she'd attempted could hold her interest. Despite arguing to herself that such a thing was ridiculous, she couldn't shake this restless sense of expectancy.

Why could she just not accept that, despite his vows to the contrary, Jack would not be coming after her? She'd all but guaranteed such an outcome by demanding he cease pursuing her unless his family agreed to a relationship between them. Which, no matter how well settled marriage might make his sister, they probably would not.

His mother was an earl's daughter—and therefore most unlikely to accept having her family name besmirched by the infamy of her son's marriage to a well-known courtesan, however genteel her origins.

Besides, Jack might think *now* that he preferred her company to retaining the position he occupied among the ton, but later, once the heat of passion cooled, would he regret his bargain? He was too honorable ever to disavow her if they wed, no matter how dissatisfied he might become with his self-inflicted banishment. The only heartache worse than living *without* him would be to live *with* him and watch the man she loved become a silent, stoic stranger, forever regretting the folly that had prompted him to make her his wife.

Even imagining it made her shudder.

A knock sounded at the door and Jem bounded in. "There be a gent to see ye—not the captain," he added, quelling the automatic leap of her pulse.

Before she could tell Jem to admit the visitor, the door opened again. There on the threshold, his gray eyes sweeping her with a glance, stood Lord Rupert.

He made her a bow. "I thought to spare you the trouble, if you had any inclination to deny me. You may go, boy," he added, with a wave at Jem.

Jem drew his scrawny body up to full height. "I go when the lady says go."

Rupert frowned, clearly displeased. "How dare you address me in such a tone—" he began, advancing on the boy.

Worried Rupert might cuff Jem for not according him the deference he expected, Belle said hastily, "You needn't wait. Lord Rupert will not be long."

With more bravery than sense, Jem stood his ground. "All right, Miss Belle. But he looks like a rum one to me. I'll be right outside, iff'n you needs anything." Passing close by Rupert, as if daring the baron to take a swipe at him, Jem proceeded to the door.

"Leave him, Rupert," Belle said in an urgent undertone as the baron turned toward the boy, lifting one hand.

Slowly Rupert lowered it. "As you wish—for the moment, Lady Belle."

As soon as Jem closed the door, Rupert sniffed. "The low quality of the staff you employ amazes me. A tart like Mae as a dresser, a half-witted ex-boxer for a butler and now that—guttersnipe!" He shook his head disdainfully. "When I have the ordering of your household, the servants will be properly trained and know their places."

Deciding not to dispute that point so as not to lengthen a visit she intended to be brief, Belle said, "I cannot imagine why you've called on me. I thought I had made my future plans perfectly clear."

"I should have returned sooner, but you were naughty, popping off to London without a word, then running back here scarcely a day after I discovered you were in the City," he reproved, reaching for her hand.

She drew it back. Neither did she offer him a chair.

A look that might have been anger flashed briefly in his eyes, but his tone remained pleasant. "As my last visit provided the impetus to end your little interlude with Carrington, I thought to give you time to get over your pique. I am still prepared to be generous, despite your temporary...defection to the captain."

"Lord Rupert, I believe I have already, in quite plain terms, refused your—your obliging offer. I am sorry you force me to state the matter so baldly, but I am not interested in a relationship with you. I shall never be interested in a relationship with you. Now, I will thank you to leave and not call on me again."

To her exasperation, he merely shook his head at her. "And I, my dear, am not interested in prolonging this tiresome game of advance and retreat. You have taunted me and tempted me and driven me mad with jealousy long enough. This time, I will not accept no as your answer."

"*You* will not accept—!" she gasped. She'd known he was arrogantly certain of always getting his way, but this time his presumption was outside of enough. "Since we do not appear to be exchanging any meaningful conversation, I will thank you to leave now. Good day, my lord."

Calmly Rupert crossed his arms. "I have no intention of leaving. Now—or ever."

The first flickering of alarm went through her as she walked to the bellpull. "I regret to part on such a note, but if you will not go voluntarily, you leave me no choice but to have you forcibly removed."

Rupert chuckled. "I didn't doubt you would try. So I took the precaution of insuring you could not."

The self-satisfied look in his eye intensified her unease, though she maintained a facade of calm as she tugged at the bell.

"Ring away, my dear, but no one will answer. Your household is in my keeping now. And so are you."

His humorous expression vanished, replaced by an intent look that mirrored the heat gleaming in his eyes as he advanced on her. Her attention riveted on his face, she backed away, until her heel bumped the parlor wall.

With a wolfish smile, he put his hands on her shoulders. "Ah, my sweet, I've waited so long."

"Let me go immed—" she got out before his mouth came down on hers.

Resisting the probing of his tongue against her firmly closed mouth, she struggled, but Rupert was surprisingly strong. She could neither break his grip nor twist free.

In desperation, she bit his lip.

She felt, rather than heard, his curse against her mouth. She had an instant to rejoice at the removal of his lips from hers before his hands tightened on her shoulders and he slammed her against the wall.

The force of the contact knocked her off balance and

nearly robbed her of breath. His nails biting into her arms, Rupert caught her before she could fall and pinned her in place with his shoulders.

Fear and fury pounded through her to the beat of the ache in her head. She tried to focus her rattled brain, create a plan, while his harsh panting breaths filled her ears. Then she heard a scrabbling sound and he pressed the whole length of his body against her.

Through the thin muslin of her gown, she felt the thick heat of his erection throbbing against her belly and realized he must have unbuttoned his trouser flap.

"Like it rough?" he growled into her ear. "I knew you would. It's going to be such a pleasure to oblige you."

Keeping her immobile with the weight of his body, he forced one of her hands down and wrapped her fingers around his naked penis. Then, before she could think how to counter that, he smashed a fist into her cheekbone.

Pain exploded in her head, blinding her, ran shrieking through her body. For a moment she battled it, until a wave more powerful than her will submerged her and she went falling, falling backward into darkness.

CHAPTER TWENTY-SIX

EARLY THAT EVENING, Jack sat in his library, Belle's note between his fingers as he inhaled its faint scent of lavender. At his mother's behest, he'd retreated here to escape the tumult of activity as Lady Anne prepared for the ball tonight in honor of Dorrie and Winston's engagement.

Soon, he thought, replacing the note on his desk. He'd been disappointed, but not surprised, to receive Belle's missive and discover from Watson, after immediately setting out to her house in an attempt to talk her into remaining in London, that she'd already departed.

He smiled. Trust Belle to act at once upon any matter she felt to be important.

He'd been half tempted to go after her then and there, armed with the welcome news of his mother's approval. But he had appointments with the solicitors about Dorrie's wedding contract, numerous parties to which he'd already promised to escort her, and the affair tonight—as much bittersweet joy as obligation—where before all the ton he would present her hand to James Winston. After that, he would finally be free to set out for Bellehaven.

He hoped this time apart had led Belle to miss him as sorely as he missed her—thereby weakening her desire to live independently and softening her resistance to accepting his suit. If so, now that he could present her assurances of his family's support, he had a reasonable chance at winning his heart's desire.

Making Lady Belle his wife.

He grinned. Failing such a victory in his first attempt, though, he might well follow through on his threat to camp out on her doorstep, refusing to budge until she finally gave in to his persuasion.

He was imagining some of the more intimate forms of persuasion he might employ when a knock sounded.

"Lord Egremont to see you, sir," the butler said.

Surprise, and an unwelcome flicker of jealousy, stirred in Jack's chest. What could Belle's good friend—his mouth thinned as he recalled the two of them tête-à-tête in her theatre box—want with him?

"Send him in, and bring us some wine, please."

A moment later, the earl walked in. "My apologies for intruding at such a busy time—and congratulations on your sister's upcoming nuptials. Winston is a fine young man."

"We are all pleased with the match," Jack replied, gesturing his visitor to a chair. He had to work at curbing his impatience as they exchanged pleasantries while Quisford poured the wine, knowing that since his personal acquaintance with Egremont was slight, the earl's call must have something to do with Belle. Had something happened to her? he wondered with a stab of alarm.

As soon as Quisford withdrew, Jack asked, "How may I assist you?"

"As I imagine you suspect, I've come to discuss a—certain lady we both hold dear. I have reason to believe you may harbor serious intentions toward her."

The jealousy intensified, along with a primitive, purely male possessiveness. "And what might your interest be in that?" he replied, an edge to his voice.

"Do you mean to marry her?" Egremont asked bluntly.

"Yes." Jack neglected to add that he'd yet to obtain the lady's consent to such a plan.

Egremont smiled wryly. "Then, much as it wounds me to have my suspicions confirmed, concern for Belle's welfare forces me to salute you." He raised his glass to Jack.

Surprised and somewhat mollified, Jack lifted his glass in return. "I thank you for having been a friend to her when she had great need of one."

Egremont set down his glass, his smile fading. "I should have been a better one. For what you believe about her and are now attempting to prove—yes, I know about your trip to Eastwold—I've suspected for years."

Disconcerted, Jack raised his eyebrows. "You seem singularly well informed."

"One of the benefits of long friendship with members of the Home Office. After learning of your quest, I decided that if your intentions toward Belle were honorable, I would offer you what I know…and an apology. From the first night I met her, she's fascinated me—not just her startling beauty, but the grace and dignity of her, the unexpected keenness of her wit. After barely half an hour of conversation—she quizzed me about some matter under debate in the Lords—I knew she was no common strumpet. By the end of that conversation I...I had fallen in love with her."

His face pensive, he swirled the wine in his glass. "Oh, I knew she deserved better than what Bellingham provided. But I was already married, and could offer her no more than the friendship which, since I'd known Bellingham for years and had a reputation for fidelity, he permitted. I knew if I found her rightful family, I might lose her altogether and I...I couldn't bear that thought. So I soothed my conscience by telling myself that, having been taken so publicly under Bellingham's protection, there could be no going back for her. I appointed myself a sort of guardian to watch over and protect her from the worst of the excesses." He sighed. "I was not always successful."

"Vauxhall," Jack said.

Egremont grimaced with distaste. "Vauxhall. I like to believe our friendship provided Belle some measure of comfort and relief from a life she despised. But in my heart, I know I should have done more. I should have done what you are doing—searched for her family, tried to restore her to the life she somehow lost. I had all the connections needed to make such an attempt. It was selfish cowardice on my part that I did not. By what I did, and even more, what I did not do, I betrayed both our friendship and her."

Setting down his glass, Egremont looked back up at Jack. "You are a better man than I, Jack Carrington. If you choose to honor me with your confidence, and I can do anything to assist, know that I will do so. Know also that I will lend whatever support I can to reestablish Belle."

Not sure what to say in the face of Egremont's disclosures, Jack remained silent. Though furious at the earl for letting Belle languish in shameful servitude for six years, he could not help also feeling a strong sympathy. Would he have the courage to pursue his inquiries if at the end of them, instead of claiming her as his bride, he would lose her forever?

Once again the earl raised his glass to Jack. "I hereby turn over to you the privilege of caring for Belle. It comes with a warning, however."

"And what would that be?"

"You know the story behind the girl Jane Parsons?" When Jack nodded, Egremont continued, "Belle maintained from the first that she was the victim of a conspiracy to traffic in young girls. She uncovered enough evidence to that effect that Lord Riverton felt justified in investigating further. The information we've gathered leads us to believe that a number of prominent, wealthy gentlemen are funding it—and Lord Rupert may be one of them. Certainly we have discovered that he is one of Mrs. Jarvis's most regular customers."

Jack's instinctive dislike of the baron intensified. "I don't find that hard to believe."

"Given Belle's involvement in bringing the affair to light—and Rupert's designs on Belle, he will bear close watching. He's recently left town, and I would not be at all surprised if he calls at Bellehaven."

Rupert at Bellehaven? Jack spit out a curse.

"Exactly," Egremont agreed. "I intended to go there myself, to check on her, but now, perhaps it would be better for you to do so."

Jack cursed again. "I cannot leave until after my sister's ball tonight."

Egremont nodded. "I'm probably being overly cautious, but Rupert has wanted Belle for a long time and won't be easily discouraged. I imagine she could use some help."

Jack envisioned the baron's face at the other end of his fists. "'Twould give me the greatest of pleasure."

"I imagine it would. Well, with the festivities soon to begin, I shan't take up any more of your time." The earl stood and deposited his glass. "Good luck, Captain."

"Thank you, Egremont," Jack replied, offering the older man his hand. "For watching over her. And for relinquishing her now."

Egremont gave his hand a firm shake. "If any man could, I believe you deserve her. God bless you both."

Thoughtfully Jack walked him to the door. Whatever the earl's failings in not doing all he could to help Belle earlier, he admired the man's fortitude now. He could only imagine what it would be like to have to stand aside and let a more fortunate man claim Belle for his wife.

"If we are shunned by society, you may not wish to acknowledge us, but if you choose to visit, you will always be welcome. Belle has a great fondness for you."

His eyes misting, Egremont nodded. "That is kind of you, Captain. Good evening."

As the door closed behind Egremont, Jack strode back to his desk. He would make sure his paperwork was in order and pack a portmanteau. Then, as soon as he handed Dorrie over to James and led his mother out for the first dance, he would leave for Bellehaven.

THROUGH A THICK, pain-filled mist, Belle struggled to wake, her head throbbing, the side of her throat on fire. Moaning, she tried to move and found her hands tethered.

Alarm evaporated some of the confusion induced by the pounding in her head. She tried to push herself upright and focus her thoughts.

She was in bed—her bed? In a night-dark room. But how had she come to have her hands tied?

Then with a jolt, the memories broke through.

Rupert.

Entering the parlor oh so casually, only to later overpower her, force a kiss on her, strike her.

What else had he forced after she lost consciousness?

Sickness and a rising fury in her gut, her mind groped past the pain to search out more subtle sensations. The bareness of her body, clad only in a shift. The sticky wetness between her legs.

"Ah, so you are awake at last," observed a voice that made her instantly stiffen with distaste and dread. "Here," Rupert said, approaching the bed with a cup in his hand, "drink this. 'Twill ease the ache in your head."

She wanted to bat the cup away, until she realized she was desperately thirsty. Still, what if the liquid were drugged? Her whole being rallied around the conviction that, however and whenever the opportunity arose, she would escape him. And she must be ready.

"I don't mean to drug you," Rupert said, as if reading her thoughts. "Come now, don't be stubborn. Take a sip."

Her throat felt so raw, she could hardly force out a sound. "Why should I trust you?"

"Touché, my dear, though I assure you, I have no desire to render you comatose again. I do regret the rather over-vigorous blow to the head, but you so agitate me, I forget caution, sense, all. I could not even stop myself from enjoying you, though next time, I promise to wait until you wake."

"Spare me the pleasure," she spit back.

"Oh, I intend to spare neither of us that. But this little episode in the arms of Morpheus did prove useful." With one finger, Rupert touched her neck, just above where the pain was most intense, and she couldn't keep herself from flinching. "I was able to accomplish one important task without causing you further discomfort."

He pulled his hand back, waving it so the candlelight glinted off his gold signet ring.

"You see it, the crested 'R'? A judicious application of heated metal just below your delectable ear, my sweet, and I have made my mark on you—indelibly. 'R' for Rupert, sealed in your flesh for all time."

Horror washed over her in a cold wave. Despite the

pain in her head, she struggled at her bonds, desperate to break free, to verify or disprove his awful words.

"Don't struggle so," he advised. "You'll see it soon enough. You must rest and regain your strength."

Tears of rage and a growing despair leaked from the corners of her eyes. "Bastard," she whispered.

"A drastic measure, to be sure, but I worried that Carrington might be besotted enough to forget what was due his name and offer you marriage. And though his fortune cannot compare to mine, wedlock might prove a powerful inducement. Though we both know that you, my sweet, were born not for lawful union but to indulge a man's secret, sinful pleasures. You are, quite bluntly, a whore—but you are *my* whore. Now that the whole world can see that at a glance, Carrington will have nothing more to do with you."

His every word was like a stone sinking her heart into a bottomless ocean of despair. For it was true. Any approval Jack might have managed to coax from his family for a betrayed daughter of the gentry would be forfeit, were she truly branded with the mark of servitude to Rupert as clearly as the French branded the "V" for *voleur* onto the breasts of their thieves.

Overcome by a sense of violation too profound for tears, she closed her eyes.

Rupert made a soothing sound. "Do not fret, my dear, it will mar your beauty but a trifle. And I shall make it up to you. Bellingham's gifts are nothing to what I will settle on you. Sumptuous gowns, the most brilliant and perfect of jewels, horses, coaches, houses in magnificent style. But you will not leave this chamber until you agree to belong to me and me only."

As he delivered that speech, the embers of her anger stirred, lifting her spirit out of its torpor of hopelessness. After he'd struck her unconscious, burned her, rutted on her—he thought a few jewels and trinkets would make the matter right?

"Then I shall die here, for I will never agree."

Rupert frowned. "I concede that you have some reason for anger, but I cannot like your attitude. Perhaps you will require a bit more…discipline to improve it. I've found your sex, being subject to flights of fancy and poor judgment, need the same strong hand one must exert with servants and animals. But then—" a gleam sparked in his eyes "—mayhap you enjoy a little…chastisement."

"Chastisement!" she sputtered. With all he had done, he had the presumption to claim *she* should be punished?

"And you will resist, you mean to tell me? Pray do, my love. Fight me with teeth, fists, nails. 'Twill make burying myself in you again all the sweeter."

She realized this verbal fencing would gain her nothing. Better to induce him to leave her alone, rest her battered body—and plan how she would escape.

And once she did… She thought longingly of her rapier. She would force the baron to a duel of honor and have her revenge—or die in the attempt. With Kitty established and Jack lost to her, the possibility that she might be wounded or killed was of no concern.

She pushed herself higher on the bed, then gasped. "Oh, my head hurts so! I think...I think I may be ill!"

"Lie still, then," Rupert advised, looking for the first time uneasy. "The feeling will pass."

So he did not relish the thought of her casting up her accounts on his pristine breeches?

She moaned again. "It's...getting worse. Please, may I not have a maid to attend me?"

Though he still looked uncertain, he shook a finger at her. "No trying any tricks. I can't allow you the use of your servants until you agree to my terms, but I brought a woman to attend you on the journey back. I'll send for her."

A different kind of fear made her stomach clench in earnest. "Where are my people? Have you harmed them?"

"What, do you take me for some sort of barbarian? They were overpowered one by one and removed to the stables, where they will remain confined, but well cared for, until after we leave together."

Relief made the throbbing in her head ease and she uttered a silent prayer of thanks.

"I shall take care to promote your speedy recovery." The heated look in his eyes intensified. "After waiting for years, one quick taste will not satisfy me for long."

If she expired in the attempt, Belle promised herself, "one quick taste" would be all he ever had. "Send the woman, please? I must attend...other needs, as well."

"Of course, my dear. I've had my cook prepare some

broth. Later tonight, or surely by morning, you will be ready for me to show you the pleasures that await us."

She didn't bother to reply. As soon as the door closed behind him, she twisted at her bonds, ignoring the redoubled throbbing in her head. But he'd done well, and the ropes had no give.

Belle's hope that she might appeal to the woman Rupert had brought withered almost as soon as the grim-faced crone entered the chamber. Telling Belle curtly that she would have to make do with propping herself over the basin provided, as no one but her master was authorized to release Belle's bonds, she stood by as Belle relieved herself, making no attempt to help with that awkward maneuver. After removing the basin, she fed Belle the broth she'd brought with utterly disinterested precision.

Feeling soiled in body and spirit, after the woman left, Belle lay back, cudgeling her mind for a plan that offered some chance of success. As the night deepened and none occurred, she fought a growing sense of hopelessness.

How could she avoid what Rupert promised for morning? Further protestations of nausea might delay him for a time, but that would buy her at best a day or so. Then a more bitter realization struck her.

Rupert would probably enjoy taking her while she was bound and struggling. Real nausea rose in her throat at the thought of what he might force her to do while she was tethered to the bed, helpless to defend herself or resist.

She fought it and her sagging spirits. If she had to, she could endure even that. Had she not, over long bitter years, perfected the ability to distance her mind from whatever indignities were forced upon her body? She would call on that skill again, if she must. Sooner or later, she would find an opportunity to break free.

Through the long night she girded herself for what would come next. At some point she must have dozed, for when a sharp noise jerked her to full consciousness, pale dawn light pooled at the bottom of the curtains.

The sound came again, a scrabbling noise as if there were a rat in the chimney. Would that he might come out and bite Rupert, she thought with vicious humor.

The noise grew louder. Then a puff of ash issued out of the hearth, followed by a slight, blackened figure that landed lightly among the fire's dying embers.

"Jem!" Belle gasped in astonishment.

The boy darted out of the fireplace, batting out the smoldering patches on his sooty clothing. His street-toughened face looked older than his years as he inspected her.

"Knew that bloke be a bad'un, soon's I seen him," he whispered. Quickly he pulled a small knife from his boot and began cutting the ropes at her wrists. "Much as I'd like to stay a spell and give him a taste of me knife, I reckon we best get you out of here afore he comes back."

"How did you get free?" Belle demanded.

His homely face broke into a gap-toothed smile, transforming him back to impish boy. "I squalled so loud, they put me in the tack room all by me lonesome, told me they'd leave me hungry until I could mind me manners. Pshaw, what lock ever held the likes of me? Soon's I knew for sure they was gone, I loped off. Then 'twere only a matter of skulking by the kitchen, listening to that bunch of hatchet-faces 'til I heared where they was keeping you. Have to own I didn't much like having to scabber down that chimney, but seemed the best way to get in without no one being the wiser."

She rubbed her raw wrists. "How can I thank you?"

His narrow face softened. "After all you done for me? 'Tweren't nothing—except for the chimney part. I hopes never to see the insides of one of them again!"

Gingerly Belle got up, relieved to find herself only slightly dizzy and the headache manageable. "You're sure Rupert's men are all in the kitchens—none above stairs?"

"None," Jem confirmed. "I ran my peepers by all the rooms on my way to the roof. Speaking of, there be a big oak on the west side what touches the house. We'll scarper out the attic window and climb down it, then be through into them woods faster'n a rat can cross an alley."

"Let me put on some breeches and get my sword." Much as Belle wished for a bath and something with which to tend her wounds, that would have to wait.

Jem stared at her. "You mean to skewer that bounder? Best let the law handle him, my lady. He's got enough men with him to collar you quick and take that blade."

"Not if you sneak back to the stables and release my servants. Do you think you can, though 'tis now daylight?"

His grin widened. "With all them shrubs and trees betwixt here and the stables? I'll be as invisible as me dear mama's ghost."

"I shall wait in the attic. Rupert must be in one of the guest chambers and probably won't wake for hours. Free Jackman's soldiers and the others, tell them to seize Rupert's men and send someone for the constable. Then come find me. I shall deal with Rupert."

Jem murmured agreement as he walked to the door. "I'll listen out whiles you get yer togs on."

When she joined him a few minutes later, dressed and armed, he turned back to her, his narrow face serious. "I ain't never done nothing more than thieving. But I'll kill the bastard for you iff'n you wants me to."

"Thank you, Jem. But that's a pleasure I plan to attend to myself."

Accepting her claim without comment, he nodded. "Reckon that's your right. Be you ready?"

"Let's go."

CHAPTER TWENTY-SEVEN

BLESSING THE CLEAR, moonlit sky that had followed the previous day's storms, allowing him to travel through the night, shortly after dawn, Jack turned his weary job-horse onto the carriageway leading to Bellehaven.

The sick feeling that had plagued him ever since Egremont's warning had driven him to ride scarcely without a stop, pausing only long enough to quaff a mug of ale at the posting inns while the sleep-stupored grooms he rousted readied him a change of mount. Within a few minutes, he would reach the manor and find Belle, perhaps share a laugh over his excess of caution, and finally release the knot of tension in his gut.

Except that no one challenged him as he rode past the gatehouse. Nor did he spy on the heights or hidden near the stables any of the extra men he'd hired.

Perhaps, thinking she no longer needed protection, Belle had dismissed them. But that didn't seem likely, since Egremont had surely urged a continued wariness while Riverton's investigation proceeded.

The innate soldier's caution that had saved his neck on more than one occasion told him to avoid the stables and approach the house by stealth. With silent apologies to his exhausted mount, Jack tethered the horse among the trees and stole forward.

He had nearly reached the kitchen—from which issued no clanging of pots, scent of coffee, or cheerful voices going about their morning chores—when he heard muffled bootsteps. Slipping behind a shrub, he drew his pistol and waited.

Jack peered into the morning mist, trying to see if the group of men stealthily advancing were Belle's servants. Then a slight, unmistakable figure approached.

"Jem!" he called in a low voice.

The boy turned and spotted him. "Cor, Captain, you gave me a start! Sure glad I am to see you, though."

"What's going on?"

"That nasty excuse for a nob, Lord Rupert, come yesterday and tried to snabble Lady Belle. I helped her get away and freed her people. Now they're gonna tie up Rupert's men whiles I meets her and she takes care of *him*."

Not if Jack had his way. "Bring me to her."

"Quiet, now," Jem admonished as he led Jack into the house and up the servants' stairs. "We don't wanna give ol' Rupert time to prepare us a welcome."

Jack hadn't realized just how great his fear had grown since riding into Bellehaven until he reached the attic and saw Belle in shirt and breeches, a sword at her side, standing with her back to them as she gazed out the attic window. Relief at finding her unharmed made him dizzy and he couldn't get her name past the lump in his throat.

She half turned and saw him. "Jack!" she cried. But after that first flash of joy in her eyes, her face grew shuttered. "What are you doing here?"

"Egremont sent me," he replied, dismayed as he watched her change before him from warmly welcoming into the remote, untouchable Belle of the early days of their acquaintance. "He worried Rupert might come here. Jem says he tried to kidnap you. Did he hurt you? Lead me to the villain and I will demand satisfaction!"

She turned to fully face him. His eyes were immediately drawn to a raw, ragged patch beneath her ear that looked like—a burn? "Lord have mercy!" he gasped.

"I believe demanding satisfaction is my right," she replied. Unsheathing her sword, she nodded to Jem. "Are all my people unharmed?"

"Yes, my lady. The sheriff be sent for and Rupert's men be soon locked up in the stables."

"You've done well, Jem. Now, let's finish this."

Jack stepped in her path. "You mean to fight him."

Her calm, cold eyes gazed at him without emotion. "'Tis a matter of honor."

Honor. Sickness punched him in the gut, followed by intense, impotent fury. Rupert must have taken her against her will, damn his black devil's heart. For an instant Jack thought of asking her to yield him the privilege of combat, but a second look at the implacable hardness of her face convinced him arguing that point would be fruitless.

"Let me stand as your second."

She paused a moment, considering. "Very well. But

only if you agree not to intervene in any way, regardless of what happens. *Regardless.* Will you swear it?"

"I swear." Though if Rupert's blade came anywhere close to Belle, Jack knew he couldn't keep that promise.

Softly they paced down the stairs to the second floor, where Jem nodded toward one of the chambers. Belle kicked open the door and strode in, Jem and Jack behind her.

"Lord Rupert," she called to the man standing before the washbasin in his shirtsleeves. The baron looked up, his eyes widening in disbelief.

"Belle! And Carrington? What is—"

"I have changed my mind about our sharing a relationship. You will be my opponent. Captain Carrington is to be my second. Name which of your men you wish to stand with you and my servants will release him."

Rupert opened and closed his mouth, clearly still astounded at this reversal of his plans. Finally he seemed to take in Belle's attire and the drawn sword in her hand. "Opponent? What nonsense is this? Carrington, you can't mean to be a party to such an outrage!"

"I believe the outrage has already been committed. If the lady wants satisfaction, I intend to let her seek it."

"See that he has a weapon," Belle instructed Jem. "How fortunate you selected the most spacious bedchamber, my lord," she said while the boy plucked Rupert's foil from his baggage and tossed it on the bed.

Crossing his arms over his chest to confine the sword hand that itched to feel Rupert's neck under his blade,

Jack positioned himself near the door, where he could block Rupert's flight—or intervene, if necessary.

"If you wish a second, speak now," Belle added.

"You cannot believe I would deign to fence against *you*," Rupert said scornfully.

"I shall take that as a no to my offer to await your second. Very well. *En garde*, my lord."

When Rupert continued to stand unmoving, Belle picked up his sword and tossed it to him. He let it clang to the floor at his feet. Haughtily he stared at her.

"Very well," she said with a shrug. "If you don't wish to defend yourself, I shall make short work of this." Whipping her sword into position, she advanced on him.

Rupert lost a little of his sangfroid. "You can't mean to attack an unarmed man."

Belle continued until her sword point nearly touched his chest. "Did you give me a chance to fight before tying me down like an animal?"

A growl issued from Jack's throat and he lunged toward the baron. Sword still trained on Rupert, Belle whipped her other hand out, commanding him to halt. "Captain, remember your promise."

Cursing, Jack stepped back and wrenched his own blade from its scabbard. "Very well. But if there's anything left of him when you're done, I claim the next round."

"As you wish," Belle said, her voice disinterested, her gaze riveted on the baron. "Now, Lord Rupert, I suggest you pick up your sword."

When still the man did not move, she jabbed the sword

forward, slicing open his shirt and drawing a thin trail of red across his chest. With a howl of pain and rage, Rupert stumbled backward.

"Shall I continue to stick you like the pig you are until you bleed to death? Or make a quick lunge and finish you at once?" she asked, as if debating whether to wear a straw bonnet or a chip hat. "Ah, I think slow will be better." With another practiced swipe, she cut through his sleeve, grazing his shoulder.

This time, the baron rolled away from her onto the floor and snatched up his foil. "Very well," he snarled as he regained his feet. "I shall fight. But don't pretend to call this an affair of 'honor.' A tart who spread her legs for the titillation of the crowd like you did at Vauxhall has none to defend."

"Stay, Captain!" Belle commanded, seeming to sense Jack reaching for his sword even though he stood behind her. "Do not force me to fight you, too. You are ready now, Lord Rupert?"

"You dare to think you can match me?" he sneered.

With that, she attacked, driving the baron, who took a precious second to react to the unexpected swiftness of her advance, toward the corner of the room. "Tart!" he taunted as, marshaling his superior strength, he pushed her back. "Harlot! This is the drab you would sully your name by wedding, Carrington?"

Fury bubbled through Jack at the first epithet, making him grind his teeth as he strained to keep immobile. By the second insult, though, he realized the baron was *trying* to draw him in and force Belle to split her concentration.

Deliberately Jack lowered his sword, making sure Belle saw him. "This lady can finish you without my help."

Something—gratitude, perhaps?—flashed briefly in her eyes and she gave him a tiny nod. Then she refocused on Rupert, following a straight lunge with a cut over, then a feint as he came toward her, then another lunge to deliver a hard blow high on his sword.

Nearly losing his grip, the baron cried out in pain as he reached down to brace his sword hand. When he looked back up at Belle, a feral anger gleamed in his eyes.

Jack's hand clenched on his sword, but Belle appeared unmoved. "*Now* are you ready to begin, my lord?"

With a growl, the baron attacked. Jack held his breath, concentrating on the clash of blades to determine how he would intervene to protect Belle, should that become necessary. But despite Rupert's furious charge, she appeared icily calm. And as she parried his final lunge and counterattacked in a series of moves as ferocious but more precisely executed than the baron's, totally fearless.

For endless minutes, they challenged each other back and forth across the narrow space—lunge, cut, feint, withdraw, check, countercheck, lunge, the baron's advantage in height and weight offset by Belle's superior technique. Until Jack realized Belle was using against Rupert the tactic he'd used on her at Armaldi's: forcing the baron to fight with all his strength and waiting for him to tire.

Her strategy was succeeding, though the baron, sweat

dripping down his face as he fought in teeth-clenched fury, seemed unaware of it. Another few moments and the baron started gasping for breath, his sword arm beginning to droop, his lunges and counters growing increasingly sloppy.

Finally, as if taking pity on Rupert's deteriorating display of swordsmanship, in a precise series of advances, Belle drove him into a corner, then drew him off balance into a lunge. With a brutal blow that would have done credit to a dragoon, she slashed her sword back, sending him to the floor and the foil flying out of his hand.

Flat on his back, Rupert reached out, fingers scrabbling for the foil that was now out of his reach. Terror filled his eyes as he stared up into Belle's implacable face.

Suddenly her expression changed, the naked hatred Jack had glimpsed the moment before she stabbed him in their duel filling her eyes. With a snarl, she pressed the tip of her foil against Rupert's already bleeding chest. He whimpered, the sound between a plea and a sob.

She would strike now, Jack knew, plunge her blade through Rupert's heart and end it. Exact revenge for whatever indignities he had forced on her bound and helpless body, for Vauxhall and for all she had suffered in the long years of her bondage to Bellingham.

Though having Belle kill Rupert would complicate matters, perhaps force him to remove her from England to avoid the law, his heart urged her to drive the blade home.

Jack gave an involuntary gasp as her hand moved. But

instead of finishing off the baron, she flung aside her sword and strode away from him.

"He's not worth the dirtying of good steel," she said as she passed Jack, tears gathering in her eyes. "Get him out of my sight before I change my mind. Jem, lend me your knife, please."

After catching the blade he tossed, she walked out.

Jack advanced, and with the boy's help, pulled the shaking baron to his feet. Half carrying, half dragging him, they herded Rupert down the stairs.

When they reached the downstairs parlor, Jack shoved the baron into a chair and ordered Jem to fetch his carriage and coachman. Though Jem shook his head in silent disagreement, he went as Jack bid.

As soon as the boy exited, Jack turned to Rupert. "You have estates in the West Indies, I believe?"

Still breathing hard, Rupert nodded.

"You have just conceived a burning desire to inspect them—and will find them so much to your liking, you shall settle there permanently. I would urge that Belle press charges for kidnapping, but I don't wish to subject her to the notoriety of a trial. Relocating to the Caribbean might be beneficial in any event, since I understand you've had dealings with a certain Mrs. Jarvis which are unlikely to sustain the legal scrutiny they are shortly to receive."

The baron shrugged, some of his arrogant hauteur returning. "So I pay a madam handsomely to insure a steady supply of unsullied wenches? What concern is it to me how she recruits her tarts, as long as they are fresh and can rut as enthusiastically as Belle?"

Fury long suppressed whipped through him. An instant later, Jack finally took the satisfaction of feeling his fist connect with the baron's jaw.

"Consider that a mild sample of what you're owed, you miserable excuse for a gentleman. You should know that, after Waterloo, I'm not squeamish about seeing men die, nor do I possess as fine a sense of honor as Belle. If I ever see you again, I won't wait to offer you a sword."

Jack hauled the baron up and held him at arm's length, pleased to note that his split lip and the bruise forming on his jaw had removed the arrogance from Rupert's face. "If, before you take ship for the Caribbean, you have an urge to reveal to anyone what occurred here, resist it. For if I hear a whisper of anything that transpired, there will be no hellhole on earth deep or dark enough to hide you from my wrath. Have I made myself clear?"

Though Rupert conceded nothing, after a moment he looked away from Jack's unflinching gaze.

Jem entered with two stout footmen. "The coachman be harnessing the horses. We'll see he gets in the buggy. You best go check on our lady."

As they pulled him toward the door, Rupert jerked free of his captors to look back at Jack. "She'll never have you now." His lips stretching into a smile that died when it encountered the cut on his lip, the baron limped out.

Praying he could find some way to repair the damage Rupert's visit had wrought, Jack took the stairs two at a time to Belle's chamber.

HER OWN ROOM was deserted. Jack continued down the hall, throwing open each door until he found her in the last bedroom. Seated at a dressing table, she was inspecting herself in the mirror—Jem's bloody knife held in one bloodied hand.

His heart dropped to his boot tops and he knocked over a side table unlucky enough to be in his path as he rushed to her. "Belle, what have you done?"

The eyes that looked up at him, full of rage and pain when she fought Rupert, were now expressionless. Blood dripped steadily down her neck from three cuts she'd scored across the burned place beneath her ear.

He wanted to wrap her in his arms, but she thrust out a hand, warning him to approach no closer. "He knocked me out, tied me down, violated me. Then he…he b-burned the mark of his signet ring into my neck. I could see the 'R' reflected in the mirror. I couldn't b-bear it."

Jack felt sickened to the depths of his soul. And if he, who was only hearing the story secondhand, felt repulsed, what must Belle be feeling?

"I can still kill him."

She shook her head. "Were I not so weak, I should have done so. But killing him cannot undo what he's done."

He wanted to wail with anguish for her. But most of all, he wanted to cradle her to him, treasure the life that others had treated with such callous disregard.

"I'm sorry," he began, pushing the words with difficulty out of his constricted throat, "that I wasn't here when you needed me."

For the first time since she saw him in the attic, her

expression softened. Her eyes full of grief and regret, she said, "You could not have known."

He stepped closer and again, she warned him away. "Don't. I...I don't think I can bear being touched."

"Please, Belle, I *need* to hold you," he said, the words ripped from the agony in his chest.

She must have seen the truth of it in his eyes, for with a tiny sigh, she made room for him on the bench. He threw himself down and gathered her in his arms, crushing her to him as tightly as he dared, his tears beading like diamonds in the gold of her hair.

At first stiff in his embrace, after a moment she relaxed, then clung to him, weeping silently while he held her, wanting never to let her go.

Afraid of what would happen when he had to let her go.

All too soon, she straightened and pushed him away. "Thank you. I guess I needed comfort more than I knew."

"Give me the right to comfort you always. Marry me."

She smiled sadly. "Once there might have been a chance for us. But this—" she pointed to her neck "—this changes everything."

"Why should it? I told my mother I intend to marry you, and she will support us. My sister will be wed at the Season's end. Why can we not marry immediately after?"

"The ton might—*might*—forgive Bellingham's mistress, were she well born enough and supported by sufficiently influential friends. But to excuse my having been Bellingham's whore and *Rupert's?*" She shook her head. "I would not have you dragged down by my degradation."

"No one need learn of what happened here."

She sniffed scornfully. "As no one learned about Vauxhall? Oh, I do not doubt you threatened Rupert, but he brought a dozen servants. You cannot silence them all. Besides, this mark will shout out the news, were you to cut out the tongue of everyone who was present."

"I cannot perceive the outline of a letter now. As the burn heals, the skin will wrinkle. No one will know."

"*I* will know," she said simply.

He knew his arguments were failing, could almost feel her slipping away. While he cudgeled his brain to find some new line of appeal, she said softly, "Could you really stand to live with me, knowing your wife had been taken by that...degenerate?"

He could scarcely bear the thought of it—because of her anguish, not his. "'Twas an abomination you resisted with everything at your command. I can move past it."

"I'm not sure *I* can. When you were here, you taught me to see loving in a new way, as something pure, giving, tender." She paused, wrapping her arms around herself as her gaze trailed off to the far distance. "Now all I remember is the ropes burning my wrists and the—the stink of Rupert on my body. I don't know if I will be able to allow anyone to touch me intimately ever again—even you."

"Then I won't touch you. My pledge, my first pledge

to you, still holds. I will never take anything that you do not gladly give."

She shook her head impatiently. "Leaving aside that you deserve a wife you can be proud of, you owe your family an heir. I couldn't promise to let you provide one."

"I have cousins in whom I have full confidence."

She rose and walked away, one hand rubbing absently at the raw marks the ropes had cut into her wrists. "You are a stubborn man, Jack Carrington."

"Do you still love me, Belle?"

She halted, looked back at him. For a long moment she said nothing, and his spirits sank. If Rupert had managed to crush every tender feeling in her, Jack might have to kill the bastard after all.

"How could I help loving you?" she said a moment later. "You who are everything that is good and honorable and noble in this world."

"Then for the love of God, Belle, marry me!"

"How can I claim to love you and allow you to marry a woman who would force you into a lifetime of exile from decent society, one whose name is a byword for carnality?"

"Is society's respect so important to you?"

"You are frustrated now—and you desire me. But later, when lust fades, you will thank me for saving you from throwing away your honor and the position of esteem you now occupy. Here in our own private heaven, Jack, we shared a beautiful dream. Don't ruin it by trying to make it into something it can never be. Leave me at least that."

"We can make that dream a reality if you'll just marry me," he insisted.

Suddenly the strength seemed to leave her and she swayed on her feet. He ran to catch her, but she pushed him away and staggered to the bed. "Please, I cannot bear any more. If you love me, grant me one request."

Tight-jawed, fearing what she would ask, he replied, "What?"

"Go. Leave me now and don't come back."

For a long moment he stood irresolute, but he had barraged her with every argument he could muster and still she resisted. More than that, he could see she was exhausted, physically and mentally driven to her limits.

"Very well, I'll go. I cannot promise not to return."

She nodded, as if that were concession enough for now.

On the threshold, he hesitated. "Shall I send Mae and Watson back to you?"

Her lips trembled and she blinked back tears. "I would appreciate that," she said, her voice a whisper.

Jack swept her a bow. "Then goodbye, my love." Grimly he strode from the room.

TOO DRAINED TO MOVE, Belle lay back, watching dust motes dance in the sunlight now pouring through the chamber windows. 'Twas only midmorning of a very fair day.

The day her hopes died.

'Twas partly her own fault, she supposed. She had underestimated Rupert's cunning and his malice. She would pay for that lapse the rest of her life.

Thank heaven Jack had granted her request. She wasn't sure she could have resisted much longer, as vehemently as she believed everything she'd told him. All she need do now was remain steadfast. In a month or a year, he would weary of her continued refusals. Some pretty, charming, well-bred girl would catch his fancy, one whose impeccable lineage would make her a suitable bride.

Then he would bless her for saving him from taking a wife who brought him nothing, not even the promise of performing on him the arts she was reputed to possess.

While she… She had a sudden vision of life stretching before her, an endless void of loneliness and regret. She wouldn't think about that yet.

Kitty would be safe. Jack would find happiness elsewhere. That would have to be enough.

She let herself sink toward the blessed oblivion of sleep. Later, when she woke, she'd order that her own bedchamber be stripped and everything in it, furniture and all, be burned. She'd dress her wounds and soak in a bath, the water as hot as she could stand it.

But she didn't think she would ever feel clean again.

CHAPTER TWENTY-EIGHT

AFTER LEAVING BELLEHAVEN, Jack stopped at the first decent posting inn, engaging a chamber and sleeping through the rest of that day and the following night. Since he'd told his mother before leaving Dorrie's party that he wasn't sure when he'd be back, there was no need to hurry. Feeling better after his slumbers, he set out again.

During his long hours on horseback, he pondered ways to solve the dilemma with Belle. While he ached for her pain and understood her reasoning, he wasn't about to simply let her go. So after arriving the following morning, he went straightaway to ask his mother's advice.

"Jack!" she cried as he entered her study. "What a pleasant surprise! I hope this means all went well at Bellehaven…" Her words trailed off as she studied his face. "It did not, did it?"

For a moment the images ran through his mind: Belle's cold, expressionless eyes; the bleeding burn beneath her ear; Rupert's triumphant face as he was led away. "No, Mama. It did not go well." In a few concise sentences, he told her what had transpired.

Though she gasped when he relayed what Rupert had done, she did not interrupt. After he finished, she remained silent, obviously pondering what he'd told her. "Do you still want her?" she asked at last.

"Still want her?" he echoed angrily, stung by the repetition of Belle's question to him. "How can you, another woman, ask me that? None of it was her fault!"

"Calm yourself," she soothed. "Of course *I* don't blame her. But many men would—'tis the way of the world. Although I reluctantly agree 'twould be best not to urge Belle to press charges, every feeling revolts against letting Rupert escape the consequences of his acts."

Jack smiled bitterly. "Oh, I believe the consequences will be severe enough. Rupert, a creature of London, forever banned from returning to England? Forced to live the rest of his days among ill-bred colonials and a handful of natives? Did I not feel that retribution worse than death, I would kill him myself. I will be tempted to do it yet…if he has crippled Belle's spirit so severely that she will never consider my suit."

"She feels strongly about the damage wedding her might do to your position, does she not?"

"Yes, much as I've tried to convince her that does not matter to me. I want to spend my life with her, if we have to flee to the Outer Hebrides to do it."

"I don't believe anything that drastic will be required. I can't help you with the…other thing—" his mother's face hardened and Jack knew she was recalling what Rupert had done "—but there is a good deal I can do about *Belle's* standing in society."

For the first time since leaving her, Jack's spirits brightened. "Tell me how!"

"After checking several sources, I discovered that the Germaynes possess some very influential relations."

"Indeed! And you would nose that about town?"

His mother gave him a reproving look. "As if I were some jumped-up Cit trying to pander influence? Certainly not! No, I shall call upon the lady of the family, apprise her in confidence of the facts, and what she chooses to do then is up to her. However, gossip mill that the ton is, society will probably winkle out the relationship eventually. If after a suitable interval the family makes no move to embrace Belle, I might have to let slip what a shame I think it that Lady Belle endured what she did, given that her mother is cousin to Lord Cowper's aunt."

"Cousin to the aunt of Lady Cowper?" Jack burst out laughing. "Are you sure?"

"My dear, 'tis too important a matter for jesting."

"Should Lady Cowper choose to support Belle, acceptance would be nearly assured. You think she might?"

His mother shrugged. "Emily Lamb was ever a dear, clever girl, and is now thought to be quite the nicest of Almack's Patronesses. I believe she might take up Belle's cause. Even if she does not, few among the ton would want to risk slighting a relation of the Cowpers."

"Brilliant, Mama."

His mother gave him a regal nod. "Thank you, my dear. I like to think not all of strategy for which you were mentioned in the dispatches came from your dear papa."

Jack's excitement faded a bit. "If this gambit doesn't succeed, your open support of Belle could still tarnish your reputation—and Dorrie's."

"'Tis possible. Dorrie and James must decide for themselves what they wish to do. As for me, if one cannot employ the assets one has to the benefit of one's children, what good are they?"

Jack kissed her hand. "Mama, you are a marvel."

She grinned at him. "I did produce two rather excellent offspring, did I not?"

A knock sounded at the door and Dorrie peeped in. "Jack, I thought 'twas your voice I heard!" Entering the room, she continued, "Mama explained why you left the party so abruptly. I do hope your errand prospered!"

"Not yet, poppet. But Mama and I are working on it."

"I wish to offer my support, as well."

"That's generous of you, little sister, but you needn't risk your reputation. Nothing shall be done until you are wed. I don't want my choices to taint your life—or to cause problems between you and your betrothed."

"It will not. As soon as Mama apprised me of what had transpired, I informed James. I told him I wouldn't marry him unless he could willingly support my family in this."

"And he agreed?" Jack asked, impressed, amused and touched by his sister's staunch support.

"Naturally."

"He must love you very much—little tyrant!"

Dorrie smiled. "He does. I had only to bid him imagine what it would be like, were we to be parted with no chance of marriage, for him to understand how you feel about your Belle. I convinced him to confide in his papa, and though he vowed to wed me regardless of whether his sire approved what you plan, after hearing Lady Belle's story, the earl announced that they would stand with us. The Winstons, you may recall, are cousins to the Ancasters and the Howards. Given our own connection to the Wentworths, the Sudleys and the Beauvales, we're already a fair way to conquering the ton, don't you think?"

Jack gave his sister a hug. "Thank you, poppet! I can't tell you how much this means to me."

She hugged him back. "As if I would *ever* give up my big brother! Family is everything, Jack."

"Grateful and humbled as I am by your support, ladies, I must warn you that, even if you succeed in establishing Belle, she…she still may refuse to marry me. From the first she's emphasized how much she prizes the independence she has won. And after this last episode, she has reason enough to be wary of men."

His mother gave him a thoughtful look. "You do want to do this, regardless of whether or not she accepts you?"

"Of course!"

His mother patted his hand. "Then let us begin. You can worry about persuading her later."

ON A LATE-SPRING morning a month later, Belle rode out to inspect the fields at Bellehaven. Grain waved its emerging tassels in the freshening breeze, while vegetables in the kitchen gardens grew in a collage of green and blossom hues. Belle found a small measure of peace in the eternal rhythm of germination, growth and harvest.

The supportive presence of Watson and Mae—Jack

must have dispatched them the instant he arrived in London—and the passage of time were helping to heal her wounded spirit as it had the scrapes and bruises on her body. Only the still-tender flesh beneath her ear had not yet completely recovered. But although even her critical eye could not now discern within the puckered scar the outline of an "R," she thought she must feel it carved on her soul forever.

She'd pulled up her mount to speak with one of the farmers, when a pony cart careened toward her. A moment later, Jem brought the vehicle to a skidding halt.

Impressed as she was by his skill at the ribbons, she was about to reprove his recklessness, when he cried, "You needs come back. A powerful lot of visitors done arrived!"

Though her pulse leapt at the news, she immediately steadied it. If Jack were calling, the boy would have said so. "Who is it, Jem? I'm not expecting company."

"Don't rightly know, my lady, but one of 'em be that silver-haired gent who visited you in Lunnon."

"Lord Egremont?"

"I expect so. You best go entertain 'em."

Not Jack. But then, she didn't expect Jack. They had nothing to say that hadn't already been said. Egremont, however, would provide a pleasant and much safer diversion.

"I'll go make myself presentable. Please tell Lord Egremont and his party that I will join them shortly." As she rode back, she wondered who Egremont had brought with him. Agents from the Jarvis case, perhaps?

A half hour later, her riding habit exchanged for a morning gown, she walked into the parlor—and stopped short. By the hearth, conversing with Egremont, stood Jack.

Shock and a painful mix of emotions—gladness, sorrow, regret, resignation—held her immobile. While she hesitated, Egremont came to her. "Belle! I'm relieved to see you looking so well. You had a…difficult time of it. I'm so sorry I failed to send Carrington soon enough."

Though Jack had yet to approach or speak to her, simply having him in the same room made it difficult for her to concentrate. "It—it wasn't in any way your fault."

"You are too gracious. Nothing can make amends for your suffering, but we have news that, I hope, will please you. The captain has discovered new information that leads us both to believe it is time for you to return to London—and resume your proper place in the world."

"My proper place?" Belle repeated. "But how—"

"No questions yet! We've brought someone who will explain it all. Carrington, if you'll do the honors?"

A tall lady, who in her agitation Belle hadn't noticed, rose from the sofa. A lady whose dark hair and familiar eyes immediately identified her as Jack's mother.

Jack's mother. Here at Bellehaven. For an instant, Belle thought she must be hallucinating.

"L-Lady Anne," Belle stammered, pulling herself together. "What a wholly unexpected honor!"

"A pleasure to meet you, too, Miss Germayne. Jack, Lord Egremont, since we've made our own introductions, perhaps you could amuse yourself with a game of billiards or a stroll about the lawn while we chat?"

"I believe we've been dismissed," Egremont said dryly.

"As you wish, Mama," Jack said. His gaze moved to Belle and lingered, triggering the automatic, immediate connection that always crackled between them and squeezing her chest with an anguished yearning. "Belle," he said softly, making of her name a caress. "Until later."

After the men exited, Lady Anne turned to Belle. "It must be very disconcerting, having your home invaded in such a manner! But I hope to shortly explain everything."

Lady Anne gestured to the sofa. Still numb with shock and confusion, Belle obediently took a seat.

"When Jack confided to me what had befallen you after your mother's death," Lady Anne began, "I was as outraged as he, and pledged to help him right the wrong that had been done you. I commenced trying to determine whom we might call upon to support us—and discovered your mother to be a distant cousin to Earl Cowper, whose wife, Emily, you may know, is both Lord Melbourne's daughter and a Patroness."

"Indeed! I had no idea of the connection. Though quite honestly, I cannot see what difference that makes, as I am a stranger to them and likely to remain so."

"Come now, child, you are a relation, however remote! Forgive me, but I took the liberty of confiding your story to Lady Cowper—a discerning and compassionate woman. She is anxious to meet you and offer her assistance. I believe she means to sponsor your introduction into society."

Belle stared at Lady Anne, not daring to believe such a reversal of fortune might be possible. "But how could she hope to win me acceptance, when all the ton knows I was Lord Bellingham's mistress?"

"Miss Germayne, be her birth high or low, no woman can fail to recognize the absolute control men exercise over her life in matters of law, marriage and finance. In one area only do we ladies rule—determining who will be admitted into society. If Lady Cowper supports you, the other Almack Patronesses will, as well. Add to them Lord Egremont and his connections, plus those of our own family, and you have already won over nearly half the ton."

"But what of Lord Rupert?" Belle asked, her hand unconsciously rising to the scar at her throat.

Lady Anne sniffed. "You needn't worry. Apparently he was heavily involved in a scandalous scheme to traffic in young girls, and escaped arrest when he returned to London only by bribing a jarvey to drive him to the docks, where he bought passage on the first ship leaving port. As for the scar, I brought you this." Lady Anne reached into her reticule and pulled out a pearl-beaded choker. "I wasn't sure of the size, but your maid can adjust it. Try it on, my dear. Ah, only wait until you see yourself in your glass! I predict you will start a new fashion."

Belle fingered the necklace Lady Anne had hooked around her neck, knowing by touch that it completely covered the scar. "I hardly know what to say."

Lady Anne patted her hand. "This has all been so sudden, I know. You needn't decide yet what you wish to do. Now, there are several others waiting to see you."

Lady Anne walked over to tug on the bellpull. Belle expected, with both anticipation and dread, that she would summon the gentlemen to rejoin them, but when the door opened a few minutes later, two young women entered.

The first was the girl who'd been riding in the park with Jack and Kitty, whom Belle assumed must be Jack's sister. The second was the young lady who'd accosted her in the theater lobby—Bellingham's daughter.

"Miss Germayne, so good to meet you at last! I'm Dorrie, Jack's sister, and *your* sister is now one of my dearest friends. My fiancé, Lord Winston and I, plus all his family, will be delighted to welcome you into society."

"As will I," Miss Bellingham said. "But first, please accept my most profound apologies! Not until I insisted the solicitors let me examine Papa's will did I learn what you had done for my mother and I. 'Twas both generous and compassionate. I can never thank you enough."

"You needn't thank me," Belle replied, feeling a bit overwhelmed. "The wealth rightfully belonged to you."

"By right, perhaps, but by law it would have been yours, had you not acted as you did. I should be even more grateful if you will allow me to play some small part in rectifying the…the wrong my father did *you*."

After a rap at the door, Watson entered to ask, "Should I show in the other folks now, your ladyship?"

"Please do," Lady Anne replied, turning to Belle.

"If you will forgive me for giving orders in your own home?"

Her mind flitting from thought to thought as she tried to comprehend the possibilities offered by this unexpected support, Belle hadn't yet found the proper reply when another lady entered the room. "Kitty?" she gasped.

Her sister halted on the doorstep, her eyes widening. Then she ran across the room and threw herself into Belle's arms. "Oh, my dear Constance, it *is* you! Until this moment, I didn't dare believe it was true!"

Not for nearly seven years had Belle been embraced by a member of her own family. Tears welled in her eyes as the girl clung to her.

Finally Kitty let her go, wiping away tears of her own. "But here I am, standing about like a watering-pot, when I meant to introduce you to your family!" She motioned to the older couple now coming toward them. "Constance, this is Aunt Mary and Uncle Thaddeus."

The gray-haired woman stared at Belle and clutched her husband's arm. "Sweet heaven, Thaddeus, how she resembles our Kitty!" The old gentleman, too, appeared astounded.

"Lord Bellingham was an infamous rogue, stealing you from us," Kitty said hotly. "Dorrie's brother said he told you Uncle Thaddeus didn't want you, when in truth he paid the innkeeper to tell us you were dead. He even had a tombstone erected for you!"

"You mean," Belle said slowly, "Bellingham never contacted you about me?"

"Contacted us?" Uncle Thaddeus said. "No! Until

Captain Carrington found us two weeks ago, we had no idea you were not buried beneath that marker. If I'd had even the slightest reason to suspect you'd survived, I should have searched the length and breadth of England for you."

"But we can be a family again now, can't we, Constance?" Kitty asked anxiously. "I know you must be angry with us for…for abandoning you, but please say you will give us a chance to start again."

"I was never angry with you. And I would love to be a family again, but—are you sure you wish to associate with me? I may bring discredit on you all."

"No longer," Lady Anne inserted. "Miss Germayne, you will shortly be received by some of the best society in London. But now, everyone, I believe we've overwhelmed Miss Germayne quite enough. If you would all withdraw to the library, I believe Watson is bringing tea."

Before leaving, Kitty hugged her, and Aunt Mary squeezed her hands, as if not quite believing Belle to be real. After they went out, Lady Anne smiled an apology. "Forgive me again for usurping your authority."

"Since I scarcely know what I am about at the moment, let me thank you for your assistance."

"There is one last thing I wished to mention to you—my son, Jack. Please, before you object, indulge me. I am not privy to what has passed between you, nor do I wish to be, but I know my son loves you. Nor does he give his affections lightly. I assure you, if any man can be loyal for a lifetime, it is my Jack."

"I don't doubt his constancy," Belle acknowledged.

"As for protecting your independence, you can have your solicitors draw up documents giving you full control over your own wealth. Jack will not object."

Belle smiled. "Nor do I worry that Jack covets my fortune, such as it is."

"Then, Miss Germayne, I must ask, do you love my son?"

"Yes," Belle replied simply. "But I don't know if that will be enough."

Jack's mother studied her for a moment. "Rupert?"

Belle nodded, relieved that Lady Anne seemed to understand, knowing she could never bring herself to explain what he'd done. Or how it made her feel.

"I won't insult you by saying I understand what you've experienced. But neither has anything in your life prepared *you* to imagine the joy of marrying a man you love and respect, sharing his life, bearing his children. If you let the...barbarity Lord Rupert committed keep you from reaching for happiness, then though you never see Rupert again, he accomplished his aim." Holding Belle's gaze, she said softly, "Don't let him win, my dear."

Leaving Belle to absorb her words, Lady Anne rose. "Jack is waiting to speak with you. This has been a morning of shocking surprises, and as I can't promise that he will not again press his suit, if you would prefer some time to compose yourself, I will send him away."

It would be better not to see Jack until she'd ordered her tumultuous thoughts, reflected upon all she'd learned and decided what she meant to do next. But knowing he was so near, the need to see him, talk with him, outweighed caution and prudence.

"I will receive him," she heard herself say.

When the door opened a few minutes later, Belle had to avert her gaze. She'd not had long to reflect, but already she'd begun to realize what an incredible gift he had offered, believing in her, traveling for weeks about England to trace her origins, enlisting his own family's support, bringing about a reconciliation with her nearest kin. For which he had demanded nothing but her love, freely given. Could she not match his courage?

She heard him stop before her. "If you cannot even look at me," Jack said, his tone wry, "then I fear whatever plea Mama made on my behalf was not forceful enough."

"Your mother is a very wise lady," she replied, gazing up at last into the face so dear to her, it made her ache.

"If that means she's recommended that you marry me straightaway, I agree."

"Oh, Jack, how can I ever thank you? But still—"

"Belle, I don't want your gratitude! Besides, whatever I saw restored to you was already yours by right, as much as the property and wealth you returned to Bellingham's family. Over the next few months, you will be able to regain your place in your family and society. Much as I still want you for my wife, I can withdraw my suit while you establish yourself in your new life. All I beg is that while you do so, you will let me stay your friend."

Belle smiled, love for him melting some of her anxiety and trepidation like the sun dispersing a morning mist. "You'll never take more than I gladly give?"

He smiled back. "Never. When I rode to Bellehaven that day, fearing Rupert might have harmed you, knowing I might never see you again, I realized that I would gladly accept whatever part you are willing to give me in your life. So, shall we let our bargain stand?"

Gratitude welled up that he was not pressing her for a decision now. "Our bargain stands."

SIX MONTHS LATER, Belle sat beside Jack as his carriage conveyed them to her house in Mount Street. So much had transpired, she mused as she studied the dear, familiar profile of the man beside her. She'd been introduced at a ball given by Lady Cowper herself, attended by all the Patronesses and every notable in the ton, including Wellington and the Prince Regent. Thereafter, no one with aspirations to society had dared slight her.

In fact, to Belle's great satisfaction, with the influence of the important connections Lady Anne had amassed added to her own charms and handsome dowry, Kitty had drawn the attention of several highly eligible suitors and ended her Season engaged to a fine young nobleman possessed of large fortune and an old, respected name.

The highlight of the succeeding summer had been attending the bride as Dorrie and Lord Winston pledged their vows, followed by a long visit to Carrington Grove. Jack had delighted in showing her around his estate. Though she'd feared the intimacy of living in the same house, he'd treated her throughout with meticulous respect.

In fact, did she not know for certain he was a man of

deep passion—and occasionally glimpsed the banked heat in his eyes—she might believe he no longer desired her.

For he had been true to his word, an ever-present friend who never demanded more. With the acceptance of society and his steadfast affection, she'd slowly begun to regain her confidence and self-respect. And as her recovery accelerated this past month, she'd begun to chafe at the limited nature of their relationship.

"Did you dance the leather off your slippers tonight?" Jack asked, breaking into her thoughts.

"Nearly," she replied with a chuckle. "Sometimes I wonder whether 'twas wise to have wanted to join the ton. We're scarcely home one night in ten, I've danced until my feet blister, and 'tis only the Little Season."

"I'm thankful to have claimed a fair number of those dances—no mean feat, given your crowd of admirers."

It was a perfect opening, if she now had the courage to take it. "Jack," she said, her heart beginning to thump against her ribs, "speaking of admirers, is…is your obliging offer still open?"

For a few, very long moments he said nothing.

"Of course, if you've changed your mind," she added, glad the dimness of the carriage lamps masked the heat rising in her cheeks, "you've every reason—"

"Of course I've not changed my mind," he interrupted. "Belle, do you mean to say you're finally ready?"

"To marry you? To be your wife in every way? Yes."

Jack seized her hands and kissed them, then gave a shout of delight, dissipating her concern that he now had reservations about wedding her. "We shall have the banns read this very Sunday."

"Well…we've waited so long, I don't think I wish to wait for the reading of the banns." She knew the instant her meaning penetrated his consciousness, for his whole body alerted and a dazzling smile lit his face.

"Sweeting, though I don't wish to deprive you of the usual pomp and ceremony, if you're of a mind to hurry, I happen to have a special license I've been saving for just such an eventuality. Do you wish to make use of it?"

"I do. For months now, I've been struggling to rid myself of the ugly memories of Rupert and what he did. Once, long ago, you showed me what loving can be. I want you to help me banish the nightmares for good, replace them with the joy and wonder only you can show me."

His fervent grip on her hands bespoke his eagerness. "We can be married tomorrow and begin tomorrow night."

"I was rather hoping perhaps we could begin—now."

"You are that sure you are ready?"

"No. But I trust you to stop whenever I ask you. Do to me whatever I tell you. Jack, I want to end tonight with you in my bed."

"As you wish, then, my dearest love." Cupping her face in his hands, he kissed her gently. "Tonight and every night to come."

Then, a grin lighting his face, he banged on the carriage wall and commanded the coachman to spring the horses.

* * * * *